SF   KAYE

FANTASTIQUE

3/95

18.95

FANTASTIQUE

FANTASTIQUE

Marvin Kaye

ST. MARTIN'S PRESS
NEW YORK

Design by PAUL CHEVANNES

Library of Congress Cataloging-in-Publication Data

Kaye, Marvin.
    Fantastique / Marvin Kaye.
      p. cm.
    ISBN 0-312-08191-X
    I. Title.
    PS3561.A886F3   1992
    813'.54—dc20   92-25164
                                   CIP

FIRST EDITION: November 1992

10 9 8 7 6 5 4 3 2 1

· ·

In memory of
My father and mother
Morris & Theresa Kaye
My paternal grandmother née Rae Rosenthal
My godparents
Edith & Joseph Cohn
My paternal uncle Al Kaye
My maternal uncles Herman and Phil Baroski
My mentor cousin
Jean Dunn
And my friends
Ila Jerom
Richard V. Mazza
and Jean Paiva

ACKNOWLEDGMENTS

Thanks to Robert Aronoff, D.M.D., for technical aid; Carole Buggé for German translation and for inviting me to participate in a Chicago City Limits mask class; Alan Warren for supplying me with a copy of *Lélio*'s French text and Faith Lancereau for her gloss of the same; Dan Wilson of the *Saturday Night Live* staff for explaining operational details of that NBC-TV show.

References: *Astral Projection*, Oliver Fox (University Books, 1962); *Beyond the Body*, S. J. Blackmore (Heinemann, 1982); *Brewer's Dictionary of Phrase & Fable*, revised centenary edition, ed. Ivor H. Evans (Harper & Row, 1981); *The Doors of Perception, Heaven and Hell*, Aldous Huxley (Penguin, 1959); *Dream Telepathy*, Dr. M. Ullman & S. Krippner, Ph.D., with Alan Vaughan (Penguin, 1973); *Georg Büchner Complete Plays & Prose*, trans. C. R. Mueller (Hill & Wang, 1963); *Harvard Brief Dictionary of Music*, Willi Apel & R. Daniel (Harvard Press, 1960); "The Hypnagogic State: A Critical Review of the Literature," D. L. Schachter (*Psychological Bulletin*, Vol. 83, #3, 1976); *Impro*, Keith Johnstone (Theatre Arts Books, 1979); *The Italian Comedy*, Pierre Duchartre (Dover, 1966); *Journeys out of the Body*, Robert Monroe (Doubleday, 1971); *Music Theory*, George T. Jones (Barnes & Noble, 1974); *Neurotic Styles*, David Shapiro (Basic Books, 1965); *The Norton Scores*, ed. Roger Kamien (W. W. Norton, 1968); *Oxford Companion to the Mind*, ed. R. L. Gregory (Oxford Press, 1987); *Plays of Georg Büchner*, trans. G. Dunlop (Vision Press, 1952); *Six Plays of Strindberg*, trans. Elizabeth Sprigge (Anchor, 1955); *Woyzeck*, trans. Theodore Hoffman in *The Modern Theatre*, Vol. I, ed. Eric Bentley (Anchor, 1955); *Woyzeck Ein Fragment*, Georg Büchner (Reclam Stuttgart, 1963), as well as John Ciardi's translation of Dante, two Passover

Haggadahs and my own *Handbook of Mental Magic* (Stein & Day, 1975).

Thanks to Jessica Amanda Salmonson for publishing an earlier version of the first chapter in *Fantasy Macabre* #11.

Structural Notes: Cuts in *Woyzeck* and *The Stronger* for reasons of narrative flow are not intended as aesthetically valid performance suggestions. All excerpted passages are used by permission of the translator, Carl Richards.

Four recordings of Hector Berlioz's *Symphonie Fantastique* were consulted for the ongoing durational, sequential, structural, and thematic musical-literary *"glasperlenspiel"* equations employed in this book: EMI C120760, The London Classical Players, conducted by Roger Norrington; EMI 4LZ626605, Philharmonia Orchestra, conducted by Andre Cluytens; RCA Victor LM1131, San Francisco Symphony Orchestra, conducted by Pierre Monteux; and London STS515423, Vienna Philharmonic Orchestra, conducted by Pierre Monteux. Also consulted: *Lélio, ou le retour à la vie*, CBS Records "Masterworks" Series MPT 38767, London Symphony Orchestra & Chorus, conducted by Pierre Boulez, with tenor John Mitchinson, baritone John Shirley-Quirk and narrator Jean-Louis Barrault.

The first five superscriptions are based on Berlioz's own "Fantastique" programme notes. The last epigraph derives from *Lélio*. In the fifth "movement" is a quatrain from the Bretzner-Stephanie libretto to Mozart's *Die Entfuhrung aus dem Serail*. This passage, as well as French, German and Italian passages in the last section, are translated at the end of the book.

—Marvin Kaye
New York—Edinburgh, 1988–1992

Trying to make amends for what is dead and cannot be changed—is this not the source of all art? From shame, suffering, injustice and humiliation, does not the creative spirit emerge *de profundis*?
—Leo Perutz, *The Master of the Day of Judgment*

Artists suffer and will always suffer, yet they should not complain. They have experienced intoxications unknown to the rest of mankind.
—Charles Gounod discussing Hector Berlioz, *An Artist's Memoirs*

Why has the spirit
From the loftiest height
Plummeted into Hell?
Within the fall is contained
Its own resurrection.
—S. Anski (S. Z. Rappoport), *The Dybbuk*

Isn't waking just another kind of dream, and all of us, sleepwalkers?
—Georg Büchner, *Danton's Death*

Alas, zero is a presumption of
the mathematical imagination, so
don't assume which dreamed it. Logic
is suppressed hallucination, see,
and bedtime tales are tepid
druggy potions anyhow.
—William H. Klein, *Alice Kills the Cat*

Time is memory, they say: the art, however, is to revive it and yet avoid remembering.
—Lawrence Durrell, *Clea*

PROGRAMME

....

DREAMS—PASSIONS

'An artist of morbid sensibility and ardent imagination plunges into deep sleep accompanied by strange visions of a beloved woman who becomes a fixed idea that he finds everywhere. At first he remembers the sickness of soul, the vague despair, the melancholy and the joy which he experienced before he saw his beloved, then the volcanic passion with which she suddenly inspired him.'

PRAELUDIUM OSTINATO

"BITCH!"

She screamed as Carl flung her naked to the floor and mounted her. Shoving her legs apart, he tore into her body, strove to, could not climax, filled her with darkness.

s
ast
tasti
ntastiq

—could not remember yesterday or sunset or the last five minutes, but every man who hurt her in the name of love stained her like secret blood; each was named Carl, a four-letter word synonymous with shame, all except the first Carl, the only gentle Carl, the one she could hardly recall because he died too soon, but the Carl who followed and every brutal Carl who came next compelled her to submit to the most degrading acts before abandoning her to pain and anger and self-loathing—

ast
tasti
ntastiq
antastiqu

Suddenly, she found herself in a nearly empty diner. A greying, pinch-lipped waitress behind the long service counter gossiped with a short, bald, potbellied policeman sitting on a red leatherette swivel stool. At the cash register, a bespectacled man with a straggly brown mustache read a newspaper and picked his nose. None of them paid any attention to her or to another woman clad in an old *Cats* T-shirt, stretched out on her side on the countertop, her face turned away from a man restlessly dreaming at the far opposite end.

Carl?

She was sitting in one of the diner booths. *Why? How did I get here?* As she stared down at the greasy surface of the table, she was surprised to see her own hands clutching a coffee cup half-filled with liquid too tepid to warm her chilly fingers. *When did I order it? When did I drink half? What am I doing here? And who—*

"LOOK AT ME, BITCH!"

Dread gripped her; glancing up, she saw Carl framed in the doorway. He moved towards her in the half-crouch of a predator stalking its kill. The waitress disappeared, the policeman vanished, the cashier was gone, the troubled slumberers faded away, the corner booths winked out. Her memory flooded back: this was the only reality she knew, a cycle of pain, a closed repeating loop of rape and humiliation.

"BITCH!"

She screamed as Carl flung her naked to the floor. He shoved her legs apart, tore into her body, strove unsuccessfully to climax, ripping her with one last despairing thrust as she cried out again and again in pain and fear and rage. Darkness filled her. She—

tasti

ntastiq

antastiqu

Fantastique

—no longer trusted tenderness or yesterday or the closed repeating loop of sunset, but could not forget that agony called love and all the angry Carls who hurt her in repeated despairing attempts to satisfy their passion before abandoning her. All except the first Carl, the only gentle Carl, the Carl who died too soon—

ntastiq

antastiqu

Fantastique

F a n t a s t i q u e

A diner. A pinch-lipped waitress argued with a fat policeman. A woman with her face turned away from a sleeping man. At the cash register, someone reading a newspaper, ignoring her.

She was sitting in a booth.

Why?

Staring down at the tabletop, surprised to see her own hands clutching a coffee cup. *Why? When did I order it? And who am—*

"Look at me . . . please?"

This gentle voice could not belong to Carl, and yet there he was *frozen till I* (marie) *raise my eyes* sitting across the booth from her, reaching out to touch her. She flinched, but the only thing he did was to lightly, reassuringly stroke the back of her hand. It ended the closed, repeating pattern. She could not understand the change in him at first, but as she stared into eyes as tender as his voice, a strange thought struck her: *This is the first Carl, the Carl who never hurt or had me, the Carl who died.*

<pre>
            antastiqu
            Fantastique
          F a n t a s t i q u e
        F a n t a s t i q u e
</pre>

—and the sunset loop of men who raped her in the name of love was nothing but illusion. Those brutal nightmare Carls were not real. Her only truth, her one reality was this first sweet Carl who never hurt or had her, this Carl who died too soon—

<pre>
            Fantastique
          F a n t a s t i q u e
        F a n t a s t i q u e
      F a n t a s t i q u e
</pre>

She gazed at him in loving wonder, *Carl who never really died at all,* and as he tenderly kissed her fingertips, she knew that until this very instant she had never felt so wholly, gloriously, vibrantly alive. The room and the restless slumberer faded away and the two of them were alone in hazy wilderness tinted with morning, but as they clasped and kissed in a perfect union of flesh and harmony and flame—

<pre>
          F a n t a s t i q u e
        F a n t a s t i q u e
      F a n t a s t i q u e
    F a n t a s t i q u e
</pre>

—something shimmered beyond the rosebud portal of romance and she was once more distressingly aware that she could not remember yesterday or the last five minutes or anything but the closed repeating loop of memory that she had no memory and *who* AM *I?*

                    F a n t a s t i q u e
                F a n t a s t i q u e
            F a n t a s t i q u e
        F a n t a s t i q u e

Whispering *I love you,* he parted her legs, gently entered, swiftly climaxed, and as her lips and tongue and teeth and breasts and limbs and hands and hips and heart crushed urgently against him, she shuddered in the sudden agony of truth as reality seized and canceled her—

                    F a n t a s t i q u e
                F a n t a s t i q u e
            F a n t a s t i q u e
        F a n t a s t i q u e

—but just before she ended, a thought wholly and independently her own darkened her dying mind.

Tenderness is the worst rape of all.

        F   a   n   t   a   s   t   i   q   u   e
            F   a   n   t   a   s   t   i   q   u   e
                F a n t a s t i q u e
                    F a n t a s t i q u e
                        F a n t a s t i q u e
                        F a n t a s t i q u e
                            Fantastique
                            antastiqu
                            ntastiq
                            tasti
                            ast
                            s

7:01 A.M.

Waking or sleeping, she was the most desirable woman he'd ever seen, but now he could not clearly recall her haunting, haunted face; the harder he tried, the further she fled down lost corridors of memory.

A painful pun fretted at him—*Après le mort, on y triste*. He cursed the radio–alarm clock that woke him playing Berlioz's *Symphonie Fantastique*.

In another room, Carl's wife stirred in sleep.

SONATA FORM

A paroxysm of noise, coldness, harsh light. Everything hurt or frightened him. He cried. When the wetness stung and he stank, some of the big people made sounds that made him feel bad, but after he was clean, his mother held him close and as he rested against her warm, soft body and she soothed him with cradlesongs, he began to learn the intimate rapport of shame.

The infant Cary Richard Markowitz lived behind his father's radio and television repair shop in downtown Scranton, Pennsylvania, with his parents, paternal grandmother, a teenage sister Rebecca Ruth and a ten-year-old brother Irving who never smiled at him. It was like having a houseful of parents. Everyone told him to behave, everyone gave him orders and warned him what not to do. Long before he learned to utter "Mama," Cary understood the meaning of the words "No" and "Don't," as well as Gramma Hannah's disapproving *tch-tch,* although it did not have the effect on him that she thought it would. The sound fascinated Cary; he tried to imitate it, but when he did, Gramma stopped, so he only practiced it when she wasn't around.

Gramma Hannah was an overweight, slope-shouldered autocrat with straggly bleached auburn hair that she parted in the middle and pulled severely sideways toward her ears. Her accordion-pleated lips generally frowned at Cary's father (her own son), who never could do anything to please her. But she smiled all the time at Cary's mother, who devoted herself to helping Gramma Hannah stand up and sit down, who plumped her pillows when she sighed and shifted her ponderous bottom on the cracked leatherette couch, who measured and sometimes had to weigh her food because the old woman was a diabetic. Gramma Hannah was born in Austria and spoke a thickly accented English that she could neither read nor write, yet she laughed at Cary's efforts to shape random noise into words. But when she did, she'd catch him up in her arms and press him to her ample breast, and he always liked that. The buttons of her dress scratched, but he still loved to burrow into the warm, generous expanse of Gramma Hannah's bosom.

Cary's slim, square-shouldered sister Rebecca Ruth, whom he thought very pretty, often had to babysit her brother. She might greet the news with a mischievous twinkle and tickle Cary into gales of deliciously tormented laughter, but on other occasions she brushed chestnut strands of hair petulantly away from her heavy-lidded hazel eyes and declared that she was "sick and tired of being stuck with the brat." Those were times that Cary did and didn't like. Once she got him alone, Rebecca Ruth's full lips would twist into a peculiar smile and she'd punish him, ordering him to do things he didn't always like— but later she'd make funny faces at him and sing silly songs that he couldn't help but giggle at. Then they'd go outside and walk three blocks to their Uncle Lou's ice cream parlor for hot fudge sundaes and a new supply of comic books. On the way home, Cary would solemnly promise Rebecca Ruth not to tell their mother about "all the crazy things we've done" because "it's *our* secret!"

Cary never shared secrets with his brother. Irving was a dour, bespectacled boy who pointedly ignored his sibling's fumbling attempts to make friends with shy offers of treasured playthings. Irving never acknowledged Cary, except when he complained to their mother that "*he* always gets special treatment," a claim that unfortunately was rooted in truth, since Abraham Markowitz displayed great favoritism toward his younger son.

Cary's father was a short, bald, potbellied cigar-stub of a man whose domestic furies so starkly contrasted with his jovial public persona that his wife secretly called him "Jekyll-Hyde." He bickered with Gramma Hannah, fought with his wife and daughter, and constantly shouted at Irving, who never seemed to be able to please his father, no matter how hard he tried. Yet Mr. Markowitz doted on Cary, who basked in his father's roughshod affection at the cost of Irving's unappeasable enmity.

The opposing hemispheres of Cary's world coexisted in an uneasy state of détente. The women kept house as neatly as the cramped conditions permitted, but clutter dominated the long fluorescent reaches of Mr. Markowitz's repair shop where mysteries in abundance rewarded prying eyes and probing fingers. Radios and TVs to be serviced, tubes, tools and electronic testing equipment all were logically, accessibly arranged, but the drawers and edges of desks and workbenches described a fleamarket of delights—from magnifying lenses, plastic puzzles, wire, thumbtacks, loose change, rubber bands and canceled checks to souvenir postcards from long-dead relatives, half-a-dozen crystal radio receivers, hundreds of dusty cans of 16mm movies (cartoons, newsreels, singalongs and a handful of full-length features like *Mutiny Ahead* starring Neil Hamilton that even knowledgeable film buffs never heard of), red-and-green 3-D glasses with no pictures to look at through them, BBs and targets without a gun to shoot them from or at, stubby pencils and notepads of half-sketched uninvented ideas abandoned after someone else marketed them—the detritus of an untrained mind, brilliant but slapdash.

Cary loved to wander through the shop examining prizes that his fingers beachcombed. If Abraham Markowitz was busy, he might snap at him to get out of the way, but more often he encouraged the little boy to explore, and if Cary unintentionally mishandled something, his father would just ruffle his hair and explain how to do it right, though if Irving accidentally brushed some worthless nondescript to the floor, Mr. Markowitz instantly bellowed at him.

By the time Cary was in second grade, his father liked to talk to him while he worked. "See how the TV picture is made up of lots of scansion lines? There are more than five hundred of them. Here's the neck of the picture tube and if you look in here you can see the electron gun. It paints the TV picture one line at a time, skipping every other space, then it goes back and fills in the missing spaces. It happens so fast, you think you see a whole picture, but your mind's really filling in the details." Cary asked lots of questions and usually got puzzling answers, but he nodded his head sagely and pretended to follow the explanation, which made his father very proud. Yet as time passed, Cary vaguely began to understand some of the things he heard: persistence of vision, wave length, frequency modulation.

On slow days, Mr. Markowitz sometimes produced a dog-eared pack of playing cards and showed Cary a game that he learned in the army. "I'm holding five cards, Cary. One of them is the Ace of Diamonds. Close your eyes. Let your finger hover over the tops of the cards. Pull out the first one you touch." Four times out of five, Cary would find the named card. His father insisted there was no trick, it was pure telepathy. Cary believed him.

When he tired of rooting through the shop's junk piles, Cary sat with tucked-up feet on the worn cushion of a battered swivel chair near a broken rolltop desk and watched his father who, surrounded by the colorful flotsam of his past, stumped back and forth along his workbench performing wonders on obsolescent Philcos, Zeniths, RCAs—calibrating, rewiring, tuning, perhaps even snipping out sections of circuits that miraculously resurrected decrepit appliances declared unfixable by other repairmen. Mr. Markowitz wore a leather work-apron over pinstripe pants, white shirt and a dark tie held proudly in place by a Masonic stickpin. As he worked, he belched, broke wind and chain-smoked foul-smelling cigars that Cary's mother vainly tried to make him stop smoking in the rest of the house.

The downstairs living quarters behind the shop consisted of a single chamber generally referred to as "the combination room" because it served as the dining area, kitchen and parlor, all in one, and when Cary was a baby, his crib was kept there, too, in a corner behind a portable screen. The upper floor had a single bathroom for six people and three bedrooms, one for Mr. and Mrs. Markowitz and a second that Gramma Hannah shared with Rebecca Ruth. Irving slept in the smallest of the three, but when Cary outgrew his crib, Mr. Markowitz ignored the protests of both boys and moved Cary into Irving's bedroom, which became even more cramped when their father replaced its cot with a double bed that had to be clambered over to reach the bureau or tiny overstuffed closet. Irving, barely acknowledging Cary's presence, slept sprawled in the middle of the bed, and if his brother accidentally rolled against him during the night, he would shove him away so ungently that Cary took to sleeping squeezed up against the wall. If Cary hoped his brother appreciated this sacrifice, he was wrong.

Sometimes in the middle of the night, Cary had to go to the bathroom. Though he hated to quit the warmth of the blankets, Cary realized the longer he waited, the more urgent the need to go, and since he didn't want to wake up Irving, he knew that delay meant an excruciatingly cautious sidle around the edge of the room. The horrible thought that this enforced slowness might cause him to have an accident on Irving's side of the bed was a strong reason to obey nature's promptings promptly.

Often, Gramma Hannah woke up after midnight and could not get back to sleep, so, wrapping herself in a faded blue cotton night robe, she shambled downstairs to the combination room, sat on the sofa and worked at the long grey wool comforter she'd been knitting longer than Cary could remember. If, on his return journey from the bathroom, he saw the forty-watt parlor light glowing below, Cary tiptoed down as far as the staircase landing and spied on Gramma Hannah through the banister, waiting to see if she'd drop a stitch and go *tch-tch*. It was a secret game he'd made up for himself and if Gramma Hannah noticed him there, as she usually did, and clucked mild disapproval because he was not in bed, it didn't count because it wasn't a spontaneous *tch-tch*.

But some nights when he passed by the middle bedroom, Cary heard Gramma Hannah snoring in her sleep like a beached whale. Then if he looked in and Rebecca Ruth happened to be awake, the two of them would tiptoe downstairs, raid the icebox and sit huddled under a quilt, munching on Ritz crackers and listening to a portable radio just loud enough so that if they put their heads together and each squeezed an ear to the speaker, they heard popular music played by disc jockeys who sounded wide awake in spite of it being so late.

Cary loved nights like these. He thought it would be unbearably exciting to walk around outside and maybe even sneak into other people's houses while they were fast asleep—but then one night Rebecca Ruth took it into her head to bring a flashlight and read scary stories from her inexhaustible supply of comic books. Cary wanted to hear funny ones like Donald Duck, but she vetoed them because "you'll laugh out loud and Mom'll hear us and that'll be the end of the Markowitz Midnight Marauders!" Her argument convinced Cary. He loved belonging to a two-member club that excluded his brother.

One night, she read Cary a story called "The Thing in the Cellar" that was so scary it even frightened her. She almost sent him back to bed without a kiss to protect him from the monster he now imagined lurked in their own basement, but then, changing her mind, she started telling him all about death and disease and going to Hell. Cary stuck fingers in his ears and made tympani noises inside his head to drown her out, but it didn't work.

"What if you died tonight," Rebecca Ruth asked, "and you could either go to Heaven for a little while and then to Hell forever, or to Hell first, then to Heaven. Which would you do?"

The answer seemed too obvious, he thought it must be a trick question, so Cary replied, "I'd go to Heaven first."

Rebecca Ruth curled her cherry-bright lips scornfully. "How can you really enjoy Heaven when you know that sooner or later the Devil's going to show up and grab you and shovel you into Hell? And once you're down there burning like a lump of coal, you'll be worse off than all the rest of the damned because you'll remember how beautiful Heaven is, but you won't ever be able to go back there again."

When Cary returned to bed later that night, he was angry at himself for not telling his sister the answer that he knew must be right. He fell asleep and dreamed that he and Rebecca Ruth were playing in the cellar. Their father came downstairs to feed the furnace and Rebecca Ruth smothered Cary's mouth against her midriff so he couldn't cry out when Mr. Markowitz obliviously scooped up Cary in the coal shovel and pitched him into Hell. The child woke up terrified, gasping for breath, but his brother Irving just rolled over in bed, smacked Cary's arm and muttered, ''Shut up, damn you!''

Several months later, at another session of the Markowitz Midnight Marauders, Rebecca Ruth surprised Cary by asking him the same question about Heaven and Hell. He was amazed she'd forgotten that she'd asked it before and was glad that this time he would not fail her morbid inquisition. But as soon as he said, ''Hell first, then Heaven,'' Rebecca Ruth smiled wickedly and Cary knew he'd fallen into a trap.

''How can you ever get to Heaven once you go to Hell? The Devil will burn you up like coal and there'll be nothing left of you but a little pile of ashes and bones!''

Later that night, Cary dreamed the same nightmare, only this time it was Rebecca Ruth who wielded the shovel. As she hurled Cary into the inferno, he screamed so loud that the Devil's blood-red lips parted and he heard a voice growling, ''Shut up, damn you!''—and then his brother shook him awake.

When Irving saw he could not quiet his hysterical brother, the older boy ran down the hall and woke their mother. She donned a robe, sent Irving back to bed, then, picking up Cary, paced back and forth along the hallway, gently rocking him against her bosom until at last he calmed down and fell asleep again.

Cary's mother was a greying, gentle-spirited diplomat who valiantly tried to maintain her volatile household in a state of equilibrium. Wary of Abraham's hair-trigger temper, Vera Markowitz seldom argued with him directly, but her perennially pinched lips and tight-set jaw unmistakably informed her offspring that Mama disapproved of their father's crude, bellicose manners. Because she hated the way her husband continually yelled at Irving and Rebecca Ruth while doting on Cary, she treated her three children with even-handed affection, taking pains never to show favoritism. When her boys fought, as they did more and more often, she refused to take sides, but devoted herself solely to getting them to lower their voices and ''make up.'' Cary couldn't understand why Mama didn't see that Irving picked on him all the time, but protests only resulted in a rebuke from his omnipresent grandmother, who adored her daughter-in-law and frequently declared for all ears, "Abie, this girlie's too good for you!"

Gramma Hannah was more or less joking when she said this, but when Cary was eight he overheard Aunt Peg tell his mother the same thing, and she was dead serious. That morning at breakfast, Irving, recently turned eighteen, dumbfounded his family by revealing that he was going to quit high school to join the army. His mother pleaded, "It's only one month till graduation! Get your diploma, *then* do what you want!" But Mr. Markowitz (who had run away from home to enlist when he was younger than Irving) just glared at his son and said, "You've always been goofy. Maybe the army will do you good." This remark kindled his wife's long-smoldering ire over the way Abe treated Irving. They fought about it all day. That night, Aunt Peg came to counsel her sister Vera. Cary, eavesdropping at his mother's bedroom door, overheard his aunt say, "He talks big. He said he'd jump off a bridge if you didn't marry him. You should've called his bluff there and then. So enough now, bring Cary and Ruth and move in with me and Max."

Now Cary liked Aunt Peg, she was pretty and smart and owned lots of albums of music that had numbers instead of names, but he was absolutely crazy about her husband, Uncle Max. He was a jolly, chain-smoking elf who told sidesplitting jokes, did magic tricks and could play guitar, harmonica and drums all at once (he'd been a one-man band in vaudeville). Uncle Max always had a smile and a bear hug for "my little shortstop." Cary never saw him lose his temper or heard him raise his voice.

As he stood there shivering in the chilly corridor outside his mother's room, Cary supposed he ought to get mad at Aunt Peg for trying to split up his folks, but how could he blame her when, to be truthful, he wanted to go and live with his godparents, *just me and Mama and nobody else.* Cary was ashamed of himself for feeling this way and doubly so because, even though he knew how much his own Daddy loved him, this was not the first time he wished that Uncle Max could be his real father.

When he became a man, Cary rarely mentioned his childhood unless he was asked a direct question. Then he would say with secret irony that it was the happiest time of his life. But there was one brief period just after his brother went away to boot camp when this was literally true. The hoped-for move to Uncle Max's never took place. Aunt Peg harangued her sister passionately, but could not persuade her to abandon home and husband—a sense of duty, however, that did not prevent Mrs. Markowitz from ignoring her mate for the next several weeks. She maintained a frosty silence that became even chillier when Irving actually quit school and signed up at the local army recruiting office. Cary, whose head was filled with wonderful stories that Uncle Max enjoyed telling him about the faraway places he'd seen when he was an itinerant vaudevillean, envied Irving a little for escaping humdrum Scranton, Pennsylvania, but mainly Cary was delighted to be rid of a brother he no longer hoped or desired to be friends with. He regretted that his mother was so upset over Irving's actions, *and leaving school a month before graduation IS goofy,* but still, for the first time in his life, Cary was going to enjoy the privacy and luxury of his very own bedroom, and he refused to feel guilty about it. It was almost as good as living with Uncle Max and at least it didn't involve him in paternal disloyalty. So by the time Irving departed in mid-June, Mrs. Markowitz was speaking to her husband again, and though Gramma Hannah seemed more forgetful and crochety than usual, the Markowitz household was uncommonly tranquil and Cary was content.

Less than a week later, his world began to darken. Cary came home one day from the playground and found the CLOSED sign on the front door. It scared him. Why wasn't the repair shop open in the middle of the afternoon? Cary rang the buzzer and soon heard his father tramping down the long work aisle. Mr. Markowitz opened the door, hugged Cary, then, laying a shushing finger on his son's lips, led him to the combination room where Cary's mother and Gramma Hannah sat on the sofa with their arms around Aunt Peg, who looked awful. Her skin was pasty white, her eyes red and puffy. She dabbed at her sniffing nose with a crumpled lace handkerchief.

They buried Uncle Max the following afternoon. Cary's mother thought her son too young to go to the funeral, so, to keep him from dwelling on sad things, decided to send him to the movies with his sister. Mrs. Markowitz waggled an admonitory finger at her daughter and warned, "Nothing scary, do you hear? There's already too many frightening things in the world without looking for more. Take your brother to something nice and funny, *f'shtay?*" Rebecca Ruth dutifully nodded, but then secretly winked at Cary, who even though he felt like crying over Uncle Max's heart attack, had to smile in spite of himself at his sister's wonderful wickedness.

As the rest of the family left for the funeral, Cary and Rebecca Ruth pulled on galoshes, took umbrellas, and sloshed three blocks to the Keystone Theatre, where they goosepimpled through a British chiller called *Curse of the Demon* and an interesting low-budget science-fiction film, *4D Man,* all about a scientist able to walk through walls, but who accidentally stuck his hand through a man's chest and killed him. They stayed and watched it a second time.

That night when their mother asked what they saw, Cary said *Sleeping Beauty,* which he and his sister actually went to in March. Before Mrs. Markowitz could voice her suspicion, Rebecca Ruth changed the subject and asked how Uncle Max's funeral went. Her question elicited an angry snort from her father and a resigned shrug from her mother, who replied grimly, "It was not pleasant. I have never approved of open casket ceremonies."

"Did you ever see such jackasses?" Mr. Markowitz thundered. "Actually closing the box while Peg was still there! How can anyone so dumb not be goyim?"

Cary didn't understand the problem. "But they have to close it sooner or later, don't they? Doesn't Aunt Peg know that?"

"I'm not talking to you," his father bellowed. "Shut up!"

With an exasperated glance at her husband, Mrs. Markowitz went upstairs. When she came down later to fix supper, she was cool to all three members of her immediate family, though after the meal she cuddled Cary for a few moments before leaving to spend the night with Aunt Peg. As soon as her mother was out of the house, Rebecca Ruth told her father she had to stay overnight at a girlfriend's studying for a summer-school math quiz. Mr. Markowitz said OK, so she ran up to her room, filled her schoolbag with makeup and hurried out.

Cary watched TV for an hour with his father while Gramma Hannah lay on the couch snoring through Ed Sullivan, then at nine-thirty he went upstairs to work on his book collection. When he shared the room with his brother, Cary had to cram his assortment of fantasy and science-fiction paperbacks into cardboard boxes that Irving pushed into remote corners out of the way of his own things. Now that Cary had the space to put his books wherever he pleased, he couldn't decide which way to set them out. The night before, he'd spent hours rearranging them according to whim, changing his mind each time he opened up a new storage carton. He was still working when his mother told him to turn out the light and go to bed.

Surveying the colorful paperbacks piled all about the room, Cary wondered which stack to tackle first. He remembered that Irving shoved one box of books high up in the closet out of sight and reach, so, standing on a chair, Cary groped around blindly on the top shelf feeling for his last carton of books. His fingers brushed against a bulky envelope that he supposed must belong to his brother. He fished it down to see what it contained. His jaw dropped when he saw the thick bundle of photos inside. The first revealed a naked woman lying on her back, knees wide apart, her hands spreading her thighs to display a gaping tunnel in the middle of her body. Now Cary's parents kept him in such sexual ignorance that although he'd noticed that Rebecca Ruth's chest was different from his, he presumed that women had penises just like men, so for one horrified instant he thought the naked lady either was a freak or had hurt herself. But the next picture depicted the same woman with a man on top of her burying his penis in the hole between her legs. Cary suddenly was flooded with early memories of how Rebecca Ruth used to "punish" him by putting his hands on the same spot and telling him to rub hard "because I feel stiff." Sometimes she even pressed his face against her midriff, and that frightened him because he couldn't breathe, but even though he pretended not to like being punished, Cary actually enjoyed massaging his sister and was sorry when she stopped letting him do it. It used to puzzle him that he couldn't feel her penis through the folds of her dress, but now as he studied the two pictures, Cary realized he had to revise his notions of female anatomy. He didn't understand why there was such a big difference in the way men and women were built, but he guessed it had something to do with what was going on in the second photo. Cary examined the rest of the packet. Most of the other snapshots were variations on the same man-into-woman activity, but one pose showed a man forcing his penis into a woman's mouth. It confused and upset Cary. *Why is he so mad at her?*

Suddenly, Cary heard his father's heavy footsteps in the hallway. Without even thinking about it, he shoved the pictures back into the envelope, kicked it under the bed, grabbed a handful of books and began to stack them on top of his bureau. Mr. Markowitz opened the door and smiled when he saw what his son was doing. "That was your mother on the phone, Cary. She said you should stop playing with your books and go to bed. You know she's the boss." His father kissed him good night and closed the door.

Cary changed into his pajamas, turned off the light and shut his eyes, but all sorts of ideas raced through his brain and kept him awake.

Thinking about Rebecca Ruth, he recollected that it felt funny sometimes when he washed himself in the same place he used to stroke her. It never before occurred to him that there might be a connection between the two things. He tentatively touched himself down there and liked how it felt. He did it again and was surprised and pleased at the result.

Maybe this is what she meant when she said she felt stiff? [No, dummy, look at the photo . . . she doesn't have one!]

He tried to picture what the tunnel in his sister's body looked like, but his heart began to beat so fast that he got scared he was going to die like Uncle Max, so, promising God that if he let him live, he'd never do this thing again, Cary forced himself to stop. Little by little, his pulse slowed. A soothing lassitude stole over his tired body, but his conscious mind, unable to shut itself down, pursued strange ideas into the twisted corridors of sleep.

Cary opens his eyes and finds himself suspended in midair high above a freshly turned mound of earth. He looks down and sees Uncle Max rising up out of a long tunnel, arms outstretched to hug "my little short-stop." Cary is so glad to see him that his heart beats faster and faster, but as Uncle Max floats closer his face melts and changes into someone else and then the features run together again and become a leering skull with sharp teeth and horns and now Satan's hands plunge deep into Cary's chest in a sensation so titanic

that he shot bolt upright in bed gasping for breath. He snapped on the table lamp and looked wildly around the room, but he was all alone. His crotch felt wet. At first he thought he must be bleeding.

After Cary cleaned himself, he put out the light and tried to sleep again, but the darkness was infested with demons. He rose, wandered into the hall and peeked into his grandmother's bedroom. He did not hear her snoring, so he tiptoed down the stairs until he saw the feeble glow of the forty-watt parlor bulb. Cary thought she'd be on the couch knitting the same grey wool comforter she always busied herself with, but instead she was sitting as still as a statue, the comforter wrapped round her shoulders like a shroud. He was in no mood to play his usual I-spy games; he went directly up to her and said plaintively, "Gramma, I can't sleep."

His grandmother, smelling of sulphur and lavender, gazed blankly at him through thick, rimless spectacles that made her eyes look as big as one of the guardian dogs in Cary's favorite fairy tale, "The Tinder

Box.'' Cary remembered how forgetful she'd become lately and was suddenly frightened that she didn't even recognize him, but then Gramma Hannah smiled and beckoned him to clamber up beside her, and as he did so, his fears faded away. Cradling him in her great fleshy arms, she crooned an Austrian lullaby that her own mother sang to her nearly seventy years before Cary was born. The little boy yawned, shut his eyes and soon fell fast asleep. His grandmother removed the comforter from her shoulders and covered him with it, then pressed her wrinkled lips to his forehead and muttered, *"Tch-tch, mein Kind! Nur die Alten und die Bösen können schlafen nicht."* She switched off the dim lamp and sat alone in the darkness with her thoughts and her son's son slumbering in her lap.

Just before dawn, the old woman's eyes closed and her head drooped upon her chest. She felt like a little girl waiting for her mother to come and take her by the hand and lead her away to some place very nice.

THEME AND VARIATIONS

"Es war einmal ein arm Kind und hatt kein Vater und keine Mutter—"

Turning east off Broadway, Carl Richards strode ten paces to the narrow entryway of the Innamorato Rehearsal Studios, opened its imitation red-leather, brass-studded door and passed through. As he climbed a steep flight of slump-bellied wooden steps, he heard the rich contralto of an actress one flight up quoting the Grandmother speech from *Woyzeck* in the original German.

"—keine Mutter war alles tot und war niemand mehr auf der Welt!"

Carl shook his head. *Either a colossal showoff or trying to psych out the competition. Or both.* It offended the actor in him and he decided, sight unseen, not to cast her. But the declamation ended just before he entered the Innamorato reception room. He scrutinized the group of fourteen or fifteen women waiting there for the *Woyzeck* callbacks to begin. Some sat studying their scripts, some stood poised in carefully "casual" attitudes, one sexy brunette in dance tights stretched her left ankle over her head *by way of advertisement,* a blonde in purple slacks did exercises that involved a great deal of bending and flexing. *As if she hadn't already warmed up at home.* Carl mentally selected one frosted-haired character actress as the likeliest candidate for the recent Teutonic effusion. *Pity. She actually looks intelligent.*

All but one of the women smiled at Carl in a way that told him they knew he was the man who would ultimately cast or reject them. A less jaded director might have imagined a silent spectrum of promised intimacy in their massed display of dimples, teeth, and upcurled lips, but Carl read the coiled-spring challenge behind each manufactured smile: *Are you going to hire me, asshole?*

But standing in one corner of the room, seemingly unaware of him, was a slim, bewitching redhead in cerise blouse and black leather skirt. She had a finely chiseled nose, high-fashion cheekbones, enticingly ironic eyes and a sensual mouth whose corners twitched up in a private smile. Carl noticed with dismay the cigarette she smoked with the mannered elegance of a Katharine Hepburn or Lauren Bacall.

Studied preoccupation, Carl thought. *Posed for maximum visual effect.* He thought her subtext was easy to read: "You're going to have to work hard to get *my* attention." But just then, she cast a sidelong glance at him, giving herself away. *Maybe deliberately?*

A niggling wisp of memory. *She looks familiar? Why?*

The narrow reception room was a drab L-shaped chamber with two paint-chipped wooden benches lining either side of the long axis and a switchboard/reception desk right-angled in the short leg. The perky ash-blonde sitting there grinned up at Carl with an overabundance of capped teeth.

"Room number three, Mr. Richards. Your A.D. is in there already." She modulated her voice to her idea of an Irish brogue. "And I'll be wishin' y' a foin, broight marnin'."

"Brenda," Carl warned, patting her hand and pressing it momentarily to his lips, "next time you wish me a good morning, this'll be a bite. All mornings should be lined up against a wall and shot."

She switched to a Scottish burr. "Och, and wad ye r-r-really be toothin' me?"

"The whole tooth and nothing but the tooth."

"Sounds like fun. Where?"

"Where? What do you mean, 'where'?"

"Where," she stage-whispered coyly, "would you bite me?"

"In a window at Macy's."

"It's a date. I'm off at four."

"Bad timing," Carl replied, releasing her hand. "My wife'll be here at four."

Her playfulness vanished. Brenda immediately changed into an adoring fan. "*NO! Really?* Diana Lee Taylor is coming *here?*"

"Uh-huh." Carl was uncomfortably aware that the atmosphere in the studio had suddenly changed. They all heard, they were all curious to see Di, *the* Diana Lee Taylor in person, *and none of them believe for a moment that she really has to audition for her own husband.*

Carl glanced curiously at the sophisticated redhead in the corner to see what her reaction to the news might be. She was watching him now, one perfectly penciled eyebrow quizzically arched. There was wit, intelligence, certainly independency in her emerald-green eyes, but something else, too, an elusive quality he couldn't quite fathom. Carl was surer now he'd seen her before, but could not think where; on the other hand, he mused, maybe her pretended aloofness—*aggravating typical personal need to be noticed-liked-loved—(forgiven?)*—merely produced in him a sense of false recognition.

He realized he was staring at her too long. Looking away, he forced his self-defense system into play. He told himself her oddly haunting, haunted smile was just another auditioner's involvement ploy, *the old Strangers-Across-A-Crowded-Room mindfuck tactic*.

The cynical thought snapped him into work mode. Hefting his briefcase, Carl hurried off for rehearsal studio number three.

The day was heating up fast. All of the windows in the audition room were cranked open, but it still felt hot and close to Carl. Jan Napier, the A.D. (assistant to the director), already had a pair of folding chairs set up behind a long, narrow Formica-top table that was angled so that the auditioners wouldn't have to watch themselves trying out in the floor-to-ceiling mirrors that lined one wall of a space primarily designed for dancers. A battered upright piano stood in one corner with its back facing out. Slung on the floor next to it was an abandoned dance belt that had been there at least a week without being cleared away, but whether out of slovenliness or squeamishness, who could tell?

"Salaam, O Mighty Ruler." The A.D. acknowledged him without looking up.

"Salami yourself, 'Shweetheart'," Carl replied out of the side of his mouth like Humphrey Bogart. He glanced appreciatively at Jan Napier's accentuated curves as she sorted photo-résumés into neat piles. Jan was that prized rarity in the professional theatre, a bright, attractive young person who possessed the enormous organizational skills necessary to be a competent stage manager and who *mirabile dictu* had absolutely no desire to act. Carl met her two summers back while he was directing a production of Albert Camus' *Caligula* in London. When his stage manager got sideswiped by a bus and had to be flown back to Massachusetts, Carl, in frantic need of a replacement, took a chance on a Syracuse University theatre exchange student recommended by a Green Room bartender and never regretted it. Jan not only had a head for the ten million details that any normal stage manager must keep track of, she could actually interpret the scribbled notes Carl dashed off like automatic writing as he prowled the dark aisles during rehearsals, pad in hand, eyes riveted to the stage, pencil point racing by feel alone. Jan's deciphering skills, coupled with her ready grasp of Carl's demanding directorial style, soon earned her a promotion to special assistant to the director. The predictably catty speculation about her success was wholly unfounded—not that Carl hadn't fantasized about his petite assistant. He liked everything about Jan: her size and shape, her close-cropped blond-brown hair, grey eyes, aquiline nose and thin lips. Features too irregular, perhaps, to qualify as beautiful, but Carl found them absolutely adorable. Jan was wearing her usual Syracuse T-shirt loose over frayed, heartbreakingly tight bluejeans. For the thousandth time, Carl warned himself never to "come on" to her, it wasn't worth the risk of losing a spectacular A.D.—his plausible rationalization of the fear that someone as young as Jan would only react to him with ridicule and loathing.

Pointless speculation, anyhow. I'm married to America's Sweetheart. Y clept.

Unsnapping his briefcase, Carl removed a sheaf of notes, shuffled them into a parody of order, sat behind the Formica-top table and reached for the Styrofoam coffee cup that his A.D. had waiting for him. Jan exchanged a porcupine glance of barely tolerated existence with him *another point in her favor, she's got no use for mornings, either.* He removed the plastic lid, muttering, "I should take this intravenously," and pretended he didn't notice Jan in the mirror silently mouthing it with him.

She handed him the latest issue of *Playbill.* "Seen this yet? You're in it."

"Thanks. Pat Clayborne said she'd placed it." The piece had indeed been planted by their press agent, but Carl wrote it himself. He opened the magazine to the appropriate page and savored it while he gulped down black coffee.

> For the past ten years, Carl Richards has been fascinating and frightening the normally jaded New York theatregoing public with what he likes to call "darkly erotic horror." His electrifying versions of *The Demon Barber of Market Street* and *Titus Andronicus* ("the most repulsive special effects outside of a slasher movie," said *The New York Times*) outraged critics but delighted the backers.
>
> As a director, Richards pays lip service to the mad genius Antonin Artaud, but his razor-honed, convoluted imagination is more attuned to the romantic mysticism of Bruckner, El Greco, Liszt and Mahler. Indeed,

when he starred in and directed Michel de Ghelderode's *Sire Halewijn* in Edinburgh, he took his lighting designer to the local art museum to see El Greco's famous painting, *Allegory,* because, says Richards, "there was no other way to explain the candlelit terror lurking in that canvas."

Carl Richards has a wild unruly shock of hair, a smooth complexion and brooding eyes like Poe's "demon that is dreaming," an effect he admits "I crafted as deliberately as I manipulate audiences because everything about me is planned and intentional. I smile like an ingenue, just with the corners of my mouth, that's why I've got crinkles instead of wrinkles. Hell, I even took my smile out of a book, Lucille Fletcher's *Sorry, Wrong Number.* The woman in it loves this man who, I quote more or less, has a quiet smile, 'not a toothy adolescent grin.' " One corner of Richards' mouth twitches. "Like this," he says, "See? Quiet."

"Quiet" *is* the word for Carl Richards. Onstage, his lungs are powerful, but in rehearsals and private life, he is a soft-spoken, improbably affluent, inescapably morose Dostoievskian scholar. The thirty-eight-year-old Scranton, Pennsylvania, native holds an M.F.A. in theatre from Carnegie-Mellon University. After five years with Powder Rocks Repertory Co. in Luzerne County, Pennsylvania, first as literary manager—"NOT 'dramaturg,' " Richards grumbles. "Only a jackass would use that pretentious title!"—later as assistant to the director, he spent several years "on the road" as a stage manager for one of the national companies of *A Chorus Line* before launching his New York career in 1979 by staging John Webster's bloody revenge tragedy, *The White Devil,* at the Municipal Stage. Later that season he mounted *Titus Andronicus* at the Rafters, a production John Simon called "infamously graphic."

The director counters, "*I* call John Simon graphically infamous. Being graphic is what *Titus* is all about! It's as if Shakespeare said to his audiences, 'You want blood? *I'll* give you blood.' And he sure does, plus some magnificently savage poetry. If that's the way Shakespeare wanted it, how else *can* it be staged?"

Despite, or perhaps because of the critical clamor surrounding *Titus Andronicus,* the five-foot-seven-and-a-half—"Don't forget the half inch! At my height, or lack of same, I need that fraction!"—director suddenly found himself "commercial." He began producing and sometimes acting in a wildly successful series of *guignols* both *petit* and *grand: The New London Midnight Ghost Review,* which opened in 1981 at the Regent Park Cinema and is still running; Emlyn Williams' *Night Must Fall* at the Clovis Rep (Richards played Dan, the honey-tongued, head-toting killer); Anthony Shaffer's stomach-wrenching *Murderer* at the Baldwin, with nurses stationed at the back of each aisle equipped with smelling salts. In 1985, his sadomasochistic portrayal of de Ghelderode's *Sire Halewijn* was the "succès de scandale" of the Edinburgh Festival.

Some ("definitely not all") of Carl Richards' critics have begun to respect the validity of his artistic vision. Opinion began shifting in 1987 when Richards announced that Diana Lee Taylor would play Mrs. Lovett in his upcoming nonmusical production of *The Demon Barber of Market Street,* which opened in 1988 to capacity houses at the Colonial Playhouse. Miss Taylor had just voluntarily terminated the six-year run of her acclaimed NBC-TV sitcom, *The Diana Lee Taylor Show,* and announced her plans to move east and become a Broadway actress. Her choice of a Carl Richards vehicle for her "legit" debut was a surprise casting coup that columnists predicted she would bitterly regret. Rex Reed: "There are some roles that, like athletic numbers, ought to be retired with the players. Mrs. Lovett belongs to Angela Lansbury and if Di Taylor thinks otherwise, she's suffering from delusions of adequacy!"

The Demon Barber of Market Street went on to win three Tonys for Best Lighting, Best Set Design . . . and Best Actress—none other than Diana Lee Taylor. Carl Richards' directing was nominated, but he does not mind being passed over. "Look what I won instead!" he grins, referring to his recent wedding with the glamorous Miss Taylor, who before leaving Los Angeles dissolved a twenty-year marriage with TV producer Milford Harrison III.

"It wasn't fair to compare Di with Angela Lansbury," Richards explains. "The Sondheim musical bears little resemblance to Dibdin Pitt's original melodrama, *Sweeney Todd,* which I followed closely when adapting *The Demon Barber of Market Street,* though I did switch the locale to nineteenth-century Philadelphia and added a few horrific touches of my own, especially the decapitation of Mrs. Lovett in full view of the audience, an illusion I discovered in an old conjuring manual."

Richards has a library full of "old conjuring manuals" because early in his career he moonlighted as a professional mentalist. He is planning soon to work theatrical magic once again with his new production of Georg Büchner's expressionistic masterpiece *Woyzeck,* a play that scholars call the first great modern tragedy. Carl Richards himself will perform the title role and there is a rumor Richards will neither confirm nor deny that Diana Lee Taylor will play Woyzeck's doomed lover, Marie.

Carl finished the article, threw the empty Styrofoam coffee cup in the wastebasket and said, "Okay, I'm ready for the first slice of ham. How many auditioners today?"

"Thirteen this morning, ten this afternoon. And your wife's coming at four."

"Yes, I know." *Not likely to forget that.* ("Since when do *I* have to audition, Carl?")

The A.D. paused with her hand on the doorknob. "Oh, there's some actor who telephoned the office late yesterday afternoon. The Shenkel Agency told him he ought to read for the Drum-Major. He claims he's an old friend of yours."

"Oh? What's his name?"

"George Bannon, I think."

"Never heard of him. Where was he when we announced general calls?"

"In Florida doing *Biloxi Blues* at a dinner theatre. Just got back."

"And he says he knows me? George Bannon?"

"I was halfway out the door when he called, so I might've misheard him. Anyway, I told him if he showed up here today around twelve-thirty, we'd try to squeeze him in before lunch."

"Good. So far, all the men we've seen are ballet dancers, not Drum-Majors."

"That's why, O Mighty Ruler, I asked him to come on down." Jan left the room to fetch the first auditioner.

Carl considered the melancholy statistic: twenty-three culled from hundreds of applicants, *many of them capable,* all competing for three parts to be played by two women. (The roles of Margret and Käthe would be doubled.) It was different with men. Good actors—Jan argued it was a unisex word, but Carl still thought in terms of actor = masculine, actress = feminine—good actors were harder to find, *they tend to keep working.* Capable actresses were never in short supply. At any casting call, one might meet five fetching Ophelias, six first-rate Kates and easily a score of superior Juliets, each with her own valid look and interpretation. One might shop for every—*any*—wavelength along the spectrums of height, weight, shape, vocal timbre, hair hue, eye color; one could and did attach subjective weight to minute gradations of humor, sobriety, introversion, extroversion, sensuality. *Apples or oranges? Which looks better on the table today?* So much available talent, but he could only afford to hire two women to play Margret-Käthe and the Grandmother.

Out of sympathy for his fellow thespians' vulnerable egos, Carl tended to run long callbacks. If an auditioner were at all promising, he exhaustively outlined the AEA* salary scale the production would operate under. *"He's talking money—I must really have a chance"*—*the addictive hope of every actor.*

That day, each of the actresses had been asked to prepare one out of three possible monologues adapted by Carl from Büchner's *Woyzeck:* the Grandmother's nasty bedtime story, the carnival barker's spiel or the drunken apprentice's sacrilegious "sermon." The latter pair of speeches

---

*Actors Equity Association, the "legit" theatre labor union.

normally were performed by men, but their content, Carl contended, was "unisexual," and he selected these particular passages because he believed that he could better tolerate their repetition than having to listen, say, to Marie's climactic repentance scene histrionically mangled over and over again, which would certainly happen if he left the choice of speeches drawn from the script totally up to the auditioners.

The door opened, interrupting his train of thought. "Gynger Morrison," Jan said, ushering in the frosted-haired character actress whom Carl suspected of "psyching out" the competition by reeling off *Woyzeck* in the original German. He picked up her résumé from the appropriate pile on the table and examined its formidable credits: three Broadway shows, one of them as Eileen Heckart's understudy; the New York Shakespeare's version of *Antigone* at the Public; tons of regional theatre where she'd practically made a career of playing John Patrick's recurring character, Opal Kronkie (another Eileen Heckart role); TV commercials; in-house industrial promotions; day-player stints on *Another World, The Guiding Light, One Life to Live;* various British, Irish, Scottish and Welsh dialects, and on the continent, Arabian, Armenian, Balkan, Czechoslovakian, Dutch, French, German, Hungarian, Italian, Portuguese, Russian, Scandinavian, Spanish, Turkish; her American accents included Brooklyn, Bronx, New England, Southern, Texan.

Now that he'd survived his wakeup coffee and seen her credentials, Carl had second thoughts about flatly rejecting Gynger Morrison. He guesstimated her age at fifty-two or -three (her résumé declared, AGE RANGE: 45–60), but her lively hazel eyes belied the creases time etched across her forehead, along her narrow face and on either side of a generous mouth that smiled so frankly that Carl decided—*hoped*—that perhaps he may have tagged the wrong culprit. He glanced speculatively from the glossy 8 × 10 head-shot that actually looked like the woman standing in front of him—*maddening rarity*—to her trim five-foot-five, 115-pound dancer's figure tastefully clothed in a white cotton blouse and charcoal grey pants-suit. She reacted to his scrutiny with a lift of her shoulders designed to make her bosom protrude provocatively.

"So?" She smiled at him archly. "Do you approve of the equipment, sir?"

"More to the point," Carl countered, "do *you?*"

"Touché. What's your opinion?"

"That all actors love good dialogue. Let's hear your speech, Miss Morrison." He resisted the urge to add *this time in English*. There was no mistaking her rich contralto, she was indeed the showoff.

If Gynger Morrison interpreted Carl's abruptness as a gentle knuckle-rap *and she does,* she did not show it. With a toss of her head, she picked up a folding chair, set it down in the middle of the room, sat in it, lowered her head for a few seconds, then, looking up, fixed her gaze above and behind Carl's head. Suddenly she disappeared and in her place was a squint-eyed, hardbitten harridan who smacked her lips as if tasting the words she was about to pronounce. She crooked a bony finger at an imaginary crowd of children clamoring for her to tell them all a bedtime story, and then the Grandmother cackled—

Come here, you little crabs, and listen to me! Now once upon a time there was a little girl who had no father or mother because they both were dead. Everybody in the whole world was dead. The little girl searched high and low for family or friend, but all she found were corpses. She gazed into the heavens and liked the way the moon smiled, so she thought she'd go there, but when she did, she discovered that it was only a chunk of wormy wood. So then she went to the sun, but that turned out to be nothing more than a dried-up daisy. She journeyed to the stars, but they were just little golden flies trapped in the spiderweb of God. The little girl thought she'd better go back home, but when she got there, she saw that the earth was really a chamberpot full of doody, so the little girl sat down and cried and cried. And to this very day, she's still there crying all by herself . . . all alone.

The old crone lowered her chin for the space of a long deep breath and when she lifted it, she was Gynger Morrison once more.

"You're right, Mr. Richards," she said. "I *do* love good dialogue. I may sound like a toady for saying it, but your adaptation of *Woyzeck* is the best I've—"

"Thanks," Carl said, curtly interrupting. "That'll be all."

The actress, who'd heard that Carl Richards was "a love to audition for," was taken aback by his summary dismissal; she tried to stammer an apology, thought better of it, gathered up her purse and hurried to the door. Out of the corner of his eye, Carl noticed Jan's involuntary protesting tic.

"Wait a minute, Miss Morrison," he said, irritated at himself for the way he'd behaved. She paused with her hand on the doorknob. "Would you mind coming back at four?"

Swift as blood rushing to an adolescent's cheeks, her smile returned. "I would *love* to, Mr. Richards." She made an exit worthy of Anastasia's Dowager Empress, complete with curtsy.

When they were alone, Jan asked, "What, pray tell, was that all about?"

"Mostly sixth sense. I don't like her."

"She read beautifully."

"You know that isn't what I mean, Jan."

"What I know is that you're having one of your cactus days. Want to talk about it?"

He held up a forestalling hand. "I quit analysis, remember?"

"Whoops Almighty! Anyhow, for the record, *I* liked Gynger."

"I called her back, didn't I?"

"Just barely. And at *four?*"

"She can read opposite Di."

"If you think that's wise." Her mouth described a rueful moue. "You could have at least asked her to demonstrate."

"Demonstrate what?" Carl looked at the bottom of Gynger Morrison's résumé where Jan's forefinger tapped the kitchen-sink heading, Special Skills. It read "Ballet/Jazz/Tap/Ballroom dancing—Fencing—Quick study—Recite English, Greek, Hebrew alphabets backwards while writing them frontways."

"Big deal," Carl said. "I can do that, too."

"Oh, su-u-u-ure you can."

"Z Y X W V U T S R Q P O N M L K J I H G F E D C B A. There, convinced?"

"What about Greek and Hebrew?"

"No, but it's the same principle. Give me some paper and I'll do her forwards-and-back stunt."

"Never mind. I'm impressed. You know the damnedest things— how?"

"The alphabet routine is used by mentalists as a 'super memory' demonstration. I used to do that stuff. Ten to one, Gynger used to work with a mindreader."

"Oink, oink!"

"What do you mean, 'oink, oink'?!"

"Why couldn't she have *been* a mindreader?"

"She's too old. There aren't many professional magicians who are women. Most of them came along comparatively recently and none of them, to my knowledge, specialize in mental. And I am *not* a chauvinist."

"Then you shouldn't call women 'Miss.' "

Carl tossed a playful punch at Jan's jaw. "Not women, kiddo, actresses. *They* prefer 'Miss,' and if you don't believe me, ask one. Now show in the next victim, 'Shweetheart.' ''

The morning came and went, and so did the auditioners. Every time the door opened, Carl felt a curious momentary tension, but after the newcomer entered and Jan introduced her, the sensation ebbed. As each woman did her speech, Carl scribbled impressions and opinions on the back of her photo-résumé, which he subsequently placed on one of three piles equated in his mind with Yes, Maybe or Reject. By twelve-thirty, when Jan suggested they take a lunch break, there were still no new headshots in the Yes stack. Gynger Morrison was the only Maybe.

Carl frowned at his watch. "Lunch already? Have we seen all the morning appointments?"

"There's one more, but she doesn't seem to be in any particular hurry."

"Hmm?"

"She was one of the first people here, but she keeps letting other actresses go on ahead of her."

"Funny. Maybe she's a little nervous."

"I don't think so. Poised to the nth." The A.D. hesitated.

"Yes? What?"

"She makes me uncomfortable." Jan shrugged. "I don't know why. Sixth sense, as you put it."

"Sixth sense? From the pragmatic *Ms.* Napier? Intriguing." Carl fished through the headshots, found one, held it up. "Is this the woman you're talking about?"

"Uh-huh. Angelica Winters."

"Well, let's have a closer look at her. Bring her in."

With a noncommittal nod, Jan left the room and a few seconds later held the door open for the slim redhead who earlier had pretended not to notice Carl.

Angelica Winters wore a cherry-red blouse, a similarly tinted lipstick shade and a figure-flattering black leather skirt that coordinated with the 11×14 model's portfolio she carried. Carl admired her smooth skin and high, handsome cheekbones. Her eyes were green as emeralds, wild as heather, but the ironic humor in them struck him as hollow. Her smile lacked warmth. Some private demon prevented her carmine lips from curling too far away from a pout. Her headshot captured the same paradox. *Pain? Passion?* Or the keen edge of cruelty?

On entering the room, the other auditioners waited for Carl to speak first, but walking over to him, Angelica Winters immediately took his hand and, with great sincerity, said, "I know I ought to call you Mr. Richards, but the first time I saw you this morning, Carl, the strangest feeling came over me that we were already acquainted."

The boldness of her approach startled him. A flood of mixed emotions. Distrust. Curiosity. Fascination.

"Peculiarly enough," he admitted, "I felt the same way. Have we met before?"

"Maybe in our dreams." The half-smile, the warm press of her fingertips were gone as swiftly as if she'd flicked off a switch.

In spite of the heat, Carl felt chilled.

Angelica Winters propped her portfolio on a folding chair that she arranged near the center of the rear wall. "I'm doing the barker's speech. This represents the sideshow tent." She paused. "Would you mind my asking you a quick question?"

He glanced at Jan glancing at her watch. "All right, if it's really quick."

"There's one phrase in my speech—'little piles of ashes and bones.' I couldn't find it in the original text. It sounds like something out of *Waiting for Godot*. Is that intentional?"

"Damn! No, it's a coincidence I should've caught. I know the exact line you're thinking of, Didi says it after Gogo's been beaten. I'll have to—" Carl spied Jan valiantly trying not to fidget. "But we're pressed for time. Thanks for mentioning it, Angelica. Are you ready to do your speech?"

She nodded. If the use of her first name struck her as a point scored, she did not show it. With one arm akimbo, Angelica gestured with her other hand at the make-believe flap of a sideshow tent and began the barker's spiel.

Ladies and gentlemen who crave pleasure, come and find it here in our little ménage-erie. Inside, you'll see marvelous monkeys in uniform. Why do we dress them up? Because stripped they're just ugly, naked beasts, but in our tent each ape is clad in fancy pants and jacket gaudy with medals. In every paw, a shiny ceremonial sword. Presto! Change-o! Chimps no more! Art transforms these little piles of ashes and bones into paragons of civilization—just like us, the chosen people whom Our Lord lovingly

sculpted out of sand and slime and shit. Up the ladder one more rung our
monkeys climb until they become . . . soldiers!

With a smart salute, Angelica Winters clicked her heels together and
marched across the room in a parody of a Prussian officer. *Good bit of
business,* Carl thought. He'd been pleased with her reading as soon as
she broke "menagerie" into two parts, catching an international pun
that he'd omitted from the tryout script because he was afraid that
"ménage-erie" printed as such would only confuse the auditioners. *But
she caught it and played it. Solid A for ingenuity.* He liked her voice,
too: a well-trained instrument that ranged from a supple upper register
down the scale to a vibrant throaty contralto.

Sloughing off her military pose, the actress reached into the air,
plucked an ebony, white-tipped walking stick from nowhere. Carl recognized it as an Appearing Cane, a standard magician's prop; he'd owned
one once. *Make that grade an A Plus.* Suddenly, the barker bellowed—

And now let's begin our *real* show! All that you've seen so far is merely
a prologue to the beginning. Step inside our tent, and we'll dazzle you
with wonders doted on by all the crowned heads of Europe! Inside this
canvas edifice you'll meet a horse as smart as a university professor and a—

The door of the room banged open. A tall, handsome, youngish man
in Levi's strode in, flung his hands wide in the attitude of a musical
comedy finale and blared a make-believe trumpet fanfare. "Ta-*da!*
Rejoice, Master Markowitz! Your fondest prayers are answered! I am
come to save your ass and—"

"There is an audition in progress!" Jan's bellow was twice her size.
The intruder clapped both of his hands over his lips and muttered a
scatalogical noun through a mouthful of fingers. The A.D. spoke again.
"Please wait outside, Mr.—Bannon, is it?"

"Not Bannon," Carl said, both angry and pleased. "A horse as smart
as a professor, and an actor as dumb as a jackass. Jan, this is an old
friend of mine, George O'Brien—who really ought to know better."

The interloper uncovered his mouth. "Look, Cary I'm sor—"

"That's Carl!" Said with the force of a slap.

A dead pause. The newcomer nodded stiffly. "Carl. Right. Look,
the receptionist outside told me you'd seen everybody by now, so I
thought—"

"George," Carl interrupted, indicating Angelica Winters, "apologize to her, not me, she's the one whose audition you interrupted."

George turned to her, but Angelica, already smiling at him with fastidious sweetness, said, "Mea culpas aren't necessary, Mr. O'Brien. It was just an innocent mistake."

Carl studied Angelica curiously, amused. When the door opened, her eyes flashed green hellfire, but now she was all candy-coated forgiveness. *Naturally. She just learned the culprit is an old friend of the director's.*

"Thanks for being a good sport," Carl told her, "but, after all, George did spoil your audition. Would you like to start over again?"

"If you really want me to," she replied unenthusiastically, efficiently collapsing her trick cane into a palm-sized packet. Then she brightened. "I know what! I'll go out and come back again later, and then you and your friend can have some quality time together."

"The problem is," Jan protested, "we're booked solid this afternoon, Ms. Winters—"

"But we'll squeeze you in somehow," Carl interrupted. "Come back at four, Angelica."

RITORNELLO

The honey-haired waitress in white silk blouse, black knee-length skirt and sheer charcoal stockings smiled pleasantly at Carl Richards and dazzlingly at George O'Brien as she served them both Ballantine's scotch on the rocks. The men were seated at a table in Mantalini's, a large Italian restaurant not far from the rehearsal hall. Carl chose it not so much for the kitchen as the fact that before Happy Hour the place actually was quiet enough to carry on a conversation.

Watching the waitress as she retreated, Carl murmured, "I wonder whether I'll ever stop wanting them all?"

"Don't fight it," George said, raising his glass, "it keeps you looking young."

"That's generous, coming from someone eighteen months older who looks ten years younger." Carl couldn't deny the sour fact that George still possessed those same boyish features he had when they were teenagers—lustrous black hair curled above snapping black eyes, a nose *not too big, not too small, just right* and toothpaste-commercial teeth in a mouth keen to smile, utter a sarcastic quip or both. Good looks that always drew women's eyes. *Away from me.* "You son of a bitch," Carl chaffed, "do you know how hard I have to work to avoid wrinkles? Of course not. You don't do anything but go up to the attic once in a while and dust off that picture that shows how old you really are."

"Am I supposed to feel sorry for Cary Markowitz, the small-town boy who married Diana Lee Taylor?"

Carl stiffened. *Vintage George O'Brien Condescending Tone Number Three.* "What's that got to do with anything?"

"It means you moan about the whips and scorns of time and here you've gone and landed a rich superstar you've lusted after most of your post-pubescent life. A celebrity, incidentally, who happens to have goosed your career along very nicely, thanks.''

"What's your point, Georgine? *I* was talking about aging.''

"Well, isn't Diana Lee Grail nine years older than you?''

"Closer to eleven, though you're dead if you ever say I told you. Anyway, there's an old Chinese curse . . . 'you should only live long enough to get what you think you want.' ''

"Oho, trouble in Paradise? Just because she won a Tony and you didn't? Tell Uncle Georgie a-a-a-all about it.''

"That file is Classified,'' Carl said shortly. George still had the power to get to him like fingernails on frosted glass. "Over to you. What've you been up to? I heard you did *Biloxi Blues* in Florida.''

"Yes.''

"Who were you? Certainly not Eugene.''

"Sergeant Toomey.''

"No kidding? Congratulations! Which dinner theatre was it?''

"Just a nonunion gig near Lauderdale. Trust me, you never heard of the place.''

George's evasive attitude puzzled Carl. An actor who lands a show-stealing role like Sergeant Toomey is generally eager to tell self-aggrandizing anecdotes about the production and his stellar performance in it, yet George skipped over the topic altogether. He downed his drink and signaled the waitress (who hadn't taken her eyes off him) to bring him another.

Carl frowned. "Since when are you in the habit of belting down scotches in the middle of the day?''

George poked him playfully. "Since you said you'd pick up the tab. What, no lectures about my scabbing?''

"No. Actors can't always be choosers.''

The refill arrived and George clinked the brim of his glass against Carl's. "To old friends and new.''

"Old friends and new? Meaning what?''

An unaccountable pause. Carl's friend seemed oddly uncomfortable. *Like he said either too little or too much.* George forced a smile. "Meaning maybe you'll hire an old buddy?''

Casting qualms hardly explained George's caught-in-the-cookie-jar expression, but Carl, ignoring the prickling sense that something was fishy, dryly remarked, "I see you haven't lost your old insouciant subtlety.''

"And you your vocabulary. Remember the button I bought you back in high school? 'Eschew Obfuscation'? *Tch-tch*. Not you, Cary. 'If you can't lick 'em, make 'em join *you*,' right?"

"I bought you a button once, too," Carl countered through clenched teeth. "It said, 'Use tact, you fathead.' "

Deliberately—*irritatingly*—misreading Carl's anger as a joke, George guffawed. "So where is it? I'll put it on right now."

"I didn't give it to you because I was afraid it'd hurt your feelings. Maybe I should've. You might've evolved into a circumcised prick, at least."

"I love you, too, Cary-Warry. So what *does* an old friend have to do to get a job offer?"

"One," said Carl, ticking off points, "pretend I don't know your work and read for me at four. Two, stop calling me by my old name. It's been legally changed for years and you know it."

"Just reminding you of your roots."

"I'm not a frigging tree."

"If I 'leaf' you alone, will you quit growling?"

"DAMM IT, I DON'T FIND IT FUNNY!"

"*Shhh!*"

Carl lowered his voice. "Sorry. But I used to hear that same kind of 'roots' crap from my folks. Bunch of hypocritical garbage. My family never set foot inside a synagogue."

"Well, you *were* born Jewish."

"Bullshit! I was born exactly four things. Homo sapiens, masculine, American—and poor. If you don't understand that, then you think like a fucking racist!"

"Don't call *me* a racist!"

"I didn't. I said you think like one. Both of you pin on name-tags, you just react to them differently. Assholes become racists. You became a liberal." Carl took a breath and continued more calmly. "I thought you of all people would understand, Georgine. There's only one religion that ever meant anything to either one of us and that's the theatre."

"That's true, anyway." Biting into a breadstick, George chewed on it and Carl's argument. "Okay, tell you what, fair exchange. Once and for all, you knock off the Georgine crap and I eighty-six Cary Markowitz. Is it a deal?"

"Ouch! ouch! and mea culpa! Old habits *do* die hard. It's a deal." Carl extended his hand. George solemnly shook it. A moody silence. Both men peered intently into their glasses of scotch. George finished his and signaled for still another. Finally, Carl took it on himself to dispel the charged atmosphere. "So . . . how's *your* clan?"

George shrugged. "Life goes on at its petty pace, what can I say? Smiley's preaching gospel in Delaware, John runs an ashram in Colorado. Lena stayed Catholic, she's got five kids and never left Scranton. Do you ever see your brother or sister?"

"No." His tone invited no further discussion. "How about your parents?"

"Mom died. Dad's 'on the road' someplace. I heard your mother passed away."

Carl nodded. "A year after we graduated. Lung cancer."

"I don't remember that she smoked."

"She didn't."

A pause. "So, how's your dad? Does he still run the same old shop in Scranton?"

"No, he can't. He—" Carl interrupted himself. "He decided to retire."

"Where to? Florida with your sister?"

Carl, abruptly turning away from George and his question, motioned for the waitress. "We'd better order. I don't have much time before callbacks start up again."

CADENZA

When Carl reentered the rehearsal studio, Jan was waiting for him with the latest copy of *Back Stage* newspaper in one hand and a folded telephone message from the Innamorato receptionist in the other.

"Exhibit A," she said, turning to page two of the newspaper. "Listen. 'Diana Lee Taylor, star of NBC-TV's late lamented sitcom, *The Diana Lee Taylor Show,* today announced she has accepted the lead in an off-Broadway production of *Woyzeck,* to be directed by her husband, Carl Richards.'" Jan lowered the page and raised her eyebrows. "You didn't authorize Pat to plant that, did you?"

"You know effing well I didn't."

"Sorry. I had to ask." She handed him the scribbled phone message. "Here's Exhibit B."

Carl got on the phone and tracked Diana to the office of her personal manager, Stuart Pierce, who tried to run interference.

"I've advised Diana not to audition for you this afternoon," Pierce declared. "You can't expect a star of her magnitude—"

"This is between me and my wife. Let me speak to her."

"I'm sorry," Pierce objected, "but this is business, not a domestic problem . . . Mr. Taylor."

"That's *Richards.* Don't pull that bullshit on me. Diana's not the only one with access to the press."

Muttering at the other end of the line. Diana took the phone. "Carl, I apologize. Stu ought to know better."

"So should you, Diana. You promised you'd be here at four."

"*You* promised you'd do Carmilla next, not *Woyzeck.*"

"Why didn't you publish that, too, while you're at it?"

"That was totally Stu's doing."

"Do you honestly expect me to believe you didn't approve it first? By the way, are we on a conference line? Is he listening in?"

"Well . . . yes."

"Good. Then you can hear this, too, Pierce—if Diana doesn't show up today, I won't cast her as Marie or Carmilla or anything else *ever*." Carl banged down the phone.

He hoped they didn't call his bluff. Diana might actually believe him, but Pierce probably already was telling her that Carl couldn't afford to back up his threat. *Which I can't.* Financing was largely dependent on Diana Lee Taylor costarring.

When Carl first decided to produce *Woyzeck,* he had absolutely no qualms about his wife's ability to play Marie, but now he was plagued by second thoughts, *mainly because she's afraid it might be wrong for her. Thanks to Mr. Pierce . . .*

Diana's manager represented all that Carl loathed. The Ivy League scion of Scarsdale conservatives. Pierce wore grey hand-tailored suits, imported neckties, Rolex wristwatch, ruby Masonic ring, diamond stickpin: *the bland ostentation of old money.*

Carl was jealous and suspicious of him. When Diana heeded the *idiot* critics who ridiculed "an over-forties woman still playing a desirable unmarried" and canceled her own sitcom, she divorced her producer husband, moved east and embarked on a brief intense round of sexual liaisons that did not, however (she reassured Carl), include her manager, *not that he didn't try.*

Pierce boasted he'd danced with his client at her East Hampton debutante ball, "back when she and I were respectable," meaning before she entered show business and he gave up law to manage some of the celebrities he'd counseled legally. "Stu doesn't realize that little remark destroyed whatever romantic chances he might have had with me," Diana told her mate. "That's the kind of thinking I ran away from when I was a girl."

Still, she trusts him implicitly. Their families, after all, were old friends, their fathers fellow Masons. Though just three years her senior, Pierce held an influence over Diana that was virtually "in loco parentis." She refused to believe her manager used his leverage to prejudice her against Carl. *He's got her half-believing I only married her to further my career.* Like all effective lies, there was a grain of truth in it, and anything Carl said otherwise made Diana worry that maybe Pierce was right.

The afternoon callbacks passed with agonizing slowness. Jan prudently did not ask whether or not Diana would show up. She busied herself, instead, with running things smoothly, doing most of the talking because Carl's attention was fragmented. Not that it mattered. None of the women who auditioned even remotely interested him.

Four o'clock arrived. Gynger Morrison returned, prompt to the instant. Angelica Winters appeared soon afterwards. The A.D. handed each of them a set of "sides"* and said, "Gynger, you read Margret; Ms. Winters, take Marie. You do both understand that you're not necessarily being considered for either one of these parts?"

Angelica nodded. "I saw the article in this morning's *Back Stage*."

You shouldn't believe everything that you read in the papers.

Jan noticed the preoccupied expression return to Carl's face. To distract him, at least momentarily, from what she punningly thought of as "the Di miscast problem," she asked with a mischievous twinkle, "Ladies, before you start looking over your scripts, do you mind if I ask you a totally unrelated question?"

"Ask away," said Gynger, puzzled. The redhead agreed with a nod.

"Tell me which title you like better, 'Miss' or 'Ms.'?"

Angelica, catching the meaningful glance that passed between the director and his assistant, spoke first. "Say that I don't have any special preference . . . is that an answer that'll get me a job?"

"It won't lose you one," Jan said dryly.

"Then that's my answer."

"Well, frankly," Gynger declared, "*I* prefer 'Miss.' In the theatre, even married ladies are addressed as 'Miss.' It's our tradition."

Angelica, smiling sweetly, said, "I guess you're just not into Women's Lib."

"Little girl," Gynger retorted with a chuckle of good-natured condescension, "I was liberated before you or Gloria Steinem were born. I played the road for seventeen years. Know what that means? Haggling with producers, shlepping my own suitcases, doing my own laundry, putting local Casanovas in their places. I know how to take care of myself, but I'm still a lady, and I don't need the sound of a cow kissing a bee—*Mmmm-izzzzzz*—to prove it."

Jan expected to see a triumphant expression on Carl's face, but her diversion was a fizzle, he'd tuned out again, his attention nervously

*A script restricted to a single character's lines and cues.

switching back and forth from his wristwatch—*five after four*—to the studio door that stubbornly refused to open.

The actresses retired like pugilists to opposite corners of the room to examine their scripts. Gynger's lips worked sotto voce as she tasted the length, sense and texture of her dialogue, while the only features of Angelica's countenance that moved were the gem-green eyes that quested swiftly from left to right, left to right, down the page, up the next, as she silently analyzed and labeled each distinct "beat"* so she could select interesting and appropriate "actions"* for all of the speeches she had to deliver.

The doorknob turned. Hoping to see Diana, Carl looked up and was visibly disappointed when it turned out only to be George O'Brien. Jan, handing the newcomer a set of sides for the same scene that the women were preparing, said, "Read Woyzeck's lines. You do realize, of course, we're not actually considering you for that part—?"

"I imagine not," George said, with a significant nod at Carl. The tall actor, strolling to the same corner of the room as Angelica, took a single casual glimpse at his script, then lowered it and waited with an air of nonchalant superiority until the women "caught up" with him. Carl wasn't fooled. *George's oldest trick. Busts his buns doing his homework, then pretends he only has to skim his script once.*

Carl nodded to Jan, who instructed the three actors to begin the scene. Immediately crossing in front of Gynger, Angelica planted herself on a spot corresponding to stage right center, thus affording herself a slight positional advantage over the other actress. With a brief angry glance at the redhead, Gynger faced Carl full-front, thus effectively negating Angelica's upstaging maneuver. The director was amused. Since Marie and Margret were supposed to be next-door neighbors gawking out of their front windows at a passing parade and the Drum-Major leading it, Gynger's strategic countermovement was wholly justifiable.

George's eyes narrowed at the women's wordless jockeying. *Uh-oh,* Carl thought, *Angelica had better watch her ass. Nobody upstages Georgy-Girl and gets away with it . . .*

The scene began. Angelica-Marie hugged the imaginary bastard son that she and her soldier-lover Woyzeck conceived together.

MARIE

Look out there, baby . . . the marchers are coming!

---

*Beat; actions = Stanislavskian terms used in motivational analysis.

MARGRET

Get a load of that Drum-Major! He's tall as a tree!

MARIE

And walks with the pride of a lion.

In his corner of the room, George O'Brien straightened his shoulders as he imagined himself playing the Drum-Major. His feet marked time.

MARGRET

Catch the way he stares at you, neighbor—like he wants to eat you up! Not that you'd mind that, would you?

MARIE

Hey, you of all people shouldn't act catty. Your own eyes are shining so bright, you could take them to the pawnshop and fool the Jew into paying good money for them.

MARGRET

How dare you?! I'm an honest woman, and that's more than you can say! A man could wear seven layers of leather pants, and you'd stare through all seven. You were the one they had in mind when they coined the phrase, "cock-eyed"!

MARIE

You miserable slut!

With convincing anger, both actresses pantomimed slamming down their windows. Margret walked to the side of the room and changed into a motionless, head-down Gynger Morrison.

Angelica continued the scene alone, talking and crooning to her make-believe child. When she reached Woyzeck's entrance cue, George, looking properly "in character" morose, tap-tapped the edge of the floor-to-ceiling dance mirror that lined one wall of the rehearsal studio. He took a few steps that put himself on the same horizontal plane as Angelica, a move that divided audience attention fairly and equally between them. Carl was mildly surprised. *Not the slightest attempt to upstage her? Verily, the millennium hath come.*

MARIE

Who's there? Is that you, Franz? Come on in!

WOYZECK

I can't. I'll be late for company muster.

MARIE

Did you chop the wood for the Captain?

WOYZECK

Yes.

MARIE

What's wrong? You look so upset.

WOYZECK

Marie, it happened again . . . only this time it was worse. Isn't there something in the Bible about smoke erupting from the earth like the fires of Hell?

MARIE

Oh, God, you poor thing!

WOYZECK

The sky screamed at me. It was horrible. I ran away, but flames followed me all the way home. Maybe it was the Freemasons? They hold their secret meetings underground. Marie, what's wrong with me? I'm afraid I'm losing my mind!

MARIE

Oh, Franz, you poor man, try to get hold of yourself. Calm down.

WOYZECK

I'll try. Look, Marie, I've got a little money saved up. Meet me tonight at the carnival. I've got to go now.

George exited, Angelica spoke her tag line and the scene ended.

"All right, once more through, please," Carl said. "This time, ladies, switch parts."

George again read well. Gynger, though still the polished professional, was less comfortable with Marie's lines than she was with Margret's. Angelica's Margret, however, was as good as her Marie, and both interpretations were as distinct from one another as they were different from the carnival barker whose spiel she'd done earlier that day.

No question, she's a damn fine actress, only . . . Only what?

After a second runthrough, Carl dismissed Gynger and asked George and Angelica to stay. "George, I'm going to read you now as the Drum-Major. Would you mind doing Marie again, Angelica?"

"I'd love to."

Jan handed each actor a new single-page side. George examined his script more carefully this time. *Sure. He knows he's got an actual chance of getting this part.* More than a chance, actually; Carl had every intention of hiring him as the Drum-Major, which, after all, was not a particularly difficult role. *Marie's tougher. Especially in this scene.* When the playwright Georg Büchner died at the tragically early age of twenty-three, he left the manuscript of his third drama in workshop disorder, a fact especially apparent in this initial confrontation between the Drum-Major and Marie. The scene demanded several abrupt mood shifts of Marie in a scant half-page. Carl wondered how well Angelica could bring it off.

But before he could find out, the door swung open and there, framed in its portal, looking cool, lovely and distant as a goddess sculpted from ice, stood Carl's wife, Diana Lee Taylor.

Diana's personality was rooted in paradox. Though by nature an intensely private woman, the deep-rooted sense of personal inadequacy that had been with her ever since she was a girl drove her into this most public of professions. The diffused love she won acting never came close to replacing the approval of a father whose conservative values she rebelliously rejected, but she could not accept the fact that fame would never be enough to validate her in her own eyes. Thus Diana constantly yearned for—and shrank from—the attentions of her fans. She reminded Carl of Mr. Chops, Charles Dickens' feisty sideshow dwarf who had "a kind of a everlasting grudge agin the Public." But Mr. Chops longed to "go into society" and Diana yearned to escape it *except when she needs an ego fix.*

Unlike Mr. Chops, Diana was not diminutive. She stood two whole inches taller than Carl, who was hypersensitive about his height. His dad used to promise him he'd be "a six-footer" when he grew up, *which was ridiculous, Mom and Dad were both short.* But as a little boy, he believed his father implicitly, so now, at five-feet-seven-and-a-half inches, he felt cheated of his birthright. His size had been especially hard to tolerate in his teens when girls seemed to equate height with desirability. Seeing Diana standing there in the doorway almost as tall as George O'Brien brought back his old feelings of physical inadequacy.

Though she was indeed tallish, Diana's most remarkable feature was not her stature. In Carl's eyes, there were several excellent candidates for that honor, from her sleek, long tawny-golden hair to her almond-crescent eyes, upturned nose, coral-tinted cheeks and generous lips capable of a radiant smile that might melt the Snow Queen (which used to be Diana's hated sobriquet, bestowed upon her by the press, until she changed her residence, image and husband in that order). Diana's fashion-model bearing was an elegant carryover from an early period in her career when she posed for *Vogue*. Her padded shoulders, correctly aligned, displayed her small breasts to maximum advantage and her slim hips and graceful derriére surmounted dancer's legs capable of standing *en pointe* indefinitely, even in flats.

As she stood there intentionally framed in the portal, Diana's characteristic ambivalence was displayed in the way her graceful pose contradicted her aloof expression, tacitly communicating a wholly different message "look at me, look at me, look at *me*."

Well-trained actors automatically observe minute physical, emotional and atmospheric detail. Carl was no exception. His senses were so finely tuned to situational nuances that sometimes he felt like a combination of Sherlock Holmes and Christopher Isherwood in *I Am a Camera,* who pretended to be a neutral observer in order to distance himself from life's painful impingements. Now as George, Jan and Angelica turned towards the woman posed in the doorway, Carl witnessed a curious crosscurrent of individual reactions.

Jan was the easiest to read. She knew all about Diana's prima donna refusal to show up but, save for a slight tensing of her mouth, kept her feelings in check. George wasn't hard to fathom, either, as he squared his shoulders, lifted one eyebrow and ventured a *"come in and meet me"* smile that produced no discernible response from Diana *but she sees him, all right.* Angelica's reaction was hardest to interpret. After a perfunctory glance at Di, she focused first on George, then Jan, then Carl, where her gaze lingered longest. In her expression, Carl could detect nothing other than razor-keen awareness. *Maybe she's just vampiring emotions for possible future acting use, like I do.*

The freeze-frame moment ended as Diana entered the room and said, "I hope I'm not interrupting?"

"Not at all, Mrs. Richards," Jan answered so cordially she almost fooled Carl. "We're *so* glad you could make it."

If Diana noticed the A.D.'s deadpan putdown *and she does,* she didn't show it. Turning to the other actors, she introduced herself graciously, which momentarily startled Carl. *She usually expects someone else to do the honors.* Then he realized she was only making a point of being sociable to snub him. *De rien. At least Princess Di finally deigned to show up.*

Taking his cue from her, Carl did not address his wife directly, but said, "Now that everyone is here, I'm ready to watch the next scene. George, Angelica, places, please."

At that moment, Angelica did something bizarre.

With a bright "I want to be helpful" smile, the redhead put her script into Diana's hands and said, "I'm sure your husband would rather hear you read Marie." Then she rounded the table and sat down next to Carl.

The director was staggered. In one bold move, Angelica had both preempted his prerogative and usurped Jan's place. Whether she did it in order to score points with Diana or out of some genuine, though misguided sense of good sportsmanship, the actress earned herself a black mark *and just when she was doing so well.*

Meanwhile, Jan stood stranded and nonplussed by the mirror wall. Half-rising, Carl offered her his seat, but she shook her head and stayed put.

George, who by now had assumed the character of the Drum-Major, began the scene with Diana.

DRUM-MAJOR

They say your name's Marie.

MARIE

Yes. Just look at you . . . brawny chest like a bull and a beard you must've ripped off a lion's jaw. You're one of a kind.

DRUM-MAJOR

Wait till you see me on Sunday! When I've got my white gloves on and my big hat with the feather, know what the Prince says? "That's a real man, goddammit!"

MARIE

Su-u-ure, he says that. "A real man," eh?

DRUM-MAJOR

And you're a real piece of woman! You and me, let's populate the whole world with Drum-Majors.

MARIE

Take your hands off.

DRUM-MAJOR

Come on, bitch, don't pretend you don't want it.

MARIE

Let go of me, or see what happens!

DRUM-MAJOR

The Devil burns in your eyes like smoldering coal.

MARIE

So what? It's all the same in the end, anyhow.

"Thank you both," Carl said. "Would you mind trying it again? This time, Di, let's see more ambivalence from Marie."

"What do you mean, 'more ambivalence'?" It was a challenge, not a question.

"I mean, show me her state of mind. It's confused, right?"

"Yes, and I'm confused, too. I don't get her last line. What's it supposed to mean?"

The question irritated Carl. If she was too lazy to think for herself, at least she could have queried him in private, not at an open audition, where they both risked embarrassment. "What do you *think* it means, Di?"

"If I had any idea," she retorted, "I wouldn't ask you. You translated it. You tell me."

Their eyes locked. The script was only an excuse; Diana was pushing for a fight that Carl refused to be sucked into. He returned her stare and said nothing.

The stalemate stretched on till Angelica tentatively broke the silence.

"You know, Diana," she said diplomatically, "I had the same trouble you're having trying to figure out this scene."

"Did you really?" Diana smiled at Carl as if to say, *You see?* "What do you think Marie's last line means?" she asked Angelica.

The other actress hesitated. "I'm not absolutely sure. Marie's attracted to the Drum-Major, but she must also be feeling guilty about Woyzeck because he *is* the father of her child. So when she says 'It's all the same in the end,' maybe she's trying to reconcile the two feelings. What do *you* think, Diana?"

"I think maybe you're right."

Angelica swiveled round to Carl. "May we have a ruling from the judge's bench?"

First she tugs Di's strings, now she yanks mine? "I think that reading might work," he said dryly. "*Now* will you try the scene again, Di?"

Diana nodded toward her new ally. "Let Angelica do it. I want to get an objective look at the whole thing."

Carl patiently agreed. Diana returned the script to the other actress, who rose and crossed to a balancing position near George. They ran the scene together and read it so well that Carl thought, *practically all they need are costumes and an audience.*

After they were finished, Diana took Angelica's place and repeated the same scene with George. It was a considerable improvement over Diana's first time through, *not as good as Angelica, though, dammit.* Finally, Carl asked the three actors to run the Marie-Margret-Woyzeck sequence once again, this time with Diana playing Marie. With Angelica and George backing her up, his wife gave her best reading of the day.

"All right," Carl announced, "that's it for this afternoon. Thank you very much, George, Angelica. We'll be in touch."

The pair left together. Jan diplomatically went out to the studio reception room "to make a few phone calls." As soon as they were alone, Diana resurrected her deferred argument.

"You threatened me today, Carl."

"Because you tried to break your promise."

"I was acting on my manager's advice."

"That I don't doubt."

"Don't start up with your childish jealousy. You put me on the spot in front of an old friend. You will never do that to me again, I promise you!"

The wide angry set of her lips, the flare of her nostrils distracted him.

He locked off an impulse to take her in his arms. Instead, he said to her, "Who's threatening who, now?"

"It was a promise. Idle threats are your department."

"And your specialty," he retorted, "is promise breaking."

"All right, that's it, Carl. I'm leaving."

"What do you mean, leaving? You're walking out on me?"

"No. I don't know." She crossed to the door. "For now. For tonight."

"Where are you going?"

"To The Plaza. I need time to think. To think about us."

He put a restraining hand on her arm. "How can you do that alone? We have to talk things out."

"Words are your specialty, Carl. I can't compete."

"Since when are we in competition?"

"Since I got a Tony and you didn't." Stony silence. Her jaw quavered uncertainly. "We-ell, that's what some of my friends claim."

" 'Friends,' my ass! *One* friend, Diana . . . and what else does 'friend' Stu tell you?"

"That you're too young for me."

"And you believe that?"

She paused. "No-o. Not really."

"Then what, 'really'?"

"That you only married me for my—"

Carl touched a finger to her lips. "Hush. You know better." No answer. "Don't you?"

Diana brushed him away. "I don't know what I know. I feel manipulated."

"By *me?* Di, I love you!"

"Sometimes I believe that."

"And sometimes you believe Stuart Iago Pierce."

"Sometimes everything gets all tangled up. My feelings for you, the feelings I *think* you have for me." A frustrated shrug. "Maybe you're right. When I listen to Stu, I get worried and I overreact. But then again, maybe for once you're wrong, Carl. What you call love, how do I know it isn't all just some sort of elaborate star-humping fantasy?"

"Jesus, there you go again! Typical counterphobic psychobabble!"

"And there *you* go again, using words on me like a club! But the first time we met, you admitted I was your sexual fantasy practically all your life. How has that changed?"

"It hasn't."

"Then Stu is right."

"Oh, for God's sake, Di! One minute I'm only interested in your money, then it's your body. Yes, I like wealth. Yes, I'm turned on by who you are, publicly *and* privately. So what's wrong with that? Do you think physical desire is wicked?"

"No, but maybe that's your hang-up, Carl."

A sharp intake of breath. "What's that supposed to mean?"

She was instantly sorry she'd said it. "Nothing. Forget it."

"No, don't give me 'forget it.' Explain."

"All right." She lowered her voice and her eyes. "It's the way you make love. Or . . . the way you can't." She waited for him to say something, angry words, tender words, *any*thing, but he just stood there without speaking. "Carl, I don't mean you're bad in bed, you're not, you're a good lover." Too many words now, the wrong words tumbling out. "But why is it so hard to satisfy you? Every time we make love, you make me feel so damned inadequate—and yet you claim you've fantasized about me all your life."

Carl turned his back on her. "The Plaza?" he said. "How can you walk into that pretentious lobby without feeling guilty about the entire Third World?"

He hated The Plaza, she loved it: an incompatibility not worth wasting her breath on. Knowing he would make no further effort to detain her, wishing he would, Diana departed.

He was staring out the window at his wife getting into a taxi on Broadway when Jan Napier returned. She patted his shoulder.

"Boss, we've got to vacate the premises. There's a dance class scheduled in here in ten minutes."

With a curt nod, Carl began packing his briefcase.

She watched him for a moment before asking with calculated ambiguity, "So, Mein Herr, are we any closer?"

"Closer?" he growled. "Who? Me and Diana?"

"No," Jan white-lied, "that's none of my business. I mean, are we any closer to having a complete cast?"

"Sorry I grumped. Yes, we've moved ahead. We've got our Drum-Major, don't you think?"

"Absotively." Jan grinned. "He's adorable."

"George would be the first to agree with you. Don't go setting your heart on him, though."

Her face fell. "Don't tell me he's gay?"

"To be truthful, I still don't know for sure. My guess is he swings both ways."

"How can you not know? You grew up together."

"Jan, I was very naive."

"Hard to imagine."

"Imagine it." Carl clicked his briefcase closed. "So, do you have some time to kill? It's Happy Hour, I'll buy you a double."

"Fringe benefits? Hallelujah! You're on!"

They left the studio and headed for Mantalini's. As they were walking, Carl said, "I've decided to use Gynger Morrison as the Grandmother."

"I thought you didn't like her."

"She's starting to grow on me."

Jan laughed. "Her stock went up as soon as she said she preferred 'Miss,' right?" No answer. "Carl?"

His preoccupied stare told her he'd turned out again. For a time, they strolled in silence. As they neared the restaurant, Jan made another tentative foray into volatile territory. "Dare I ask what we're going to do about casting Marie?"

"We don't have any choice in the matter. We have to wait until Di decides to get in touch with me about it."

"How do you know she will?"

"She has to," he said, trying to make himself believe it. "She wouldn't just break the story to *Back Stage*. She must've gone national with it."

"Well, when she does make contact, what then? How do you feel about her interpretation of Marie?"

"It has promise," Carl said guardedly, opening the door to Mantalini's. "With a little directing, she'll do beautifully."

Without commenting on how much directing she thought Diana actually would need, Jan entered the bar and sat on a stool next to Carl. He ordered a glass of white wine for her and scotch for himself. After they toasted the success of the production for the third time that week, Jan cautiously asked his opinion of Angelica Winters.

Carl stared into his glass as if the future could be divined in smoky swirls of scotch. "Well, the lady *is* an excellent actress. She could easily double Margret-Käthe."

"I sense an 'only' coming."

"Yes. I've got odd vibes about her. She's complicated."

"Bottom line, boss?"

He swallowed an ounce of scotch. "The bottom line is . . . I think we're not going to use Miss—*Ms.*—Winters."

Raising her glass, Jan said, "I'll drink to that," and did.

IDÉE FIXE

4:30 A.M.—For the third time in as many hours, Carl Richards aimlessly wandered the thirteen-room penthouse he tried to think of as home, though it really belonged to his wife. Just before they wed, Diana urged him to give up his studio at 67th and Amsterdam. At that time, it sounded sensible enough for him to compromise to the extent of subletting the place short-term to an actor-friend who needed crash space, but now Carl realized his wife's insistence was not based on confidence in the probable longevity of their relationship, but stemmed, instead, from her *ridiculous* insecurity over holding onto her new husband. Well, tonight Diana was sleeping at The Plaza; tomorrow she might just as easily decide to oust him from "their" home. His refusal to worry about it was due partly to "work mode" preoccupation with casting, but it also reflected his ongoing discomfort with the grand-scale luxury of a duplex that struck him as only slightly less decadent than the legendary Plaza, which Carl considered a monument of *nouveau riche* ostentation.

He stopped in front of the open door of Diana's sleeping quarters, remembering that it was the focus of their first marital disagreement—

"Separate bedrooms? How come?"
"Because I need my privacy, Carl."
"There aren't enough rooms in this labyrinth for you to go to be alone?"
"That's not the point. I have my own room and you've got yours. What's wrong with that?"
"Nothing, if I were your guest and not your husband!"

—which was precisely the way Carl now felt: like a visitor liable to be asked at any time to vacate the premises.

Surveying Diana's plush, designer-coordinated bedroom, Carl shook his head at its not-slept-in-by-mere-mortal neatness. *Skeleton key to Di's sexuality,* he mused somberly. *God forbid she should ever muss a sheet.* He stepped into the chamber and picked up a rumpled pullover she had uncharacteristically flung across the otherwise immaculate counterpane. An odd concession to entropy, he thought; her wardrobe cost thousands of dollars, yet she usually curled up at night in knockarounds like the Mets sweater she wore in colder months or the old *Cats* T-shirt that Carl now pressed against his cheek, wistfully smelling her scent.

He carried it with him into the study, drank a pony of Courvoisier he hoped would help him sleep, then went into his own bedroom and turned on his "white noise" machine, adjusting it till it was barely audible. He switched off the light and lay down, clutching Diana's nightwear like a security blanket.

Earlier, Carl had spent hours reviewing his options in case Diana refused to work with him again. He'd drafted and torn up so many cast lists (none of which included Angelica) that his wastebasket bulged with crumpled sheets of paper. Weary of it, yet still unable to sleep, he continued to think about the show while the soft slow plash of the sound machine's simulated waves whispered to him in the dark.

Am I dumb not to use Angelica? Another producer might say so, but Carl firmly maintained that his single most important *toughest* directorial duty was to forge each new cast of players into a coordinated ensemble. It was a hard task because so many American actors either were poorly trained or seduced early on into a posturing there's-only-one-true-way-to-do-this-MY-WAY inflexibility, *especially Strasberg and Yale alumni.* Bitter experience taught him that an A-Plus performance from such an actor usually aggravated the rest of the cast down to B-Minuses, *and then some stupid critic will praise the prima donna and pan everyone else busting their buns to buoy up the arrogant shit!*

Startled at his own vehemence, he clamped off his sudden flood of spiraling rage. *Hardly fall asleep like that.* What did Gramma Hannah used to say in German? "Only the old and the wicked cannot sleep." Settling back on his pillow, Carl concentrated on the soothing ocean tides, breathing rhythmically to a deliberate system once taught him by an acting teacher . . .

in-two-three-four
hold hold
out-two-three-four

Inhale, hold the breath, exhale. Monitoring the heartbeat and match-

ing the count to the tempo of the pulse as it adjusted to the steady surge
and ebb of artificial surf.

in-two-three-four
hold hold
out-two-three-four

His thoughts spooled backward; he saw that his moment of dispropor-
tionate anger over difficult actors was really directed at Diana. Which
wasn't fair, because no matter how hard Di was to

three-
four-
hold-
hold

deal with in private,
at rehearsals she was completely professional. Her TV-acquired time-
is-money discipline made her a dream

hold hold
out-two-three-four

to work with.

Though she'd certainly shown some temperament that afternoon, but
a reading isn't a rehearsal. Carl realized that Di's behavior reflected her
nervousness because she had been unprepared to read Marie, but he also
knew that if she decided to take the part, she would put in

two-three-four

plenty of
homework on it.

hold hold
out-two-three-four

But was Angelica such a risk, really? True,

dream to work with?

he'd noticed a little bit
of friction between her and Gynger Morrison, but then again, Gynger
pulled the *"deutsch-sprechen"* bit earlier, *and that evens things out,
doesn't it?*

two-three-four

Or maybe it doesn't. He played back and catalogued his various
conflicting impressions of Angelica.

in

Was she a risk or not?

hold hold

What problems did he foresee with her? What—

"Makes me uncomfortable."

Jan Jan

—the attractions?

And what did Di ask? What love means.

in-two-three-four

hold Love? Do I know? *hold*

What *do* I like

out-do-I-like

about Angelica Winters? *Familiar territory?* Yes. Intelligent, sophisticated, evidence of wit, probably passionate. *Like me.* But that haunting thing in her eyes? *Pain? Irony? Anger*—or a telltale trace of cruelty?

Cruel words come too easy.

"Like a club, Carl."

What was the club? *Counterphobic.* Meaning? "An impenetrable defense that masks an inner woman afraid of falling in love because intimate commitment threatens the boundaries of Self."

Di?

No need to keep counting. By now, the breathing rhythm was automatic. Behind closed eyelids, Carl watched colorful spangles sparkle-dancing like some living theatre curtain studded with precious gems. His thoughts bled together like the glinting patterns in his head.

Di. No star-humping fantasy. *Tenderness the wor*rriter*ritory?* Yes. Superficially self-confident, secretly self-damning, the kind of irresistible woman *Who?* unable to love because she *WHO?* doesn't love Herself

"you love . . ."

love Hersell

"the way you love . . . the way you can't"

love Hell

"inadequate . . ."

"LOOK AT ME, BITCH!"

The ringing echo of something very important. *Cary* the whisper and suddenly the sounds stop. Cut off. No murmurs of the bells and the sea long dead. A smoky inner looseness. Ghost limbs striving to escape from their encasement. A red glow high up in Carl's forehead. Rushing up upup upupup and in the darkness shortshovel ready sssssscreaming loose and andand andandand safe away—

—in bed?

—above?

Yes. Clarity returns. Suddenly *the way a head is clear* and Carl

is split in half Austria
        Hungary,
               indivisible yet distinct. Half of him in bed relaxed, immobile. The other Carl, hovering just beneath the ceiling, staring at minute crevices and canals in the off-white plaster . . . and now outside flying swiftly through the night, untrammeled, exhilarant, speeding towards distant fireflies of promise. Someone with eyes as big as saucers calling to him and *gentle* Carl stops short above a field that looks like almost any place in New Jersey. Dewdrops like huge emeralds on the grass*diamond* and *I don't like this place.* NO!
    BRRRRRRRIINNNNNGGG

    Carl's pulse skittered up the scale to minor panic. Suddenly heavy with himself, he threw back the covers and leapt out of bed.
    He reached to shut off the alarm, wondered why it went off ten minutes early, sluggishly recalled it was a clock-radio and never rang, finally deduced it was the phone that woke him.
    BRRRRRRRII—
    A froggy croak. "Hello?"
    "Carl, I wanted to catch you first thing."
    Di. "You certainly did that."
    "I know. Sorry I woke you. Look, I've been up all night thinking."
    "Uh-huh." It was all he could do to concentrate. "Thinking."
    "Yes . . . look, Carl, I hear you struggling with the hour. Meet me this afternoon at Stu's. Three o'clock, okay?"
    "Uh-huh." He yawned in echo. "Stu's."
    He hung up and stared stupidly at the telephone. *Damn. When they shoot you at dawn, at least they don't expect you to keep an appointment later.* He rang up The Plaza, fought with the operator to be put through to Miss Taylor, finally got his wife back on the line.
    "What took you so long?" she asked with a trace of sympathetic amusement. "Three o'clock, Carl."

    Stuart Pierce's suite was on the sixth floor of an office building at the corner of 58th and Broadway, a short cab ride from The Plaza for Diana and a seven-minute walk for Carl, who spent the earlier part of the day on the phone conferring with Jan Napier on a variety of production details blissfully unrelated to casting. He left the apartment early and began to stroll along Central Park South.
    It was a sultry, overcast day. The weatherman predicted a fifty-fifty

chance of precipitation, but the lurid light that broke through soot-smudgy clouds promised better odds of a storm. Carl had on a short-sleeve blue shirt, faded Levi's and a tan leather jacket. The last umbrella he'd purchased from a street vendor was already broken, he dumped it in the trash on the way out. Turning south, he went to Uncle Sam's, a shop across the street from Carnegie Hall that specialized in canes and sturdily-made parasols. Five minutes and one forty-nine-dollar bumber-shoot later, Carl continued west along 57th Street, secure in the knowledge that his outlay of cash was positive insurance that it wouldn't rain.

He was only a block away from Pierce's office building, but still had plenty of time before the meeting. On an impulse, Carl crossed Broad-way and entered a huge corner bookstore that extended halfway to Eighth Avenue. Aptly named Coliseum Books, the two-level amphitheatre of popular, "classic," specialty and nonfiction literature was one of his favorite mid-Manhattan loitering spots, second only to the theatre collection at the Lincoln Center Library.

Normally, Carl might have headed straight over to a long aisle bounded on the left by murder mysteries, snail-crawling it to the far end and heading back down the opposite side where a vast array of science-fantasy was stocked, *everything from Asimov to Zelazny—and beyond, as Mr. Kubrick might put it*. Today, however, he walked directly toward the back of the bookshop.

Carl flattered himself that he had "a semi-photographic memory." By this he meant he could re-picture the position and length of lines in a playscript so vividly that memorizing dialogue never daunted him. His talent had useful geographical applications, too (he never got lost in a new city), but there were also drawbacks. In New England, he said he felt the country "drawing in" and in California, Carl cracked the old joke about the ocean being on the wrong side of the road, but the western shoreline really did make him nervous. Now, though he'd never before browsed in the Coliseum's occult section, he knew precisely which shelves to examine along the rear wall.

He found the books he wanted and began to scan their spines back-wards . . . ZOROASTERISM . . . YOUR PAST, PRESENT AND FUTURE LIVES REVEALED . . . X-RAYING THE SOUL . . . WITCHCRAFT FOR THE MODERN CHRISTIAN . . . VAMPIRISM AND LYCANTHROPIC WORSHIP IN THE EAST . . . UNLOCKING THE SECRETS OF THE TAROT . . . TRAVELING THROUGH TIME AND THE MULTIVERSE . . . SPIRITUAL SURVIVAL AND MODERN MEDIUMSHIP . . . RITES AND TOTEMS OF LUCIFER AND LILITH UNREPEN-

TANT . . . THE PRACTICAL HANDBOOK OF PHOTOGRAPHY FOR GHOST HUNTERS . . . *Almost there—*

He felt a hand on his arm. Turning, he saw a woman wearing a jade pants-suit, sunshades and an uncertain smile. Angelica Winters raised her dark glasses. She was even handsomer than he remembered. Her slim eyebrows curved quizzically over bewitchingly viridescent eyes; her high-fashion-model cheekbones perfectly complemented her delicate mouth and chin. The tip of her tongue darted between her lips. "I'm not invading your privacy, am I?"

"No, not at all."

Her lacquered fingernails traced a mischievous path down his forearm. "So, sailor, come here often?"

"No. Yes. I mean, yes, I come here a lot, but not this part of the store."

She took away her hand. "Really? That's surprising."

His arm tingled where she'd touched him. "Why? Because of the shows I direct? A lot of people make that mistake. I'm more interested in fantasy fiction than—" Carl stopped. "I don't want to say something that might offend you."

"You won't. Pardon my frankness, but most of these 'true supernatural' books are horseshit."

"You speak like an educated consumer."

She shrugged modestly. "I've studied a bit."

"Studied what?"

"Magic."

"Really? I used to do magic."

"No, I don't mean conjuring. Magic."

"Oh. I see." Said flatly. Carl knew many self-styled adepts in the theatre, and they all bored him. *Psychological need to play Little Miss reMark(er)able, Miss Winters?*

The redhead indicated the shelves of occult books. "So if this isn't your thing, what brings you here?"

"I had this weird dream last night."

"And you want to translate it into a winning lottery ticket?" The twitch of a smile that she instantly stifled. *Disturbed by the spontaneity?* "So what happened in this dream, Carl . . . or would you rather not talk about it?"

"No, I don't mind. It was very sharp, for one thing. I mean it was unusually full of detail, like really being there."

"You're describing a lucid dream. Actors have them a lot."

"Yes, but there was more to this one. It was kind of—uh—split level." Carl faltered to a self-conscious halt, but Angelica was already running a finger along the shelves of books.

"Here," she said, pulling out four volumes and handing them to him, "start with Oliver Fox and Bob Monroe. Fox interprets everything theosophically and Monroe's a pretentious windbag, but at least they'll convince you you're not crazy. Susan Blackmore here leans toward psychological explanations, and this one—" tapping the fourth book, a digest-sized softcover—"is mostly full of the crap I mentioned, but it does describe some good step-by-step induction techniques."

"You've lost me. Induction techniques for what?"

"Out-of-body travel. Isn't that what you were looking up?"

"Yes, but I didn't tell you that, did I?"

"You said 'split-level' and I knew just what you meant. You were in bed and someplace else at the same time, right?"

"Right! Has that ever happened to you?"

"Once in a while."

"How can you tell what is and isn't real? I mean, it seems to be really happening, then it gets all mixed up like—well, like a dream."

"It does get complicated." She patted the books. "After you've done a little reading, you'll start to understand the difference. Then the next time you have a 'split-level' dream, you'll be able to control it better."

"Well, I'll take your word for it." Carl accepted the books and turned to go, but Angelica caught at his sleeve.

"Wait. Would you like to talk about it some more over coffee—my treat? No, that sounds like a bribe. We'll go dutch, okay?"

"Well," said Carl, not liking the fact that he liked the idea, "I *do* have a little time before . . . before my next appointment."

They went to Rosie Stirling's, a popular, determinedly undistinguished deli on 57th off Sixth Avenue, choosing it because it was close by. A bespectacled bald-headed waiter sporting a straggly brown mustache greeted Carl familiarly. He showed the pair to a corner booth, took their orders and came back so fast with a bottle of Beck's and Angelica's espresso that she said, "You know, Carl, some days I've sat here ten minutes without seeing a menu. Is it always this good, being rich and famous?"

"Rich I wouldn't know. Famous comes in lots of sizes. Before I married Di, they used to treat me anonymously, too."

"You brought *her* here? *Here?*"

"Once." His tone warned her to drop it.

Angelica prudently busied herself, isolating a tiny amount of sugar on the tip of her spoon and dribbling it into her cup. "My first husband said that when I do this, I look like an analytic chemist."

"First husband? How many times have you been married, Angelica?"

"Two and a half. The half was common law, sort of. Currently single."

"Divorced?"

"The second time. My first husband—would you believe his name was Carl, too?—my first husband died young."

"I'm sorry about that."

Angelica frowned. "Why do men always say that? As if they were personally responsible." Her remark irritated Carl, but she gave no sign of noticing. She finished stirring her coffee. "There. Story of my life. Restrict sweetness to small doses."

"You're not a diabetic, are you?"

"No, just an actress. The first rule you learn is stay trim or stay off the couch." She sipped primly. "So tell me about yourself. What sign were you born under?"

Her cynicism amused him, but her question made him cringe. "Superior Radio Repairs," he quipped. "My father's shop."

A brittle smile. "Meaning you don't believe in astrology."

"I don't believe in belief, Angelica."

Her eyes widened. "That sounds *so* clever. Maybe someday you'll tell me what it means." Before he could take offense, she abruptly switched topics. "Was last night the first time you ever experienced a 'split-level' dream?"

"No. I used to have them long before I ever heard of astral projection."

"That term's passé, Carl. Nowadays they're usually called obies. O.B., for 'out of body'—though nobody knows if anything actually leaves the body. Maybe it's all in the mind. I don't like to think that, but most things I grew up believing turned out sour, so why should the afterlife be any different?"

The cynicism of True Hope. He smiled with unmistakable condescension. "That's what's called reasoning from insufficient data. I'm impressed, though, Angelica. You've quite the analytical mind."

"I'm *ever* so flattered." Her nostrils flared; her lips thinned. "You know, just because I believe in astrology doesn't automatically mean they shortchanged me at the brain bank."

Her sudden sharpness jolted him. "This wasn't such a good idea, after all, was it?" He started to rise.

Angelica clasped his arm. "Carl, no, I'm sorry!" Her panic was as sudden as her pique. "That was world-class stupid of me!"

"Why? Because it was rude—or because you think you just screwed yourself out of a part?"

For one livid instant, Angelica's eyes blazed, then she regarded him with mingled regret and defiance. "Guess I deserved that. Look, for whatever reason, I'm sorry. Okay?"

"Yes." He sat back down, feeling sheepish. "I'm sorry, too. You *were* on the right wavelength, I *was* patronizing you. Truce?"

She took the hand he offered. "Everybody says you're sweet."

"I am. I work at it."

"Oh, yes, I know. I noticed that about you right away." She still held his hand.

A dangerous silence. Carl felt caught up in something not altogether pleasant, a thing with its own perverse logic. Opening his palm, Angelica lightly ran her fingernail along the groove of the heart-line. "So, hokay, sveet guy," she said in an accent like Maria Ouspenskaya in *The Wolf Man*, "crossing geepsy's palm with silver and telling to her all your weird dreams . . ."

Which he did.

They never got around to discussing Angelica's out-of-body experiences. She sidetracked the conversation, rousing Carl's suspicions with an oh-so-casual remark about how much she admired Bruckner, El Greco, Mahler—*straight out of* Playbill. But then, as they talked about movies and TV and popular music, he was delighted at how many oddly eclectic opinions the two of them shared: they both liked The Limeliters, Stephen Sondheim, Karen Akers, Emerson, Lake and Palmer; they both loved L.A. *Law, Cheers, Northern Exposure* and *Sisters;* they both adored Laurel and Hardy, Monty Python, *Fawlty Towers* and Mel Brooks but loathed most of Woody Allen's films and all of Robert Altman's and—

Suddenly, Carl noticed his wristwatch.

"Oh, Lord, it's after three o'clock! I've got to meet Diana!" Sliding out of the booth, he grabbed the check. "I'll take care of this."

"That wasn't the deal, Carl."

"It is now. Thanks. I enjoyed this."

"So did I." She indicated his package of books. "Maybe after you've read those, you might want to talk some more. . . ?"

A critical second's hesitation. "M-maybe."

She immediately knew he'd reerected a barrier. Her lips twisted into a wintry smile. "Well, if you decide yes, my number's on my résumé, Carl."

Up at the cash register, he glanced into a mirror and saw her still sitting there, watching him intently—*how?* Flirtatiously? Bitter because he'd suddenly distanced himself? Was she sending him genuine signals, or just trying to get him to cast her? *All of the above? None of the above?* How much of Angelica was real, how much play-acting? The first moment he set eyes on her at audition, he knew she was a kind of woman who calculated her every word and gesture, yet, breaking pattern, she'd lashed out at him self-destructively. The two behaviors didn't mesh. The contradiction made Angelica undeniably intriguing, a puzzle-box that might hold treasure or a serpent poised to strike. *Or both.*

As Carl left Rosie Stirling's Deli and hurried west to meet his wife, he silently but firmly reaffirmed his earlier decision not to risk casting the talented, enigmatic Angelica Winters in *Woyzeck.*

Though her husband arrived late and seemed preoccupied, Diana greeted him with a conciliatory hug and Stuart Pierce shook hands with a wooden cordiality that suggested he'd been warned to treat Carl with respect. The dapper manager took his place behind a great oak desk and gestured for the others to sit down.

"Just for the record, Mr. Richards, I've advised Diana not to do this show with you. I say this without animus or malice. I simply believe, on reflection, that it's not the best career choice for her at this time."

"You mean," Carl said, affecting a casualness he did not feel, "there's a new offer on the table that you want Di to accept, instead."

"A star of her magnitude always has a variety of available options."

"Cut to the chase. Yesterday's argument is going to cost me. How much?"

Before Pierce could reply, Diana interrupted. "Stuart—no! That's not why we're here!"

With a sigh, Pierce folded manicured hands over the silk vest covering his middle. "Pardon me for misunderstanding, but when you called to set up a three-way meeting, I naturally assumed you wanted me to renegotiate terms."

"Not for money that Carl doesn't have."

Pierce shrugged. "Then do you really need me at this stage?"

"Oh, yes, you're part of this. I want you to pay attention." She faced Carl. "I don't know if you managed to get any sleep, but I was up all night thinking."

"About the show?"

"That, too, but mostly about us. Our problems . . . personal problems."

The color rushed to his cheeks. "Di, not in front of him!"

She gestured impatiently. "Look, I've been rehearsing what I want to tell you for hours. Now for once, just trust me and shut up . . . okay?"

"Okay." But he was still afraid of what she might say, angry that Pierce would hear it, too.

"Your threat didn't make me come to callbacks," Diana said. "Stu called it a bluff, but what I care about is that you gave me an ultimatum and that's not your style. I decided it was my fault, I pushed you into it when I let Stu run that story in the press." Pierce began to protest, but she rounded on him. "And now that it *has* appeared, you have nerve enough to ask me to change my mind? Why? Just to cause Carl trouble?" The manager tried to break in again, but she overrode him. "You haven't exactly made your feelings about Carl a secret. You ignore him every which way. I never even heard you use his first name. Yesterday you deliberately called him Mr. Taylor."

"I already apologized for that," he replied. "The point is, Diana, I represent you, not your husband."

"The point is, Stu, he *is* my husband. I expect you to stop treating him like my enemy." She turned back to Carl. "You've been right all along, I *do* pay too much attention to my friends and not enough to my own common sense. But the bottom line is, I need a man like you, mister. I want us to work."

Recognizing a cue, Carl rose, went to her and said, "Di, if we were alone, I wouldn't be groping for words to tell you—"

"Hey, like the song says, 'Don't talk at all, show me!' " All at once, Diana was on her feet and in her husband's arms. The warm flex of her body excited Carl, but he didn't trust the *happening too fast* sudden reconciliation. Diana was obviously staging the scene for her manager's benefit. *Should've trusted her, though. She'd never discuss our real problems in front of him.*

"I hate to spoil a good love scene," Pierce said drily, "but might I introduce a modicum of business into this alleged business meeting?"

"We're listening," Diana said, one arm round Carl's waist.

"I still advise you not to get involved with this project."

"And if I do, you won't represent me?"

Fat chance of that.

"I'm not saying that at all," Pierce hastened to reply. "I'm merely going on record for your husband's benefit."

Still chokes on my name. Let him.

"Your objection is noted, Stu, but I'm not going to renege." She waited, heard nothing. "Carl, the next line is yours, I think. Do you still want me to play Marie?" When he did not instantly reply, she said, "Look, if you don't think I'm right for it, just say so. I know you've had second thoughts about it, don't tell me you haven't."

"Only after you started to become all sorts of insecure about it yourself." Addressed to her, but really meant for Pierce's ears. "I still think you can do it, but if you don't believe that, too, it's doomsday . . . and now you've got the next cue. This has got to be your decision, Di."

"Don't I know it, pal." Her voice cracked, her thumbs twiddled, her eyes sought the ceiling. Carl recognized the line and its accompanying fidget as one of his wife's most endearing mannerisms from her old network television show. A familiar-yet-still-novel thrill ran through him as he remembered as if for the first time the cosmically amazing fact that Diana Lee Taylor, *the* Diana Lee Taylor actually deigned to marry Cary Richard Markowitz of Scranton, Pennsylvania! The miracle of it made inner distances foreshorten, incompatibilities dwindle; he felt the urge for intimate communion with his dream-goddess . . . but then Angelica Winters' cryptic smile broke into his thoughts unbidden.

NO! Carl promised himself yet again, *I positively will not cast her— not even if Di turns down the part!*

His wife was speaking to him. "I realize Marie would stretch my technique, and that's fine, I like a challenge, but I've already had my honeymoon with the New York critics, I can just picture them sharpening their stilettos. I can't risk any bad reviews at this stage of my career—"

"My point exactly," Pierce murmured.

"So," Carl said, "you're going to turn down the part, after all?"

She shook her head. "Uh-uh. If I bring this off, I'll be able to land any part I want next. I know you're a good director, so if you think I've got the range to do Marie, I'm going to trust your judgment. And you had damn well better be right!"

Amen! Carl turned to Stuart Pierce. "Let me use your phone and call my office. I'll tell them to send over the contract right away."

Diana put her hand over the telephone. "Wait, before you do, I've got one condition." Carl stiffened. "Relax, I'm not going to usurp any of your precious directorial prerogatives, I just want you to provide us both with a little extra insurance."

"Insurance? What do you mean, 'insurance'?"

"I mean a smart understudy. Someone I can watch and learn from."

An ominous silence. He summoned the courage to ask the question he already knew the answer to. "Di, do you have someone particular in mind?"

She nodded. "That sweet redhead who handed me her script."

A thing with its own laws and logic.

Arriving home after a quiet dinner at Le Festin de Pierre, Diana, radiant with romantic promise, slipped off her shoes, curled up on the living room sofa and sipped Dom Perignon. Carl, sensing that she was in a receptive mood, delicately suggested she might wish to change her mind about Angelica Winters.

"Why? Do you know something I don't?"

If I say Angelica deliberately manipulated her at auditions, Di'll be insulted. Nobody likes to admit they've been used. "It's like this," Carl said, appealing to her sense of professionalism, "I've never known you to take artistic shortcuts. Wouldn't you rather develop your own characterization?"

"Carl, this script is tough. First Marie says one thing, then she goes and does something exactly the opposite."

"You know people like that, don't you?"

"Sure. They mystify the bejesus out of me. I've got to find a way to get inside Marie's skin, justify her, make her me, find elements of myself in her."

"I agree. That's why you can't go carbon-copying Angelica Winters."

"I never said I would! I just want the benefit of her common sense.

Yes, I admit that I'll be watching how she interprets her lines—her timing, her business—but when I do Marie, you'll see, Carl, it'll come out completely different.''

"I believe you, Di, but will she? Put yourself in Angelica's place—won't she think you're just vampiring her interpretation?''

Very carefully setting her wineglass on the veined marble top of her coffee table, she replied, "No, but even if she did, she'd put up with it. What actor wouldn't rather be an understudy than go without a job?'' A reediness in her voice warned Carl that so far as Diana was concerned, the subject was closed, or had better be.

Angelica Winters was hired.

4:30 A.M.—Carl stared up at the ceiling, hoping his rhythmic breathing would help him sleep. He tried to remember what his grandmother used to say.

Nur-die-Bö-sen
können schlafen
nicht-two-three-four

Something like that. Beside him in the darkness, Diana slumbered with her thighs pressed against him, tempting Carl to mold himself against her in the manner of nestled spoons. In his mind, the same dreary litany repeated itself over and over and over again—

ailurefailurefailurefailurefailurefailuref

—though at

least his failure was not due to any kind of masculine inadequacy, *not impotence,* Carl reassured himself. He remembered all too well the emasculating locker-room propaganda drummed into little boys' heads by the mothers, sisters, aunts and sexist elementary-schoolmarms who metaphorically rock the American cradle—*What are little girls made of? Sugar and spice and everything nice! What are little boys made of? Spit and shit and half a wit!* Growing up ashamed of his coarse, truculent father *and hateful brother,* men the arrogant loudmouths of the world, using fists instead of brains and when little Cary read books instead of going outside to play because the neighborhood boys teased him because he didn't know how to catch a ball or swing a bat—*and yea, verily, the world shall be saved by Jesus Christ in a catcher's mask*—Mr. Markowitz, this same doting father, cracked one joke repeatedly, "Let's take his pants down and see if he's really a boy!'' *Well, fuck you, Pop, I learned more about manhood than you ever could've taught me.* Early on, Carl assimilated the Eleventh Commandment preached by all the goddesses-in-his-midst: Thou Shalt Not Cheat Us Of Our Orgasm(s)! As he reached puberty, he trained himself to delay the moment of release so that someday, if some incredibly generous woman actually permitted him entry, he would be worthy of her. Now that he was grown up, he knew he'd trained himself well; he was proud of his ability to stay erect indefinitely while his appreciative lovers repeatedly came. So, earlier that evening, Carl toiled tirelessly in

two-three-four

side Di as she enjoyed multiple climaxes, until she finally *cried, "Hold (hold), enough!"* out

two-three-four

of sheer exhaustion. But as he drew away from Diana, she said, "Hey, there, laddie, how about you?"

"I'm fine." *Hold hold*

"Mister, I've faked too many times not to know the difference."

"It's all right, angel, I'm satisfied, really I am."

"Jesus, Carl, what's wrong with me? Some men probably get off just watching me on TV in G-rated Nice-Nelly clothes! You've got it all . . . why isn't that enough? Why am *I* not enough?"

Answer the question, Mr. Richards. Why *isn't* she enough?
in-two-three-f—
Answer the question, Carl. Why isn't *she* enough?
tch-tch-three—
Answer question, Cary. Why isn't she *enough?*
tch-thr—
m
Answer, *Why?*
tch
Answer m
t
Answer m
e,
BITCH!"

She screamed as Carl flung her naked to the floor. Shoving her legs apart, tearing into her body, striving unsuccessfully to climax, ripping her with one last despairing thrust while she cried out again and again in an agony of blood and flame and the intimacy of—NO!

Carl shot up in bed, heart pounding with the immediacy of nightmare. He saw by the radio-alarm's glowing face that he'd only been asleep for a moment. The bedroom was still dark. His sudden movement hadn't disturbed Diana, she was sleeping more deeply than usual. *Poor baby, I guess she really was up all last night.*

("I need a man like you, mister.")

He stroked her hair, his physical yearning for her quelled by a wave of paternal protectiveness *because she looks so little-girl-lost angelic.*

Outside, the Manhattan skyline glimmered with the first ghostly flush that comes before dawn. Carl remembered something he'd read when he skim-flipped through the books he'd bought at the Coliseum: "Adepts know that the best time of day for out-of-body travel is that cosmically mysterious moment immediately preceding sunrise when, often, spirits of the old and sickly quit their bodies for good." *Like Gramma Hannah.*

Carl needed to understand this upsetting-exhilarating phenomenon that stole over him sometimes as he teetered on the borderline of sleep. Maybe if he could control it, it might lose its power to frighten him, *but how do I will it to happen?* The book that Angelica recommended contained numerous techniques for inducing "astral flight," but all but one were too complicated to absorb from a single desultory look-see. The exception was a simple suggestion to "choose a place to go and then imagine the various points along the route that you will have to pass in order to reach your goal."

He didn't have any special destination in mind, but he closed his eyes, anyway, and tried to imagine himself floating up to the ceiling, through the window, out above the street. Nothing happened. *Naturally. Too much too soon.* The trained actor in him took over: *Pull everything inside first, then open up. Three deep breaths, hold. Imagine something beautiful. Five medium breaths, now . . . hold . . . something beautiful . . . seven shallow breaths . . . hold hold . . . someone beautiful . . . breathe steady steady . . .* regulating the rise and fall of his chest, picturing the air as visible vapor flowing through his nostrils, narrowing his concentration to a slim filament of awareness . . .

. . . and now, examining each sensory strand separately, meticulously, one faculty at a time—the cool night breeze ruffling his hair, the warm contrasting touch of soft womanly skin . . . her perfume faintly mingling with perspiration and the musky afterscent of desire, the interlayered bittersweetness in his mouth . . . calm breathing and the occasional rumble of early traffic that rode by, rustling the overhanging treetops of Central Park . . .

. . . red glow high up inside his forehead . . . ringing, and the smoky looseness of phantom limbs striving to free themselves . . . and Carl *awake and lucid* feels himself rising, indivisible yet distinct, one Carl still in bed, the other Carl opening doppelgänger eyes and staring, amazed, at the ceiling's retinal cracks and crevices.

Pilot to navigator—where to?

'Choose place. Imagine.'

Navigator to pilot—where to?

'Go. Points to pass to reach goal.'

This time, Carl notes his route precisely: soaring high above the street, flying west along Central Park South, crossing Columbus Circle, Ninth Avenue, Tenth, Twelfth, and now the brisk invigorating air of morning welcomes him down the silver line of the Hudson as it empties into the basin of the Upper Bay. Past the Statue of Liberty glowing in the waning darkness, he follows the beckoning down a waterway bordered east and west by Staten Island and New Jersey. A dock. On the banks of the Sound, a boundary park with walkways and a playground. The detailing and dimensionality are extraordinary: he sees each shaft of grass distinctly, even to the dewdrops glistening on every tip.

Carl finds himself in a nearly empty diner. A greying pinch-lipped waitress behind the long service counter gossips with a short, bald, potbellied policeman sitting on a red leatherette swivel stool. At the cash register, a bespectacled man with straggly brown mustache reads a newspaper. None of them notice him or a woman sitting in one of the diner booths staring down at the greasy tabletop, a coffee cup clutched in her hands.

Wondering who she is, filled with the sudden urgent need to find out, Carl draws closer, tries to see her face, but she will not raise her head.

"Look at me . . . please?"

She gives no sign of hearing him. Drinking the rest of her coffee, the woman rises, goes to the cash register, pays her bill, walks out. Carl pursues her round a corner, up a flight of stone steps to the vestibule of an old apartment building. She stops to unlock the front door that Carl penetrates, passes through. Upstairs now, up a second flight, a third, trailing her into a parlor dominated by a bookcase crammed with fashion magazines and softcover playscripts. On the left, a long narrow kitchen. The woman walks through an arch with the splayed skin of an animal tacked over it. Carl follows her into a small bedroom overlooking Staten Island and the Sound. A dresser. A closet. Every object hard-edged, infinitely complex. *Real.*

The telephone rings. She answers it. He cannot make out the words, just her anger. She slams it back on its hook.

Her face is still in shadow. Now as she kicks off her shoes and sits on the bed to remove her stockings, Carl drifts closer.

"Look at me . . . please?"

Perhaps she hears, perhaps she senses him, perhaps it is merely chance, but at that very moment she looks up and Carl
instantly recognizes

her

his half-remembered dream-lover, whose haunting, haunted features are no longer concealed from him in secret corridors of thought

her

emerald eyes luring him down the river's long glistening skein into

her

outstretched arms, and now as Carl's heart beats ever faster and faster and his passion begins to uncoil, he reaches out to clasp

her

naked in a perfect union of harmony and f

antastique

antastiqu

ntastiq

tasti

ast

s

sss

sssss

SSSSSSS

SSSSSSS

NO!

A dark serpent of primal force surges suddenly up from her bosom, slashing sharply into Carl's chest in a sensation so titanic
that he whipped
back instantly through time and all the long miles, plummeting heavily

into his own body. With a cry of terror, he sat bolt upright in bed, gasping for breath.

Diana woke with a start. "My God, Carl, what's wrong? Did you have a bad dream?"

"Yes."

"What was it?"

"Nothing. Go back to sleep."

He went into the bathroom, shut the door, switched on the light. Baring his chest, Carl studied himself in the mirror.

No visible wound.

But Angelica's addictive venom was already seeping, drop by bitter drop, into the darkest chambers of his heart.

A BALL

'The artist attends a festive celebration, but cannot find his beloved. To his fervid spirit, her absence makes all seem hollow
and false—but ultimately, in his time of greatest despair, She
appears!'

VALSE EN 5/4

The young policeman adjusted the stand of the tabletop mike. "All right, ma'am, now remember to face this way and keep your voice—"

"My dear boy—excuse me, 'Officer'—I learned microphone technique long before you were born. I acted on the radio."

"Okay. Switching on, then."

chk

STATEMENT OF GYNGER MORRISON

Q: Statement taken at 1:07 A.M., Saturday, May 13, at Wyssamisson County Courthouse by Officer John Wilbur. Please state your full name and address.

A: Gynger Faye Morrison, Ten Downing Street, New York City. Don't look at me funny, I'm not making it up. Ten Downing Street is a real address in Greenwich Village.

Q: Relationship to the victim?

A: None. We're both in the cast of *Woyzeck* at Powder Rocks Rep.

Q: Voyt-seck?

A: W-O-Y-Z-E-C-K. It's German.

Q: Did you see what happened tonight?

A: The stabbing? No.

Q: Where were you?

A: Off right.

Q: Where's that?

A: Okay, if I say right or left, I mean from the viewpoint of an actor onstage facing the audience. So off right is the backstage area to the right of an actor onstage facing the audience, see? I was off right changing my costume.

Q: In your dressing-room?

A: No, I work O.P. It's faster to make a quick change right from there.

Q: Where's O.P.?

A: Bubbaleh, you're going to need a lexicon. O.P. is short for the backstage working area known as the Opposite Prompt Side—to distinguish it from the Prompt Side. Wait, I'll explain. Backstage at Powder Rocks, you've got your light control booth, your sound panel and your act curtain ropes off left, and the mens' dressing rooms and two of the kids' dressing rooms are on that side, too. So when the show's running, the stage manager—Jan Napier—cues the technicians and prompts the actors on her side of the stage, which is why it's called the Prompt Side. So at Powder Rocks, the side of stage just off right is also known as the Opposite Prompt Side. If your company needs an assistant stage manager, you station him—her—O.P. In our show, we've got two women's dressing rooms and a property table off right, so I cue the other gals and check that the props are preset correctly.

Q: So you're the assistant stage manager?

A: Uh-huh. Head of props, too. There are so many short scenes in *Woyzeck,* it's a real bitch to cue. Jan needed help and I certainly didn't object to a few extra bucks. Carl was going to pick . . . somebody else, but Jan's a sweet kid, she named me, instead. Insisted on me, actually.

Q: Let's get back to tonight.

A: Okay. After I finished my bit as the Grandmother, I had two short scenes to change into my next costume, so while Woyzeck—that's Carl—was murdering Marie, I was standing O.P. pulling the Grandmother's skirt over my head and off, which is why I didn't see anything till I heard this—God, this awful cry, I'll never forget it!—and I looked and there she was stretched out on the stage floor where she's supposed to be, because she's dead. Blackout—but when the lights came up on the next scene, Carl hadn't cleared. He was there on the floor with her, holding her in his arms, saying her name over and over again. Well, Jan rang down the curtain fast. For all that most of the audience knew, that's how the show's supposed to end. They applauded, but there was no curtain call—maybe they thought that was an intentional Carl Richards touch.

Q: What happened after the curtain came down? What did Richards do?

A: You'll have to talk to Jan about that. I didn't see much. Everybody panicked, everybody was milling about, it was chaos. Bill Evans, he doubles the Captain and Karl the Fool, Bill starts telling everyone how once he did Shakespeare's Scottish play and an actor was murdered onstage, but our show's worse because this sure isn't our only casualty. I'm trying to shut him up when Jan tells me to get Lyla and Frank and Myne—they're the local kids we jobbed in to play the children's roles— Jan says get them the hell out of there, so I herded them across the road to the Sweet Tooth and phoned their families and treated them to waffles and ice cream while we waited for their folks to come and pick them up. That's why I can't tell you much about what went on afterwards down at the theatre.

Q: Tell me this—did Richards have any reason to want to hurt her?

A: What are you saying? That Carl actually meant to kill her? Come off it, you don't know Carl.

Q: Look, all I'm trying to do right now is establish, if I can, exactly what did happen. No, I don't know Richards, I don't know any of you people. Anything that you can tell me about whatever's been going on with you folks might possibly help me.

A: Okay, I'll try. This may take a few minutes.

Q: Take all the time you need. Tell me whatever you remember, facts, impressions. You never can tell what might be important.

A: I was picking up bad vibes about this show right from the start. There was tension between Carl and Di, there was something going on with George O'Brien. Whenever the cast went out for a bite after rehearsal, George wouldn't say much, he'd just sit there and hit the bottle. Jan was having some kind of trouble about George over at Equity—

Q: Where?

A: Equity, Actors Equity, the actors' union. Jan had to miss several hours of rehearsal the first week, she asked me to fill in for her. There was a complaint against George from some producer in Florida. I don't know the details, it was none of my business, but I heard that much from a friend at Equity. You can't keep things secret in a small theatre company. Anyway, things really started heating up by the end of the week. On the night of the cast party, Carl—

Q: What night was this?

A: Saturday night, end of the first week. The night before we came to Pennsylvania.

Q: What was the exact date?

A: Let's see, we've been here two weeks, today's the thirteenth, tomorrow is the fourteenth, counting backward—okay, I'm talking about Saturday night, April 29th. This was a humongous bash, you'd think we were a million-dollar Broadway musical—I mean, we're talking hordes of famous guests, catering by Le Festin de Pierre—Beluga caviar, Dom Perignon, Godiva chocolates, music by Peter Duchin, and he was actually there, not just his orchestra. This was not Carl's party, it was a Diana Lee Taylor media event . . .

Tydings, a huge upscale discotheque on West 53rd Street half a block east of the Hudson, has a pair of hundred-foot-long bars sandwiched between outer rows of black plastic banquettes and a central line of small Lucite tables designed to accommodate two at a time comfortably, more as a hardship necessity. A large raised rectangle for dancing at the rear of the great long room is surmounted by an overhanging, steeply raked balcony that provides a dramatic vantage for watching the psychedelically lit couples below. The mezzanine's comparative seclusion is generally employed for private conversations and/or discreet foreplay.

Gynger and Jan arrived together. Despite the difference in their ages, they'd become fast friends during the first week of rehearsal. Gynger understood that Jan, an orphan, probably needed a mother *but she'll just have to settle for an older sister.* Gynger missed her own kid sister, Kitty, a successful San Francisco attorney; Jan looked a little bit like her.

Gynger handed her slicker, umbrella and galoshes to a buxom checkroom attendant, glanced at her hairdo in her compact mirror and decided a swift repair trip was indicated. Jan's close-cropped brown-blond locks were undisturbed by the high winds. *I'd kill for hair like hers!* Jan undid her plastic babushka, shoved it into a raincoat pocket, checked the garment and accompanied her friend into the ladies' room.

"Well," Gynger said, adjusting her makeup at a lounge mirror, "the storm doesn't seem to have dampened attendance. Did you see that crowd?"

"Just a few intimate friends coming to wish Her Majesty well," Jan replied drily.

"Oh, Lady Di's not so bad when she stops playing herself."

"Yeah, Gyn, I guess not, only—well, I don't know."

Oh, yes, you do know, hon . . . a bit of a crush on the bossman, haven't you?

They saw Carl almost as soon as they entered the main room. He was sitting at a Lucite table having what appeared to be a serious talk with

George O'Brien, but though both men seemed intent, Carl's eyes kept darting restlessly about the crowd from face to face to face. He gave Jan and Gynger an acknowledging nod. George glanced around, saw who it was and flashed them a half-hearted smile.

The women maneuvered past a knot of people clustered around one of the many food tables. "What's wrong?" Gynger asked Jan. "Carl looks like he's reading him the riot act. Or are George's problems still classified?"

"Gyn, no shop talk, please. I want a drink."

At the nearest bar, Jan vied for the attention of one of the determinedly unhurried bartenders as Gynger peered curiously at the contained pool of blinding white light in a far corner of the club. She said, "Looks like an Eleven O'Clock News team decided to cover us."

"Yes. NBC promised to interview the Snow Queen. Her old network—" Jan interrupted herself when the bartender deigned to recognize their existence. "Bombay Sapphire martini, stirred, not shaken, served straight up, two olives. Gynger?"

"Jack Daniels, rocks." She looked quizzically at her friend. "Since when did you understudy Sean Connery?"

"Carl taught me Bombay Sapphire."

"I'll bet." A pause while the bartender made their drinks. "Here's our poison. Come on, Jan, let's go gawk at royalty."

Drinks in hand, they threaded their path through the throng packing the long, crowded room. They jostled for places in a semicircle of spectators standing outside a concentric ring of TV technicians taping Pia Lindstrom, who was sitting at one of the black plastic banquettes with Diana Lee Taylor, interviewing her.

"I can't hear them, can you, Gyn?"

"No. I didn't expect to. TV performers usually let the mike do the work. Stage-oriented people have to remember not to project and break the microphone."

Pia asked a question that prompted one of Diana's wide-eyed, million-teeth-flashing smiles. Jan stiffened. "Why does she always have to grin like that?"

"Honey, that smile's one of Di's most popular trademarks."

"It looks so phony."

"No, I don't see phony. More like fear." A technician waved at Gynger to lower her voice. "See? I'm not even near the mikes. Let's wander."

Q: "Fear"? You're saying she was afraid of somebody?

A: Everybody. No, I don't mean that literally. Just that whenever Di switched on that big smile of hers, all Jan could see was what we actors call "indicating"—in the sense of indicating an emotion with a signpost, instead of really feeling it. But Jan's a kid with a lot of life experience not logged in yet. She doesn't know what it's like to be deep-down scared and not allowed to show anything but self-confidence. That lightswitch grin was just a place for the little girl inside Di to hide behind. I never saw her turn it on when she was really focused on her acting.

Q: Let's get back to the party. So far, I notice you haven't mentioned Angelica Winters. Didn't she show up that night?

A: Oh, yes. Actors love delayed entrances. She made one. Deliberately, I'd guess.

Q: You don't sound fond of her.

A: I can't add up my feelings about her one-two-three. You meet someone carrying around that much bad kharma and how can you not pity them? Angelica never willingly dropped her mask, certainly not in front of me, probably not even in front of her own mirror, but even so, God! the pain!

Q: She was sick, you mean?

A: For all I know. But no, what I'm saying is—a very angry, very frightened lady. Why I can't tell you, and I can't prove I'm right, but I know I am . . . and after a while, I even started to see a few things in her that I admired. But still—

Q: Yes? But still?

A: But my first impression was—well, less than terrific. This was at callbacks—auditions—for *Woyzeck* and we were all in the waiting room, maybe a dozen actresses, and Angelica was chatting ever-so-sweetly to the other gals—a word here, a phrase there—planting insecurity like seeds.

Q: What was she saying?

A: All the pertinent literary poop about the play and Büchner, the author—basically, showing just how smart she was and how well *she* knew the show. That might not sound like much to you, Officer, but you've got to understand, some actors are hypersensitive about their lack of formal schooling and *Woyzeck* isn't exactly a household word. These ladies were nervous already. Angelica was strafing them intellectually, making them feel completely unprepared. I saw what she was up to and when she got around to me, I just blitzed her by spouting

Woyzeck at her in the original German. Later on, when we auditioned together, Angelica tried to upstage me, but I handled her then, too.

Q: When did your opinion of her start to change?

A: I wouldn't say change. Modify, maybe. A kind of chilly respect, watching her operate like *All About Eve,* right from the first.

Q: What did she do?

A: Nothing obvious. We were all busy learning our lines and blocking, but there were undercurrents—George's trouble with the union, a couple of tense exchanges between Di and Carl—and meanwhile, here'd be Angelica asking Carl all these nitpicking questions he loved to answer about his adaptation of the play, while the rest of us'd be standing around waiting with our thumbs—twiddling them. Sometimes she'd give him some perfectly innocent little gift, a pencil or a cup of coffee, perfectly innocent, understand, and Carl would thank her, but he wouldn't look directly at her, and maybe when he took it from her, their hands would touch and maybe not, but it'd all take just a little longer than it should have.

Q: Didn't his wife notice?

A: No. Totally not. She treated Angelica like her younger sister. I mean, there are two dressing rooms for women on the O.P. side and I figured Di, being a superstar, would get one and the rest of us—me, Angelica and little Lila—would be bumping bottoms in the other. But Di invited Angelica to share hers. Insisted on it.

Q: Why are you shaking your head?

A: Because Angelica manipulated that to happen. The same kind of mindgames she pulled at audition she played on Diana, undermining her confidence, making her all sorts of vulnerable.

Q: Did you actually see any of this, or are you just guessing?

A: I wasn't in their dressing room, no. But look, Di's Marie started off okay, but then she began to lose faith in herself. She'd bicker with Carl and he'd tell her to take a break while Angelica stood in for her. Di would watch Angelica, then she'd try it her own way and Carl wouldn't like it, so she'd get upset and go to her dressing room and Angelica would have to calm her down. Then Di would come back and act like an Angelica clone and Carl would be satisfied. Oh, and listen to this—on the second day of rehearsals, Carl announces that *Woyzeck* runs too short, so he's going to add a curtain-raiser to the bill, a one-act by Strindberg called *The Stronger.* It's just a few pages long, but it's a great monologue for one actress with a second actress sitting and listening to her, reacting but never saying anything. Naturally, Diana has the lines and Carl casts Angelica in the silent role—but would you believe that when we got to Pennsylvania, the two of them actually switched and Di got the nonspeaking part?! Granted, there was a reason for it, but still—

Q: What was the reason?

A: Because Diana unexpectedly had to miss part of the second week of rehearsals. This came about at the cast party right after Pia interviewed Di. Carl was livid. He called Jan over and—

Gynger didn't recognize the man in the monogrammed white shirt and hand-tailored grey suit sitting with Diana, Carl and Jan. The discussion they were having looked bitter, yet Carl, intent though he was on what the well-dressed man was saying, still darted occasional glances about the crowd.

"Who's he looking for?" George O'Brien grumbled to himself as he passed by Gynger's table on his way to the bar.

"George," Gynger asked, catching his sleeve and pointing to the man in grey, "who's that, do you know?"

"Him? That's Di's manager."

"Ah, so that's the mighty Stuart Pierce. They all look like they're planning a funeral. You know what they're talking about?"

George gave a contemptuous snort. "As long as it's not me, I don't give two shits. You seen Angelica anywhere?"

"No."

"I have to talk to her." Emptying his glass, George went back to the bar for a refill.

The meeting broke up a few minutes later. Jan rejoined her companion, Gynger, who cocked an eyebrow at her. "Well, is this another deep dark mystery, or do I find out who died?"

The A.D. replied, "Carl's furious at Di. NBC okays Pia's interview, but expects a favor in return. The Snow Queen's manager tells her she's got to do it, so she jumps to say yes without even discussing it first with Carl."

"What's this big favor?"

"Hosting *Saturday Night Live* next week."

Gynger's jaw dropped. "But my God, we're opening the week after! How many rehearsals will she miss?"

"That's what the conference was all about. She's staying in town for a Monday morning meeting with the writers, then she flies to Avoca . . . Scranton–Wilkes-Barre Airport. We'll be into overtime Monday night, you can bet, but at least she promised to pick up the tab. She rehearses with us Tuesday, then the rest of the week, Wednesday through Saturday, she's back in New York.''

"Terrific. Carl must really be upset.''

"Try 'white-hot,' Gynger. Not that he shows it.''

"Well, come on, let's go see if we can cheer him up. General morale and all that.''

"I'm game.''

They went down one long side of the room and found Carl talking with Perry Cooke, a popular Sunday *Times* columnist. Carl gestured for them to sit by him on the upholstered bench.

"Perry, I'd like you to meet one of my talented cast members, Gynger Morrison. You already know my assistant Jan.''

Gynger shook hands across the table with a balding gentleman of perhaps sixty with crinkling smile-lines at the edges of his eyes and mouth. She immediately liked Cooke.

"Miss Morrison, Carl here has been sharing with me some of his views why people become actors.''

The director nodded. "I say men do it mainly to defy the system, while women want to fit into it, control it.''

"What do you think, Miss Morrison?'' Cooke asked.

"Well, I do know men like that,'' Gynger admitted, "but then again, there are others who are only looking for an easy ride. They usually don't last long. The profession winnows them out.''

"What about the women?'' the columnist prompted.

"That, my dear man, is what I would call an essay question, and this isn't my interview.''

The journalist smiled encouragingly, but Carl spoke first. "Gynger, feel free to expound. That's why I called you over.''

"Ah, well, in that case, how can a lady resist?'' Her lashes fluttered. "American women—when you're brainwashed from birth into thinking your Number One priority is the looking-glass, is it any wonder if you start behaving like Alice in—

A: But you don't need to hear all that. What I'm leading up to is, during our interview, I noticed Di across the room whispering to her manager. He nodded and left the party. A little while later, she did, too. I'm not implying anything, understand, just telling you what I saw.

Q: Did Richards notice her leave?

A: Oh, he noticed, all right.

Q: What did he do?

A: Nothing. Finished his interview.

Q: After the interview, what did Richards do?

A: Went to the balcony to sulk. We were sitting together, the three of us, me and Jan and George. We figured one of us should go upstairs and talk to Carl, try to cheer him up, but George was too sloshed, so . . .

"Oh, no, sweetie, not me," Gynger declared. "You're officially his gadfly. This is your job."

"I don't know what I'd say to him, Gyn."

"Don't say anything, Jan. Let him talk."

She fidgeted. "What if he doesn't want to?"

George smiled sourly. "He's always got something to say."

"And if not, you can just sit with him," Gynger suggested.

"I don't like to intrude on his privacy."

"Worst'll happen," George slurred, "he'll say, 'piss off.' "

"Okay, okay, I'll give it a try." Jan fluffed her hair, smoothed her dress: absent gestures in another woman; for her, significant telltales. She went to the balcony . . . only to come back down scant seconds later, irritated.

Gynger's eyebrows rose. "What's wrong? Did the bossman tell you to get lost?"

"He didn't even see me. He's up there with Angelica."

"Angelica? I haven't seen her all night. Where'd *she* come from?" Gynger wondered.

Staring at the balcony, George muttered, "From Hell's back porch."

Q: None of you saw Winters arrive?

A: No, but a few minutes later, we sure saw her leaving. George called her, but she brushed right past him without stopping. He got up to go after her, but his legs were too scotch-wobbly.

Q: Did Richards leave with her?

A: Uh-uh. He stayed in the balcony maybe ten minutes, then he hurried on down, blew me and Jan a kiss and left the party, too . . .

SCENES IN THE COUNTRY

'One night in the country the artist shares a duet of surpassing sweetness. The music and the surrounding scene combine to produce an unaccustomed calm in his heart, even as they tinge his thoughts with bitterness. The melancholy anticipation of deceit torments him. The music resumes, but it is no longer a duet— one of the voices is silent. The sun sets . . . solitude . . . the foreboding rumble of distant thunder . . .'

NOCTURNE IN A♭

As he walked out of Tydings, Carl turned up the collar of his overcoat, reached into a pocket for a crumpled cap he'd bought in Edinburgh, adjusted it over his eyes, opened his new umbrella and stepped into the storm-slick night.

Perfect weather for the mood I'm in.

He slogged east in the bitter stinging rain, reflecting on the tribulations of the first week of rehearsals. The initial stages of any production are predictably chockful of directorial headaches, but this time the usual problems involved in learning the new cast's strengths, weaknesses and idiosyncracies were compounded by George's union difficulties, Diana's moodiness *not to mention her latest little surprise* and—especially—Angelica's invidious attentions: her oh-so-casual gifts; her conspiratorial nods each time Carl interpreted some textual nicety, acts of hubris that admittedly flattered him, though had they come from another actor, say Gynger or George, he would have found them offensive; most of all, those increasingly intimate occasions when Angelica's eyes met his and lingered there a fraction of a second too long. Carl was cynically certain it was all a deliberate campaign on her part and was equally convinced that she held some delusive preconception of what he was "really" like. Yet in spite of dour common sense and every one of the emotional alarm bells that Angelica rang, he still felt drawn to her.

As he entered the Ninth Avenue parking lot, a horn honked at him. Through the rain streaming off the brim of his cap he saw a pair of headlights blink. Sloshing across the asphalt to the passenger side of an old VW, he opened its door, tossed his new umbrella in the back and slid in beside her.

Fretted tension. For a long awkward moment, neither of them spoke.

Angelica removed a pack of Virginia Slims from her purse. "Would you like one?"

"I'm allergic to cigarettes."

"Oh." She depressed the knob of the dashboard lighter. "I'll crack a window, then."

That won't help, Carl thought, but said nothing. He'd watched her during rehearsal breaks and knew she was one of those ironclad compulsives who smoke to mask inner tension. He understood her present need, *and besides, it's her car.*

Half-opening her window, Angelica checked to see whether the rain would spray inside, found that the storm was slowing to a gentle whispering drizzle. The lighter popped out. She held it to her cigarette, inhaled, returned it to the dash and asked, "Well, where to? Any special place or should I just drive?"

"Maybe we ought to sit here a while."

"And do what?"

"Talk."

"Talk about what? Whether your wife's having an affair with her manager? Uh-uh, not your style. Production problems? How we're going to rehearse around Di? You'll cover that on Monday, and anyway, that's work, this isn't. You could tell me what's going on with George O'Brien—but that's none of my business. So? Name a topic and we'll talk." She blew smoke through the window and waited. He made no reply. After a longish silence, Angelica said, "All right, Carl, we're both feeling awkward. Do you want to just say good night and go home?"

"Not really."

"Well, for the record, neither do I." She took a long drag on her cigarette, glanced at Carl and frowned. "My smoking *is* really troubling you, isn't it?"

"Yes."

She crushed the butt in the ashtray and thrust the key into the ignition. "I don't smoke when I'm driving. Okay?"

"Okay. So where to?"

"Who knows?" Rolling up her window, Angelica switched on the motor, shifted into gear, pulled out of the parking lot into Ninth Avenue and turned south. When they reached the turnoff for the Lincoln Tunnel, she took it.

Carl raised his eyebrows. "Crossing state lines turns this into a federal offense."

"I doubt that you're eligible for the Mann Act."

"But why New Jersey?"

"Just because it isn't New York?"

He nodded. "I buy that. When I was a teenager, one of the things I really liked to do was ride around with my friends and see places I'd never been to before."

"So we'll do that now?"

"Sounds good to me."

A quick smile, then her eyes returned to the road as the VW emerged from the garish yellow glare of the tunnel. They rode round a curve and thrilled to the lights of Manhattan twinkling on the other side of the Hudson River. Another mile and then Angelica steered onto the New Jersey Turnpike. As the traffic separated into lanes and thinned out, she said, "All right, now, driver's privilege—I get to ask a personal question."

"This car has interesting 'house rules.' What do you want to know?"

"Why you like directing better than acting."

"Suggesting by your tone that you think acting is the be-all and end-all?"

"For me it is."

"It was for me, too, at first. Then I learned directors and producers control the final product."

" 'Product'? You sound like an M.B.A. candidate."

Carl was amused. "Artists turn up their noses at business, then wonder why their careers don't go anywhere."

"But why are men always so hung up on control?"

The remark irritated him. "I don't know about 'men,' Angelica, I only know about me. Why do *I* find control important? Maybe because when I was a kid, I was always being bossed around—mother, grandmother, sister, brother telling me what to do, what not to do. Especially what not to do."

"Do you stay in touch with them?"

"My mother's dead, my sister lives too far away and I don't talk to my brother."

"What about your father?"

"What about *your* family?"

"No siblings. My father died when I was twelve."

"And your mother?"

"I don't like to talk about her."

"And I don't like to talk about my father. But monologues only work at auditions, Angelica."

" 'You tell me yours, I'll tell you mine'? Maybe next time. Let's start out slow.''

Carl stopped himself from asking what, precisely, it was they were starting upon. Meanwhile, up ahead, the turnpike split in two, the right route for buses, trucks and general traffic, the left for cars only. Angelica eased into the left lane.

"Well, so far," he remarked, "we haven't gone anywhere I haven't already been to."

She gave his leg a quick playful squeeze. "A touch of my hand, and ye shall be upheld in more than this—see there?" Angelica pointed to an exit sign that suddenly loomed in the headlights. She switched on her blinker signal and steered into the right lane.

"Random choice?" Carl asked.

"Absolutely. Are you game?"

"Sure, why not?"

She drove onto the exit ramp, stopped at the tollgate, let Carl pay, headed for an intersection and turned left. They drifted down a long, straight block of wooden salt-box cottages lit by old-fashioned street-lamps.

"Ever been here before?"

He shook his head. "It's quaint. Where are we?"

"Seacliffe. One of the pleasanter Manhattan bedroom communities, so I'm told. Maybe if we're lucky, there'll be a greasy spoon that's still open downtown. I could use some coffee."

"Are you sure there *is* a downtown?"

"We'll find out."

They followed the street as it skirted the low glistening bank of a wide bay. A strangely familiar feeling began to steal over Carl. *Déjà vu to the Nth.* After a few minutes of riding, they reached a lighted intersection. On one corner they saw a chrome-buckled trolleycar diner with a blinking neon sign in its front window repeatedly declaring, "Open 24 Hours!"

Angelica parked in front of the Seacliffe Grille and shut off the motor. "This all right?" When he did not reply, she looked at him and noticed the peculiar expression on his face. "Carl? Something wrong?"

"I'm not sure yet. Let's go inside."

She locked up the car and they entered the almost-empty diner. A skinny waitress stood behind the long familiar service counter cracking her gum and gossiping with a hefty bald graveyard-shift worker in plaid shirt and dungarees.

Same place, different people.

They sat down in a diner booth, ordered cherry pie and coffee and waited silently till the waitress returned with their food. Angelica tasted a mouthful and put down her fork. "Well? Are you going to clue me in on what's bothering you?"

"I'm trying to integrate new data."

"Such as?"

"Something I know you don't think I know."

"You sound like a cross between the Oracle of Delphi and a computer." Her lips twitched nervously. "Speaking of which, there was a time I honestly believed I *was* a computer. Right brain, left brain—disk drives A and B. My thoughts were my software. All I ever learned in school, data files reducible to ASCII Code. Falling in love? Computer virus." She paused, got no reaction from him, resumed her banter. "I was raised Catholic. That was my command program. When I 'lapsed,' I just switched operating systems, CPM to DOS. Hey, how long do I have to keep up this stupid analogy before I get a readout from you?"

"The readout, Angelica, is that I've been here before and so have you."

"How do you mean? Figuratively? Literally? And where is 'here'? Seacliffe? This diner?"

"Both. This isn't some place you just drove to by accident, is it? You live here. Nearby."

He expected an apology or some kind of rationalization, but instead, astonishingly, Angelica was angry. "What did you do, Carl, look up my address on my contract?"

"I didn't see your damn contract! Think back—Coliseum Books, remember? The dreams I told you about?"

A sharp intake of breath. "*This* diner?"

"Yes."

Angelica exhaled, surprised and sheepish. "All right, you caught me. I *do* live in Seacliffe. My apartment is just—"

He cut in. "Just around the corner. I could take us there without you showing me."

Half-lidded eyes studied him. "I like that idea, Carl."

Carl led the way up a worn stone stoop to the vestibule of the same apartment building he visited in his sleep. Angelica opened the front door and they went along a short hall to the foot of a steep staircase. Still in the lead, Carl climbed one flight, another, another, turned right on the third landing, walked to the far end of a hall where there were two doors, pointed to the one on the left and said, "This is your apartment, right?"

"Yes." Angelica unlocked the door.

Carl entered and recognized the cozy parlor with the large bookcase crammed with magazines and softcover playscripts. He indicated a short passage left of the entry. "Doesn't that hall lead to your kitchen? With the bathroom on its far side?"

"You're still batting a thousand. Make yourself comfortable, okay? I want to get out of my party things. I won't be long." Angelica walked through an archway he already knew led to her bedroom.

He began to inspect her books. Actors' shelves are generally stocked with scripts they've appeared in; Angelica's were no exception. Curious to learn some of the other roles she'd played, Carl browsed systematically, working backward through the alphabet: *Wedekind*'s Lulu. *Figures*. Alice in *Dance of Death*, yes, *Angelica'd be spectacular*. Gertrude in *Rosencrantz and Guildenstern? Bit of an age stretch*. Carl glanced at the next script and shook his head. *Boy Meets Girl? No way*. He pulled it out, flipped to the character listing and saw that the name of one of the leading male roles had been pencil-changed from Robert to Roberta. *Well, okay, I guess that could work*. He reinserted the volume and was about to withdraw the Neil Simon script next to it on the shelf when Angelica returned, fetchingly clad in a lime-green skirt and matching short-sleeve blouse.

Tacitly admiring her ensemble *(green is certainly her color)*, Carl pointed to a spot above the arch and asked, "By any chance, Angelica, did you ever have an animal skin tacked up over there?"

The question startled her. "No, but—curiouser and curiouser—I've got a pet wolfhound that's getting very old. After Vulcan dies, I'm going to have his coat removed and hang it on that wall." Carl stared in astonishment. "Don't look at me like I'm crazy, it's an old Indian custom."

"And of course you're an old Indian."

"It's meant to honor the memory of a faithful animal companion." Angelica's eyes narrowed. "Do you have a problem with that, Mr. Richards?"

"Only if we get married and *I* die first." Carl, who couldn't resist the wisecrack, was relieved, surprised even, that it struck her funny. It occurred to him that this was the first time he'd ever seen Angelica really laugh. Her display of humor was generally restricted to a controlled uptilt of her lips. He knew that the most arrestingly lovely women paradoxically often were the most insecure over their looks, childhood ugly ducklings who grew up yearning to be magnificent, constitutionally unable to accept that they'd actually succeeded. Now as Angelica's lips curled away from her gums, they revealed a slightly uneven overbite. He found the girlish openness of this expression perversely appealing: it seemed to reveal an unguarded glimpse of the "real" Angelica. *Maybe when she was little,* Carl speculated, *someone insensitive kidded her— and now no man under the sun could ever convince her what a wonderful smile she's got.*

"So," Carl asked, "where is he?"

"Who?"

"Your wolfhound Vulcan. He's awfully quiet."

"He's not here. I kenneled him with my cousin Katy."

Carl did not ask her why; he was sure he knew the reason. As Angelica honed in on the tension between him and Di during rehearsals, she must have decided there might be a chance of luring him to her apartment. Maybe her dog was overly protective and she didn't want him underfoot.

Ego-stroking theory. Carl's inner demons tried picking holes in it, but did not succeed. He could not discount the fact that she had deliberately brought him to Seacliffe. The why of it troubled him, though. Was Angelica really attracted to him, or was she only using him to advance her career? A little of both? Yes? No? Something more complicated?

Definitely more complicated. Carl thought of the coiled serpent in her bosom. When would she unleash it again?

Is that what I'm waiting—hoping—for?

Yes. No. And more complicated.

Choosing a place on the end of a small burgundy sofa, Angelica motioned for Carl to join her. "Getting back to what started all this," she said, "your obie tells me what I already knew. We're linked. I felt it the first time we met. You did, too—remember?"

"Linked? Maybe." He sat down next to her. "I seem to have read your mind, anyway."

"Not necessarily. You might have glimpsed the future."

"Come on, you don't honestly believe that?"

"Carl, you saw Vulcan's coat on that wall. That hasn't happened."

"But it's in your mind."

"How can you believe in telepathy, but draw the line at prophecy?"

"My father used to play a telepathic game with me that worked. He was an electronic repairman. Once you understand radio frequency, thought transference becomes logical—banal, even.''

"Maybe so, except for one thing. Telepathy tests have worked in spite of electrical shielding."

"I didn't know that. But if it isn't electrical interchange, how do you explain thought transference?"

"I don't have to, Carl, I just accept."

Sure. You were raised Catholic.

Angelica abruptly rose and crossed to a window overlooking the bay. She shoved the sash open with a bang. "I need a cigarette. I'll stay over here." She lit up and stared out into the rain-scoured night, patently ignoring him. *The same pose as at callbacks—Madonna Preoccupado.* All the taut lines of her face and body straining toward some distant point.

He knew it was a pivotal moment, one that would probably determine the growth or death of their relationship. Carl didn't trust himself to speak. He wasn't sure if he really wanted anything from her, and if he did, what price he was willing to pay for it. He thought about telephoning Diana at The Plaza. When Angelica tossed away the remnant of her cigarette and turned toward him to ask whether he'd read the books he bought on her recommendation, Carl weighed whether to answer the question or ask, instead, to use her phone.

He decided to reply. "I haven't had the time to, Angelica. I skimmed them to learn how to induce obies deliberately, but I didn't pick up much."

"Obviously, you picked up a few things if you came here without my knowing it."

"Well, it *was* the clearest obie I ever had—but still, I slipped in and out of control . . . in and out of consciousness."

"When you're in the middle of an experience," she nodded, "it's hard to judge what's true and what's a lie." She held her hand out to him. "Come with me to the other room. I'll guide you through a lucid obie."

"Is that really possible?"

"We're linked—remember?"

He followed Angelica into her bedroom. He saw the same narrow closet, the same tidy mahogany dresser, the kingsize bed that took up almost the whole width of the room . . .

"What is it, Carl? You remember something else?"

"Not the way you mean. It's just this bed, it reminds me of the one I used to have to share with my brother."

"The two of you aren't very close, are you?"

"What did Oscar Wilde say? 'Family is the true ferment of the artistic spirit, provided one escapes it.' "

Some fleeting ghost of bitterness crossed her face, a hurt-angry look that roused conflicting emotions in Carl. Wanting—*needing?*—to protect her. Needing—*wanting?*—to get as far away from her as possible. Expecting her to lash out for all the irrelevant men that ever hurt her, *and how do I know she'll do that?*

Old song, new singer. That's how.

The moment and the memories die with the dimming of the lamp. A gentle murmur. "Take off your shoes, Carl. Lie down. Close your eyes." Her fingers brush his brow. "Tighten your forehead, now release the tension. Move down, do the same with your eyes. Squint. Hold. Release. Now your mouth. Your chin. Your neck." Her fingers lightly caress each feature as she names it.

Carl's eyes open. "Jacobson's progressive relaxation. I learned an interesting variation on it once in an acting class."

"Hush, not now. I know it's hard, but you have to relinquish control, Carl. Turn off your mind."

"I *do* have trouble with that."

"Tell me a secret. Shh. Close your eyes. Trust me."

Trouble with that one, too.

Cloaked in shadows, her hovering nearness dominating his senses, he allows her to guide the tension from his body. Neither seeking nor avoiding intimacy, her fingertips stroke and press him as other arms stir inside sleeves of his own flesh. Through closed lids, a red glow high inside his forehead—*the pineal gateway?*—that he read about in one of the books he bought. *Gateway to what and where?* But Carl ignores this last-ditch momentary upwelling of protective sarcasm . . . and now

his thoughts start to drift in w i d e   c o n c e n t r i c
s
i * l
r c

s l o   w   l   y   at first, up and around and through
then swirling swifter swifterswirlingswifterswifterswifter
and the long pitched vortex spins him dizzily
through the echoing chambers of darkness
where someone croons half-remembered songs
and whispers half-forgotten names

F   a   n   t   a   s   t   i   q   u
F   a   n   t   a   s   t   i
F   a   n   t   a   s   t
F   a   n   t   a
Fantastique
ntastiq
tasti
ast   cha
s   and the secret tunnel whirls

h*im*

plosion

up in s   *z*

i d e.   *r a*

n   *o   n*

ecstasy   *f   do*

freedom   *decrescendo*

serenity   *diminuendo*

solace   *morendo*

ll

A   i   o

liberating b   w → and
he soars through a smoky web of tendrils twisting over and around and
under him. Euphoria. Glorious freedom. The mists tatter; far beneath,
through shimmering tangles of force, he sees her bending over him, one
hand resting on his thigh, the other stealing over her own bosom,
capturing her breast. The twinned sensation of altered focus:

High angle long shot, Angelica beneath him, remote as passion carved
in marble;

Low angle closeup, through shut eyelids, Angelica above him, his
flushed skin sensing her burning desire—

NO! Terror! Escape! Hurtling up through hostile ceilings, resistant
walls, ghostflung into the harsh night where an old woman waits for
him—

Zurück, Mein Kind!

The sudden salvation of a mundane question—*If I open my eyes, will I see Angelica in two places at once?*

The urgent need to know prompts h*im*

                              plosion, and suddenly

               p

HEAVY, Carl whips e

               d

                    back into himself.

Instant monofocus: Angelica, startlingly near, her curled tonguetip touching the cupid's bow of her parted lips, green narrowed eyes transfixing him: predator and prey balanced on the dangerous cusp of chance as

rrrring rrrrring

                        the shrilling telephone shattered the moment and its options.

In the bathroom, splashing water on his face, Carl tried to decide. Spend the rest of the night with Angelica or go home and try to rest before the long afternoon ride to Pennsylvania?

As he returned to the bedroom, Angelica was just hanging up. Whiplash tension in her neck and spine. "I'd better drive you back to Manhattan." Said with finality: no choice in the matter.

Though neither spoke during the return journey, the silence was not so much strained as empty. Not until they pulled out of the Lincoln Tunnel and turned east on 42nd Street did Angelica address Carl. "Did you travel out of body?"

"Yes. Briefly."

"How was it compared to other times?"

"Sharper. Not totally. There was still some subjective distortion."

"It's hard to keep an obie 'pure.' They happen on the edge of sleep. Even if you start out awake, you can drift into dream state without knowing it. But the more you practice, the easier it becomes to tell what's real, what's fantasy."

"Once you were going to tell me about your experiences out of body."

"Another time. We're here." She pulled up in front of his building and switched off the motor and headlights. "Sit a moment?"

"Sure."

She stared out the windshield. "You're very easy to be with, Carl."

"Should I be flattered? You sound surprised."

"I expected different. I pictured you intense. Too much so."

"Why'd you think that?"

"Things I'd heard about you."

"From whom?"

"I don't mean 'heard' literally," she said quickly. "I meant from things I read about you. You know what you remind me of?"

"What?"

"An Ibizan hound."

"If that's a compliment, it's the weirdest I ever got."

"Now let me explain," she said, stroking his forearm. "Ibizan hounds are mood sponges. If you feel perky, so do they. If you're in your dressing room studying lines, they'll curl up quietly in a corner."

"I rarely curl up in corners."

"All that I'm trying to say, Carl, is I appreciate your coming with me tonight, your wanting to come with me." She squeezed his hand. "And I also appreciate that you didn't ask me any questions."

"About your mysterious phone call? That's none of my business."

"Most men would've thought differently."

"That's like saying most blacks tap-dance and chomp watermelon. I'm not responsible for what other men may or may not have done to you. I've been down that route, it's bad, and I don't ever want to travel it again, okay, friend?"

In the pale glow of the streetlamp, a cynical smile tugged the corner of her mouth. "Is that what we are, Carl—friends?"

"If that's what you want."

"Is that what *you* want?"

"Unfair parry."

"Why? Because you asked me first?"

"No, Angelica, because you set this up."

She opened her purse, rummaged in it and found a cigarette.

"Angelica, please don't smoke till I leave."

"Will that be soon?" Instantly wincing, she clapped her hand on his. "No, pretend you didn't hear that! I'm sorry! I get nicotine-edgy."

"That's not why you snapped. Right from the start, you've been pulling strings—"

"Excuse me! I pride myself on *never* pulling strings!"

Translation: no one ever caught you at it. "Fine, have it your way—

but at least admit that whatever we're skirting, it's something other than friendship.''

She dropped the cigarette back inside her purse and clicked it shut. In the movement's play of light and shadow, a diagonal bar of darkness crossed her face, hiding all but her mouth. As she spoke, he watched the supple flex of her lips. ''Carl, maybe you and I mean something different by friendship. I used to have this friend, we did things together, movies and shows and sometimes I'd cook for him, and sometimes he'd cue me when I had a new part, and sometimes I'd listen to his problems and sometimes we'd make love, but we weren't lovers—''

''In that case,'' Carl interrupted, ''you weren't really making love.''

''What would you call it?''

''Sexual accommodation.''

''No, it was more than that. It was friendship.''

''The kind you think we can have?''

She shrugged. ''Who knows?''

''So what happened to this friend of yours?''

''There were things he started to want I just couldn't give him.''

''Such as?'' *Commitment?*

''No, please, this car is too small for three people. I don't want to talk about him anymore.'' She fidgeted. ''I am *dying* for a cigarette!''

''That's my cue to leave, I think.'' He unlatched his door and was about to open it when Angelica, throwing her arms round his neck, kissed him with savage intensity, her teeth catching the end of his tongue. The pungent tang of strawberries and blood. Just as abruptly, she let him go. Only her eyes still held him; no calculation in them now, no pretense. Desire . . . but something else, too . . . *what?*

Something he'd probably never understand.

Carl drew a ragged breath. ''Is *that* what you call friendship, Ms. Winters?''

''For want of a better label? Yes.'' She smiled, but it was not the sweet unguarded grin that had captivated him earlier. ''So, Mr. Richards? Will it do?''

A long pause. ''I'll let you know in Pennsylvania.''

After she drove away, Carl slumped hands-in-pockets against the low stone southern boundary of Central Park across the street from his apartment building and tried to make some sense of the evening. Angelica, despite her protest, was undeniably a string-puller, yet even so, her underlying motivation was shadowy. If she merely wanted to use him as a stepping-stone, would she put her foot in her mouth quite as often as she did? *Possibly.* Yet her offer of extended friendship sounded genuine: a seductive notion and probably a perfect blueprint for pain. But underneath all the other questions and doubts, one tiny detail worried at him, a niggling thing Carl couldn't quite bring to mind, something he'd seen or almost seen . . . *and what in hell was it?*

When Carl let himself into his apartment, he was startled to discover his own bedroom light burning. He entered and found Diana on top of the covers, wide awake, wearing the bottom half of china-blue silk pajamas, her tawny-golden hair provocatively curled over her breasts, concealing them. She smiled tentatively. "You must've stayed till the party's bitter end."

"I thought you were going to The Plaza." *With Pierce.*

"I changed my mind."

"Why?"

"Because I want—I *need* you to understand what I did. Why I agreed to host *Saturday Night Live*."

"Simple. You owe NBC a favor."

"Carl, open your eyes! I did if for you!"

"For *me?*"

"They promised me if I do the show, they'll put me in a Carl Richards–type sketch, maybe even something about *Woyzeck* if they can work out an angle. It'll be good publicity."

"But why didn't you discuss it with me first?"

"Because Stu told them I said yes without asking me. Don't you see? If I contradicted him, they would've thought *I* reneged."

"Okay, I understand. But does this finally suggest something to you about your dear Mr. Pierce?" *Like fire the bastard?*

"It was wrong of Stu," Diana conceded, "but look at the plus side—at least now he's finally accepting you."

"I missed a station along this line of reasoning."

"He wants to help you. Us. The show."

"Yanking you away for nearly a week, that's *helping?*"

"I don't have to miss that many rehearsals. I figured it out. Listen to me, Carl."

"All right, I'm listening," he said, slipping off his shoes.

"As soon as we get settled at Powder Rocks tomorrow—tonight, actually—we can work our scenes together. Monday—"

"Wait," Carl interrupted, "I thought you had to stay here for a production meeting Monday?"

"I arranged it with them. Monday morning, I'll be on a long-distance conference call to NBC for a couple of hours. The rest of the day, you've got me, ditto Tuesday. From Wednesday on I'm in New York, but look, if you make next Saturday the company day off instead of Sunday, I'll only miss three days instead of four, and if that should run us into union overtime, I'll personally pick up the tab. So how does that sound? Not so bad?"

"Not *so* bad." He removed his jacket, hung it in the closet.

"And while I'm gone, at least you've got Angelica."

"True."

"You know, I've been thinking about her—maybe you ought to switch the two of us around."

Carl, busy extracting cufflinks from his shirt, fumbled one onto the floor.

"Clumsy!" Diana chided. "What I mean is that from now until Wednesday, I'm going to be totally concentrating on Marie's lines and blocking, and the rest of the week I'll be busy learning *shtik*. Maybe you'd better reverse me and Angelica in *The Stronger*. Give her the speaking role."

Carl put the retrieved cufflink on top of his dresser and sat down beside her on the bed. "You really wouldn't mind doing that?"

"I suggested it, didn't I?" Diana leaned against Carl's shoulder. Her long sleek hair slipped away from her bosom. "What do you say, pal? Won't I come off smelling like roses?"

"Mm-hmm. The more I think of it, the better I like it. We can work up a special press release—'The Sound of Silence—Diana Lee Taylor, true and generous artist, says there are no lahge parts, only lahge actors.' " Carl ran his thumb lightly over her breast. "Cut to a reaction shot, lady."

"Mmmmmm. I love it . . . ."

His fingertip circled her nipple. "Which? My idea, or this?"

"Both." Twining her arms about his neck, she kissed him. Without thinking, Carl nipped the tip of her tongue between his teeth. Diana shoved him away, her eyes wide with surprise. "Hey, mister, that hurt!"

"I'm sorry, Angelica." A wincing pause. Carl groaned, "I do not *believe* I said that!"

"Two Freudian slips of the tongue, Mr. Richards?" she scolded, mock-seriously.

A tumble of rationalizing words. "I don't know why her name popped out of my mouth. Maybe because we were just talking about her?"

Merry laughter. "Carl, you look so adorable when you're minused!"

"Minused?"

"Nonplussed. Now come here and see if you can kiss me without giving me the Purple Heart. Or is it the Purple Tongue?"

"Di, it's late . . ."

"So what? We don't have to be on the road first thing. Suddenly you're too tired?"

"No-o."

"All right, I understand. Fear of flying."

He nodded. "You could call it that."

She guided his hand down her body. "How about a short solo hop—please?"

Afterward, still clinging to him, Diana whispered, "You came that time."

"Yes."

"*In* me . . . and you were *so* hard." She gazed up at him languidly. "I love you, Carl." Silence. "Carl?"

"Hm?"

"Penny for your thoughts?"

"Don't waste your money," he said, kissing her cheek. "My mind's a blank."

DIVERTISSEMENT FOR
CHAMBER ENSEMBLE

I. Prelude in D

So many silences, Diana reflected, peering sidelong at her husband in the rear of her stretch limo rolling through the age-tempered foothills of eastern Pennsylvania. Carl stared pensively out the window at the lush green division of the Delaware Water Gap sparkling in late Sunday afternoon sunshine. They were en route to Powder Rocks, a village on the north branch of the Susquehanna River midway between Wilkes-Barre and Scranton.

Must be his 'You Can't Go Home Again' mood. On the few occasions that Carl mentioned Pennsylvania to her, it was with a curious mixture of pride and sorrow. "When Texans brag about their home state," he said once, "Pennsylvanians just smile. We don't like to take candy away from babies." But then he grew sad. "I still miss P-A—but, Di, I could never live there again."

So many places I can't reach. But that was one of the very reasons why Carl fascinated her: a welcome change from her grey unflappable "ex," Milford Harrison III, with his grey Italian suits, imported silk ties, handcrafted Oxfords from Oxford and fussy-neat grooming that reminded her of a Schweppes spokesman. Not that she'd object to Carl spending a bit more effort on personal appearance. He had no patience with material things. He hurried through shopping as if the time he took choosing clothes was subject to a surcharge. As for hair style, Diana tried, but could not wean him away from the West Side tonsorial museum he patronized. Its decrepit barbers did nothing to tame the wild unruly mane he claimed made him resemble Berlioz. She tolerated this posturing—*it sure matters to him how* I *look*—because, she told herself, *Carl's shallows way outclass Mil's depths.*

Just then, the chauffeur asked for directions. Her husband surfaced long enough to reply, then sank back into himself.

He's got so many locked-off places. But at least when Carl tuned out, it was because he was caught up in fantasies of his one true mistress, the theatre. *Damn sight better than Mil's endless parade of peachmuff Lolitas.* No affection lingered from her first marriage, just residual pain and a lot of anger. *Why'd they all have to be so fucking young?*

Catching a glimpse of herself in the rear-view mirror, Diana raised both hands to her forehead and stretched the skin on either side of her crinkled temples. Proper nutrition and exercise kept her body trim and in tone, but emotions were dangerous luxuries capable of eroding her skin's smooth planes and textures. An actress who smiled or frowned too wide or often groomed herself unwittingly for character roles.

Anyway, she mused guiltily, *what right have I got to resent Mil's cheating? Look how I lied to Carl.*

After her divorce, Diana embarked on a brief, intense round of bed-hopping, *not as much as the toilet-newspapers claimed, but enough, enough.* On one ill-considered occasion, she slept with Stuart Pierce, once only, never again, but Diana knew that would be two times too many for Carl. *A pity.* She considered Pierce a good friend and manager. *Just in the sack, he's a washout.* She wondered why she gave herself to Pierce that one time. Maybe because he reminded her of her ex-husband? More likely, she thought, because they both reminded her of her father. *And what if they do? Carl's better for ME than all three of them put together, even with all his closed-off places.*

Still, she reflected, it *was* a thrill when a man, any man, climaxed inside her, *even old One-Two-can't-make-it-to-Three Stu.* Carl always satisfied her in bed—*he stays hard, and Oh God, where'd his tongue take lessons?*—but it took him so long to come, Diana felt woefully inadequate. *Not last night, though—*

"What?" Carl asked, suddenly turning to her.

"Hm? Was I thinking too loud?"

"I felt you staring at me."

"Sorry. You've been preoccupied. I missed you."

"I was thinking about the show."

"I figured."

He stroked her cheek. "If you want to talk, Di, we can talk."

"We just did." She appreciated his offer and the tenderness of his touch, but his mind wanted to go elsewhere. "Back to your thoughts, pal. I'm going to use you as a pillow, all right?"

"Climb aboard."

Carl tapped the partition and told the driver to watch for a turnoff in five miles. Diana slipped off her shoes, stretched out, and lay her head on his lap. Gazing up through shaded lids, she studied the look in his deep-set dark eyes. It reminded her of an expression she saw on someone else's face last night at her party, possibly George O'Brien. *Old friends, similar habits?* The miles sped by. The monotonous rhythm of the wheels lulled her.

When the tires crunched gravel, Diana rubbed her eyes, yawned, sat up and stared dubiously out over a parking lot at a large rust-red barn-like building they were riding toward.

"That's *it?*"

"I didn't promise you Paper Mill Playhouse," he said drily.

"Does this place even have indoor plumbing?"

"It has clean rest rooms and air conditioning. Behave yourself, Little Miss Superstar. These people are old friends."

She lowered her head. "Di-Di pwomises not to embawass DaDa."

"I may throw up."

"Kin-ky. Kiss me quick."

"Any more lip and I'll leak that remark. Imagine the roles they'll offer America's Sweetheart then."

"Something even better than a whore with a bastard whose lover knifes her to death? I'll call Stuart first thing." She saw Carl wince. "Hey! I can't even mention his *name?*"

"Sure you can. Just don't expect me to like it."

The chauffeur guided the limousine into a parking space.

"Anyway," Carl said, "let me prove to you that Pennsylvania does have professional plumbers. You up to making an entrance?"

"Now or never, pal."

After half an hour's worth of ceremony and a guided tour of every crevice, aperture and niche of the Powder Rocks theatre, Diana left Carl to sort out logistical problems with Jan Napier and rode on to their hotel in Wilkes-Barre.

When the question of living arrangements came up during her contractual negotiations, Carl said that the cast would be rooming across the road from the theatre at the Luzerne Motel.

"Totally unacceptable," Stuart Pierce objected. "Do you really expect *the* Diana Lee Taylor to stay anywhere but at a first-class hotel? How would that look to the public?''

"I see your point," Carl reluctantly conceded. "I'll have Jan reserve a suite at the Sheraton-Crossgates on Public Square.''

Diana was surprised Carl chose Wilkes-Barre over Scranton, where his father lived; Powder Rocks, after all, was roughly equidistant from either city. However, she said nothing. *Read the posted warnings, Di— off limits, off limits, off limits.*

After leaving a message on Pierce's answering machine that she'd arrived safely, Diana unpacked, showered, dined in the hotel restaurant *(Decent food and no autograph hounds, wondrous!),* then rode back in her limousine to Powder Rocks for a quick runthrough of her four main scenes with Carl. On her way into the theatre, she met Jan Napier on her way out with Gynger Morrison. Gynger hailed Diana.

"We're celebrating, Di. Carl just appointed me assistant stage manager. Join us for a nightcap?''

"I'd love to, but I have to run lines with Carl.'' She saw an odd look pass between the two women. *What? Do they think I'm too stuck-up to drink with them?* "Look, maybe I can meet you later.''

The younger woman nodded. "Sure. You and Carl.''

Message received, little girl. Pointedly ignoring Jan, Diana addressed Gynger. "Where are you headed? I thought Pennsylvania's dry on Sundays.''

"There's a private club across the road. George O'Brien told me they sell one-night memberships for a couple of dollars.''

"Carl knows where it is," Jan volunteered.

"I'm sure he does.'' Diana's lips smiled. Her eyes did not.

The women said goodbye. Arm in arm, Jan and Gynger crossed the parking lot, heads close together. Diana wished she could hear what they were bee-buzzing about so intently. It irritated her that her star's status shut her off from that easy camaraderie that bound the rest of the cast together. Not that she wanted to be close with Carl's *young young young* stage manager. She distrusted her. *I ought to introduce the little bitch to Mil. Except she's already way over the hill for him.* But Gynger was different; Diana rather liked her. *Pity she's Jan's bosom buddy. Guess I can't trust her, either.*

Diana crossed the lobby and entered the theatre, a large proscenium space with several hundred seats lit only by the exit signs. She paused nervously at the back of the house. Empty theatres gave her the shivers. "Carl?'' Squinting, trying to see. "Hey! Anybody home?''

There was a rustle up near the stage.

"Di?" A woman's voice. "That you?" She saw Angelica coming up the aisle toward her. She wore a dark red short-sleeve blouse hanging loose over an old pair of jeans.

"Angelica? What were you doing down there in the dark?"

"Waiting for you. I dozed off."

"Do you know where Carl is?"

"Poking around backstage. Join me while I fix my face?"

Diana followed Angelica into the "ladies" off the lobby. Pausing to tug a few rumples into place, Angelica sat down at a mirror, opened her purse and fished for tissues and cosmetics.

"Diana," she asked, opening a tube of lipstick, "do you *really* want me to do the lead in *The Stronger*?"

"Yes. Do you mind?"

"Mind? I'm thrilled!"

"I've got so many things to worry about already," Diana said, "what with learning Marie, plus a monologue and umpteen *Saturday Night Live* sketches. You're doing me and Carl a favor, and I know you'll do a spectacular job with the part."

"You're incredibly generous—I don't know to thank you. But then, I always knew you'd be special." Angelica snapped her lipstick back inside her bag, rose and gave Diana a quick peck on the cheek.

Diana was charmed by the sisterly kiss. "Tell you what. Do two things for me and we'll call it square."

"You've got 'em. Number one?"

"While I'm gone, take notes for me, okay? You know, Marie notes . . . fine points, timing, business, any insights you—Carl might have on playing her."

"I already planned to do that. Next favor? You did say two."

Diana pressed her hand. "Just be my friend, okay?"

"That was also on the agenda. So now what do we do? Pick nicknames?"

"You already know mine. How about you? Angie?" Diana frowned. "Uh-uh. That sounds like short for a heart condition. How about if I call you Angel?"

Angelica laughed. "You'll be the first!"

As they entered the theatre together, Carl was onstage, setting up a pair of folding chairs under the work light.

"Di," Carl said, "let's hold off our scenes till tomorrow. I want to run Angelica once in *The Stronger,* and that's it, okay?"

She nodded. "If you're comfortable with that."

"Perfectly." He faced Angelica. "Just talk to Di this time through. Give me basic word sense, nothing more."

"Got it. No emoting." Angelica handed her copy of the Strindberg script to Diana. "Would you hold book for me?"

Carl stared at her. "You *already* know your lines?"

"I'm a quick study."

"The understatement of the century."

The edge in his voice irritated Diana. She remembered her husband's unreasoning prejudice against Angelica and how she had to push him into hiring her. "Carl," she demanded, "what's your problem? Lots of actors have memories like sponges."

"Di, I only told her about the switch a few minutes ago!"

Angelica said, "I began learning the part last week."

"Why?"

"So in case Di goes up on her lines, I can cue her."

"See? She was just being helpful." Diana glared at Carl. "You've seen *All About Eve* too often. Now may we do the scene and get the bejesus out of here?"

"All right, go ahead."

Sitting on the folding chairs facing each other, the women established "in character" eye contact and began. Angelica spoke.

Well, well, well, if it isn't little Millie! What a surprise, old friend! To find you, of all people, sitting here alone, drinking all by yourself the night before Christmas. How sad! You remind me of a bride I saw once at a hotel. She was off in a corner reading a comic book while the groom was shooting pool with the best man. I thought, well, there's a doomed marriage if ever I saw one.

Both women were playing actresses who'd worked in the same theatre ensemble until Angelica's garrulous character quit in order to get married.

You think I maneuvered to get you kicked out of the ensemble. That's not true, but if it makes you feel better, Millie, go ahead and believe it. I'm blessed with a little girl and boy and a husband who adores me. All you've got is your acting.

But as Mrs. X prattled on about her marriage, she gradually realized the truth, that her husband was passionately, obsessively in love with the silent Ms. Y. This, Diana guessed, was why Carl chose the script as a curtain-raiser for *Woyzeck*: *Two different ways of paying off jealousy. Spitefulness or murder . . . quick death, slow death, which is worse?*

Looking directly into Diana's eyes, Angelica spoke her lines with great conviction.

> When you and I were first becoming acquainted, Millie, I was so terrified of you, I did everything I could to get close to you. I couldn't afford to have you as my enemy, so I moved heaven and earth to become your friend. I invited you to our home, but my husband seemed to dislike you. I was *so* happy when I got him to change his mind. Oh, how you must have both been laughing at me!

God, she's good! Diana wondered whether she'd made a major tactical error by turning over the opening spot in the show to an actress this talented, but her conscience rose shakily to Angelica's defense. *Hey, you asked her to be your friend . . . why don't you behave like one?*

Angelica spoke the play's closing lines.

> I used to think you were so strong, Millie, but now I realize that I'm the stronger. You took my husband's love, but you couldn't hold onto it. Everything you touch turns to dust. You play at emotions without knowing what they are. You have no children—you're just a barren child yourself. But you're a good teacher, Millie. You taught my husband how to love. Now you have to sit here all alone on Christmas Eve while I go on home to love him.

A thought that eluded Diana earlier that day suddenly clicked into place. She recognized exactly where she'd seen Carl's moody-pensive expression before.

II. Scherzo in C Minor

Two roads diverged in a carmine mood,
And I, sorry I cannot choose both—

Staring out the limousine's rear window at the sparkling waters of the Delaware rushing into yesterday, Carl felt a familiar coldness steal over him. In the scene, yet on the sidelines observing life with calm disapproval, *I am a chimera* analyzing beats and objectives, wondering how to play each moment. *Going through the* (e)*motions.*

Out of the corner of his eye, he sensed Diana's stare. He turned to her abruptly. "What?"

"Hm? Was I thinking too loud?" She sounded guilty, he had no idea of what. "Sorry. You've been preoccupied. I missed you."

"I was thinking about the show." *Liar.*

She nestled in his lap. "Back to your thoughts, pal."

Tapping the partition, Carl gave a direction to the driver, then, absently stroking his wife's hair, sank back into his seat and psyche. He replayed the past evening—the party at Tydings, Pierce's aggravating announcement about *Saturday Night Live,* the allegedly happenstance ride with Angelica to Seacliffe, the diner he'd visited before in dream (?), the niggling wrong detail he'd almost seen at Angelica's apartment *and what was it?,* the semi-erotic out-of-body experience—above all, Angelica's searing kiss and the twin-edged betrayal of lovemaking with Diana afterward.

Consider the lilies:

Diana. *The* Diana Lee Taylor. Grail-symbol. Mummer.

Angelica Winters. Sorceress. Traducer.

Two roads converged in a carmine wood,

And I—

Seek the one less traveled by?

After sending Diana on ahead to unpack, after waving to Jan, who was already busy on the box office telephone even though it was Sunday, after meeting with the Powder Rocks theatre owners, after speaking with Gynger and gabbing with the antediluvian caretaker, Carl wandered backstage and reintroduced himself to old inanimate friends hanging on wardrobe racks and hiding in prop or makeup bins: a lopsided wire-mounted beard he made for a production of *Oedipus at Colonus,* his Cothurnus mask from Millay's *Aria da Capo,* a tattered commedia dell'arte smock he once wore while playing Molière's miser, the GOD IS LOVE cushion he suffocated Mrs. Bramson with in the last act of Emlyn Williams' *Night Must Fall*—

Just before she touched him, he recognized her scent. He turned; his breath caught. Her lips, *so close,* were the same sensual shade as the sheer blouse she wore tucked inside her tight black jeans. Carl, seldom impulsive, reached out to embrace Angelica, but she frowned and fell back a step.

A chilly wave of embarrassment and irritation. His first thought was that he'd fallen for seduction's oldest mindgame—*"Just wondered if I could interest you, Mr. Richards. Thanks for the ego boost. Ta-ta!''*—but then he heard a man's voice close by calling Angelica's name.

"Over here," she called back, then, speaking to Carl in a low voice, said, "George followed me over from the motel."

The tall actor emerged from a space between two flats. With a nod to Carl, he said, "Once more, to tread the boards at Powder Rocks! Feels like nothing that ever happened since then and now is real. Like I'm still waiting to start my life."

"I certainly know that feeling," Carl said. "Listen, Georgie, I've got something important to discuss with Angelica. Catch you later, all right?"

A barely perceptible pause. A strained smile. George turned and went out the way he came in, saying to no one in particular, "I've got to unpack, anyway."

After his footsteps died away, Angelica said matter-of-factly, "You hurt his feelings."

"Him? He never used to be so thin-skinned."

"He's a mystery." She lowered her voice. "Gynger's poking around in one of those dressing-rooms." A strained pause. A barely perceptible smile. "Platonic has its points, doesn't it?"

"So I've heard. Have you decided that's what you want?"

She curled her fingers round his. "What do you think, Carl?"

Staring at her, trying to fathom his own tangled feelings, he couldn't decide whether her wide, frank eyes were calculating or merely bold. She drew his hand to her breast, resting it there. Her nipple hardened against the soft flesh of his palm.

A long breathless silence. Making no move to move away, he asked, "How'd you like to switch roles with Di in *The Stronger*?"

Angelica's green eyes glinted. "You're offering me one of the performances?"

"I'm offering you *all* of the performances."

A frown; she shook her head decisively. "Uh-uh. I don't need Diana Lee Taylor mad at me."

"But this was Di's idea . . . ask her yourself."

Angelica quickly released his hand. "Why? Is she here?"

"Pardon me," a new voice interrupted.

Carl whirled and spied Jan, clad in Levi's and a French-cut tie-dyed rainbow T-shirt, standing in the wings. *How long has she been there?* he worried. *What did she see?*

The A.D. approached. "We need to talk, boss." She indicated Angelica. "Privately."

An instant that felt like a century. "Well," Angelica said, "if anyone needs me, I'll be in one of the dressing-rooms." She gave Carl a fleeting glance and walked out.

He waited, breath held, until she was gone. "Okay, Jan. What?"

"Val Snyder finally returned my calls."

Carl relaxed. This wasn't about Angelica. Snyder directed the troubled production of *Biloxi Blues* that George did in Florida.

Jan said, "Val's directing *The Apple Tree* in Seattle. That's why it took so long for my messages to catch up with him."

"So what did he say about George?"

"That at first he was great to work with."

"Never mind 'at first.' How about 'at second'?"

"A mess. He was late for rehearsals. He arrived so hung over he couldn't remember his lines or business."

"Incredible!"

"Chief . . . there's more."

"Something worse?"

"*I* think so," Jan replied dryly. "He decked their A.D."

"Decked? *George?*"

"Put him in the hospital with a broken jaw."

"How come?"

"Who knows? Val didn't. Anyway, the A.D.'s suing your pal, and to top it all off, George quit before the end of the run. Val says you're nuts to use him." She paused. "Instructions, Holmes?"

"No, Watson, take off. I've got some heavy thinking to do."

"Well, I wish you joy of the worm. Aloha."

As she exited, Carl sat on a stool and pondered. To his recollection, George never drank anything stronger than an occasional glass of wine, but recently, he'd noticed him tossing back one scotch after another. Still, it hadn't affected his work habits; he hadn't missed a rehearsal, he showed up on time, *except last Friday, but that was the subway, he said.* George did seem unusually moody of late, but all in all, as far as *Woyzeck* was concerned, Carl saw no danger. *So far.*

Nevertheless, he worried about his boyhood chum. Ever since they'd both entered theatre, George prided himself on consummate professionalism. *What happened in Florida?* Carl wanted to ask him point-blank what the fight was all about, but there'd always been strict boundaries between them, "don't-cross" lines that George expected him to respect.

Carl hated to admit it, but this was one time when Diana's attorney-manager, Stuart Pierce, might actually be able to help.

Someone coughed. Carl looked up and saw Gynger Morrison, her hair tied back with a red bandanna, her yellow scalloped-edge dress reminding him of a gypsy seer. A line creased her forehead.

"Yes?" he asked. "Problem?"

"The big off-right dressing-room is for the ladies, right?"

"Except Di, the smaller room is hers. I told you that."

"Yes." Gynger pursed her lips. "You'd also better tell Angelica. She's setting up a beachhead in Di's space."

Her tone annoyed him, but he stifled his reaction. Gynger was Jan's friend, after all, and he was still worried that the A. D. might have seen him holding hands with Angelica earlier. Carl made a split-second decision. "Gynger, I've been meaning to ask you . . . Jan needs an assistant. It pays extra. Interested?"

En route to the hotel, Carl surprised Diana by asking for her manager's aid in checking out George's legal problems. She agreed to talk to Pierce. Then it was her turn to startle Carl.

"Tell Gynger *I* invited Angelica to share my dressing-room, okay? By the way, what did you think of Angel as Mrs. X?"

Angel? "She . . . gave an adequate reading." *Angel??*

" 'Adequate'? Come on, Carl, you're not deaf and blind! Do you think I'll melt if I hear the truth?"

"The truth? She's better than adequate. Satisfied?"

Ever-so-casually, Diana asked, "How much better?"

Watch out . . . "Almost as good as you, if you had time to rehearse." Swiftly sensing danger, he added, "As Mrs. X, I mean."

A chuckle. "Flying colors, pal. You should enter politics."

"Why?"

She tapped the tip of his nose with her forefinger. "You'd get to lie to more people."

III. Chaconne in G $^\sharp$

After he finished unpacking, George set up the mini-gym that he took with him wherever he went—stretch-stirrups, weighted lifting clamps, Styrofoam pressure grips, a set of bracket-mounted elastic pulls and a floorstand boxing bag. When he was done, he sat on the edge of the motel's double bed, opened the top drawer of the nightstand, took out a local phone book and by sheer force of habit, started to look up the location of the nearest Roman Catholic church. When he caught what he was doing, he threw the book down.

Damn. Old habits die hard.

Long ago, George turned his back on the paternalistic hierarchy of priests, bishops, archbishops, cardinals and Pope that he considered criminally conservative, yet no matter how enlightened-radical he told himself he'd become, he could not escape the fear that his rebelliousness was speeding him down the proverbial primrose path. He'd tried it all: cynicism, iconoclasm, eastern solipsism, but deep down nothing ever allayed his childhood-instilled terror of damnation. *Want to see a happy Catholic? Open a coffin.*

George dropped the telephone directory into the desk drawer and slammed it shut, then, reaching across the nightstand, unwrapped a plastic cup, poured several ounces of scotch into it and drained it in one swallow. He picked up the phone, dialed, got no answer, hung up. Stretching out on the bed, George closed his eyes for a few minutes to rest.

He woke nine hours later: 7:00 A.M. Monday morning, when the front desk rang his room.

The first day onstage at Powder Rocks was a tough one for George. Diana was spending the morning in her hotel room on a long-distance call, so Carl concentrated on scenes not involving Marie. His itinerary called for everyone to be "off book" so he could start drilling for pace and tempo. With Murphy's Law perverseness, the other actors were practically line-perfect, but George had a gargantuan headache that wouldn't go away and let him concentrate.

"George," Carl said after his fifth blown cue, "you're holding us all up. Pick up your book."

Face flushing, George retrieved his script. He glared at the rest of the cast, daring anyone to look at him, but with one exception, the other actors studiously studied their shoes. Angelica, however, returned his fierce glance with a frown.

At the midday break, Carl spoke privately with him. "For God's sake, what's the matter? I've never known you to have memory problems. Your lines are easy. You don't have that many."

"You don't have to remind me who's the 'Stah,' Cary-baby."

"Call me that one more time, Georgina, and you'll be out on your ass. And don't expect Equity to help you out . . . not after what you pulled in Florida.''

"Okay, okay, I'm sorry! I've got a stinking headache. I swear I *had* these lines.''

The director beckoned Gynger Morrison to join them. ''After lunch,'' he instructed her, ''find someplace quiet and cue George till he learns all his lines and entrances. Take all afternoon if you have to, but get him off book.''

Carl headed up the aisle. George watched his old friend meet Angelica in the lobby. The pair left the theatre together.

Later, Gynger Morrison turned out to be a great help to George. She showed him a mnemonic trick for making mental connections between the last words of his cues and the first words of the Drum-Major's speeches. After the two of them had worked for a little over an hour, George felt confident to return to the rehearsal.

The pond scene, the murder scene, was running. George sat down next to Angelica and watched. He noticed with cold fury that Carl's wife was still holding her script.

MARIE

I'm cold, Franz.

WOYZECK

But I feel your hot breath. Your eyes burn into me like coals. I'd sell my soul to kiss your fiery lips one more time. Tomorrow, though . . . that's when you'll be cold, Marie.

MARIE

What are you talking about?

WOYZECK

Nothing.

MARIE

The moon's rising. Look, it's so red . . .

WOYZECK

Like a bloody knife.

"Aren't we *all* supposed to be off book?'' George asked in a loud stage whisper. He ignored Angelica's sharp warning hush. ''What? Is there a different set of rules for Madame Superc— OW!''

Onstage, Carl and Diana stiffened, but stayed in character.

Angelica put her lips close to George's ear and murmured, "Remember what they say about Caesar's wife."

"That pinch hurt!"

"It was meant to. Now behave yourself!"

That evening, the company dined at the club across the road. At a large round table presided over by Carl and Diana, George sat next to Angelica, with Jan and Gynger across the table. Bill Evans, who played the Captain, and Vincent Swailes, who doubled as Andres and the pawnbroker who sells a knife to Woyzeck, were also there. The only missing actors were the three young local jobbers whose first rehearsal wasn't till the following day and Joel Roye, an elderly character man who, still worn out from Sunday's bus ride, went directly to bed.

Dinner was done. Over dessert and coffee, the performers were telling one another how each of them first entered the profession.

"Your turn, George," Gynger said. "Why did you decide to become an actor?"

He set down his glass of scotch and shrugged. "It looked so easy. I was brainwashed by all those MGM musicals where Judy Garland and Mickey Rooney decide to put on a summer show in a barn, and after maybe five minutes of montage, out of that hat, it's that big first night! Who knew from cattle calls and idiotic directors? Present company excepted."

Gynger turned to Carl. "Speaking of present company, what brought you into theatre?"

"Not 'what'—who. George talked me into joining ninth-grade drama club. Which took guts. Boys who want to act are automatically labeled fruits." Carl laughed, not without bitterness. "In those days, I was so naive, I didn't even know what 'fruit' meant."

"Naiveté in a boy is refreshing," Diana observed.

"Uh-uh, Di, not when you're such a geek you don't even know what they're calling you." Carl's hands balled into fists. "I didn't find out the meaning of 'fruit' till this girl in my English class—" he hesitated. "Well, she called somebody that, but our teacher overheard her—"

George held up his empty glass. The waiter ignored him.

"And?" Diana prompted Carl. "What did your teacher do?"

"He made the girl stand up. He asked her if she knew that calling a person a fruit is the same thing as calling him a homosexual. She turned every shade of red. So did I. I couldn't *believe* that's what 'fruit' means! I almost laughed out loud!''

Carl's wife squeezed his arm. ''Well, mister, if you're a fruit, you sure overcompensate.''

George abruptly muttered, ''Excuse me,'' got to his feet and stalked out of the room. An embarrassed silence. Jan shot Carl a quizzical glance, but he shook his head. After a discreet interval, Angelica rose and excused herself, too.

Angelica found George in the bar ordering another drink. ''Don't,'' she warned. ''Carl's already upset enough with you.''

''Too bloody bad.''

''It will be if he fires you.''

''As if you give a damn.'' He reached for his refill.

''I give a damn that you're screwing things up!'' She yanked away the glass, spilling scotch. A deadly pause, but George was no match for Angelica's bridled fury. ''Come on,'' she commanded.

George watched the taut flex of her black leather skirt as she exited, then followed her out.

They walked along the side of the highway and listened to a poolside concert of frogs.

''Hard to picture you and Carl as boys,'' Angelica remarked.

''To quote Lady Di, 'Naiveté is refreshing.' We used to spend hours in my attic room. The ceiling slanted at an angle. Carl would hit his head a lot. I used to drive him crazy putting on show music and tap-dancing right in the middle of the floor without ever bumping my head, even though I'm taller. I'd make up crazy movie takeoffs and put them on tape, doing all the voices and Carl would groan his head off, but he'd always listen and he'd always end up laughing. He was a great captive audience. Mostly, though, we'd just spend the time talking about movies and science-fiction and shows we wanted to act in.''

''Did you ever talk about sex?''

George shook his head. ''No. Carl had his problems and I had mine. Sex was a factor only once.''

''I'm listening.''

''I saw this notice in the paper that Barter Theatre was looking for apprentices. I got Cary to take a bus with me to Philadelphia, where they were holding tryouts. We met this young actress there, I still remember her name, it was perfect—Marge Tallant. We all liked each other and the three of us were accepted into the company, but it cost thirty bucks a week room and board. Only thirty dollars, but Carl's folks didn't have it, and even if they did, they wouldn't've let him go. It killed him that he couldn't spend the summer with Marge.''

"Did you go?"

"No, I stayed home, too. End of story."

Angelica broke stride. "I think not."

George sighed. "No, there's more. Marge wrote to me that fall and invited us both to visit her."

"And did you?"

"Uh-uh. I never told Carl." He stopped. "I'm tired. Let's go back."

In George's room, Angelica watched him drain the rest of his scotch in a single swallow.

"What are you trying to do, kill yourself?"

George lay back against his pillow. "Maybe."

"How long have you been drinking like this?"

"Since Florida."

She frowned. "Whatever happens to you won't be anybody's fault but your own."

"If you say so."

"I do." Angelica stared into her hands. "I definitely do."

He watched her. Neither moved a muscle.

Time passed. George began to snore. Angelica rose, switched off the light and slipped out of the room.

On Tuesday morning, George woke when Jan Napier rang his extension. "You're late, George! It's almost ten o'clock!"

"Oh, shit! Be right there!" He stumbled out of bed, fumbled on his clothes and ran out, unshaven, unkempt, sprinting to the theatre in record time. The auditorium was empty except for Jan sitting on the stage sipping coffee as she busily transferred notes from her prompt script to Gynger Morrison's clipboard pad of "things to do."

"Where is everybody?" he asked breathlessly.

"In back of the theatre on a photo shoot. Pat Clayborne's down for the day and brought a columnist. Carl's pissed at you. You look hideous."

"Thanks, Jan. I love you, too."

"Sorry. Comb your hair, then get out there."

He ran to the washroom, splashed himself awake, hurried outside.

Everyone was standing by a wide wooden loading platform. George recognized Perry Cooke, the balding *Times* columnist, talking to Gynger, and also saw Stuart Pierce speaking quietly with Angelica. *Why don't I trust that guy?* Pat Clayborne, the company's plump, straw-haired press agent, was setting up a pose of Marie (Diana) looking into the distance with Woyzeck (Carl), knife raised, standing behind her. As Pat snapped the photo, Carl signaled George to come over. He did so; the director guided him several feet away and out of earshot.

"For Christ's sake, where've you been?"

"The front desk forgot my wakeup call."

"Buy yourself an alarm clock!"

"Will you get off my case?!"

Carl's face flushed. "Damn it, rehearsal time's precious—you know Di leaves tonight."

"Don't blame *me* for that."

"Yesterday, you held us up not knowing your lines. This morning, you don't show up. You lied about your 'nonunion' gig in Florida— you quit an Equity show without giving notice—"

"That's none of your business!"

"No? The only reason the union grievance committee doesn't have you up on charges is because Di pulled a thousand strings."

"Tell her I'm grateful."

"You're not grateful, you're hung over. You look like shit the morning after. Go take a shower."

"What about the photo shoot?"

"We'll manage without you." He tapped George's chest smartly. "And if you don't ease up on the sauce, friend or not, we'll manage without you permanently."

George glared at Carl as he walked away. Slouching back to his motel room, he rooted out a new bottle of scotch, opened it, then caught a glimpse of himself in the mirror. A long pause. George returned the bottle to his suitcase, walked over to his boxing bag and began to pummel it systematically.

His fifth punch broke the bag.

IV. Contredanse

After breakfast, waiting in the Sheraton lobby for the limousine to arrive, Carl reviewed his production journal.

THURSDAY, MAY 4

1. RUNTHROUGH SCENES 1–13, MAKESHIFT PROPS. SET TEMPI.
2. LUNCH: TECK PROBLEMS, MISCELLANEOUS TROUBLESHOOTING.
3. RUN 14–26, PROPS, TEMPI.
4. RUN STRINdBERG.
5. DINNER BREAK.
6. WOYZECK SPEED RUN.

Carl glanced at his watch. *Wonder what's keeping the driver? Maybe I'd better wait outside.*

In front of the hotel, rain streaming from the overhanging marquee ricocheted off Carl's cheeks. He shaded his eyes and peered up the street. No sign of the limo, but a block away, a bright patch of sunshine shone down on midtown Scranton storefronts. Odd that all the shop windows had "Closed" signs in them, but the door swung open and Cary tramped down the long work-aisle into the combination room, where Gramma Hannah sat on the sofa with her arms around Aunt Peg. Uncle Max waited for him in the place that shifted and—

STOP! STOP!

Stopped.

Darkness lit by random patterns.

Interpret.

Phosphenes: "Phos + phainein = bright images produced behind closed eyelids, usually the result of retinal stimulation."

So, status report:

In bed. Not Thursday; early Wednesday. Still dark out. Can't move arms, legs. Someone whispering in the corner of—

STOP!

Stopped. Stopped.

Factor.

Transfixion: "Transfixus pp.→ transfigere = Rigidity of limb sometimes experienced at the borderline of slumber."

Interpret:

Body asleep, mind awake, easy prey for hallucinative sounds, voices,

atmospheres. B
                    u
                         t "The adept recognizes hypnagogic symptoms (loss of
motor control, half-audible whispers, the ominous sense of threatening
presences) as mortal atavisms that, conquered, permit us to engage in
lucid out-of-body travel."

So? Make use of it!

Effortlessly rising, drifting out over Public Square, but instead of the
bandshell, Uncle Max in the great tunnel calls, *my little shortstop,
come*—NO!

Stay in control!

*Pro-*JECT!

~~~~~ Traveling northward.
                    Following the Susquehanna. ~~~~~
                    Reaching the theatre.
                    Across the highway.
               Into the motel.
          Along empty corridors.
          Her room.
          Impasse. You can't come in.
               You can't come in.

But the third time he tries, something yields a
                                        n
                                             d Cary passes down
the long work aisle into the combination room where Gramma Hannah
sits with her arms round Aunt Peg.

Tch-tch, mein Kind, so long you've stayed away?

NO! Whipping out, away from them, away from the shifting place
where Uncle Max beckons, hurtling backward, streaking along the river
route again, down, down in the motel court come down, hammering at
the door of her privacy when suddenly A
                    FIRESPHERE OF MOTTLED
FORCE RAGES INTO THE CORRIDOR, ITS FIERY TENDRILS
WHIPPING OUT TOWARD HIS CHEST AS CARY, PULSE RAC-
ING WILDLY, SCREAMS
                         a
                              n
                                   d Carl opened his eyes on a sunny
Wednesday morning.

He rubbed his eyes, sat up. The night-terrors were gone; so was Di, she'd flown to New York; last night's make-believe lovemaking a memory he'd rather forget.

The wages of guilt prepaid.

A grueling day ahead: crowd scenes to rehearse, "make-do" props to try out, problems to pinpoint and drill. Carl rose, showered, dressed and rode to the theatre.

The rehearsal began well. George showed up on time, bleary-eyed but letter-perfect; Angelica, filling in for Diana, already knew all of Marie's dialogue and business. The entire cast, for that matter, was so well prepared that Carl handed the prompt script to Jan so he could focus on his own lines and blocking.

But it was hard to concentrate. Angelica was deliberately avoiding him. Except for their scenes together, she did not speak to him all morning, and though normally she remained aloof from the rest of the cast, today, during breaks, she engaged in conversation on the far side of the house, *wherever I'm not.* He tried to attribute her behavior to discretion, but the tautness of her stance, the way she avoided direct eye contact suggested she was having second thoughts about their "friendship."

The one true constant of liberated women: ambivalence.

Adopting the only possible strategy, Carl ignored her, too. It worked. As they broke for lunch and he conferred with Jan and Gynger, out of the corner of his eye he noticed Angelica glancing back at him uncertainly as she walked up the aisle with George.

Early afternoon. He'd sent Gynger out to buy a suitable knife and other props. Partly to allow time for her to return before continuing *Woyzeck,* Carl scheduled a solo rehearsal of *The Stronger.* He wondered how Angelica would handle being alone with him—but she arrived in the company of Lyla Dean, a gangly twelve-year-old local they'd hired to play one of the children.

"I asked Lyla to fill in for Diana. Do you mind, Carl?"

"No . . . Ms. Winters."

Ignoring his coolness, she motioned Lyla to sit down; after a brief get-in-character pause, Angelica began. At first, Lyla seemed overawed, but Angelica played to her as if she really were her nemesis, Ms. Y, and soon the girl began reacting to her like a seasoned professional.

In spite of himself, Carl had to admire the redhead's skill in drawing a performance from the twelve-year-old. And whenever he stopped the scene to direct Angelica, she never disagreed, but immediately implemented his advice. *A far cry from Diana* . . .

Carl had her run the scene once more, this time uninterrupted. The other actors, returning, sat down and watched. At the end, some of them applauded. Angelica blew them a kiss.

That wonderful smile again! "Okay," Carl said, "places, everyone, for *Woyzeck,* scene fourteen." He turned to compliment Angelica, but she'd already disappeared backstage.

Woyzeck continued: the barracks scene, the Doctor's lecture, the barracks yard, the tavern, again the barracks. Carl lurched upstage to the pawnshop and bought the knife (temporarily, a wooden paint stirrer), exiting as the children entered with Angelica-Marie and Gynger, back from her prop-purchasing safari. Gynger, as the Grandmother, told her mean-spirited bedtime tale, and then it was time for Woyzeck's entrance.

WOYZECK

Sst! Marie!

MARIE

God, Franz, you scared me! What do you want?

WOYZECK

Come with me, Marie. It's time.

MARIE

Time? What for?

WOYZECK

You think I know?

"Musical bridge," Jan said from a seat in the auditorium. "Scene twenty-two. A forest path by a pond."

MARIE

It's too dark to see. Where's town? That way?

WOYZECK

Why? You're not going there. Come, sit down.

MARIE

I have to go, Franz!

WOYZECK
Aren't your feet sore by now? You should rest.

MARIE
What's wrong with you? You're so different.

WOYZECK
Do you know how long it's been, Marie?

MARIE
Us? Two years, Pentecost.

WOYZECK
But how much longer will it last?

She rose to her feet, vaguely alarmed. Woyzeck stealthily removed the wooden paint-stirrer from his pocket and tested its blade with his finger.

Meanwhile, one part of Carl's awareness, that split-screen faculty Stanislavskians call "the superobjective," remained aloof. He was simultaneously musician and instrument, observing and shaping his performance "in medias res." Angelica's computer/brain analogy came to mind, but this was a different condition: *Both hemispheres directly functional. Left brain full-speed, right brain studying left brain unobserved.*

So, layer on layer =
Remembering Büchner's lines, cues—
Performing Büchner's lines, cues—
Remembering knife business—
Performing knife business—
Observing personal performance—
Adjusting personal performance—
Listening to Marie—
Watching Angelica—

Her taut breasts,
Sinuous hips,
Strawberry lips,
Haunted eyes.
Eve the innocent.
Lilith the Bitch.

"Carl!" Jan called out. "You still in there?" Normally, she was not supposed to cue an actor unless he requested it by saying, "Line."

Carl shook his head to clear it. "Sorry. My mind wandered."

"It seemed a little long for you to pause for effect," the A.D. remarked, adding mischievously, "even for you, boss."

He growled mock-resentfully, "Don't be a smartass." Her wisecrack referred to his idiosyncratic dramatic silences. Like Olivier's exaggerated Ronnie-Roberts-on-ice "The Play's the Thing" pirouette, Carl's long pauses were easy critical fodder; they'd been parodied in *Forbidden Broadway* and he fervently hoped *Saturday Night Live* would kid them, too. *Say anything you like, just say* something!

"Well?" Jan asked. "Do you need the line?"

"No. We'll pick it up from the top of the scene." He turned to Angelica. "Sorry. My concentration's off."

She smiled sympathetically. "You must miss Diana."

Carl gave her a sharp look. She pretended not to notice.

At a little after five, he dismissed the cast and returned to the business office with Jan and Gynger to see the results of the elder woman's prop-hunting sojourn.

"No luck finding a barrel-organ, but I got a tip on an antique fair in Reading that might have one. Otherwise, I got everything you asked for." She rummaged in the first of two large shopping bags and lined up a set of steins, metal beer mugs, and a small wooden keg on the desktop.

Jan indicated the keg. "That needs aging."

"Uh-huh," Gynger nodded, removing from the other bag a lather cup, strop and straight razor, as well as a pistol and a knife for the pawnbroker scene.

Carl passed judgment on each: "Yes, yes, yes, yes and no."

"No to my knife? But it's so elegant!"

"That's the trouble, Gynger," he said, pointing to the colored-glass gems studding its hilt. "It'd be fine if I were doing *Richard III,* but Woyzeck buys it because he can't afford the pistol. Get me an ugly sharp knife and blunt the edge."

"I'll look for one tomorrow."

The three of them went to dinner, still talking shop. As they entered the club, Carl instinctively checked the bar.

"Looking for someone?" Jan asked.

"George," he lied. "I hated coming down so hard on him yesterday."

"You had no choice."

"Jan, if it'd been anyone else, I would have handled it more diplomatically."

"Well, at least he was sober today," Gynger observed.

As the company reassembled after dinner, a chunky photojournalist from the Luzerne County Record arrived to take pictures, but when Carl told him that Diana Lee Taylor was not there, he began to pack up his equipment again.

"If you come back Sunday," Carl suggested, "she'll be here."

"I can't come Sunday."

"Sorry, I forgot most people don't work Sundays."

"That's right," the photographer said, snap-shutting his camera case. "Most people go to church."

Watching him leave, Jan murmured, "Well, if he's what's waiting for me upstairs, I opt for Hell."

"Damn," Carl swore, "I wanted him to take some pictures with George. Smooth things over."

"Can't win 'em all, boss." Jan raised her voice. "Okay, places, everybody! Once over lightly, and we're out of here."

At the evening runthrough, Jan stood in for Carl as he prowled the aisles checking sight lines from the outermost and center seats of the first and last rows; snapped his fingers to indicate when the tempo must be picked up; admonished actors to "*Pro*-JECT!" At rehearsal's end, he gave notes, dismissed the cast, held a brief meeting with Jan and Gynger, then at last his long day was done.

Angelica was nowhere to be seen. He loitered in the lobby, but that made him feel so pitifully adolescent, he finally left. She wasn't at the club, either, and he couldn't bring himself to ring her room. Carl ordered a brandy, sat in a corner booth and faced the door. Four company members—Gynger, Jan, Bill Evans and their senior character actor, Joel Roye—joined him. Two hours, three brandies and four hundred theatrical anecdotes later, Carl gave up, called a taxi and went to his hotel.

He stuck his tongue out at himself in the bathroom mirror. *Go to sleep. Di's probably in dreamland by now.*

As he got into bed and turned off the light, a sudden random memory—a trip with his parents and Irving (home on leave and looking undeniably natty in razor-creased khaki and polished brass) to the farm of the Sandermans, friends of his mother. Cary and Irving stayed inside listening to music with the Sanderman girls, Claire, eight years older than Cary, and Barbara, two months younger than he. Outside, the two sets of parents sat beneath a tall maple tree enjoying the warm summer evening, wondering why ''the children want to stay inside and sweat, they know those songs by heart.'' But the music made them dance, and after dancing a while, Claire led Irving off to her bedroom while Cary and Barbara curled up on the sofa and kissed like movie lovers—except even then, in spite of puberty's fires, Cary felt nothing. When the visit was over, he promised he'd write Barbara, because, well, isn't that what you're supposed to do?

Only I never did.

Anyway, Carl reflected, that must've been the only time he and Irving ever shared anything remotely close to—what?—a ''brotherly'' experience?

This was more typical: whenever Cary got new clothing instead of the usual hand-me-downs, Irving was instantly jealous.

''Cary, let me borrow your new shirt.''

''But I haven't even got the pins out.''

''Mom, he's acting selfish again!''

Cary would try to explain he just wanted to be the first to put it on, after that Irving could wear it to his heart's content, *but that wasn't the point, was it? Anything I ever got he thought of as an Amazing Technicolor Dreamcoat (and whose fault was that?). Surprised he didn't want first dibs on Barbara, too.*

Carl enters the long hall. Huge windows bordered with ghostly billowing curtains; sconces gripped by living arms.

No, false! Cocteau's Beauty and the Beast—*wake up!*

The white curtains melt. Translucent plastic walls. The disembodied limbs dwindle into a beast stalking him on the far side of the contracting-expanding-contracting channel.

Carl inches his way downstairs. The feeble glow of a forty-watt bulb.

All grown up, mein Kind? Komm, setz dich!

They wait for him in the combination room on the sofa, their faces and bodies completely muffled in grey wool.

Mein Kind, so long you've stayed away?

Gramma, I'm sorry.

So long you've stayed away.

I can't go. I won't!

Tch-tch.

Carl struggles free of the dream. His eyes snap open. He sighs, glad to be back in his Wilkes-Barre hotel room.

After breakfast, waiting in the lobby of the Sheraton-Crossgates Hotel for his limousine to arrive, Carl reviews his production journal.

THURSDAY, MAY 4

1. RUNTHROUGH SCENES 1–13, MAKESHIFT PROPS. SET TEMPI.
2. LUNCH: TECK PROBLEMS, MISCELLANEOUS TROUBLESHOOTING.
3. RUN 14–26, PROPS, TEMPI.
4. RUN STRINdBERGman.
5. DINNER BREAK.
6. WOYZECK SPEED RUN.

Outside, rain streaming from the overhanging marquee ricochets off the pavement. Carl remembers that he left his new, expensive umbrella in the back of Angelica's car. *Damn, it must still be there. Hope she drove to Pennsylvania.*

Shading his eyes against the rain, Carl peers up the street. No sign of his limousine, but a few blocks off he notices a great shaft of sunshine beating down on midtown Scranton storefronts. *Not the first dime-sized Pennsylvania thundershower I've been caught in.* Still, he feels a little like Al Capp's unspellable hard-luck cartoon character, always walking around with a gloomcloud hanging over his head and—

and?

Scranton?

A sin so great, the angel*ica already knows Di's line*s hold their breath. What's that shining so bright? Take down your hands, Marie. Let me see.

''That's the suspicion scene, Carl. We're doing the accusation scene.''
What's wrong with my concentration?
''You must miss Diana.''
''Yes, yes, yes, yes and no.''
''No to my knife?''
''Mom, he's acting selfish again!''

The front door had a ''Closed'' sign on it.

Tch-tch, mein Kind.

so long you stay away?

NO! Whipping out, streaking along the river route again, down, down in the motel court come down, hammering at the door of her privacy when suddenly A FIRESPHERE OF MOTTLED FORCE RAGES INTO THE CORRIDOR, ITS FIERY TENDRILS WHIPPING OUT TOWARD HIS CHEST as the alarm bells begin to ring a

n

d

R

I

N

G,

yanking Carl awake. He fumbled for the telephone. ''Hello?''

A click. Dead air.

He slammed down the receiver. Carl had a dull headache. He glared at the time (7:00 A.M.), then out the window.

Well, it actually is raining.

Twenty minutes later, semi-fresh, he dressed, breakfasted, called his driver and waited in front of the hotel. Peering anxiously into the rain, Carl pinched himself, winced. Across Public Square he could see the Wilkes-Barre bus terminal. *Terminal déjà vu.* A crooked grin. *First and only time I was ever glad to see* that *place!*

The limousine arrived. Carl settled himself inside and spread his production journal open on his lap.

THURSDAY, MAY 4

1. RUNTHROUGH SCENES 1–13, MAKESHIFT PROPS. SET TEMPI.
2. LUNCH: TECK PROBLEMS, MISCELLANEOUS TROU-BLESHOOTING.
3. RUN 14–26, PROPS, TEMPI.
4. RUNTHROUGH STRINDBERG.
5. DINNER BREAK.
6. WOYZECK SPEED RUN.

He switched items 4 and 6.

V. Intermezzo Discordare

7:03 A.M. Her telephone rang.

The voice on the other end spoke first. "Why haven't you done anything?"

"How do you know I haven't?"

"I know."

"I haven't made up my mind yet. *If* I decide to play, I'll be in touch."

"*When* you decide to play, I'll know."

A click. Dead air.

She put down the phone. In spite of the earliness of the hour, she lit a cigarette to steady her nerves.

VI. Two-Part Inventions

Carl needn't have rearranged Thursday's schedule. Angelica stayed close all day. She brought him coffee, asked questions, cast casual, innocent glances at him that, cumulatively, were neither casual nor innocent. Her behavior—*perversity squared!*—disturbed him more than her reserve, partly because—*O my manly ego!*—she'd usurped his initiative, but mainly because her growing power to influence his moods and feelings unsettled Carl.

It was one of those going-through-the-motions days. Angelica's acting was subdued; George stumbled along like a somnambulist; the other actors played every theatrical style from Shakespeare to Noël Coward, *anything but Büchner.*

After lunch, Jan stood in for Carl as he staged the fight between Woyzeck and the Drum-Major. That, at least, went well. George's big fist looked deadly chopping down "slow-mo" onto her collarbone. When the routine was refined, Carl became Woyzeck again and Jan coached him through the sequence, beginning slow, gradually accelerating tempo until the fight looked thoroughly convincing.

As they finished, the rest of the cast returned from their midday meal. Jan announced the schedule shift that freed everyone but Angelica for the evening. The cast was delighted, all but George, but then, he'd been cranky the whole day long. *Probably from going on the wagon,* Carl surmised.

The quick-time runthrough that afternoon was a monumental fizzle. It began smoothly enough, with Woyzeck-Carl and his commanding officer (Bill Evans) moving and saying their lines as if they were characters in a silent movie projected at sound speed. But Joel Roye, who played the Doctor, couldn't adjust to the harried tempo; neither could Vincent Swailes (Woyzeck's friend, Andres). Their sluggishness, like glue dribbling into a precision mechanism, began affecting the other actors. To Carl's chagrin, George, normally a whiz at jaw-breaking patter, was the worst casualty. *Is he slowing down deliberately?*

The rehearsal limped to an end. A chewing-out would only make things worse, so Carl dismissed the cast. As they began to disperse, his irritation suddenly surfaced in a misplaced dispute with Jan, who picked that unpropitious moment to criticize his own performance.

"Your concentration was way off today, chief," she said, "especially in your scenes with Marie."

"But that's when I felt the *most* focused," he argued.

"Sahib, you always tell actors if it's not coming across, it doesn't matter how it 'feels.' "

"This time"—the director in him vexed at his unmuzzleable actor's ego—"I trust my experience over your opinion."

Jan bit her lip. "We need a referee." She turned to her new assistant, but Gynger, not wanting to get caught in the middle, muttered, "I really wasn't paying attention to those scenes."

Carl noticed Angelica hovering nearby. Jan stiffened as he beckoned her over and addressed the redhead by her character name: "Marie, how'd you think our scenes went today? Was I off?"

She ignored Jan's arctic reserve. "I wouldn't say that."

Carl permitted himself a tiny smile. "What *would* you say?"

"Dare I presume?"

"Presume away."

"The right colors are there, but you're too restrained—maybe it's my fault. You've got to shake us up, Carl. I mean, the whole cast is pussyfooting around so-veddy-civilized, while here we are, my God! practically doing Brecht."

His eyes widened. Angelica had just overstepped, trespassing into directorial (*my*) territory, *though damned if I'll rap her knuckles in front of Jan. Besides, she's right.*

"I've been thinking along the same lines," Carl admitted, turning to Gynger. "Do you know how to set up a mask workshop?"

"Uh-huh." The older woman ticked off the requisites on her fingertips. "Masks. Costumes. Hats and wigs. Hand props. A large mirror. Do you just want half-masks, or doesn't it matter?"

"Whatever. Tonight after dinner, see what you can find downstairs, then if you have to, ride into town in the morning and supplement. We'll do a mask session tomorrow afternoon."

"Speaking of dinner, can we break?" Jan asked. "Gynger and I are ravenous, and afterwards we've still got to run Strindberg."

"If I do it now," Angelica suggested, "we'd all have the night free." She glanced briefly at Carl.

"One of us has to stand in for Di," Jan groused.

"Without Di," Angelica said, "I'd just as soon run it solo."

A short, uncomfortable pause. The director made up his mind. "Yes. Jan, go eat. Gynger, set props, then beat it."

Jan looked at Angelica, at Carl, at Angelica again. "Fine," she said shortly, striding out. Gynger quickly arranged the required furniture and hurried after her friend.

A swift, satisfactory runthrough: Angelica brought new textures, richer emotional colors to the role. Carl tried to imagine Diana achieving similar results without strong direction, but knew she neither possessed Angelica's range nor technique. *Maybe some day she will. Maybe.*

The rehearsal ended. Carl wondered what, if anything, to do next, but Angelica, head cocked to one side, took the initiative.

"Well, friend, game for another ride? Same house rules."

"In home territory? Hard to take me where I've never been."

She curved an eyebrow. "Is that a dare?"

"Do you want it to be?"

Frank challenge in her eyes. "I think so." She came closer. "I *think* so."

Carl felt the same way.

That morning's rainshowers were long past, but the parking lot was still a swamp. Carl threaded his way through the puddles to her car, glanced in back for his umbrella, didn't see it, turned to ask Angelica about it, and was surprised to see her holding out her ignition keys for him to take.

"Do you mind driving, Carl? You know the way."

"The way to where?"

"Wherever you want to take me."

"Uh—your insurance?"

"It's okay."

He took the keys and got behind the wheel, suspecting her of deliberately catering to some stereotypical idea of Ye Male Ego: *kiddies love toys, men love cars.* On the other hand, maybe she just wanted him to shoulder the responsibility for—?

You know what, Mr. Richards.

Adjusting the visor, Carl wheeled out onto a two-lane country blacktop. He drove cautiously, following the road's gradual downgrade till it brought them to a broader highway.

"Last night you traveled, didn't you, Carl?"

Her question momentarily puzzled him. Then he understood. "How did you know that?"

"I sensed you outside my room. Why didn't you come in?"

"Your door was blocked. Something stopped me—attacked me. Sort of a floating ball of lightning. That make sense to you?"

Her lips tightened. "Maybe." She rooted through her purse for a pack of cigarettes.

"Angelica, please don't smoke."

"I *have* to. I'm not trying to be difficult, Carl, it's just I get very tense. I'm an addictive personality."

"I sort of guessed that."

"Did you also guess I'm an alcoholic?"

Several seconds of utter silence. "No-o."

"Sorry. I shouldn't've just blurted that out. A *recovered* alcoholic. Smoking lets me cope. I know you're allergic, but—"

"That's not why it bothers me, Angelica."

His tone stopped her. "What, then?"

"My mother died of cancer. Lung cancer."

Angelica took the unlit cigarette from her lips. "She was a smoker?"

"No. My father was. She pleaded with him to give it up. He refused to. After she died, he finally quit."

"I see. And you blame him for her death." It was not a question. "Is your father alive, Carl?"

More or less. "He lives near Scranton." A longish pause. "I haven't seen him for years. I suppose I feel a little guilty about that."

"What do you mean, 'suppose'?"

As they rode down the last steep hill into the outskirts of Wilkes-Barre past gas stations, shopping malls and garish fast-food restaurants, Carl told Angelica about his lucid nightmares: the false wakings, the dark tunnel guarded by his Uncle Max, the meetings with his aunt and grandmother and especially her sad, chastising words that he understood all too well . . .

Carl drove into the Sheraton-Crossgates lot, found a spot, parked, shut off the motor and faced his companion. "For years, Angelica, I've avoided my father, but at least I lived far off. Now I'm just twenty miles away. No wonder I'm having guilty dreams."

"Maybe you weren't dreaming, Carl."

"I went back to my old home, I walked through my father's shop— places that no longer exist. The people I saw are dead. *(Why wasn't Mom there?)* That's not an obie, that's a nightmare."

Angelica tapped his knee twice for emphasis. "Listen to me. *Carefully.* You might have been scrying."

"Scrying? That's a kind of crystal-gazing, isn't it?"

"Not the way Oliver Fox uses it. Bob Monroe calls it 'Locale Two.' You bought their books. Didn't you read them?"

"I skimmed."

"You mean you skimped. You're playing with dangerous stuff. That floating lightning thing . . . Carl, please, *be careful.*"

"Spare me the instant Maria Ouspenskaya replay. What did Fox mean by 'scrying'?"

"He was having a simple obie, but then it changed."

"Changed? How?"

"He soared up into the heavens." Angelica shook her head. "No, Carl, not literally, not space travel. Fox said it was a forbidden thing— scrying. He claimed he was punished for it."

"This is getting too metaphysical for my taste. Are you saying that Fox . . . that *I* crossed to 'the other side'?"

"Carl, all I'm saying is, most obies are as harmless as taking a bus to Philadelphia. Please be careful!"

" 'Dere are some tings man is not meant to meddle vith.' "

She glared at him. "Let's go inside. I'm dying for a cigarette."

The maître d' led them to a secluded table in the rear of the restaurant. In lieu of Ballantine's scotch, which they didn't stock, Carl chose Cutty Sark. Angelica ordered a half-bottle of Jadot Beaujolais. She noticed Carl's expression and said, "I can allow myself a little wine now and then."

"I didn't say anything."

"You didn't need to."

The waiter served their drinks. Angelica raised her glass. ''So, shall we toast?''

''To what?''

''Guilt. Innocence. Take your pick.''

''So far, we're both innocent.''

A wry smile. ''Hardly, Carl.''

''Other than thoughtcrime, what?''

''Nothing. Everything.'' She stared into her goblet, frowning. ''Carl, we're being watched.''

He turned and saw George O'Brien in a smart cocoa tweed jacket with elbow patches, his collar open, his tie loose, at the bar peering intently into a highball tumbler he picked at as if trying to remove a speck.

''Wonderful,'' Carl groaned. ''He looks smashed.''

''He saw us. We can't ignore him.''

A sigh, half-regretful, half-relieved. ''The only discreet thing we can do is ask him to join us.''

''Yes.''

Carl clinked his wineglass against hers. ''Well . . . to innocence.''

The three of them spent an hour in strained, desultory tabletalk. After dinner, Angelica said she wanted to go to bed early, so if George wished, he could ride back with her to the Luzerne Motel.

After she waved goodbye to Carl, after she pulled out of the hotel parking lot, Angelica turned to her passenger and snapped, ''All right, actor, quit acting. You're not drunk. Why were you spying?''

''What makes you think I was?''

''Wilkes-Barre? Carl's hotel?''

''Coincidence. I lived around here once, too, remember?'' He winced. ''My head's killing me. Let's not fight. I need a friend.''

In the dim glow of the dashboard, Angelica's expression was implacable. ''I sincerely hope you find one.''

The amber message light was blinking. Carl dialed the front desk and learned Diana had called twice that evening. He got an outside line and phoned New York. She answered on the first ring.

''Rehearsal must've run late,'' she said. *Too casually.*

''I ran into George downstairs in the bar. Had to sober him up. I just put him in a cab.''

''I think you'd better replace him, Carl.''

"Di, I can't fire my oldest friend."

"No? You'd rather ruin my show?"

(Your show?) "Tomorrow, I guarantee you, George'll shape up. I've got an understudy coming in from Philly just to scare him."

"Maybe that *will* work," Diana conceded.

"George'll hate me for it, but he'll do an about-face PDQ."

"Good." She yawned. "This day's been grueling."

"How're the skits coming?"

"Fun, but they're hard work. Don't forget to watch. So, other than George, how are the rehearsals? Is Angel—"

"She's fine, but today was generally sluggish. Tomorrow, though, I'm going to shake everybody up."

"How?"

"We're going to do a bunch of mask improvisations."

"That I won't mind missing. Masks are weird. They scare me."

"Me, too, a little."

Diana yawned again. "Well, pal, time for beddy-bye."

"Yep. Night-night." He blew her a long-distance kiss. In his mind, Angelica's features overlay hers like a mask.

VII. Toccata-Impromptu Marziale

PREPARATIONS

DOWNSTAGE LEFT: A six-foot-long, three-foot-wide table covered with full-face masks, half-masks, vizards, dominoes, their empty eye sockets staring blindly up into the flies.

STAGE RIGHT: Bonnets, caps, derbies, high hats, shakos, Stetsons, wigs double-piled on a table of the same size. Up left of table, a huge costume rack laden with gowns, jackets, topcoats, feather boas, military uniforms.

UPSTAGE REAR: A large mirror. To its left, another three-by-six table bedecked with colorful things: artificial flowers; baby dolls; baskets; castanets; cap guns; pinwheels; plates; purses; rubber hatchets, maces; a Winnie-the-Pooh cuddly.

CENTER: Carl faces downstage. Except for the new understudy whom Jan briefs in the back, the cast is seated in the front rows.

CARL [*addressing the cast*]

Our species not only thinks, but thinks about thinking—and yet even geniuses draw only on a small part of their total mental capacity. Today, we're going to explore some of that unknown inner territory. What you experience may be closer to voodoo than Stanislavski.

The speech, adapted from Carl's old mindreading act, was like Chevreul's Pendulum, that parlor amusement in which a ring dangling from a string mysteriously swings in circles or back and forth. *Tell an actor it's magical and it works. Explain the mechanistic principle behind it and it fails.* Mask work was similar: to succeed, it was wise to "psych out" the participants.

He studied faces. Some were eager, some skeptical. The kids looked nervous. Angelica seemed fascinated. George chewed a thumbnail and glared, *pissed at me over the new understudy.*

CARL

Like hypnosis, mask improvs work best when the actors open themselves to suggestion. Will anyone help me demonstrate by letting me hypnotize them?

Gynger Morrison raised her hand. Receiving a nod from Carl, she climbed the three steps at the side of the proscenium and joined him onstage. She was wearing a milk-white blouse, charcoal tights, dance flats and a convincingly innocent expression.

Carl told Gynger to clasp her hands and imagine she could not pull them apart. She strained, but could not separate them.

CARL

All right, Gynger, relax. Now you can open your hands. Good. You're an excellent subject. Now close your eyes and imagine you're in a time machine that's taking you into the past. You're six years old and you're in school. The teacher is speaking to you: *Say your alphabet, Gynger.*

Her feet pigeoned inward. Her voice piped high and thin.

GYNGER
A B C D E F G H I J K L M N O P Q R S T U V W X Y Z.

CARL
The time machine is starting up again. But now it's running in the

opposite direction. Old years six you're. School in you're. You to speaking is teacher the: *Gynger, alphabet your say!*

GYNGER

Z Y X W V U T S R Q P O N M L K J I H G F E D C B A.

An appreciative murmur. Jan, busy conferring with George's understudy, glanced up at Carl and smiled. *First time all day.*

CARL [*To Gynger*]

When I say three, wake up. One, two, three. [*To cast*] Gynger was just in a light trance. Trances are normal. Driving a car on "automatic pilot" is a kind of focused trance. So are mask improvs.

He strode to the downstage left table and picked up two masks, a crackle-textured face, black with streaks of silver, and a Punchinello head with long, crooked nose.

CARL

When I call you up to improvise, the first thing you do is pick a mask. There are two kinds. "Punch" here covers the entire face. Half-masks like this other one leave the mouth free to speak. Not that every mask talks. Some don't utter a peep. Notice I talk about them as if they, not you, are responsible for their actions. Primitives believe gods and devils inhabit masks and possess the wearers. In his book, *Impro,* Keith Johnstone claims certain masks provoke virtually identical behavior, no matter who puts them on. This is where the "voodoo" comes in.

Carl paused to let them weigh the impact of his words. Everyone seemed suitably impressed.

CARL

After you put your mask on, go to the costume rack and the hat table and dress up any way the mask likes. When you're done, I'll bring you the mirror. Take a good look at yourself. You'll feel the mask beginning to take over. Let it. Next, go to the prop table, take anything the mask wants, then start improvising with your scene partners. One word of caution: some masks are friendly, some are cranky, a few are downright dangerous. If I tell you to take off your mask, *take it off immediately*.

Carl asked for two volunteers to improvise with Gynger. Joel Roye lumbered to his feet. Carl was pleased. Joel and Gynger were both veteran actors, *they ought to get things off to a good start*. Joel was a great bear of a man who moved with the elephantine grace of an Oliver Hardy, whom he resembled. As he joined Gynger at the mask table, a fiddlefoot-eager Bill Evans trotted onto the platform to be third participant in the scene.

PREPARATIONS

JOEL ROYE—takes a pallid vizard that makes him look like the statue in *Don Giovanni*. He dresses in an opera cape, top hat and white gloves and completes his ensemble with an ebony walking stick and an artificial rose that he places in his hatband. He epitomizes the British toff, or dandy.

GYNGER MORRISON—covers her eyes with a silver sequined domino, wraps a silk skirt round her hips, shrouds bosom and shoulders with a bandanna and gaudy beads and selects a wicker basket filled with plastic toys. Her appearance suggests the saucy commedia dell' arte wench, Franceschina.

BILL EVANS—picks a pugnosed animal mask that hides his face. Covering himself with shapeless burlap, he bypasses the prop table and shambles over to wait with Gynger and Joel.

CARL RICHARDS—brings the mirror, shows each ''mask'' how it looks, sets the glass ''up center'' and exits.

LAZZI

FRANCESCHINA enters, sees no one, flounces coquettishly.

THE TOFF enters grandiosely, courts FRANCESCHINA.

FRANCESCHINA at first ignores, then encourages, then spurns THE TOFF.

At this moment:

THE BURLAP BEAST enters. He tries to make friends with THE TOFF by lightly thumping the floor, the tables and, especially, THE TOFF's back.

THE TOFF valiantly tries to woo FRANCESCHINA, but is frustrated by her flirtatiousness and THE BURLAP BEAST's rhythmic interruptions.

CARL

All right, good scene—take off your masks.

Peeling away the pretend faces, the three hung up their costumes and returned props and masks to the tables. Bill Evans, blinking, seemed disoriented; Gynger guided him to his seat.

CARL

Not a bad beginning. Notice no one felt impelled to speak. All right, who wants to go next?

GEORGE [*Rising*]

How 'bout you and me, Cary—just for old times?

Carl's jaw clamped. *Keep cool,* he cautioned himself. *George needs to lash out. Let him.*

CARL

Okay, George, like you say . . . for old times.

He told Jan to come up and monitor the scene, then began to ask for another volunteer, but Angelica was already heading for the stage.

PREPARATIONS

GEORGE O'BRIEN—chooses a gold full-face mask with down-turned mouth and beetling brows. A strong mask, potentially cruel.

CARL RICHARDS—wants the mask George picked, but settles for an odd schizoid overlay, wearing the crackly black half-mask on top of the white statue face Joel Roye used. Carl dons striped ambassadorial trousers, a vest, tuxedo jacket, florid tie. Plopping on a fright wig, he goes to the prop table, tucks a bag of play money into his belt.

JAN NAPIER—holds the mirror up to Carl. He works his mouth, squares his jaw in keeping with the minstrel travesty he sees. Shoulders back. Stomach out. Feet splayed wide.

LAZZI

MASK sees HER split face, vertically divided: half steel, half pearl. Emerald eyes. Red hair crowned with mistletoe. Lips blood-bright like rubies. MASK kneels worshipfully before HER.

SHE shoves him away. MASK f

          a
          l
          l
           s
            a
             n
              d

                    MASK

laughs LAUGHS laughs LAUGHS laughs LAUGHS laughs—
then paws the sack of money off his belt and offers it to HER.
SHE accepts. MASK reverently kisses HER hand. SHE pushes
him away. MASK f

          a
          l
          l
           s
            a
             n
              d
                    MASK

LAUGHS   laughs   LAUGHS   laughs   LAUGHS   laughs
LAUGHS—

                At this moment:

THE GILDED MAN enters, brandishing an ax in his gloved fist.
THE GILDED MAN clutches MASK by the shoulder and spins
him away from HER.

SHE laughs   laughs   laughs   laughs
           LAUGHS   LAUGHS   LAUGHS

    and   LAUGHS   LAUGHS   LAUGHS
        laughs   laughs   laughs   laughs

                At this moment:

MASK rips off THE GILDED MAN's golden face and, with a cry
of rage, presses it over HER face.

                At this moment:

Laughter of invisible fiends. A thunderous voice.

JAN

Take off your masks!

MASK froze. His shoulders slumped. Energy slowly bled from his
body. MASK was dying—

JAN

TAKE OFF YOUR MASKS!

Carl obeyed. He squinted; the work lights suddenly were too bright.
When he was able to open his eyes again, he was startled to see Angelica
holding George's mask in her hands. Then he remembered he'd yanked
it off himself and held it over her face.

That was a damned good scene. Jan should've let it run.

He continued the workshop, but when all the actors had their chance
to improvise, Carl declared a break and motioned Jan over.

"How come you cut my scene off so fast?"

"George was just about to hit you with the ax."

"It's only plastic. He wouldn't've hurt me."

"Carl . . . you didn't see his face."

Jan and Gynger put away the masks, costumes and props and readied
the stage for *Woyzeck*. When the cast came back, Carl said, "We open a
week from tomorrow. Jan will explain what this means logistically."

Kneeling on the apron, Jan scanned her clipboard. "Tomorrow we
all have off. Sunday, it's two or three runthroughs with Di. Monday
and Tuesday, tech-dress—sound, lights, props, costumes, makeup.
Wednesday, Thursday, full dress rehearsals. Ditto Friday, except we'll
have a preview audience, including local press."

"So our first audience is in seven days, not eight," Carl declared.
"When Di returns day after tomorrow, we've got to have a SHOW she
can just slide into. We're now going to do another runthrough. I want
you to tap into that raw power the masks had."

Jan called "Places." She stepped off the apron and waited for the
actors to assume their opening positions, then said, "Music up. House
lights off. Stage up. Music out."

Woyzeck began soaping the Captain with a lathery brush.

CAPTAIN [*Sputtering*]

Slow down, take it easy, you're making my head spin! You'll live at
least another thirty years, Woyzeck. Break that down into days and

hours and minutes. What the hell are you going to do with all that time? Haven't you ever thought about that?

WOYZECK

Yes, Captain, I have.

CAPTAIN

Thinking about time is painful. Our suffering seems endless. But we're not eternal, our lives are done in an instant. Yet it takes twenty-four whole hours for the world to revolve. So slow, so fast. I see a windmill and feel awful. Know what I mean, Woyzeck?

WOYZECK

Yes, sir, Captain.

When the scene ended, Jan said, "Lights down, music up." Bill Evans exited. Angelica entered with Myne Reid, the local drama student who played Woyzeck and Marie's illegitimate son.

Marie crooned a lullaby about the jewelry her last "client" gave her. Woyzeck entered. She clapped her hands over her ears.

WOYZECK

What's that sparkling between your fingers?

MARIE [*Shows him*]

Franz, I'm only human.

WOYZECK

I . . . understand. Here, Marie—my salary, plus a bit extra I earned shaving the Captain. Take it.

MARIE

You're always so good to me, Franz.

WOYZECK

I'm due at the Doctor's and I've got to chop the Captain's wood. I'll see you later. [*He exits.*]

MARIE

I'm so rotten, I ought to stab myself. The world stinks . . . and when we die, we go to Hell.

In the wings, Carl shuddered. The mask session was paying off. At last, his whole cast was acting with that nightmarish intensity Büchner demanded.

The rehearsal reached the play's first explosive climax: Woyzeck discovering that Marie has slept with the Drum-Major.

WOYZECK

Bitch!

MARIE

Sooner a knife in my breast than your hands on me!

Woyzeck reels into an empty field. (Jan: "Music cue—Henry Brant, 'Signs and Alarms.' ")

WOYZECK [*Prone on ground*]

What are you saying down there—*in* there? Stab the bitch? Yes! "Stab the wolf-bitch dead!"

(Jan: "Blackout. Music fade. Lights up on fight scene.")

Woyzeck's friend Andres enters the tavern and warns his pal that the Drum-Major is bragging about his success with Marie.

ANDRES

Here he comes. Leave him alone, Franz. He's drunk.

DRUM-MAJOR

I'm a real man! Stay out of my way, or I'll shove your nose up your ass! Everybody get drunk! [*To Woyzeck*] Hey, knucklehead, I'm talking to you!

LAZZI

WOYZECK stares insolently at the DRUM-MAJOR and deliberately whistles in his face.

According to the script, the Drum-Major had another threatening line of dialogue and Woyzeck was supposed to whistle again, but George jumped the cue and yanked him to his feet. As George's fist slammed into Carl, Jan's warning flashed into his mind:

"—you didn't see his face."

VIII. Double Fugue & Bridge with Double

I'm alive again. I don't know how. I don't care why. Alive.
suspended
He's here, too, of course, but I don't have to deal with him yet. He and his world frozen-fixed until I open my eyes. Behind closed lids, bits of new awareness caught like flies in aspic.
MY name (marie) MY face
I see what he sees: Daddy's high cheekbones. The dangerous blade of Mama's nose. My own scarlet lips. Fear's locked rectus.
I open up my eyes. The floodgates gush and I'm drenched in the deluge. Gulls shrieking above the bright morning harbor. Women and their wind-chime laughter. The dry crinkle of old folk chatting, the off-key chattering of happy children. The snaking queue in front of the aquarium, the Day-Glo tourists shopping in the festive malls, streaming up and down the decks of docked vessels, boarding water taxis, dancing at the pennant-flapping bandstand gazebo, lunching in the outdoor Greek café where he sips retsina and watches me toy with the stem of my goblet. The texture of the cool, smooth glass. Bracing salt-air, the sharp scent of garlic, a muffled thrilling strum of bouzoukis, sweet mavrodaphne's tang, his gentle handstroke in the sunlight.
"Look at me . . . please?"
He hates his crow's-feet and large nose, but those are accidents of time. I'm afraid of his youthful face, its absence of posted warnings. *Shoals and eddies.*
Light banter. A thousand tangents, as radiantly wrong as the rose he bought when I wasn't looking and gave me as we said good night at the elevator. In bed, his steady breathing on the other side of the wall soothed me in the dark.
Last night? How can I remember that?
How can I forget?
I shut my eyes, open them again and the day is nearly done. The cars rush by us as we walk the highway's long curve around the mountain's broad base. Below, the haunted lake gleams crimson in the dying sun. At a break in the chase of headlights, we hurry across the road and up the steep walled lane to the inn, where life is literally skittles and beer.
Another blink. Another afternoon. Driving home. On the car radio,

Khachaturian's *Spartacus*. He reads the tale of the wolf-girl whose lover kills her. I can't see the road for tears.

Another blink and he's gone.

We never said goodbye

|
|
|
|
|

Carl *who?*

Neat incision in the fabric of the night, too deep and dark to see my fingers as I dabble them inside. When I try to pull them out again, a bone-cold fist on the other side clutches me tight. I can't yank my hand back fast enough. The thing draws me into the black hole wide enough to drink in canceled worlds

|
|
|
|
|

alone on a cracked leather sofa in an L-chamber with pale green walls. An owl radio perches on a nightstand, its knob eyes turned to murmuring voices emerging from its speaker-beak.

The short leg of the L is an alcove with a locked closet and a broad wooden bureau whose top is covered with postcards from long-dead relatives, plastic puzzles, loose change, a set of red and green 3D glasses, a stubby pencil, an empty notepad. Two other doors, one to the bathroom, the other to an outer corridor, are both shut.

An empty meal tray positioned across the cranked bed has five playing cards arranged on it side by side, facedown.

"The Ace of Diamonds!"

Cary's fingertip hovers blindly over the pasteboards, drifts down, instinctively touches one card, turns it over.

The wrong Ace.

"Give it to me, goof!"

The old man snatches it away, sees what he's holding, cries out, tries to throw it away, but the card's blackness seeps through his fingers, puddling on the floor, running up the walls, darkening the ceiling, blotting out sight, sound, taste, smell, touch, choking off oxy

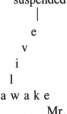

      sm of noise,
harsh light, coldness. The sweet intimacy of *tot und schlafen nicht*

suspended

e

v

i

l

a w a k e

Mr.

Richards?''

Carl tried to open his eyes, but the bright light hurt. He squeezed them shut again.

"Mr. Richards? Are you awake?"

He groaned. "That was a yes."

"Mr. Richards, who is President of the United States?"

"Wrong." He opened his eyes. "Who is on first."

The resident smiled. "Can you tell me the President's name?"

"Bush. My head hurts. How about some ten-dollar aspirin?"

"We'll see what we can do." Gesturing for the nurse to follow him, the physician left the room.

A familiar footstep.

"Jan?"

"Yours faithfully." She touched his cheek sympathetically, jerked her hand back when he winced. "Sorry. I meant it as a nice-nice."

"Thanks. Work on your technique." His mouth puckered grumpily. "Where's my old pal George?"

"Sleeping it off."

"Smashed again? Terrific. How bad did my bosom buddy rack me up?"

"Nothing broken. Bruised jaw, minor lip laceration, you'll have a little trouble with your lines. Ice packs and tetracycline. The doctor's worried about concussion, but I told him how thickheaded you are."

"I love you, too."

"Which reminds me." Jan picked up the bedside phone and dialed Operator.

"Who are you calling? Not Di!"

"Sorry, sahib. She's waiting by the phone. Here."

Diana Lee Taylor motioned her manager out. Pierce went into the other room, carefully lifted the telephone extension and listened in.

"Hang in there, pal," he heard her tell Carl, "I'm on my way. I'll be there in a couple of hours."

"Di, don't be silly. Stay in New York."

"You don't *want* me to come?"

"No need. I'm still among the living. Save your energy, you'll need it tomorrow. Live TV, remember?"

A long, long pause. "All right," she said at last, "I'll see you Sunday. Sleep warm." She replaced the receiver on its hook.

Reentering the room, Pierce pointed to the dial of his thin gold Rolex. "Diana, if we're going back and forth to P-A tonight, we'd better get started."

"We're not going."

Pierce made no comment. He watched as she poured herself a snifter of Rémy Martin. Skittering a few drops of cognac on the polished sideboard, she raised the glass to her lips, took a sip. Another. He waited for her to evolve the thing she was wrestling with into words.

"Tomorrow after the broadcast, Stu," she instructed, "I don't care how late it is, I want to go straight to Pennsylvania. Please arrange transportation."

"Diana, I'll drive you there myself."

"Uh-uh. I wouldn't dream of imposing."

Pierce smiled. "It'll be my pleasure."

IX. Eroticon

Jan ordered a taxi for Carl and rode along with him to the Sheraton-Crossgates. She wanted to accompany him to his room and fix him an icepack, but he wouldn't let her play nursemaid. Bidding her good night at the elevator, he stepped into the car; it ascended—2, 3, 4, 5. Without a sign she'd noticed Angelica Winters sitting by herself in the cocktail lounge, Jan left the hotel.

On the fifth floor, Carl watched the electric indicator flash 5, 4, 3, 2, Lobby. Part of him wanted to go to his room, shut off the lights and worry at the tangle in comfort and darkness *(What's wrong with George?)*, but downstairs he'd spotted Angelica in the bar, her face half-concealed by her hand, her eyes daring him to look anywhere else.

Time, like energy, flows in quantum packets: in the splinter-second it takes a tower to topple or an envelope to drop, Carl—forefinger poised to summon back the lift—delved for emotional answers.

DIANA

Always more than an erotic centerfold in his mind's seraglio, she was at one time a towering obsession that occupied every passionate niche of his being. A file cabinet in his desk had two manila folders filled with photos and press clippings about her; long before he met her, he used them to piece together in his imagination a model of what Diana Lee Taylor was "really like." This long-distance profile of her proved to be remarkably accurate, but on the occasion when their respective careers brought them to the same private party at The Players theatre club, the discovery turned out to be curiously flat. Seeing Diana for the first time produced in him little more reaction than a kind of clotted curiosity as he watched her "working the room" with her trademarked smile, *The Snow Queen presiding over Court Antarctica*. But then, true to her mythical namesake, She approached him.

"Hear you've got a crush on me, mister."

"Guilty. Do you find that childish?"

"Uh-uh. I admire your taste."

"Enough to have dinner?"

"Possibly . . ."

The dangerous intoxication of an adolescent fantasy suddenly fulfilled. After a giddy courtship lasting a few indiscreet weeks, they were married . . . and now, scant months later, here he was teetering on the slick brink of unfaithfulness. Now that the obsession George scornfully referred to as Diana Lee Grail had been—*too easily?*—appeased, was Di, after all, just a display of conspicuous consumption on the part of a hopelessly bourgeois male ego? *(Little Cary dowsing now for guilt?)*

ANGELICA

Consummate mask-wearer, *anyone's guess where the poses end, where the person begins*. That was something they had in common, of course, but that was not what had drawn Carl to her. *Something simpler, something more complex.* It didn't matter that Angelica Winters was an emotional minefield; he'd realized that the very first time he laid eyes on her. But even if he walked away from her tonight, he knew she was an electrochemical riddle he had to solve. She slashed across his future like a razor.

The splinter-second ended as the elevator doors (2, 3, 4, 5) opened. The envelope dropped, the tower fell—Angelica emerged.

"Surprised to see me?"

He shook his head. "I expected you."

"Ah, how sure of yourself." She stroked his cheek. He winced. "They stitched your lip, I see."

"Why? Does it turn you off?"

"*Au contraire.* Kissing it could be kinky. Does it hurt?"

"Bearable."

"And you knew I'd come?"

"I saw you in the bar. I was just trying to decide whether to go back down and join you there."

"Not a good idea. Neither is standing out here talking."

"True." He led her to his suite. Before she could stop him, he dialed room service and ordered Veuve Cliquot and two glasses.

"You're inviting gossip," she warned him. "You can bet the staff knows Diana's not here."

Carl frowned. "Knee-jerk rebelliousness at living in a fishbowl." He picked up the phone again. "I'll cancel."

"Uh-uh. The damage is done. Think of something else."

They discussed it. Moments later, when the waiter's tap came from the corridor, Angelica, making sure to leave the door open, entered the unlighted bathroom and hid behind the shower curtain.

Carl stood aside as a young black-jacketed bellhop, glancing curiously round the room, crossed to a polished oak sideboard and set on its gleaming surface two long-stemmed champagne flutes and an ice bucket with an orange-labeled bottle nestling within.

"*Two* glasses?" Carl inquired. "Why?"

The waiter wrapped a towel around the flask's neck and popped the cork. "Didn't you order two, sir?"

"I ordered a *new* glass. One that hasn't been used before. I don't want to drink other people's germs."

An amused smile. "Mr. Richards, we *do* wash our glassware."

"I'm sure. I still want a new glass."

"I don't think we can find one this time of night, the stores are all closed."

"Never mind, I'll use a plastic tumbler from the bathroom." Carl feigned embarrassment. "I'd appreciate it if you don't tell anybody how finicky I am." He handed him five dollars, knowing perfectly well it was too small a bribe to ensure his silence.

The bellhop left. Carl peeked to make sure he wasn't lingering on the other side of the door. "All clear, Angelica. By morning, I'll be famous. 'Patron Saint of Fussbudgets.' " No response. "Angelica?"

"Un moment," she intoned in French.

Half-gratified, half-irritated because the waiter took away both flutes, Carl crossed to the sideboard, unwrapped the plastic tumbler and filled it with wine. He heard Angelica emerge from the bathroom, turned to offer her champagne, halted.

The dim lamplight that spilled across the threshold silhouetted Angelica as she stood naked in the bedroom's gapped doorway. She looked curiously like a little girl trying to play a grown-up game, uncertain of the rules.

Which makes two of us. A story Carl once read came to mind, an oddly relevant non sequitur about a tourist who, aflame with curiosity over strange sounds heard behind a locked hotel room door, experienced disillusionment when he discovered what was on the other side. A similar let-down, then, suddenly seeing Angelica unclad. Another tale came to mind, a Pierre Loüys comedy of naked lovers who felt no passion for one other until they put their clothes back on. But Angelica's abrupt disrobing didn't strike Carl as an ill-advised amatory impulse; he saw it, rather, as a deliberate stratagem to minimize intimacy. *The more she pretends to open up, the more she hides herself from view.*

Carl studied the naked woman with cauterized detachment: whipcord neck; rippling interplay of creases radiating from her collarbone. Matchstick arms. Anorexic ribs. Cupcake breasts. Lacquered fingernails and toes, trim ankles, hips without a trace of cellulite. His appraising gaze arrowed upward.

"Like what you see?" she asked, pivoting, her heavy-lidded eyes watching him warily.

"I'm hardly indifferent," he lied, continuing his inventory. Shoulder blades squared like epaulettes. Fine down dappled with tiny scars bristling the ridge of her backbone. The lambent flex of muscled calves. Paired elliptic cheeks pitched lower than the slacks she wore implied. *Like most women—*

Carl immediately censored himself. *Like most* people, *Angelica's better-looking with her clothes on.*

Another oblique recollection: watching a potbellied ape at the Edinburgh Zoo eating peanuts while urine trickled from its pale white penis. *Our animal origins, nature reminding us of the fact. (Why Di never takes off all her clothes when we make love?)*

But it upset him to think about her.

Carl followed Angelica into the bedroom and swiftly undressed. Switching off the light, she clutched him with a ferocity devoid of tenderness. They coupled with the swift warlike stroke that satisfies the flesh but numbs the heart. He felt almost incidental to her climax.

Afterward, lying next to him in the dark, bodies not touching, Angelica murmured, "You didn't come."

Instead of answering, Carl said, "If you want a cigarette, go ahead. I'll survive."

"Thanks. I don't need to smoke just now."

The moment was heavy with expectation. She waited for him to say something he had no words for. He groped for an approximation. "Angelica, I—I rarely do."

She took a deep breath between each separately inflected word. "What . . . works . . . best?"

"Nothing guaranteed."

"Passive? Active?"

"On occasion."

"Which?"

"One or the other. Sometimes, neither."

Wintry detachment. "Carl, what's wrong with you?"

He stiffened. Her question, implying that *he* was sexually dysfunctional, almost spurred him to retort, "You're what's wrong," but, stifling the wish to wound this suddenly promiscuous stranger, Carl tried to answer her honestly. "Hard for me to turn off the world, tune it out. Aware of every sound, texture, scent. Tang of your lips. Interplay of limbs. Warm skin, night air. Rough sheet prickling bare knees. Distracted by a wayward hair-strand. Data input never quitting." *Ditto, guilt.*

Turning and propping herself on one elbow, Angelica said, "Familiar territory. My 'I-am-a-computer' fantasy, remember?"

"Uh-huh."

"Ever consider therapy?"

"What?" A short burst of laughter. "A sex surrogate?"

Angelica smiled wryly. "Besides me, you mean? No, but if you like, I can recommend a really fine Reichean."

Her offer irritated him. "I can just picture me and the orgone."

"You read Orson Bean's book?"

"Yep. Full of lip-service to Love, but seething with hate."

The tilt of an eyebrow. Her sharp indrawn breath told him she was angry—*hold hold*—but Angelica, slowly exhaling, abandoned her pique. Touching him for the first time since they'd made love, she said, "Mr. Richards, you *are* a challenge."

"And you're not, Ms. Winters?"

"At the moment, I am not the issue. You satisfied me. I obviously disappointed you."

"No, you didn't."

"For a good actor, that was one piss-poor line reading."

Instant contrition. "Angelica, listen. Pleasing women—*knowing* I pleased you is my main turn-on. I don't need—"

"Hush." She squeezed his lips shut. "I don't believe you. Even if I did, it works both ways. Lie down. For once, shut off your mind."

He gentled her hand away. "No. You're not oblig—"

"Shhh! No words. Right brain only." Leaning across him, nipples brushing his cheek, she flicked on the FM, tuned in muted chamber music. "Close your eyes, Carl. Focus on your senses. How I smell and feel. The rhythm of my breathing. The way I touch you. Don't look till there's nothing in your mind but me."

Whoever that is. But he did as he was told.

Angelica lit the bedside lamp, briefly eclipsing its moonfire as she mounted him. Her copper tresses grazed his thighs. The cool coupled bondage of her palms, the torrid harmony of her lips *hold hold* him in a rosebud jail of shame. Their twinned *im*pulses spiral them swiftly upward in a sudden tidal surge of

F

  L

    I

      G

        H

          T

as, with terrifying abruptness, AngeliCarl are flung from their linked bodies upUP*UP* into voluptuous Space where the scrying lovers join the spectrum's fiery tongues, visible and heat-hidden, swirling up and over, around and down and int

|

|

    BITCH!

The universe shrieks. Angelica wrenches herself away from Carl. Dark winds batter them as they plunge headlong into the socket of a cosmic whirlpool s   l   o   w   l   y   at first, swiftly picking up speed
as the cone's concentric rings contract
and they merge in a free-fall rush
of ecstasy and terror.
Just as abruptly,
the vortex
ends
in coarse gritrock underfoot . . .
sscrrrp-sscrrrp

A sharp incline. The basalt columns remind Carl of Fingal's Cave in the Hebrides. This, too, a cavern: vaulting green-black pillars; unhealthy florid light. The scrape
sscrrrp-sscrrrp
of naked feet receding down a sharp slope glistening with parallel freshets of blood.

Proceeding cautiously along the rocky passageway, Carl suddenly comes upon a pulsing sphere of radiant light that reminds him a little of the fiery globe that attacked him outside Angelica's motel room. But that was a bright mass of concentrated fury; this dull amber thing pocked with brown, streaked with black, flickers like a dying battery.

Carl approaches it and glimpses, half-hidden within its mottled depths, the silhouette of a small child.

Who are you, little girl? Why are you hiding?

—don't look at me—

But as the creature shies away from him, the curling mist clouding its surface thins and the child inside is clearer now. Her head rests on folded arms, her arms rest across bent knees. She rocks upon her haunches, keening.

He tries to coax away her misery. "Look at me . . . please?"

She glares at Carl. The force of her mistrust jars him.

—go away—

"I won't hurt you."

Their eyes meet. He imagines he sees a momentary flicker of belief. "Please . . . I promise I won't hurt you."

She trembles. Fear? Or the fear-choked yearning for hope?

"NO!"

A brutal hammerhead of force spins Carl around, shoving him away from her.

A FIRESPHERE OF MOTTLED FORCE looms in the baleful crimson wash that lights the cavern.

Its white-hot tendrils lash out at his chest. Carl leaps aside. His enemy attacks again—B

U

T NOW the child-thing's amber glare shifts up the spectrum to rainbow rage. The swift bitter serpent lashes out with fan

an

antastiqu

ntastiq

tasti

ast

s

sss

sssss

SSSSSSS

gs that slash and stab repeatedly into the tormented monster's heart. A long lamenting cry of agony and grief as Carl's

eyes

snAP

OPEN.

Angelica shrinks from him, rolls to the far side of the bed. A long silence. Both gasp for breath.

"Well," she murmured, "that worked."

"What?"

Matter-of-factly: "That worked. Didn't you . . .?"

"Oh. Yes." He waited for her to speak, but she remained mute. "Angelica, didn't something happen to both of us just now?"

"I don't want to discuss it."

"*I* need to."

"You scryed and took me with you. All right?"

"But where did we go? What *was* that awful place?"

Her voice jittered up an octave. "How should *I* know?" She flung herself out of bed, went to the other room, returned with the champagne, drank straight from the bottle until it was empty. Her hand shook as she set it down. "I'm leaving now, Carl."

"After what you drank? Don't you dare try to drive!"

"I'll take a cab, then. I just need to get away from you!"

Stung by her sudden change in attitude, Carl turned sarcastic. "Away from *me?* Even though we're linked?"

Angelica shuddered. "Especially because."

Alone, staring into the night, Carl wondered why the same ominous word kept running through his mind.

Dead . . . Dead . . . Dead . . .

MORENDO

Early Saturday afternoon.

Carl, his jaw still aching, drove northwest along Route 309. A familiar fear looped over and over in his mind:

—tor, heredity factor, the hereditary fact—

The road graded steeply upward. Carl shifted Angelica's Volkswagen into second and voiced his concern. "I was having lunch with Ed Warren, a playwright I know, and Pam Mills, the comic. We found out that each of us has a parent in a rest home, so Pam says, 'My mother's got this mental condition, they tell me it's probably hereditary, but I can't remember what it's called.' Well, Ed and I began to laugh, but Pam glared at us and said she wasn't joking, she really was scared. Then all of a sudden, there's this funny-spooked expression on each of our faces. Spontaneous loss! Not one of us could think of the word 'Alzheimer's' . . ."

Carl automatically "held" for the chuckle he might have gotten had Angelica been there with him in the car. But he was alone.

Partly as vocal exercise, partly to keep himself company, he often soliloquized. The ego-critic in his head argued it was because he, like most other actors, disc jockeys, newscasters, singers, was in love with the sound of his own voice.

Occupational necessity. Beckett notwithstanding, if language is inadequate, it's because you don't work with it enough.

—And when you do, Carl, it becomes a weapon.

The thought made Carl wince. If Diana hadn't gone to New York to host *Saturday Night Live,* she probably would have insisted on accompanying him on this long-overdue *guilt* trip to see his father, *except I would have tried to talk her out of it.*

That was the truth of it. *And the irony . . .*

That morning, as Carl was on his way to breakfast in the hotel's coffee shop, the desk clerk handed him a sealed envelope that contained a note from Angelica. It said that she'd kept her promise and taken a cab, so her car was still in the Sheraton parking lot. Would he drive it back to the theatre for her?

Carl telephoned her motel room. "Morning. Mind if I borrow your wheels for a few hours?"

"You didn't have to ask," Angelica murmured sleepily. "Going to visit your father?"

"Yes." He wasn't surprised she knew what was in his mind. "Care to come along?"

"*Très* indiscreet."

"I could pick you up in back of the theatre. Nobody'll be hanging around there today."

"Carl, you've got to work this thing through with your father. I'd only be a distraction."

"Maybe you're right. See you later, then." He hung up the phone and stared out the lobby window at the overcast sky. The threatening weather suited his mood.

. . . the irony. *And the truth.* Carl steered round a slow-moving produce truck. Once, when Di asked about his father, he told a bare minimum of facts and quickly changed the subject. In spite of common sense, in spite of Carl's deep love for his father, he still could not forgive him for the way he treated—*killed*—his mother: feelings he could not share with his wife.

*Then why did I invite—*want—*Angelica to come with me?*

("Because we're linked, Carl.")

He was half-sorry, half-relieved that she'd said no. Angelica was right, of course: it was a pilgrimage that had to be made alone. Still, she'd been a bit too glib. Was her refusal rooted in sensitivity, or did it really mean she wanted to distance herself from him?

It bothered him that it bothered him.

Carl braked for a red light. An abrupt tangent of memory: that frustrating long-ago summer when he *(Cary Richard Markowitz)* couldn't afford to go to Virginia to apprentice at the Barter Theatre with Marge Tallant.

"She was a young actress George and I met at auditions in Philadelphia," Carl told his imaginary travel companion. "Marge was the first attractive woman who ever paid attention to me. During the bus ride back to Scranton, I couldn't shut up about her. I should've known better than to get my hopes up, though. My mother doused any plans I had of apprenticing. I spent the summer working a cash register at a local supermarket. At least George stayed home, too. I hate to admit that pleased me, but if I couldn't go, I didn't want him lording it over me theatrically, plus I imagined him and Marge getting together. Not that George was especially interested in her, but our friendship was so competitive, I figured he'd go after her out of pure spite.

"Anyway, that winter," Carl continued, "I discovered that when Marge returned in the fall, she invited me and George to visit her in Philly . . . only he never showed me the letter. I was furious with him, but I never let on I knew. To this day, I'll bet he doesn't realize I found out. I was afraid if I ever opened my mouth, our friendship would be kaput and I couldn't afford that." His bruised lip twinged. "Now I'm not so sure."

He stared morosely through the windshield at the greying horizon. *Even now, the memory still hurts.*

The traffic signal blinked green. Carl shifted into drive gear and glanced at a road sign that named the village he was passing through.

DALLAS: POPULATION—2,679

Carl estimated another four or five miles to the home, but just beyond the town's far edge, the highway curved in a wide easterly arc and some fifty yards further on he recognized the gloomy iron gates he drove through one melancholy November afternoon when he and Rebecca Ruth first brought their father to Fairview. (Their brother, refusing to accompany them, told them, "Do what you want with the old bastard.")

Distant thunder.

The far-off mutter made the old man shift restlessly in the worn leather armchair where he drowsed. The TV next to his hospital bed glowed soundlessly. His crank-adjustable meal table stood beside a nightstand where a brass owl perched, its elongated beak a radio speaker, its eyes, dial-knobs that stared benignantly across the dingy room at a mahogany bureau whose broad top held a flotsam of objects: plastic puzzles, a deck of playing cards, loose rubber bands, a pencil stub on top of a blank notepad, an electric razor much in need of cleaning, a magnifying glass, a red-and-blue model racing car, a paper pair of red-and-green 3D glasses, age-yellowed souvenir postcards from dead relatives, several recent tabloid newspapers and two brittle, out-of-date, unread issues of the large-print edition of *Reader's Digest*. A pile of wrinkled clothing lay strewn on the same cracked leather sofa that his mother used to sit on in the "combination room" of the home where he used to live in Scranton.

There were two doors in the room. One opened onto the bathroom, the other led to the corridor. The hall door opened.

"Dad?"

Mr. Markowitz opened his eyes and smiled uncertainly.

"Dad . . . it's Cary."

The tremulous smile turned to tears.

At the floor nurse's suggestion, Carl signed his father out—*like a library book*—and drove him to a shopping mall for brunch. Mr. Markowitz chose a Chinese restaurant that sincerely tried to find a pair of chopsticks for his son, but failed.

Carl's father said, "I never used to eat Chinese. Your mother told me I'd like it, but I wouldn't listen to her."

That's for sure.

"Your Uncle Max finally kidded me into trying it." His face fell. "I miss Max."

"Dad, here's the soup." Carl unfolded and tucked a napkin under his father's chin like a bib. The old man spooned some wonton soup into his mouth and made a face.

"It doesn't taste right."

Carl silently agreed. *Package-frozen from the supermarket.* "There's nothing wrong with it, Dad."

"If you say so." The old man ate silently for a time, then glanced up. "Cary, did you hear? Ernest Hemingway shot himself."

"I heard." No point mentioning the suicide happened in 1961.

"Do you know why he did it?"

Carl chewed a rubbery wonton. "Who knows? Maybe he was sick. Maybe writing got too hard for him."

"No, that's not it."

"What's your theory, Dad?"

"Things never stay the same."

"You mean, people die?"

The old man shook his head. "I mean food tastes different. Flowers don't smell right. Even music—I don't know how to describe it." The waitress collected the soup bowls. Mr. Markowitz smiled at her and said, "That was very good, Miss."

The spring roll was flaccid, the pepper steak salty, the rice gummy, the sweet-and-pungent chicken rubbery-bland, but Carl's father cleaned his plate, said he was full, let the waitress clear away, then stared down at the stained linen tablecloth, perplexed. After a moment, he looked up, scowling.

"Dad, is something wrong?"

"She certainly takes her own good time, doesn't she?"

"Who? I don't understand."

"That waitress. When's she going to bring our food?"

Carl blinked in astonishment. He remembered what his father's attending physician once told him: "An Alzheimer's patient's day is a series of unrelated moments, a necklace without string to arrange the beads on. It's like walking into a movie partway through and never finding out how the film started or what comes next." *But how can he forget he just ate?*

What does it matter? He did.

Carl felt like crying, blocked the impulse by forcing himself to observe his parent objectively: *Starting from the floor, feet too swollen for shoes, that's why he's wearing shabby grey slippers.* (Buy him a new pair!) *Potbelly, but nothing like the one he had when I was a kid. Puckery skin on fists that used to crack walnuts. Fringe of white hair, otherwise bald. Forehead still relatively unlined, left lid droops over his eye, how come I never noticed that before?*

Carl patted his father's hand and said, "I'll tell her to hurry with our food."

Back at the rest home, Carl fetched a battered cardboard box of checkers from a table beneath the television, which, still turned on, ribboned storm warnings across the bottom of its silent screen.

When Carl was a child, his father was virtually unbeatable at checkers. Now, however, after a confident opening, the old man's memory faltered and he had to ask whose turn it was. He took a few therapeutic jumps, then, staring intently at the board, advanced one of his son's pieces. Carl, who suddenly felt very old, said nothing.

The game became virtually Carrollingian. With conscience mildly twitting him *(I had to beat him fair and square when I was a kid),* Carl deliberately overlooked opportunities and sacrificed men with bland surprise. But Mr. Markowitz missed chances, moved out of turn and twice again switched colors, flipflopping his opponent's sacrifices into liabilities. Losing ultimately proved so difficult that when he finally brought it off, Carl felt like a tactical wizard.

Now at least, Dad still retains his title: Undisputed Checker-Champ.

"Best out of three?" Mr. Markowitz asked. "Maybe you'll win next time."

"It's getting late, Dad."

His father looked crestfallen. "You're not going to leave me so soon, are you, Cary?"

"You don't want me to have to drive in the rain, do you, Dad?"

"No," his father reluctantly admitted. "It looks like it's going to be a pip of a storm, too. You watch out for those bastards in the other cars."

"I will, Dad, I promise."

Leaning on a cork-tipped cane, Mr. Markowitz hobbled with him toward the corridor door. As they walked past the memory-cluttered bureau, he tugged at his son's arm. "Look, Cary, here's everything that's left of all my junk. Not like the good old days, huh?"

Carl smiled wistfully. "I loved rooting through your stuff in the shop."

His father tapped the racing car on the bureau top. "I bought you that when you were a little boy, remember?"

"Sure, Dad."

"I got a kick out of it, too, it used to run so good . . ." Without any warning, the old man lowered his head and began to cry.

"Dad, what's the matter?"

His chin trembled. "I miss your mother."

Carl put an arm around him. He wanted to say something comforting, but couldn't find the words.

So sometimes language is *inadequate, Cary-Warry?*

Carl took a startled glance backward. He'd dreamed he was in this room so often that suddenly he wondered if he were actually there or still asleep. The green walls, the hospital bed, the silent TV, the cracked leather couch where Gramma Hannah died all seemed solid enough . . .

His father was speaking to him. "Know what your brother said to me? That if I'd only stopped smoking when she asked me to, your mother might still be alive." He clutched his son's hand. "You don't think he was right, do you, Cary?"

With muted irony, Carl replied, "Since when was Irving ever right about anything, Dad?"

The old man snorted contemptuously. "He always *was* goofy."

Out in the corridor, they waited for the elevator to arrive.

"You'll come and see me again tomorrow, won't you, Cary?"

Carl had an interminable rehearsal scheduled the following day, but "tomorrow" had no practical meaning for his father. He said, "I'll be here, Dad," and felt infinitely wretched for lying.

The afternoon sun was almost gone. The coming squall bramble-dusted the road. As Carl drove to Powder Rocks in the failing light, a storm of emotion threatened to overwhelm him. He distanced himself from his feelings by rehearsing *Woyzeck* aloud.

"Captain, dear God won't single out a poor worm just because no one said Amen before it was made. 'Thus spake the Lord: Suffer the little children to come unto me.' "

Stark bone-fingers suddenly raked the sky. Carl shivered at the child-hood image still lodged in his mind by Rebecca Ruth: "Know what lightning is, Cary? A skeleton ripping open the clouds. If that's just its claws, can you imagine what the rest of it looks like?"

Yes, Sister Dearest, I certainly can.

Yet underneath the justified resentment, not gratitude exactly, but a begrudging acknowledgment that her well-remembered torments forced him to adopt protective tactics: transforming what frightened him into an alliance with fear that not only forged his identity but led, ultimately, to a profitable career.

But I'm still afraid . . . why?

The lightning beckoned him onward.

He expected the theatre lot to be deserted, but several cars were parked there, and the office lights were on. Carl pulled into a parking space just as the clouds burst. He sat behind the wheel and waited for the downpour to slacken before crouch-scurrying to the front door.

Gynger Morrison, standing in the vestibule, spotted Carl. She caught his arm and spun him round. "Don't go in there," she warned, elbow-guiding him toward the building's rear entry. "Press."

"Press? Today? How come?"

"We're getting soaked. Come on." She hustled him to the loading platform, through the stage door and to his dressing-room. "Wait here, I'll pry Jan loose."

"Do you mind telling me what's going on?"

"Jan will." Gently, deliberately, Gynger shut the door.

Jan arrived a moment later, her youthful face creased with unfamiliar lines. "Chief," she began, "I think you'd better sit down."

The vague, ominous thing he'd tried to ignore all day.

"Angelica was supposed to have lunch with him," Jan said. "When he didn't show up, she went to his room and found him sprawled across the bed. The doctor said he's never seen such a massive coronary. He was clutching a phone book. Maybe he wanted to call for help, but he didn't have time to."

Carl knew just what she was trying to tell him, but refused to allow it to compute. "Jan, who are you talking about?"

"Do I really have to say?"

His eyes closed. She tried to take his hand, but he drew back from her touch. "He was going to call for help?"

"Possibly. But the doctor is convinced he couldn't have suffered much."

"It happened that fast?"

"Like lightning."

Details first, grief later. Item One: dealing with the press. Carl followed Jan to the business office, where Pat Clayborne, their PR liaison, waited with reporters and photographers wolfing down coffee, pastry and sandwiches Pat bought for them.

—Yes, of course I'm upset. George O'Brien was my oldest friend.

—No, opening night won't be delayed. George's understudy, Dean Russo, will take over the role of the Drum-Major.

—Yes, if you want a quote from Diana Lee Taylor, you can have one, but not tonight, she's in New York doing live television. She doesn't need this kind of shock just before she goes on.

—No, I had no idea that George had a serious heart condition.

—Yes, I would have risked hiring him anyway. He was a superb actor.

Eventually, after Pat Clayborne lured away "the working press" by offering to stand them a round of drinks across the road, Jan sat down with Carl and briefed him on the welter of legal hassles, labor union red tape and funeral logistics that she and Gynger had to cope with all day.

"We've got those things pretty much under control, but you've got to phone George's sister."

"You haven't told Lena yet!?"

"Relax, she knows." Jan handed him a scrap of paper with a Scranton phone number scribbled on it. "She asked that you call her."

"Why?"

"She's his executor. She'd like you to personally handle George's effects."

The manager of the motel unlocked the door and let Carl enter first.

"Everything is the way it was, Mr. Richards, except that they let me get rid of the phone book. It was all crumpled and torn when they pried it out of his hands." The manager fidgeted. "Will this take very long? I can't leave the front desk untended."

"You don't have to stick around," said Carl, "I'll make an inventory of his things and see you get a copy before shipping anything to his sister."

"Thank you." He left Carl alone.

According to Camus, he thought, *two options: Pray for the mindlessness of a stone, or drown. . . .*

Carl noisily began to pull out bureau drawers. He inspected their contents and jotted down what he found on a sheet of motel stationery. He kept it up as long as he could, but grief finally got the upper hand and he sank onto the bed.

This isn't how the movie was supposed to turn out. . . . where's the big finale where we both win Tonys on the same night, Georgie?

He wept until tears grew inadequate. Then, wiping his eyes, Carl rose and continued taking inventory. He finished up the bureaus, sorted through a large valise sitting on the luggage rack, then, turning to the closet, opened it and began sliding garments to one side to count them.

Something he saw made him stop.

Inside, leaning up against the rear wall, was the same expensive umbrella he'd bought at Uncle Sam's on 57th Street, the one he hadn't seen since the night of Diana's party, the one he'd left in back of Angelica's car.

Mosaic tiles of memory began to click into place.

Entering the club, Carl saw Dean Russo, George's understudy, at the bar with Bill Evans. The two actors were talking to one another in low tones. As Carl walked by them, Evans squeezed his arm sympathetically.

Angelica was sitting by herself in a corner booth staring moodily into a glass of red wine. The planes and angles of her face and throat were taut; she might have been carved from marble.

Carl dropped her car keys on the table next to a half-empty bottle of bordeaux. He stood there, reluctant to stay, unwilling to go.

"People are watching," she said, not looking up.

True. He returned to the bar and addressed the understudy. "First thing tomorrow, Dean, we're walking you through the Drum-Major. Are you up on your lines?"

"Yes, but I don't know the fight yet."

"Okay, go see Gynger, she's in the office, have her show you the prompt script." He turned to Bill Evans. "Go with him, you can help him work through it. I'll see you both get double overtime." *Di can afford it.*

He watched the grateful actors leave the club, then walked back to Angelica's booth. He sat down opposite her.

"You're angry." She did not look at him.

"Angry? No, just a rage of curiosity. Did you play Daisy or Rowena? You're such a consummate actress, I can picture you doing either one." *Virgin or whore.*

Angelica refilled her glass. "I have no idea what you're talking about."

"I'm talking about how you and George manipulated me."

For the first time, she looked up. "I told you once before, I am *not* a manipulator."

"Translation, you never got caught before." Ignoring her stare and tightening lips, he said, "That night we went to your apartment in Seacliffe, I saw something that bothered me. I forgot what it was till now. I was looking at a shelf of playscripts of shows you've acted in and noticed a copy of *Biloxi Blues*."

"So?"

"So that's the same show George got into so much trouble with in Florida."

"So?"

"So you were in it, too. Probably playing Rowena, the prostitute." Angelica said nothing.

"Another thing about that time in your apartment. We were interrupted by a middle-of-the-night phone call. George, right?"

Angelica said nothing.

"The way he barged in on your audition—strategy pure and simple."

"That's ridiculous."

"Ridiculous? He wasn't scheduled to read for me till just before lunch. Jan told me you sat around all morning in the waiting room letting other actresses go before you."

"Why would I want to mess up my own audition?"

"Correction. The director's oldest friend spoiled it. Instant sympathy and a probable callback."

She drained her glass and got to her feet. "Look, Carl, we both know what a rich fantasy life you've got. From now on, keep it to yourself." She took a step, wobbled, nearly tripped. He tried to steady her, but she flung him off.

"Don't push me away!" Carl snapped. "You're not crossing the highway at night, not in your present condition!"

"If you feel you have to play watchdog, fine. Just don't touch me."

"You've got it."

He followed her out. She walked ahead of him, not once looking back to see if he was still there, until

with sudden ferocity, Angelica pulls Carl inside her room and shuts the door.

Limbs snarled in garments frantically torn away. *Strawberry pinch and the rank aftermath of wine*. Teeth nipping at secret rims and curves. A sharp epiphany of ecstasy

beside him with the light switched off, he saw in the spill of neon creeping through the jalousie blinds the glint of pupils staring masklike at the ceiling.

Carl tried to, could not understand his overpowering need—*addiction*—for Angelica. He harbored no illusions; nothing that just passed between them had anything to do with love. And yet (this moment, at least), he felt connected to her in a way he'd never experienced with Diana or any other woman in his life. The irrationality of it disturbed him, but it was true.

Now, studying Angelica in silhouette, he was filled with wordless pity for this perverse, twisted enigma of a woman. He gently stroked her cheek and chin with the back of his hand.

She pushed him away. "I don't like that."

"After what we did?"

"I don't mind being used. Just don't be affectionate."

"I don't understand."

"*I* do!" An exasperated tongue-cluck. "Sorry, you don't deserve that." A long pause, he thought she wasn't going to say anything else, but then she spoke again. "Maybe I met you too late, Carl. Maybe too soon, I don't know. The timing is all wrong."

"Bad timing? The story of my life, but what's that got to do with a little basic tenderness?"

"You remind me of my first husband. I told you, his name was also Carl."

"That's what this is all about?"

"I don't like to talk about my past."

"So I've noticed. Though I've not exactly been reticent about my-self."

"That was your choice."

"Yes. My choice to satisfy *your* curiosity."

She sighed or shuddered, he wasn't sure which. "All right, you want to know about me? Picture a serious little girl with big eyes, skinny arms and legs. I used to play stickball in the backyard or chase fireflies with the other kids. Then I turned thirteen and my body started changing. More and more, I'd go off by myself and write things on a big yellow legal pad. What I thought, how I felt, first stabs at poetry. Things I couldn't talk about in the house."

"How come?"

"Because one day my mother came into my room and saw what I was doing. She snatched the pad out of my hands, read some of the personal things I'd written and tore up the paper, saying, 'Nice Catholic girls don't do this sort of thing!' "

A moue of disapproval, but Carl said nothing.

Angelica's voice hardened. "After that, I made damn sure she never saw anything I wrote. I'd go to a park bench and scribble. That's where I met Carl. He'd sit across from me and pretend to be doing homework, but if I looked up fast enough, I'd catch him watching me. He was two years ahead in school, so I was totally flattered. Finally, we met. I let him see some of my writing.''

''Which he liked?''

''He loved everything about me. If I could've gone to a store and ordered the perfect man, they would've sent him.'' A long silence. ''Then he died.''

Carl was surprised. ''I thought you married.''

''When I was seventeen, we ran away together. Then he died. End of story.''

''Well, it's more than I thought you'd ever share.''

''You make me want to.'' She absently stroked his leg.

The gesture amused Carl. *She can be tender, too, as long as she's in control.* ''Angelica, if I ask about your second husband, will you bite my head off again?''

''Harlan is easier to talk about. You saw the scars on my back?'' A mirthless laugh. ''How could you miss them, right? He put them there.''

''That bastard!''

''Figuratively and literally.'' She fumbled on the nightstand for her purse.

''You're going to smoke, aren't you?''

''I have to.'' Finding and lighting a cigarette, she sat up in bed. ''It's easier to talk about him. The only pain he caused me was bodily.''

''He beat you?''

''That, too. Calling me a bitch was Harlan's way of saying hello. He hated everything about me, the way I think, the way I speak, my cooking, my clothes, my acting, everything! He hit me. Burned me. Night after night, he raped me and he—'' She stopped. ''I can't.''

''Then don't.''

Exhaling a lungful of smoke, Angelica got out of bed and peeked through the blinds. ''It's blowing up again.''

''Intermittent storms, they said.''

She dropped the slat into place and ground out her cigarette. ''Thanks for not pressing me. I realize you've got this impulse to find out what makes me tick.''

''More than an impulse, Angelica.''

''I know. Our basic incompatibility.''

''Incompatibility? We who are linked?''

''I hear your sarcasm. But look at us right now, this minute. I tell you about myself and you're calmer—''

"And you're more and more agitated."

"If that's not incompatible, what do *you* call it?"

He shrugged. "Adjustment, maybe."

"Maybe."

A thoughtful pause, then Carl said, "Tell me about the half."

"The what?"

"You told me once you were married two and a half times."

Angelica nodded. "An arrangement of convenience . . . at first."

"You're talking about George now, aren't you?"

"Yes. I tried to help him feel the way he wanted to feel. No, that's wrong. The way George thought he was supposed to feel."

"What in God's name was in it for you?"

"Safety. Control. I set the terms, he accepted. Only it didn't work out. He began to want more."

"More? Sex?"

A short laugh. "Sex was irrelevant. He started to become proprietary. He wanted me to really marry him."

"That's why he punched out your A.D. in Florida?"

Angelica stiffened. "You've known all along, haven't you?"

"Nada. Zip. We were told George put someone in the hospital. Draw me the rest of the picture."

"He was your friend. You fill in the blanks."

Carl's eyes were sufficiently adjusted to the dark to make out her profile: the pencil-arced eyebrows, the fine-chiseled nose, high cheekbones, downturned mouth. Beneath her studied independency, the haunted undertones: anxiety and sorrow and—*what else?*

"When did George start drinking so heavily?"

"Around the same time that I stopped."

Stopped? Try "slowed down" . . .

Angelica said, "It was a little before we did *Biloxi Blues*. They cast me first, and yes, as Rowena. Frankly, I hate Fort Lauderdale, but I was looking for a way out. Only George auditioned for them, too, and landed Sergeant Toomey, so we trouped our problems to Florida."

"Did you know he had a heart condition? I didn't."

"Neither did I." Each word stressed with subtle vehemence.

Thoughts that neither cared to share. Angelica lay back down beside him. Carl sensed the muscles of her body rippling with tension. "Are you going to fire me?" she asked abruptly.

"Should I?"

"No. You need me."

"Personally or professionally?"

"I can't answer that, Carl."

"Then how about the one question we've both been avoiding?"

She shuddered. "Don't make me say what you already know."

"That's why I found you drinking at the club?"

"Why do you *insist* on spelling everything out?" She crumpled into a foetal lump of misery. "Damn you, Carl! I *swore* no man would ever make me cry again."

"You don't think I blame you for what happened? *If* it happened?"

"You blame me, all right. You think me capable of anything."

"Only to the extent you want things you can't have, so you find ways to get them."

The actress stared at him a long appraising moment. "That's true of both of us."

"Admitted." He ran his fingers lightly along her cheek, down her throat, over the rise of her breast. "There's something I want tonight," he said. "Maybe it's too kinky for you."

"Don't be too sure. What is it?"

"To fall asleep with you in my arms."

Angelica nudged him away. "I have a real problem with that."

"So I've noticed. One part of you does."

She clasped his arm with nails that cut. "You're not my shrink, Carl. Make love to me all you want, but don't ever try to interpret me."

"Since when did we ever make *love?*"

"Do you want me to call it something cruder?"

"No."

"You came before, didn't you? Isn't that enough?"

"If *I* said that, I'd be a male chauvinist pig."

"What are we having, a debate? I only mentioned it because—"

"I know why. But there's more involved here than indoor plumbing."

Her eyes closed in momentary exasperation. "Why do you have to make sex so complicated?"

He groped for some approximation of what he didn't fully understand himself. "Try to follow my logic. There was this time I found a box of pornographic photos in my brother's closet. One of them showed this woman performing oral sex on a man. I didn't know what they were really doing. I was so naive, I thought he was—I thought he was awfully angry at her."

"Maybe he was," she murmured.

"Don't you see what I'm trying to say?"

"Not really."

"Tenderness upsets you. The lack of it frightens me. That's our real incompatibility, Angelica."

A sardonic laugh. "Oh, Carl, 'The horror, the horror, the horror.' " Glancing over her left shoulder at the luminous dial of the clock, she regarded him through slitted lids . . .

Carl stiffened. "What are you doing?"

"Don't you like it?"

"Yes."

An ironic smile. "If it upsets you, I'll stop."

"Hush." Exhausted by the day's jagged anguish, warmed by her intimate touch, Carl succumbs to sensation.

Deep regular breathing. Lightning flickers.

She must have brought an animal into the room, a cat or dog or monkey, *not sure what. Too dark to see.*

And anyway, I'm dreaming.

The click and whirl of dice. A snake? spine rattling like a Jacob's ladder*sss*

Carl opens his eyes, sees the threatening smudge drifting down from the ceiling. He leaps out of bed, runs to the door, opens it, dashes through.

Darkness and the whirl of dice. Carl opens his eyes and sees the threatening smudge drifting down from the ceiling. He leaps out of bed, opens the door, dashes through.

The whirl of dice. Threatening smudge, out of bed, leaps the leaps the ceil

Click and whirl *snake?* No, warmblooded: small wet mouth closing over left thumb, sucking like a child. Thick pouting lips, sharp teeth *standing naked before the gates, obsidian and ivory, Angelica clasping the double-bladed knife, lips parting lips how red red red how red it is*

it is

"Like a bloody kni

s

sssss

SSSSSS

SSSSSSS

A deafening clap of thunder. Carl's eyes snap open. The dream-beast gnaws his thumb a fraction of a second too long.

Discovering himself alone in bed, he shivers. The absence of body warmth reminds him of death. He sees Angelica at the window.

I hate it when you don't believe me Carl

What are you talking about

you going through my things

sister said

You think I killed George

No

when we were both in Hell

I know what's wrong, Carl thinks. *She had a dream and doesn't know it isn't real.*

He woke and found himself alone in bed. He shivered. He saw a ribbon of light beneath the bathroom door, heard the sibilance of running water.

Angel's washing up.

Angel? He never called her that. *Someone does. Who?*

It took his sleep-clogged memory several seconds to recall that Angel was his wife's nickname—

Di!

Carl suddenly sat bolt upright. *Omigod!* Flailing the sheets out of the way, he kicked his legs over the side of the bed, stood up, fumbled at the nightstand, almost knocked over the lamp. He switched it on. The glare blinded him. He squinted at his wristwatch.

Angelica, emerging from the bathroom, heard him groan.

"What's the matter, Carl?"

"It's four in the morning!"

"So?"

"So I forgot to watch Di host *Saturday Night Live.*"

"Is that all?"

" 'All'? Do you know how she'll react when she finds out?"

The redhead yawned without covering her mouth. "No idea."

"She'll be so far beyond furious, Webster will have to coin a new word for it."

"Tell her you forgot. It's not as if you didn't have your hands full."

"How very true."

She regarded him frostily. "Schoolboy regrets?"

"I'm worried."

Her eyes narrowed. "About your wife."

The storm raised its voice. Suddenly, out in the corridor of the motel, they heard footsteps. Someone rapped at Angelica's door.

"Who the hell can that be so early in the morning?" Carl wondered sourly.

"Looks like we're about to find out." She hurried to the closet to put on a robe.

"Wait, don't just open up! Ask who it is!"

She went to the door. "Who's there?"

A muffled voice on the other side. "Stuart Pierce."

Carl gaped. "Pierce? What in hell is he doing here?"

A second, shriller voice: *"Carl!"*

A shock wave of recognition. Whirling, he glared at his lover. "You incredible bitch!"

Angelica shook her head with vehement denial. "You can't seriously think I set this up!"

Carl's hands balled into fists. "Bravissimo, Ms. Winters! Cut and print."

MARCH TO THE
SCAFFOLD

'The artist imagines he has killed his beloved. He is present at
his own execution—the crowd rejoices—a last thought of love,
cut short by the fatal blow.'

ALLA BREVE

chk

Q: State your full name and address.

A: Juliet Alais Napier. Everyone knows me by my initials, Jan. Ninety-four Smith Street, Brooklyn. Need my zip code?

Q: No. Relationship to the victim?

A: We're both involved in Carl Richards' production of *Woyzeck*. I'm his assistant director slash stage manager. Tch. Poor choice of phrase.

Q: Bringing up the question, why was that prop knife so sharp?

A: It wasn't supposed to be. Gynger showed Carl several possible choices, but he wasn't satisfied with any of them. Yesterday he bought one himself. Gynger tried to dull the edge—obviously not enough.

Q: Did you see it happen?

A: The actual stabbing? No.

Q: Incredible. A packed auditorium, yet nobody sees a damn thing.

A: There's a reason. Carl faces three-quarters upstage so the audience can't actually see him stabbing Marie. The only angle you might catch it from is off right. Did you ask Gynger?

Q: I'm asking what you saw.

A: From where I was standing, Carl's back.

Q: And that's all?

A: I knew something was wrong.

Q: Why?

A: They were struggling. That's not how Carl staged it.

Q: Were they having an affair?

A: Ahh . . . I'd say so.

Q: Why?

A: Things I saw. Almost saw. Backstage, the two of them together, thinking they were alone. The night George punched him out, I drove Carl from the hospital back to his hotel. Angelica was waiting for him in the bar. Lady Di was in New York.

Q: Lady Di, meaning Mrs. Richards.

A: Diana Lee Taylor. Anyway, next morning, Angelica's car still wasn't back.

Q: That was when, last Saturday?

A: Mmm-hmm. The night George died.

Q: Boy, you folks've had your share of grief.

A: George. Lady Di. Now this.

Q: Did Mrs. Richards know what was going on?

A: At first, no. But after she got back from New York, well . . .

Q: Details?

11:30 A.M. Sunday morning. The cast had just completed its first runthrough of *Woyzeck* with Diana Lee Taylor back in the role of Marie.

"We'll run the Strindberg piece now," Carl announced. "The rest of you can go to lunch."

With the prompt script on her lap, Jan sat with Gynger in the rear of the auditorium discussing various production details. They kept their voices low, so they wouldn't disturb the actors.

Onstage, Diana sat down at a small table. Angelica entered and spoke the first lines of *The Stronger*.

Well, well, well, if it isn't little Millie! What a surprise, old friend! To find you, of all people, sitting here alone, drinking all by yourself the night before Christmas. How sad! You remind me of a bride I saw once at a hotel. She was off in a corner reading a comic book while the groom was shooting pool with the best man. I thought, well, there's a doomed marriage if ever I saw one.

"Something's wrong," Gynger whispered. "Did you see the look Di just gave her?"

Jan nodded. "The Ice Princess sure looks her age today."

From the prop basket she was carrying, Angelica removed a doll and a toy pistol and showed them to Diana.

Millie, just look at the presents I bought my babies. Here's a doll for little Lisa. It opens and shuts its eyes. The gun's for Michael, naturally.

The actress pretended to load the weapon, aimed it, and pulled the trigger. Instead of flinching, as the script specified, Diana watched with narrowed eyes and rigid spine.

"Something is definitely not kosher," Gynger observed.

"Shh."

Were you afraid? You didn't actually think I was going to shoot you, did you? Come on! You can't believe I'd do that! It's far more likely you'd want to put a bullet through *my* skull, don't you agree? I got in your way, and you've never forgotten it, have you? Not that it was my fault. You think I maneuvered to get you kicked out of the ensemble. That's not true, but if it makes you feel better, Millie, go ahead and believe it. I'm blessed with a little girl and boy and a husband who adores me. All you've got is your acting.

Diana stood up abruptly. She brushed past Angelica and strode downstage. "I need to talk to you, Carl. Alone."

He rose from his seat in the front row. "Di . . ."

"Now."

"All right. Front office." Turning, Carl crooked his finger at Jan. She indicated Gynger quizzically, but he shook his head. Jan handed the prompt script to her friend and followed the director up the aisle. Diana went up the other aisle.

Onstage, Angelica stood as motionless as a gravestone.

Q: So then what happened?

A: So the three of us went outside—

Q: Outside?

A: We could hardly hear ourselves think in the office, all the phone lines were jammed. Aftermath of Lady Di's *Saturday Night Live* appearance. We went out back and she delivered her ultimatum—Carl had to get rid of Angelica.

Q: What did Richards say? Did he argue?

A: No. He asked me if Gynger is a quick study.

Q: Meaning?

A: Meaning how fast could she learn the Strindberg monologue? It was crazy. There wasn't time to replace Angelica, but Lady Di wanted her OUT and Carl seemed perfectly willing to go along with her on it. Commonsense deduction . . . she'd found out about the affair. (Laughs)

Q: That makes you laugh?

A: Sorry. It's just that later on, Carl asked me privately to call NBC and get him a videotape of Lady Di guest-hosting *Saturday Night Live*.

Q: That's funny?

A: It's just the notion, she'd probably sooner forgive Carl for adultery than missing her on TV.

Q: So Richards said he'd fire Winters.

A: What choice did he have? Only he didn't have to, because when we got back to the theatre, Angelica had already split. Gynger guessed she went to her room, but she wasn't there and her car was gone, too. I figured maybe she'd quit . . .

He wondered if she'd be waiting for him in the Sheraton bar.

Sunday night; Di was already upstairs. To avoid gossip, she'd coldly agreed to let Carl sleep on the sitting-room sofa. Still, he felt it prudent to linger in the lobby till she'd gone to bed.

Brandy sounded appealing. He entered the bar and there she was, sitting in a booth, her fists clenched round the stem of a half-empty goblet of red wine, face set in stone. Carl ordered a Hennessy, brought it to her table and sat down. "I knew I'd find you here tonight."

"I took a room."

"In *this* hotel?"

"Calm down. I put it on my own Visa, I wouldn't charge it to the company." Angelica sipped. "She wants you to fire me."

"Of course. Why did you take a room here?"

"Instead of slinking off into the night? No guesses, amigo?"

"I should interpret *you?*" A mirthless laugh. "Get real."

"Carl, I did *not* set you up."

"Amazing how Pierce knew just where to bring her."

"He's been spying on both of us."

"Not that he isn't capable, but I don't believe you."

"Why not?"

"Why should I? You lied to me about George, you—"

"I did *not* lie! It was none of your business."

"All right, then let's stick to business. You're history."

She grasped his arm. "You're actually handing artistic control over to your wife?" The last word pronounced scornfully.

"It's *my* decision," he lied, pushing away her hand. "I don't care what the union says, or how much it costs. I want you gone."

Cold. Abrupt. Finished.

Taking his brandy with him, leaving the bar, ringing for the elevator. Two. Three. Four. Five. No more Angelica. Profound relief. Except . . . tossing restlessly on the sofa, Diana in the other room, her door left ajar, yet in spite of anger and his sense of betrayal, he still feels closer to Angelica, *literally closer* . . . WHY?

Sixth sense . . . Angelica . . . room next door?

Thin spill of light beneath maid's accessway . . . if he opens it, won't she be on the other side, wai

*aaaa*AAAAAAHHHHH!''

"DI!"

—to the theatre, Angelica had already split. Gynger guessed she went to her room, but she wasn't there and her car was gone, too. I figured maybe she'd quit. Nobody saw her again till next morning.

Q: Monday.

A: Yes. Our first tech-dress rehearsal. I didn't know what to do. There we all are, bright and early but no Carl, no Lady Di, so for an hour I'm trying to keep the cast busy, sending them to put on costumes and makeup so we can see how they "read" under the lights. Gynger's on the office phone trying to track down Carl. She finally traces him to the hospital. Bucks County General.

Q: Where he took Mrs. Richards.

A: Right. I kept busy working light cues, setting sound levels, et cetera, but there was no point running anything for the cast, there's hardly a scene without Woyzeck or Marie in it. I finally declared a long lunch or laundry or whatever break, told everyone to stay either in the theatre or the motel or the club so we could round them all up again when Carl got back. He showed up at four, Angelica in tow as Di's replacement. He drafted Gynger for the silent part in *The Stronger*. That night, you can damn well bet we rehearsed overtime.

Q: So he and Winters arrived together.

A: Yes.

Q: Did they seem . . . friendly?

A: Uh-uh. Pure glacier. The rest of the week, that didn't change. Then—

Q: Yes?

A: Nothing.

Q: Looks like you had something else to say.

A: Probably not important.

Q: Anything you can tell me, I'm listening.

A: Last night—

Q: Friday?

A: No, Thursday night. I forgot it's already Saturday morning. What time *is* it now?

Q: Almost three A.M. What about Thursday?

A: Both of them got drunk.

Q: Richards? Winters?

A: Yes. Not together. We had a grueling dress rehearsal. Most of us went to the club. Carl was at our table, Angelica off by herself in a booth. Carl never drinks out of control, but this is one time he did. I offered to drive him back to the Sheraton, but he didn't want to be alone so I put him in my room. I was going to bunk with Gynger. Bill Evans helped me take Carl out, but he pulled away from us for a moment and spoke to Angelica, she said something back, then he was ready to go.

Q: Did you hear what they talked about?

A: Uh-uh. The only thing I heard, afterward, was Carl muttering to himself under his breath, the same thing over and over again.

Q: What?

A: "Two and two is four. Two and two is five. Two and two is six." On and on.

Q: Meaning?

A: Meaning he was drunk.

Q: What about Winters? How drunk was she?

A: Not as far gone as Carl, but bad enough. No way I could let her drive.

Q: Drive? Wasn't she staying at the Luzerne with the rest of the cast?

A: That's what I thought. But when I offered to help her to her room, she handed me her car keys. I found out the day she disappeared on us, she checked out of the Luzerne and into the Sheraton . . . would you believe in the room right next door to Carl's suite?

Q: Convenient.

Alone in darkness, resting across Jan's bed, clothes still on, room spinning, but thoughts steady. *How drunk do I have to be?*

Angelica. Just like before. Bury the truth.

Truth? Foreign concept.

No. Worse. Manipulates truth.

No. Worse. Manipulates herself. Add up the same column of figures, her answers come out different every time. Worst manipulation of all.

Integrate.

So, layer on layer =
    Eve the innocent.
    Lilith the bitch.
Still want her, Mr. Richards?
No, of course not. No!
What was she just saying about . . .
". . . have to talk, Angelica . . ."
". . . not a priority . . ."
Priorities? What did she say?
"Mine is playing Marie. Yours is a wife in the hospital."
So, layer on layer =
    Lilith the innocent.
    Eve the bitch.
Still want her, Cary?
Yes
Beside me in the dark.

Q: So you drove Winters to her hotel.

A: Actually, I ended up spending the night with her in her room.

Q: Oh? I got the impression you weren't particularly fond of her.

A: No, we certainly weren't friends. But Angelica was in no condition
to be by herself. She—well, what happened is she begged me to stay.

Q: Begged? That doesn't fit the picture I've built up of her.

A: It surprised me, too.

Q: Maybe she was afraid of something?

A: Oh, come off it! Like, scared of Carl?

Q: Would you say she was frightened?

A: Not in that sense.

Q: What sense?

A: That she feared bodily harm.

Q: But she *was* frightened?

A: She didn't want to be left alone. She was like a little girl. For
once, I felt sorry for her.

Q: So you decided to stay. Then what?

A: First off, I get her upstairs to her room and she goes straight to
the bathroom. I figure she's going to be sick. I'm not sure if I should
leave or stay with her till she makes it to bed. I figure I'd better wait,
I don't want her passing out and banging her head or something. So
then the water starts running, I mean she's turned on the shower. I hear
her yelp like she's hurt herself, so I call, "Angelica," but she doesn't

answer, so I decide I'd better take a look, just in case. I find her stark naked, one foot up on the rim of the tub. She's shaving her leg, only the razor slipped, blood is running down into the bathwater.

Q: Sure it was an accident?

A: It was just a nick. I dabbed it with peroxide, stuck on a bandage and talked her out of doing the other leg. I found her a nightgown, got her to bed and that's when she grabbed my hand and begged me not to leave. I thought I'd just sit with her till she fell asleep, but she kept on talking and finally I decided I'd better—

Q: What was she talking about?

A: Nothing that made sense.

Q: Such as?

A: "I'm not like her, I'll never be like her!" and I'd ask her who she meant, but she'd shake her head and refuse to answer. Then she started in on saying how George was dead and it was her fault and she was supposed to be Di's friend, but she'd killed her, too. I tried to get through to her, I said it wasn't her fault that George had a heart attack, and Lady Di only had a minor stroke, she's going to pull through just fine, but then she started in on how Carl is dead, too. I tried to convince her that he's perfectly okay, but I couldn't make a dent. Absolutely everything was Angelica's fault. So, all in all, one hell of a night . . . look, Officer, I'm ready to collapse. Can I leave soon?

Q: Just a few more questions. Did Richards or Winters do anything unusual yesterday?

A: Besides the stabbing, you mean? No. Neither talked to the other except for their lines during final dress run, but I didn't have time to monitor them every minute, we were all jam-packed getting ready for the preview, the whole cast and crew.

Q: Okay, so we're back to the stabbing. Did—

A: I already told you, I didn't see it, I couldn't see it, not from the angle I was standing.

Q: Afterward. You rang down the curtain—

A: I had to. The lights came up on the next scene, but Carl hadn't cleared. He was still there, sitting on the floor with her, cradling her head and saying her name over and over again.

Q: So you lowered the curtain, and then what?

A: Ran over to Carl and that's when I saw she was all bloody. I chased Bill Evans outside to see if there was a doctor. I warned the rest of the cast to stay away and then I got Gynger to shuttle the kids someplace else.

Q: And Richards? Were you with him when—

A: I couldn't pull him away. He kept calling her, trying to wake her up. Bill brought a doctor. She checked for vital signs. Said she detected a faint pulse. That's when Carl grabbed Angelica up in his arms, calling her as if she could actually hear him and . . . and next thing we know, Carl's unconscious . . . the doctor . . . she can't . . . couldn't wake him up, he . . . some kind of, he was in some kind of coma, she said . . .

Q: You want a tissue?

A: Y-yes.

chk

too dark to see . . . where's town?

not going there

Two and two is four is five is six. Add her up, different answers every time:

> innocent = bitch
>> soul to kiss your fiery
>>> like a
>>>> bloody
>>>>> knife

> |

Morning came too soon for Carl, this of all days, the worst day of all: press preview day, *but where the hell am I? Whose bed am I in?* The room was similar to Angelica's, it must be the Luzerne Motel. For one panicky moment, Carl worried that something foolish must have happened between him and some irrelevant woman, then he recognized the promptscript and the briefcase on a chair and remembered where he was: *Jan's room, she must have stayed overnight with Gynger.*

Where's Angelica? Hotel. Diana? Hospital. George? Dead.

And tonight . . . ?

11:30 A.M.: Speed runthrough. The late call is a dispensation to allow the overworked cast a little extra sleep. Carl arrives, head aching; judging from Angelica's taut forehead and determinedly uncrinkled temples, she is also hung over.

This time, the double-tempo runthrough surges along brilliantly. Angelica delivers her Strindbergian monologue with the pyrotechnic brilliancy of a Martyn Green singing a Gilbert and Sullivan "patter" song. The rehearsal's emotive content is deliberately low. "Save your energy," Carl urges his cast.

Bits of horseplay creep in, welcome tension-relievers. Angelica displays an unexpected burlesque flair, though never in her scenes with Carl. She hurries briskly through them without giving him eye contact. This does nothing to improve his mood or pressure headache.

1:45 P.M.: A lunchtime mercifully free of production crises. Angelica tags along with Jan and Gynger. Carl goes to the office and calls the hospital. No change in Diana's condition.

3:00 P.M.: Final tech-dress runthrough. Last chance to adjust sound and light levels, troubleshoot unforeseen hassles. Except there aren't any. Though Carl has never subscribed to the "poor dress rehearsal, good performance" cliché, the unlikely absence of petty problems unsettles him. He feels a bit like Captain Queeg, ringed by a tight circle of compliance to keep him from seeing what's really going on aboard the USS *Caine*.

4:45 P.M.: During his end-of-rehearsal remarks, Carl's penchant for the nautical gets the best of him. He calls the show a tight ship and thanks Jan publicly "for holding a steady helm."

He cautions Vincent Swailes, the actor playing the pawnbroker who sells Woyzeck the knife, to take care handling the blade. "It's still sharp. Gynger did her best to blunt the cutting edge, but please be extra careful."

4:54 P.M.: Jan declares dinner break. Carl approaches Angelica, but just then one of the Powder Rocks box office staff calls his name. "Mr. Richards?"

"What?"

"Bucks County General for you on eight-two-six-five."

Hurrying to the office.

Dr. Russell: "Your wife's awake, Mr. Richards. She's asking for you."

Returning to the auditorium. Hails Jan—Angelica within earshot—"Di's awake. I've got to get over there."

"Don't cut it too close."

"You can borrow my car, if you like."—Angelica.

"No, thanks. I already called a cab."

Walking up the aisle, knowing she is watching him—how?

Sad? Angry? Resentful?
All of the above. None of the above.
Two and two is six.
6:19 P.M.: Di holds his hand. A long, troubled moment searching one
another's eyes. The nurse declares, "That's enough for now, mustn't
tire the patient. You can come back tomorrow, Mr. Taylor."
Goodbye.
8 P.M.: Signs in as Jan calls "half-hour." Electric unrest backstage,
a company of professionals coming up to Concert Pitch.
Hurries to his dressing-room, puts on his makeup, dons costume.
Does physical warmup, tension-relaxation. Vocal warmup, alignment
of "air bag," lung capacity, sonority, embouchure: diction, diction,
diction.
Knock on door. "Strindberg up in five minutes, Carl."
"Thanks, Jan."
8:35 P.M.: Standing in wings, watching Angelica's trim attractive
figure from behind as she stands, head down, focusing on her offstage
beat, and what does it matter whether she lied or used him? he wants to
take her *now* with furious passion and tenderness but in the auditorium:
crackling of program pages, murmurs, coughs. Jan cues the opening
music and . . . *quiet* . . .
  . . . *quiet* . . .
The curtain rises. Sharing the caress of Angelica's voice: Strindberg.
The curtain falls. Applause.
A hushed pause. The program claims the interval between plays will
be "one minute only," but actually lasts ninety-five seconds; timed that
long to produce minor restlessness before the musical passage from Berg's
Wozzeck shoves the audience pell-mell into Büchner's tragedy: starting
softly, building swiftly to an ear-shattering climax as the lights switch off
and the curtain rises, discovering Woyzeck lathering the Captain.
Scene two. Marie tries to hide the earrings her latest "client" gave
her.

WOYZECK
What's that sparkling between your fingers?

MARIE [*Shows him*]
Franz, I'm only human.

WOYZECK
I understand. Here—my salary. Take it, bitch.

MARIE

Y—you're always so good to me, Franz.

WOYZECK

I'll see you later. [*He exits.*]

MARIE

I'm so rotten, I ought to stab myself. The world stinks . . . and when we die, we go to Hell.

Offstage, Carl notices Jan's odd glance. *What's wrong with me? Cutting lines, ad libbing.* No time to dwell on it, the scene with the Doctor comes up immediately, then, after that, Woyzeck's first hallucination, followed by the carnival tent sequence, bodies pressed tightly together—

> *Her taut nipples,*
> *Sinuous hips,*
> *Strawberry lips*
> *Haunted eyes.*

"Sooner a knife in my breast than your hands on me!"

Carl in an empty field: "What are you saying down there—*in* there? Stab the bitch? Yes! 'Stab the wolf-bitch dead!' "

MUSIC: "Signs and Alarms."

Angelica sits with a Bible on her lap, leafing through its pages. She stops and reads a passage.

"And the Pharisees brought a woman taken in adultery, but Jesus said, 'I do not condemn thee. Go and sin no more.' " Oh, God, forgive me!

PAWNBROKER

It's good and sharp. Want to cut your throat? You can die cheap, but

too dark to see. Where's town? That way?

WOYZECK

Why? You're not going there. Come, sit down.

MARIE

I have to go, Franz.

WOYZECK

Aren't your feet sore by now? You should rest.

What's wrong with you? You're so different.

Do you know how long it's been?

MARIE

Us? Two years, Pentecost.

But how much longer will it last?

I'm cold.

You can't be cold. I feel your hot breath. Your eyes burn into me like coals. I'd sell my soul to kiss your fiery lips one more time.

What are you talking about?

Nothing.

The moon's rising. Look, it's so red . . .

Like a bloody knife.

The moment of the murder.
Their eyes meet: Carl Angelica
A moment without secrets or answers.
Her hand closes over his.
no
alive again
Noise of the mob. Shouting. Applause.
Holding her in his arms, crying her name over and over.

A n g e l i c a
A n g e l i c a
A n g e l i c a
A n g e l i c a
A n g e l i c a
Angelica
Angelic
Angel
still a pulse . . . ''

Carl suddenly knows how to save her:
choose place imagine route to goal
Clutching Angelica to his chest,
slipping into unconsciousness,
plummeting into the vortex,
scrying downward, seeking
the basalt corridors and
bloody vestibule of
H e l l

*

DREAM OF THE WITCHES' SABBATH

'The artist finds himself at a Black Sabbath in the company of spirits, fiends and witches who have come to help at his funeral. His Beloved appears—howls of infernal delight as she dances the Dies Irae. The orgy only awaited *Her* coming.'

FANTAISIE-IMPROMPTU

Larghetto

—*mouth*—

Gravity. Compressing. Quadrants. Angles. Smothering. Matted folds. Sensing, not seeing . . .

Angelica?

Howling. Plucking claws. Apparitions that rip and tear . . .

spinning away . . .

Slants. Shafts. Bars. Angles. Honeycomb. Golden spiderwebs . . .

sscrrrp-sscrrrp

cavern . . . steep down-slope . . . spattered blood . . .

Angelica?

"Angelica?"

Angelica!

"*Tch-tch.*"

The last time here, the firesphere and the dull amber glow of Angelica's aura, but now, sitting on a rock, resting against an upthrust shoulder of stone—

"Gramma Hannah?"

"*Nu*, it's that long ago, you have to ask? Kindele, geben Sie mir . . . what's it, 'Umarmung'?"

"A hug." Smothering in the comfort of her ample bosom . . . so different . . . *why?*

Sense of touch!

"Gramma, you're really here!"

"Schlimozzle! You're here, I'm here."

"But what are you *doing* here?"

"Sitting. Better I ask why you're here. Here you don't belong."

"I'm looking for someone."

"She has a name?"

"Angelica Winters. I have to find her."

Familiar prune-wrinkling of lips. "That girlie's not for you."

"You *know* her?"

A shrug.

(Trying not to show impatience) "Gramma . . ."

"It's *so* important, Cary?"

"Yes."

A reluctant nod to the left. "Down that way, there's a place, better you shouldn't go through."

"Go through? A door?"

"I said, 'a place.' If it had a door, it should stay locked."

"Will I find her there?"

"What you'll find, you'll find, *hm?*"

Twinge of pleasure. "You always used to say that."

"*Nu?* Old dogs don't learn new tricks. Go, if you have to."

"I have to."

Watching him hurrying away. "*Tch-tch.*"

Memory loss. Wandering in a grey-white haze. Noise. Coldness. Harsh light. Everything painful:

cradlesongs

whiskers that scratchkiss

sharp ugly laughter

eyes that don't smile

the last kiss

no!

raging

twisting

away away

splashing

into icy water

CaryCarl

Angelica

whyWhere?

DROWNING!

Swift river. Whirling toward rapids. Rag-ends of nightmare. Gramma Hannah's receding voice: "Gebt die Hoffnung auf, all jene, die hier entreten."

All ye who enter here abandon Hope.

Allegro

A hot dry wind plucks Carl out of the waters of chaos. It hurls him up a long high chimney-shaft and spins him round and round its rocky sides.

Here the smoky crimson light pales from scarlet to lavender, deepening again to crimson as the cycle of engorgement continues. Cloudy wisps and streamers snake through the cavern, capriciously hiding, revealing, concealing a blurred collage of beautiful women blown past in the opposite direction . . .

Esther Martha Mary Miriam Naomi Sarah Rachel Rebecca Ruth
EstherMarthaMaryMiriamNaomiSarahRachelRebeccARuth
Esthethariamiarachelecc*Angelica*

He calls to her. The wind dies down; she drifts closer. Carl sees her now: kaleidoscope of features . . . upturned nose like Diana's . . . Barbara's sleek black hair . . . slim hips like Jan's . . . tiny breasts like Marge . . . a stranger's lips twisted in an odd smile . . .

haunted eyes . . .

"Angelica?"

Rushing into his arms, her body melting like burning wax . . . and now her fingers lengthen into gouging claws; her teeth grow needle-sharp as they pierce his neck. She shifts down his body. Carl sees the stiff little penis emerging from the folds of her FLINGS HER OFF and the whirlwind springs up again *come back!* spins her out of reach.

The gale suddenly whips round one hundred and eighty degrees, hurling Carl up the flue like looking-glass Alice ejected from the rabbit hole. Just as abruptly, the wind dies. Gravity rights itself.

Carl pitches headlong into a swamp.

Of vomit.

Allegro assai

But when he opens his eyes, he finds himself instead inside a huge cocktail bar bathed in glowing psychedelic colors. The vast plaza recedes into perspective infinity.

Carl shudders at the things perched upon the barstools: huge roaches, maggots and birds of prey smoking clotted sticks of dung; swine as big as men burying their snouts in steaming bowls of blood; savage bitches feeding off the flesh of pale trolls with brooding sullen eyes and wild unruly hair.

The most unsettling thing is the silence. The beasts and monsters chatter at one another, yet Carl hears nothing. *Like watching a TV show with the volume knob turned off . . .* and now the picture breaks up into hundreds of rushing modules slanting vertically one line at a time, skipping every other space, shifting so rapidly that his eyes and brain are unable to follow or assimilate the patterns.

No persistence.

Mosaic tiles click into place. A single detail of the fresco fills in: Angelica struggling in the grasp of an enormous cuttlefish. Its slimy pincers tear her skin. Each new wound reveals raw tissue riddled with cancer. A grand guignol pantomime; Carl cannot hear her screams.

"LET HER GO!"

Shouting as he runs runs

        runs

          runs to rescue her, knowing loud angry words won't make the monster release her . . .

              . . . except they do.

        The squid-thing

      melts into a seething pool.

Standing naked before him, Angelica streaks thick handfuls of muck over her wounds.

"Help me, Carl."

He smears her with grease. Her lips draw near. She smiles wickedly.

"Our secret, Cary . . ."

He opens to her kiss. Her tongue darts down his throat, thickening and splitting into a million thirsty mouths sucking his body's vital fluids.

Carl batters her with both fists.

He suddenly smashes into the swamp.

Alone.

Facedown in vomit.

Allegro

"So you flop funny. Now get up and clean yourself off."

A stocky middle-aged man helped him to his feet. He had twinkling brown eyes, bristly salt-and-pepper hair and clean-shaven pink Santa Claus cheeks. He wore a smart three-piece grey business suit and gleaming oxfords. One manicured hand curled around the handle of a large black salesman's sample case on casters. A pair of initials, JP, were carved in its leathery side.

His warm, comforting smile seemed familiar. "Haven't we met before?" Carl asked.

"Not exactly yes, not exactly no." The salesman suddenly raised his voice. "How about a little rain? He's covered with barf."

A solid sheet of water drenched Carl.

"A *little,* I said! Look at him now, he's practically drowning!"

An intense glare of infrared light. Carl was instantly dry.

"That's better!"

"Who are you yelling at?"

The salesman put a finger against his lips. "Shh. I know the manager." He winked at Carl. "Want to see a show?"

"I've got to find somebody."

"The actress, right?"

"You know her?"

"By reputation."

"Can you tell me where she is?"

A disinterested shrug. "Downtown, maybe someplace else. You'll find her. That's a foregone. So what's your hurry?"

"She's dying."

"Some folks are dead long before their bodies."

"Meaning what?"

"It's not worth the debate." He patted Carl's back with a manicured hand. "Look, you could use a breather. Why don't you hang out with me for a little?"

"And do what?"

"We'll have a good time. I'll take you to the thee-ayter."

"That's where I know you? 'A shoeshine and a smile'?"

An eruption of merry laughter. "Bull dicky! I'm the salesman Willy *wanted* to be." The man gave Carl's shoulder a friendly squeeze and turned him around.

Carl saw the playhouse . . .

THE COMBINATION ROOM
Movies! Variety Acts! Stage Shows!
& the World's NEWEST Sensation:
TALKING PICTURE RADIO!

"Movies?" Carl wondered.

"We'll skip that. They're running *Heaven's Gate* totally uncut." The salesman winked. "Just in case you had any doubts where you are."

They went inside.

The posh lobby glinted with gilt, but the red carpeting was patched in many places, and one of the purple barrier ropes was so frayed it hung from its brass fittings by a few strands of velvet. The theatre itself smelled mildewed, but its large scale and the decaying elegance of its appointments suggested bygone days of grandeur.

"Looks like we've got the place to ourselves," Carl observed. "Do you like the middle or down front?"

"Sit wherever you like," said the salesman. "I'll be onstage. I'm the orchestra. Watch my sample case, will you?"

Carl nodded. "By the way, what kind of things do you sell?"

"Stuff you might need. Ask me later. It's show time!" He hurried up the aisle and took his place behind a set of drums positioned to the right of the proscenium opening.

A spotlight came on. Fitting his mouth to a wire-held, sound-amplified harmonica, "JP" began playing a medley of Stephen Foster songs. The spot swept across the closed curtain, stopping at an annunciator, which read HOME SWEET HOVEL. The salesman ruffled a tattoo on the snare drum, blew a fanfare, then, swiveling on his stool, struck a chord on a small upright piano and began to play "Old Folks at Home."

The curtain rose.

LAZZI

JUDY enters, carrying a crying baby. She soothes it
    with cradlesongs.

PUNCH enters holding an oversized knife and fork. He wears a bib
    round his neck. Sitting down at the head of the dinner table, he
    pounds upon it with his fists.

JUDY ignores PUNCH. She bares a breast the size of a watermelon
    and nurses the baby.

PUNCH roars angrily and pounds the table.

At this moment:

THE SAD CLOWN enters leading a live turkey on a leash. The bird
    wears a blanket with its name embroidered on it: "SADIE."

PUNCH grabs the turkey and wrings its neck.

THE SAD CLOWN bawls.

PUNCH tears off a drumstick and beats THE SAD CLOWN over the
    head with it. PUNCH puts the rest of the bird on the table and
    begins to eat it up.

THE SAD CLOWN goes to JUDY. She pats him on the head and
    hands him the baby. JUDY exits. THE SAD CLOWN, still
    crying, throws the baby on the floor.

At this moment:

FRANCESCHINA enters in a silk skirt, bandanna and gaudy beads.
    She carries a wicker basket.

THE SAD CLOWN runs and tells her what happened.

FRANCESCHINA runs behind PUNCH and beats him till he throws
    up everything he ate. She takes a magic wand from her basket
    and waves it over the mess. A flash of light. The resurrected
    turkey jumps off the table.

THE SAD CLOWN hugs FRANCESCHINA. They dance.

PUNCH pounds the table and roars.

THE SAD CLOWN scoops the baby off the floor and dumps him on
    the table. He and FRANCESCHINA exit together.

PUNCH eats the screaming baby.

The salesman rapped a syncopated rim shot on the drums. The stage
lights went off.

A clock chimed midnight.

Onstage, a pair of flashlights clicked on. Two children sat down on
a sofa and covered themselves with a grey wool blanket.

Music started playing, a 1952 Georgia Gibbs Hit Parade favorite:
"Kiss of Fire."

As the song got louder and louder, the cellar door slowly swung open.
A sudden burst of amber light from the portal, then a strong wind
stripped the blanket away from the children and sucked it through the
open door into the basement. The flashlights whirled right after it.

The little girl clung desperately to the sofa, the boy held onto her,
but his weight made her fingers slip. She batted her brother frantically
with one hand until he lost his grip and caromed across the floor into
the cellar. The door slammed shut, cutting off his scream.

The salesman counted—"One, two, three, four, five"—then played the ride-out strain of Scott Joplin's "Weeping Willow" on the piano. Suddenly he was sitting beside Carl.

"So, junior, how'd you like the first part?"

"I've seen it before."

"You want novelty? Just watch this next number . . ."

The spotlight shone upon the annunciator. The sign changed.

MAXIE, PATSY, JEKYLL & HYDE

Carl asked, "Don't you have to go back up there and play?"

"Not in this scene. Shhh, here comes my favorite character!"

Sprightly music.

A midget in bright green knickers, vest and curly-toed shoes tap-danced onstage. From the opposite side, a tall, voluptuous blonde joined him. They performed a duet.

Now the third member of the team appeared, a short, fat comic in a leather apron. He tried to keep up with his partners, but they were too skillful. He took a colossal pratfall.

The salesman slapped his knee and laughed.

Onstage, the fat comic's face turned beet-red. A white angry V appeared upon his forehead. His brow bulged, his nose began to sprout, his jaw widened and he changed into Punch. Leaping to his feet, he brandished a slapstick in the shape of a phallus and, shouting an obscenity, pummeled the midget till the little man fell down dead.

The tall blonde dropped on her knees beside him and wept. Punch tore off his apron and prepared to pounce on her as the curtain descended.

"I told 'em they should change the ending," the salesman said. "It'd be funnier if the little guy hauls off and clobbers the comic . . . What do you think?"

"Either way, I couldn't care less," Carl answered impatiently. "I've wasted enough time, I've got to leave."

"Not yet, or you'll miss the best part!"

Tympani thundered. The curtain rose. In the middle of the stage on a raised platform stood a twelve-inch console Philco black-and-white television that displayed a test pattern in the shape of a Maltese cross. Despite the smallness of the screen and the set's distance from him, Carl saw its picture with the keen optical resolution of an eagle.

An invisible announcer proclaimed, "This theatre is proud to present for the very first time the Eighth Wonder of the Entertainment World—Talking Picture Radio!''

The test pattern vanished. Sinister music. A strange word glowed on the TV screen—

Vourdalak

"What's that mean?" the salesman wondered.

Carl explained. "That's a vampire that only preys on members of its own family. Sometimes spelled 'wurdelak.' ''

"Aaw, I didn't know it was going to be monster crap! Let's get outta here.''

Onscreen, an actress appeared. It was Angelica.

"No, *wait . . .*''

An older woman with green eyes, drawn cheeks and chopped raven-black bangs joined Angelica. From the vehemence of their manner, they seemed to be arguing violently, but none of their words came out of the speaker.

Carl complained, "Why don't they turn up the sound?"

"They haven't worked out all the bugs."

Onscreen, Angelica picked up a knife and began to approach the other actress as the TV picture broke up into random snow patterns.

"Well, that's the show, junior. Let's go meet the cast.''

"I'd rather skip that.''

"But they're expecting you!" The salesman snapped his fingers and they were backstage. Before Carl could argue, his companion steered him to the head of the reception line.

The cast was waiting for him: Punch and Judy, The Sad Clown and his turkey, Franceschina and the girl under the grey blanket, the midget and his tall blonde partner.

"Where are the others?" Carl asked.

"What others?"

"The women on television.''

The salesman's shoulders heaved. "Who knows where they broadcast from? They might not have been live. Here, say howdy-do to every-one.''

Punch tried to hug Carl, but he wouldn't let him.

Judy squeezed Carl's hand briefly, then very quickly stepped away.

The Sad Clown ignored him.

Sadie tried to peck him.

Franceschina winked flirtatiously.

The girl beneath the blanket stuck out her tongue.

The midget tap-dancer patted him cordially and introduced his partner. The tall blonde kissed Carl's cheek.

Punch ran around to the end of the line and tried to hug Carl, but he wouldn't let him.

Outside, the middle-aged salesman wheezed and put down his sample case. "This is getting heavy. Mind pushing it along for me for a little while?"

Carl grasped the handle and wheeled the bag. "Where to?"

"Next level." The salesman indicated a circular sinkhole several yards in the distance. Carl walked over to it and peered inside. He saw the top of a long metal chute.

"Is Angelica down there?"

"Possibly." The salesman sat on the edge of the slide. "Me first, then send my case down and I'll catch it. Be careful not to jostle it."

"Which reminds me, what's inside?"

"I'll have it open by the time you hit bottom. *Geronimo!*" Whooping like a child playing Cowboys and Indians, the salesman disappeared down the chute.

Carl followed after him.

Lontano

Bleak rolling tableland in every direction. Several miles away, Carl spies a gloomy city fronted by a pair of huge iron gates with flames erupting from the peaks of the crenelated reconnaissance turrets.

"That's where we're headed," the salesman says.

The older man now wears a military field uniform, a World War II service cap slanted jauntily across his forehead, a top sergeant's chevrons on the sleeve of his khaki jacket.

He waves his hand at his open sample case. Carl looks inside and sees two webbed strands of bullets, extra rounds of ammunition, hand grenades and a disassembled M-1 rifle with bayonet. The noncom removes the firearm's components and puts them in Carl's hands.

"Better snap this together, soldier. Get ready to move out, double-time speed run. We attack at dawn."

"Attack?!" Carl points at the fiery gateway. "Against *that?*"

"Son, the glory is not in the doing, but the dying."

"Bullshit!" Carl drops the rifle parts back inside the sample case.

"What are you doing, mister?" the sergeant bawls. "Mutiny ahead?"

"I came here to save a life, not to throw mine away."

"You're in no danger on this level."

"How can you know that?"

"Haven't you already come through fire and water, claws and teeth?"

"Yes. And theatre."

"So bullets and knives won't hurt you, either. You'll have to go down a lot deeper before you're in any real danger. Now pull yourself together, soldier, and assemble your rifle."

"What if I refuse?"

"Then you'll have to return without her."

Carl instinctually knows this is the truth. A moment to weigh options, then he picks up the M-1 and starts snapping it together.

Dawn.

The sergeant, marching beside Carl, says, "Our mission is to find and destroy the I.M."

"What's that?"

"Infinity Machine. It's the mainframe programming device down here."

"What does it do?"

"Grinds out guilt. Shame. Loneliness as a punishment, loneliness as a reward. Unreality. Company HALT, One-Two!"

They'd been marching less than a minute, but had already reached the fiery gates of the city.

"Dis mus' be de blace," the sergeant quips.

The rasp and aching groan of time-worn cogs and rusty gears. The portcullis ascends. From the city's grim interior issues a squad of enemies led by two knights.

The taller is clad in shiny black mail. The smaller figure is fitted into a constructivist metal frame resembling a forklift. Closed visors shield their helmed faces.

Carl snaps a shell into the rifle's chamber and waits for the order to fire. The sergeant says nothing.

The enemies advance. Carl glances impatiently at his stocky comrade. He is leaning on the butt of his rifle, its bayonet thrust into the ground.

"Hey! Aren't you going to fight?"

"I can't."

"But you brought me here!"

The sergeant wipes moisture from the sweatband of his cap. "It's not my battle, Cary—the main reason I'm here is for moral support."

"You're telling me I have to fight them all by myself?"

"That's the ticket."

"How come?"

"They're your enemies, aren't they?"

Carl recognizes them.

An Anglo-German gym teacher who deliberately mispronounced his name.

A sloppy boy who sat behind him in school and taunted him because Cary sounded like a girl's name.

A black girl in pigtails who called him a big red Jew.

The homeroom teacher who wouldn't listen when he groped to explain why he couldn't put his hands together and pray to Jesus.

A jock who called him a fruit because he was an actor.

All of the girls who hurt him saying No.

All of the women who hurt him saying Yes.

Carl fires round after round, blasting faces, necks, chests, privates, kidneys, shattering the air with screams, splattering the plain with blood.

None of them fight back . . . until the small knight in the metal frame advances and smashes him to the ground with a single blow of her forklift fist.

"You're not worth the effort." She strides through the gates and disappears inside the city.

The black-helmeted knight retreats after her, beckoning—*daring*—him to follow.

Carl turns to ask the sergeant what to do, but the landscape is breaking up into unconnected lines. He can't find his friend. Groping blindly for him, his fingers penetrate something warm and sticky. A shriek of pain.

Carl pulls back his hand, sees what's in it. He flings it down in horror and disgust.

Dies Irae

Passing beneath the raised portcullis. *No other option.*

Ringing in his ears.

City of the dead, smelling of sulphur and lavender.

Acres and acres of tombs. Every gravestone's neon-bright inscription bidding Carl to inspect its legend.

Reading the nearest ones:

ICI LES NEIGES
THEY NEVER NOTICED THE DIFFERENCE
SHE LOVED ME, BUT I LIVED
COGITO ERGO PECCAVI

Off in the distance, one great vault: the black knight entering it, expecting Carl to follow . . .

Only one step needed to reach it . . .

Now!

Neat incision and the ringing growing shriller, a cold fist drawing Carl into "someplace very ni

|
|
|

Sempra senza strigendo

The honey-haired waitress in silk blouse, knee-length skirt and sheer charcoal stockings smiled pleasantly at Carl and dazzlingly at the helmeted black knight as she served them both tumblers of scotch neat. The men were seated at a corner table in a restaurant whose walls were chess-tiled in ivory and ebony.

Watching the waitress retreat, Carl murmured, "I've stopped wanting every woman I see."

"Verily, the millennium hath come," the knight said. "If that's true, there's only one thing left for you to do—"

Carl laughed sardonically. "What? Grow up?"

"Grow old."

" 'Life sucks, and then you die,' huh?"

"Something like that."

"Not nearly as bad as 'Life sucks—and then you live.' "

"Hey, am I supposed to feel sorry for the small-town boy who married the Ice Princess? Forget it." The black knight removed his helmet. He had lustrous hair curled over snapping black eyes, a nose *not too big, not too small, just right,* toothpaste-commercial-white teeth: good looks calculated to draw women's eyes—

Away from me.

Carl was not surprised at the knight's identity. "I thought I recognized your Number Three Condescending Tone, Mistress O'Brien."

"My world and welcome to it." George downed his drink and signaled the waitress, who had not taken her eyes off him. She immediately brought a refill.

George clinked the brim of his replenished glass against Carl's and said, "Well, what shall we drink to? How about old and new friends?"

"I'm trying to find a friend."

"I know."

"So, old friend, what do I have to do to get you to help me?"

"One," George said, ticking off points on his fingers, "make sure that you know what you want. Two, are you absolutely certain that you want it? Three, if you do find it, are you really going to recognize it? Four, do you know where you have to look for it? Five—"

"Six, pick up sticks!" Carl interrupted. "Look, Socrates, I'm not in the mood to sit around listening to your brand of hemisemidemicallipygian wisdom. How about some simple questions and answers, instead?"

George peered into his glass. "Well, well, well, life goes on at its petty pace. Smiley's still preaching gospel in Delaware, John's ashram doubled its membership, Lena bought me a nice Mass . . . and you still use words like a club." He looked up. "Q and A, that's what you want? All right, pal. On one condition."

"What?"

"I do all the asking."

Carl looked skeptical, but said yes.

A cozy parlor with crammed bookcases, several well-worn armchairs, small breakfast nook, crackly imitation leather davenport. Standing catercorner by the green-shaded window, a large loom threaded with the woolen beginnings of a grey blanket. Above it on the wall hung a Wise Old Owl clock, its hands stopped at seventeen minutes past ten.

"Like to do this shrink-style?" George asked, indicating the davenport. "You could stretch yourself out on that and free-associate."

"No, thanks, I'll perch over here." Carl sat in one of the armchairs.

"Whatever fits." George kicked off his slippers, loosened his bathrobe and lay on the couch himself. "So bring me up to date."

"Angelica is dying."

"That's her business."

"What?"

"That's her business."

"I'm trying to save her!"

"From what?"

"Aren't you paying attention? I told you, Angelica is dying."

"Maybe that's what she wants."

"I can't accept that."

"Not your decision, pal."

"But it's my fault."

Propping himself up on one elbow, George asked, "You don't honestly believe that?"

"I held the knife."

"Cary . . . both of you held the knife."

"How do you know? You weren't there."

George winked. "Maybe I was there in spirit. Look, forget about the mea culpas. You tell me that she's dying." He cocked an eyebrow. "What good's it going to do for you to follow her? I mean, you could die, too."

"I have to take the risk—I'm trying to rescue her."

"Ho-o-o-ow noble," he drawled. "You're the one who ought to be wearing armor, Mr. Markowitz, not me. Hasn't it occurred to you that she's down here because this is exactly where she belongs?"

"Cut it out!" Carl snapped. "I know how much you cared for her—"

"Kee-rect, pal," the dead man interrupted, "and look where it got me."

"Georgine, just what are you trying to tell me?"

"That the lady knows her own mind."

"And doesn't want me to bring her back?"

George gave the question serious consideration. "No, I won't go that far. I can imagine Angelica actively wanting you to follow her here . . ."

"Yes? I sense there's a 'but' coming."

"You bet. But do you remember Dr. Seuss's 'Thing One and Thing Two'? Her wanting you to follow after her, that's Angelica Number One . . ."

"And Thing Two?"

"Can you honestly imagine Angelica permitting you—any man, for that matter—to treat her like some helpless damsel in distress?"

"All right," Carl conceded, "maybe I shouldn't use the word, 'rescue.' "

"You're missing the point."

"The point is, I want her to come back with me."

"Back from where?"

"Why are you making this so damned difficult? Back from wherever she's hiding."

"And what makes you think that's a place that you of all people can find, Bonne Homme Richards?"

"I was hoping you could help me. I've searched for her in a few places. I thought I found her a few times, but I was wrong."

"A few places?" George echoed.

"Yes."

"Try to describe them."

"I don't remember all that well. Okay, wait, first off, there was this rocky tunnel, kind of a . . . what do I call it? Vestibule? Back porch? You know the spot, you were there, George."

"What do you mean, I was there?"

"I don't mean recently. Last week."

"Last when?"

"Week. The night you died."

George covered his mouth and yawned. "You can't expect me to remember that far back."

"But it was only last week!"

"Last week, last month, last year, last century, what difference does it make? Dead is without clocks." He yawned again and sat up. "So is that one of the spots you thought you saw Angelica?"

"I don't think so . . . I can't remember."

"See? That's the way it is down here, everything runs together. Where else did you look?"

"I think I was in a cocktail bar. Was there . . . some kind of movie theatre?"

"You're giving me a general idea, anyhow. Down."

" 'Down'?"

"The way you're headed."

"Figuratively? Literally?"

He gestured noncommittally. "How would you answer that one, Mr. Markowitz?"

"That you *would* make a good shrink, answering a question with a question."

George chuckled. "The way, they say, to see the way."

"Jingle-jingle-jingle. What way?"

"To what you're after."

"Not what. Who. Angelica."

"Sure about that?" a new voice suddenly asked.

Carl swung round, but saw no one. Far off, he thought he caught the faint clamor of an alarm clock.

George gave no indication that he heard anything out of the ordinary, but repeated the identical concern. "Are you sure that's what you're really after, Cary?"

—Sure about nothing.

A change of venue.

Carl and George stand upon a small, barren knoll. A bitter nipping chill. Below them, a stark, twisted forest devoid of greenery; instead, a tangled network of black branches and sharp thorns. At the edge of the hill, a boulder and a painted wooden sign, the lettering so flaked and blistered by the harsh wind that Carl can't make out its inscription.

"What's that say?"

" 'Loupin'-Off Stane.' For jumpers." George struck a pose and declaimed, "Three roads diverged within a bluidy wood. It's up to you to choose."

"Tell me something I don't know already."

"Okay. I'm the three A's. Back the way you came—*all* the way back, I mean—we could call that . . . what? Philadelphia."

Wryly: "Let's not."

"Well, you know where I mean." George pointed into the forest. "That's where you've been heading up to now."

"But there's a third way I can travel?"

"Yowzah, Mr. Markowitz. Remember the Monroe Doctrine?"

"What are you talking about?"

"Bob Monroe's book . . . out of body travel . . ."

It came to him: "The place he calls Realm Three?"

"For want of a better label."

"Ever been there, George?"

"If I was, I don't remember."

"I'll find her there, you think?"

"I don't know what you'll find, pal. I'm just pointing out that you have another option."

"What's the point if she's not there?"

"How do you know she isn't? Maybe when we fall asleep, that's where we wake up."

"Hmm," Carl mused. "The third realm? Maybe it's worth a trip. How do I get there?"

George nodded at the sign. "The Loupin'-Off Stane. That's where you start."

Carl approached the boulder, mounted it. He glanced back at his friend. "You think I might find her there?"

George shrugged. "How should I know? But whatever you find will be just as important."

"You know that for a fact?"

The actor laughed. "Of course not."

Staring into the twisted wood.

Not the secret of the thorns.

?

No!

(And why so great a No?)

Hush

     two three four

             Hush

And

  Pro-JECT!

       ~~~~~ Southwestern route

            Following the riverbank

            At the water's mouth.

            Caesarean sections.

          Into the slice.

       Wave length.

         Impasse. You can't come in.

         Modulating. Fixed

                ~~~~~ neat incision in the

fabric of the

     |

     |

     |

     |

     |

morning sun and the songbirds in the air sweet with flowers.

The landscape shimmers into view. His breath catches. Everywhere he turns, he encounters vistas of such indescribable beauty and grandeur that Carl's eyes well up with wonder and tears . . .

Oz and the Land of Heart's Desire
Camelot and the Magic Kingdoms
Tayside and Narnia-in-the-mirror
Pennsylvania and the Highlands of Faërie
Leaf and stone and the lost lane-end

found . . .

In the distance, amber mountains tipped with silver beckon him. In the cloudless summer sky, flocks of geese draw patterns as he ambles down the slope of a country lane improbably bordered by tulips. His path leads him past blue hay tedders and ox carts dotting the fields of clover, wheat and maize that patch the farmland with warm primary blocks of yellow, rust and apple green.

The miles pass quickly, the long temperate afternoon slowly, but here there are no abrupt transitions, one foot must follow the other, step by step . . . and yet he neither tires of walking nor of gazing with admiration and wonder at scenery ever more and more magnificent: trees with leaves of milk and silver, cerise cornstalks, chattering rills of mignonette, heather as black as leather.

So far, he sees no sign of life.

Twilight. The foothills dance with color. Now the road switches back and forth, circling and returning in its upward march, but never very steep.

He reaches a broad plateau rippling with tall grass. Beneath the mountain's dappled shelf, he sees a sparkling orchard heavy with jewel-fruit. The trees' golden boles are clustered on either side of a crystal cottage with onyx roof and walls fashioned from silver.

Sitting in front, holding an earthen bowl on her lap is a young woman whose features seem somehow familiar to him . . . high cheekbones . . . eyes like emeralds . . . a sensuous upward quirk at the corners of her mouth . . .

Now, in a single dispensation, one step abridges the distance, bringing him to her side.

She smiles at him. "I was sure if I waited long enough, you'd come."

"You know me, then?"

"Not your name." She lets her smile grow wider. "Does it matter?"

"Not in the least . . ."

Happy that he has spoken literal truth; he neither knows nor cares about his own name.

She sets the bowl on the plain wooden bench she's been sitting on and rises, smoothing her skirts. The garments she wears are a short-sleeved scarlet blouse, licorice jumper and ruby pumps. Her only ornaments are a pair of golden maple leaves that hang from earlobes half-hidden by the rusty tresses that sweep and curl along the graceful line of her long neck down to the squared set of her firm, narrow shoulders.

She rests one hand softly on his arm. "Are you hungry?"

"I never stopped wanting you."

A peal of merry laughter. "Then you *are* hungry!" She runs to the nearest tree, plucks a bright jewel from a low-hanging branch, returns to the porch of her cottage, places the fruit in the bowl and offers it to him.

"Half for you, half for me," she says. "You have to do the dividing."

"Why?"

"I like the idea."

"Will you always?"

"Ask me when 'always' comes."

He takes the bowl, but she does not release it yet.

Their hands bracket the uncloven jewel.

"You've made me hungry, too," she says, moistening her lips.

*

Coming together beside the jewel
loved me regardless   strangers that i loved
never time to tell me   it was all so sensual
the way they smelled there   the tastes and the colors
but all of them crucified   hunger without Salvation
trying to give them what who never hurt or had me
dedicated to give pleasure of your dediction
Coming together inside the jewel

*

Once upon a time, on an amber mountain on a grassy plateau in the middle of an orchard, there dwelt in a cottage of crystal, onyx and silver a beautiful woman and her mate, and this is their story.

They lived on jewel-fruit and nectar and spent their mornings tidying up the house or building small useful things. Each afternoon, they wrote sad songs and funny stories to sing and tell at suppertime. Sometimes they made love at twilight, and always just before dawn and afterward, they fell asleep in one another's arms.

Once a month, while he stayed behind to tend their cottage and the orchard, she went off to town to sell some of their jewel-fruit and bring back good things for her husband to eat and drink. Although she never stayed away from home for more than one night, he was always fearful that something bad might happen to her while she was traveling.

"What if you never come back?" he worried. "I can't live without you."

Before every journey, she did her best to reassure him. "Bad things never happen in this country."

"Do you promise me that you'll come back home safely tomorrow?"

"I promise," she always answered him, kissing him on the cheek.

But as soon as she went away, the sunshine lost its brilliance, the clear blue skies greyed to slate, the resplendent golden trees looked lusterless and if the birds nesting in the orchard branches still sang, he did not hear them. Even the delicious-smelling dinner that she always prepared for him on the night before she left for town tasted bland and dull when he had to eat it all by himself.

After the darkness fell on those bleak days when she was not at home, their normally cozy cottage always felt either too warm or too cold for him, and every shadowy corner of the house hid a lurking threat.

On those uneasy nights, he stayed awake as long as he could, composing romantic ballads and comical tales to please her when she returned, but at last, when he could not keep his eyes open any longer and had to go upstairs to bed, he lit a tall candle and placed it on the sideboard, there to burn all through the night. Yet even so, just before dawn, he dreamed of blind things eating his flesh and when he woke up screaming, the sharp pricking sensation of ravining teeth would last a fraction of a second too long.

He never told her of his night-terrors because at first, he forgot all about them in the lamb-soft happy days that followed her return. But as the long months elapsed, his nightmares grew ever more terrifying until, at last, he silently resolved never to fall sleep again while she was not there in the house with him.

One morning, upon returning home earlier than usual from the market, she found him dozing in a parlor chair, the cream-white pages of a new tale she'd written for him resting on his lap. She fetched a woolen comforter to cover him, but her shadow slanting across his closed lids jolted him awake.

With a cry of horror, he jumped out of his chair, spilling the loose sheets of her manuscript on the floor. He ripped the blanket from her hands and threw it into the fireplace, where a few grey embers still smoldered.

Then his mind cleared. He stammered an apology, but she took his hands in hers and stared deeply into his troubled eyes for a long appraising moment.

"You've been hiding something from me," she said. "You shouldn't, you know." Not an accusation; just a statement of fact.

She went out into the orchard, picked a ripe jewel-fruit, brought it back and insisted that he share his black dreams with her.

Afterward, she asked him why he never once suggested going with her when she went to market.

"I didn't think you wanted me to come," he told her truthfully.

Her lips pursed thoughtfully, but she volunteered no comment.

When it became obvious she was not going to speak, he asked, "*May I come with you next month?*"

"I don't want to think about it now," she answered, stooping to pick up the pages that he'd scattered on the floor. "We'll talk about it next month."

The weeks elapsed. The tales she wrote were droller than ever, the ballads he composed wonderfully poignant and always in a minor key. They made love as passionately as ever, but no longer at twilight, only at dawn. When they shared laughter, he felt supremely happy, but small unpredictable silences began to spring up between them, and those were times he found profoundly unsettling.

When the end of the month drew near, he noticed her working longer and harder to complete all of her tasks, so he began to match her efforts. On the afternoon before the day she usually went off to market, he proudly announced that for the first time since he'd come to stay with her in the crystal cottage, he'd actually caught up on all of the household chores he'd promised to complete.

He thought this would please her, but she acknowledged his

news with an expressionless nod and said, "I suppose that means there's no reason, then, why you shouldn't come along with me tomorrow."

He felt hurt. "Don't you want me to?"

"Of course I do." Her smile appeared a fraction of a second too late.

Seagulls snatching morsels of food from the gleaming bay. Women and their brittle laughter. The dry chatter of old folk, the snaking queue, the children in the festive malls. Docked vessels, water taxis crossing the broad harbor, pennants flapping.

Lunching with her in an outdoor café, sipping resinous wine. The cool, smooth texture of the goblet. Touching her soft fingers.

"Look at me, please?"

Her unfamiliar frown suddenly reversing direction. "We should have done this before, Carl."

"Carl?" Puzzled.

"Well, don't you know your own name, mister?"

Laughing at the notion.

Joining her.

The day nearly over.

Walking the road's long curve around the broad base of another mountain. Below, the deep lake crimson in the dying sun. Reaching the steep lane, hurrying across the road, following the high stone corridor into the street and the cobbled plaza leading them to the old inn. Dining there for an hour and then to their room.

Shutting the door, Carl casually asking, "I wonder who he is?"

"Who?"

"That man staring at you downstairs."

"I didn't notice."

"I thought I saw you smile at him."

Rolling down her dark stockings. "I didn't notice him, I said."

"Well, he was watching you."

"What did he look like?"

"Tall, thin, curly black hair. Good-looking."

Nodding, stripping off her dress. "I think I know the one you mean."

"I'm sure you were smiling at him."

"The only man I smiled at was you. Now come over here and fuck me."

Shoving her legs apart, tearing into her body, striving to, failing to climax, but afterNO!new song he's written, the ballad of a wolf-girl whose loverNO!cries and

|

|

|

|

|

lived on jewel-fruit and laughter and made love at twilight and just before dawn and *afterwa?*NO!

*

Once upon a time, on a mountain on a plateau in the middle of an orchard, there dwelt in a cottage of crystal, onyx and silver a woman and her husband. Once a month, she went off to market to sell their jewel-fruit and bring back good things for him to eat and drink.

He stayed behind to tend their house and garden and was always afraid that something bad would happen to her while she was away.

"What if you never come back to me? I can't live without you!"

"Yes, you can. If you had to, you'd manage," she said, trying to reassure him. "But stop worrying! Bad things rarely happen in this country."

"Promise me you'll come back safely tomorrow?"

"I'll try," she said, kissing his cheek.

She went away. The sun went behind a cloud, the skies turned slate-grey, the trees looked lusterless, the birds forgot how to sing. The tempting dinner she'd made the night before seemed bland and dull.

When darkness came and every corner of the house turned threatening, he stayed awake as long as he could, but when he couldn't keep his eyes open any longer, he went upstairs, lit a candle and set it by the side of his bed to burn all through the night.

Just before dawn, he dreamed she was feasting on his blood while blind things ate his flesh

because I'm dead?

and woke up screaming.

Her return brought back laughter and drove away the nightmares.

But one morning, coming home earlier than usual from her journey to market, she found him fast asleep in an armchair. She fetched a grey blanket to cover him, but her touch jolted him awake. He knocked her aside and pitched the blanket into the fireplace.

She wept, more hurt by his attitude than any pain he'd inflicted. His mind cleared. He took her hands in his and apologized. For a long appraising moment, they stared deeply into one another's eyes.

He went out into the orchard, picked a ripe jewel-fruit and brought it back. They shared it and his wife understood the things that frightened him.

"I didn't think you wanted me along on your trips," he said truthfully.

She laughed. "I didn't think you'd want to come with me!"

"So then it's settled?"

"Of course!"

He adored the market town. There were so many things to do—side streets to investigate, bookshops to browse through, inns to revel in. He loved the crowds, the music, the colors, the exotic and familiar foods, the brandies and chocolates, the flowerstalls. He'd buy her roses and she'd blush.

They began to take trips to market more frequently, two or sometimes three times a month, and when they went, they'd stay over for two nights instead of one. The cottage and the orchard began to show signs of neglect.

In the tavern where they always stayed, he persuaded her to stay up late and play draughts and darts and skittles with women of all sizes, shapes and colors. One night, after they'd both drunk too much of the landlord's dark rum, they stumbled upstairs and flopped into bed with a slim mulatto prostitute named Beatrice.

The next morning when he woke, his bed was empty. He staggered downstairs and asked his host where she'd gone, but the only thing the publican knew was the due amount for their room and board, so he settled up and returned home, hoping he would find her waiting for him there . . .

. . . where, reaching the grassy plateau, he sees, sitting in front of the crystal cottage with an earthen bowl on her lap, a little girl whose face looks familiar to him.

Smiling up at him, the child says, "I was sure if I waited long enough, you'd come!"

"Then you know me?"

"Not by name." Her smile becomes a grin. "Does that really matter?"

"No, not at all."

"You must be hungry." Placing the bowl on the bench, she skips over to the nearest tree. She looks up into its branches and cries out in disappointment.

"What's wrong?"

"I can't reach!"

"But I can, see?" He grasps a jewel on a low-hanging limb and pulls it off.

Delightedly, she returns to the porch and offers him the fruit in the bowl.

Half for you, half for me.

?

Because it pleases me.

*

Coming together beside the jewel
Coming together inside the jewel

*

Once upon a time, on an amber mountain on a grassy plateau in the middle of an orchard of jewel-fruit, there dwelt, in a cottage of crystal, onyx and silver, a gentleman and a little girl.

She spent her mornings tidying their house while he made delightful toys for her to play with, and in the afternoon they planted flowers or harvested their fruit, and after supper, they sang songs and played games that she almost always won. When he tucked the little girl in at night, he told her wonderful stories of mischievous elves and fairy princesses who looked a lot like her.

Their time together was indeed enchanted, but slowly the gentleman began to realize that the little girl seemed destined to remain the same size forever. Mourning her destiny, he waited for the sad moment when she asked him why she didn't grow taller, yet she never gave him the slightest indication that she yearned to grow up.

But instinctually, the child understood his concern. One evening at bedtime, she nestled in his arms and said that she knew she was never going to get any bigger, and she hoped it didn't bother him, because she didn't mind it at all, "and do you know why I don't?"

He shook his head. "Tell me."

"Because I'll always be your little girl!"

So then he knew for sure that she thought of him as her father, and that pleased him greatly.

But when it was very late at night, the memory of his long-missing wife haunted him. He wondered where she might have gone and fervently hoped that she was still alive. Sometimes when he woke up just before dawn, in that transfigured moment when the world seems to be holding its breath, he remembered her with such poignant clarity that he wept.

Except for this one secret sorrow, his years together with the child passed as easily as the seasons. Once a month, he went into town to sell the jewel-fruit in their orchard and to buy pretty clothes and dainties for the little girl. He generally took her along with him, but there were times when she preferred to stay behind and play by herself. On those days, he always left at first light, walking as swiftly as he could, and when he got to town, he only did the absolute minimum of trading and necessary shopping so he could return home to her before it grew too dark.

But after many years, a fateful market day came when he did not come back before dusk. Their suppertime arrived and went, but she had to dine alone. Not till long past her bedtime did the gentleman return.

He found her cozily curled in a parlor chair with a grey blanket over her lap, fast asleep. He lifted her as gently as he could and tiptoed upstairs with her in his arms, but after he'd tucked her snugly in her bed, she opened up her eyes.

"Daddy, where *were* you?"

"You know where I was, silly!" He tried to tickle her, but she refused to laugh, so he stopped. "I went into town, remember?"

"But why'd you stay away so long?"

"I saw someone."

"Who?"

"Someone who left me a long time ago. Your mother."

The little girl frowned at him. "That's not true," she declared. "My mother lives in Heaven. Why would she want to come back again?"

"The next time I see her," he promised, "I'll ask her that for you."

"No, don't! She's *not* my mother."

"Who is she, then?"

"She's someone mean and bad. She wants to take you away from me."

"Why do you think that?"

"I just know," she said darkly. "Promise me you won't talk to her again?"

"I didn't talk to her today," he replied. "I saw her at a table in the harbor restaurant, but when I got there, she was gone. I looked all over for her, thought I saw her in the crowd, followed for a while, but then she went into the forest on the other side of town. I couldn't catch up with her. I got lost in the woods, that's why I'm so late."

"See? She wanted to take you away from me."

"But why?"

The little girl shook her head and refused to talk about it anymore.

One month later, he tried to persuade her to stay at home on the day he went to market, but she insisted on accompanying him, and ever after that, whenever he went into town, she always came along.

Never again did he see his wife anywhere, but with increasing frequency, she began to appear to him in dreams and every time she did, she wore a long black cloak with a hood that completely hid her face . . . and yet he still recognized who she was . . .

Angelica.

Waking one night just before dawn, he was sure he heard someone under his bedroom window calling to him. He leaped out of bed and hurried to the casement, threw open the sash and peered outside.

Standing on the grass below looking up at him was a figure dressed all in black. Pale hands rose to the hood and tossed it back, revealing

her

face

Angelica

Swiftly putting on his clothes.

    Starting down the stairs.

        Stopping himself.

            Returning to the second floor.

                Going to his child's room.

                    Finding her bed empty.

                Again hurrying down the stairs.

            Searching for the little girl.

        Not finding her in the cottage.

    Rushing through the door.

Into the orchard.

Gone!

   Gone!

      Gone!

         The woman in black waiting for him.

            Angelica!

               Angelica!

                  Angelica!

What's wrong?
The sky screamed at me. Flames followed me all the way home. Maybe it was the Freemasons? They hold their secret meetings underground.

Yes.

Where? Smoke erupting from the bowels of the earth?

Yes.

Then into the woods . . . ?

Yes.

PREPARATIONS

IN THE CENTER OF THE FOREST: A glass casket.

TO THE RIGHT OF THE CASKET: Weeping derbies, high hats, shakos, Stetsons, wigs, gowns, jackets, topcoats, feather boas, military uniforms.

LEFT OF CASKET: Mourning foxes, squirrels, rabbits, ferrets, weasels, wolves.

DECORATIONS: Black flowers; black baskets; hatchets, maces.

STATIONED ROUND THE CASKET: Seven sentry dwarves.

INSIDE THE CASKET: A naked child with a face of uncommon beauty. She slumbers.

AT ONE END OF THE CASKET: A raised guillotine positioned above the sleeper's head.

DOWN CENTER: A woman wearing a black robe, its cowl pushed back to reveal her features.

WOMAN IN BLACK

You can rescue her or you can have me. Not both.

CARL

Why not?

WOMAN IN BLACK
No one is allowed to live both yesterday and today.

CARL
Why not?

WOMAN IN BLACK
Don't be selfish again. Choose. Her or me?

CARL
There's no choice. I can't let her die.

WOMAN IN BLACK
Amen.

Leaving her forever.
Approaching the coffin.
Kneeling at her side.

Kissing her lips.
Her darting tongue.
Kissing her nipples.

And

B   I
at a word T
C
tHe knife descends,
cutting off all sound and light
all smells and tastes
every sensation
and both of
their
hea
*
*

'Erst geköpft, dann gehangen' . . .''

northeast 〰〰〰

the riverbank

the water's mouth

the slice

Modulating

〰〰〰 neat incision in t

he network of tangled branches, thorns rammed through both of Carl's wrists.

"Sidetracked by stigmata," George O'Brien sarcastically observed. He tore him off the tree.

Carl dropped to the ground, bleeding, gasping for breath. George waited for him to gain control, then helped him to his feet and steered him down the aisle of gnarled trunks toward the border of the forest.

"Where?" Carl panted.

George replied lugubriously, " 'There is another shore, you know, upon the other side.' "

A deep cutting in a sheer wall of volcanic rock.

"Where are we going?"

"The only way left, pal, unless you've decided to go back."

"No."

"In that case," George said, gesturing toward the dark passageway, " 'Lay on, Macduff.' "

"You'll come behind me, then?"

"For the first lap. After that, you're on your own."

The tunnel swiftly narrowed. Soon, they had to sidle between the cliff's sheer faces.

Over his shoulder, Carl asked worriedly, "Are you sure this is the right way?"

"It's a way. Pretty soon you're going to feel the wall on your left shelving out again. It's the beginning of a side channel."

"Do I follow it?"

"You do."

Almost immediately, Carl's outstretched hand happened upon the detour. Relieved to regain a little breathing space, he took a few steps to the left and waited for George to catch up with him.

Silence. Carl waited several seconds.

"George?"

Silence.

He returned to the spot where the path branched off, but couldn't find the place.

Ridiculous! It was only two or three steps . . .

No opening. A solid wall of rock.

The end of the first lap.

After that . . .

'—on your own.'

Groping in the darkness.

Other openings . . . go in?

Round about?

?

'—on your own.'

Faint green glow.

Fiat lux.

Seeing the cavern he's in for the first time.

Turnings every which way.

Burnished walls.

A mirror maze.

Hundreds of distorted faces.

His own.

Spinning every which way.

"And find myself the hero."

Trapped within a wilderness of reflections, suddenly he hears the menacing purr of a great snuffling beast prowling somewhere in the labyrinth.

Running through twisting passages, clambering over rockslides, hurrying under hanging limestone needles, brushing past stalagmite daggers, ducking through rough-hewn doorways, desperately trying to escape, trying to escape, but every dodge he attempts just brings him closer and closer to the questing beast.

At last, rounding a blind turn, Carl enters a long hot tunnel and there, lurking at the far end, the savage cacodemon Elephairo rears up on hairy hind legs, drooling at the sight of him.

He whirls about, hoping to escape the way he entered, but the fiend fills that exit, too . . . not the creature's mirror-twin, but the identical horror blocking off both ends of the shrinking passage.

Lowering its snout, the beast charges, meaning to skewer Carl upon its ivory tusks.

Lowering its snout, the beast charges, meaning to skewer Carl upon its ivory tusks.

In the mirrors now:

                  Burning Rose-Petals.
                  Communion of Champagne and Steel.
                  Mutuus Peccavis.
                  The Wrong Ace.

The maze darkens.
nd why so great a n
        tch-tch
          Flinging himself at the mirrors
            Meeting gelatine resistance
              Smashing the barrier
                Escaping the beast
                Escaping the beast
                  Breaking into the
                  Altar of the God
                    of the Trolls:
                      The Great
                          Boyg
                          and
                            dank reek of musk,

its hot breath foul. Body studded with lumps and leathery knobs.

Total darkness.

                         CARL

Get out of my way.

                         BOYG

Get out of my way.

                         CARL

Let me through.

                         BOYG

Let me through.

                         CARL

Step aside.

                         BOYG

Step aside.

CARL

Move!

BOYG

Move!

CARL

It's just my echo.

BOYG

It's just his echo.

(*A moment of silence.*)

CARL

Who are you?

BOYG

The Great Boyg.

CARL

What do you want?

BOYG

What do you want?

CARL

I asked you first.

BOYG

The Boyg wants nothing. The Boyg only gives.

CARL

Gives what?

BOYG

Truth.

CARL

Whose truth?

BOYG

The truth of the trolls.

CARL

Get out of my way.

BOYG

Do you worship me?

CARL

No.

BOYG

Then what do you want?

CARL

Angelica.

BOYG

Why?

CARL

To save her.

BOYG

From what?

CARL

Death.

BOYG (*Laughs*)

A devout worshipper, after all!

CARL

What do you mean?

BOYG

My followers always lie.

CARL

I told you the truth.

BOYG

Whose?

CARL (*Uneasily*)

Who *are* you?

BOYG

The Great Boyg.

CARL

You're wasting my time . . .

BOYG

The Boyg tells everything.

CARL

The Boyg says nothing.

BOYG

The Boyg reads your heart.

CARL (*Nervously*)

If I have to, I'll go back to the maze—

BOYG

Too late.

CARL

Please let me through . . .

BOYG

The Boyg knows what you really want.

CARL

Hush.

BOYG

A new way to enjoy old pain.

CARL

Hush!

BOYG

Winning love with sacrifice and sorrow.

CARL

Shut up!

BOYG

The pleasure of punishment. The intimacy of shame.

CARL

STOP!

BOYG
'Erst geköpft, dann gehangen,
Dann gespiest auf heise Stangen,
Dann verbrannt, dann gebunden
Und getaucht; zuletzt geschunden'.
LISTEN, GOOF!

CARY (*Screaming*)
NoooooooooOOOO!
"Tch-tch. Such a big No?!"
A sudden flood of brightness.
The Boyg begins to dwindle and melt.

BOYG (*Gasping*)
. . . too strong . . . women behind him . . .

A small, cozy chamber, furnished with armchairs, tables, a cracked leatherette sofa. On one wall: large flat oblong covered with a sheet.
Lamplight and the moon.
In one corner of the room, a short flight of steps leading upward. On either side of the staircase, two watchdogs with eyes as big as saucers.
Cary's mother at the window, looking into the night, ignoring him.
His grandmother, resting on the sofa, smiling up at him, patting the cushion next to her. "Nu, Cary? So come and sit a little."
Shaking his head. "I can't, Gramma. I've got to talk to her alone."
Rising from the couch, lips pleating like an accordion. "An old lady you're chasing out? Oy, kindele, the things I do for you."
"Gramma, I'm sorry."
"Shhaah . . . enough with sorry! Come, give a last hug."
Burrowing into Gramma Hannah's generous bosom, the buttons of her dress scratching. For one precious moment, feeling warm and comforted . . .

Alone with his mother.
"Mom?"
No sign she's heard him.
"Mom?"
Not turning round to look at him. "What do you want?"
At a loss for words.
His mother staring bleakly into the night.
"What are you looking for out there?"

"Somebody I used to know."

"Who?"

Sighing. "A boy."

"Me?"

"I don't know you."

"Turn around and look at me!"

Turning.

Waiting for her to say something.

Shrugging. "Who are you?"

"Don't you recognize me?"

"You seem familiar."

"I'm your son!"

Turning back to the window.

"Which?"

Nothing left but the sheet on the wall.

Twitching it aside from the great oblong thing it covers.

A mirror.

Surface swirling with scansion lines.

The lines coalescing into clouds of steam.

Glimpsing faces in the clouds.

Faces twisted in pain.

Mouths screaming.

No audio.

Lap dissolve.

A trinity of skulls.

Three sharp sets of teeth embedded in a trinity of women, ripping at their bleeding flesh.

All three of the women . . . Angelica.

CARL

I have to go to her.

BOYG (*Dying*)

'Erst gespiest auf heise Stangen . . .'

CARL

I *want* to go to her!

BOYG

Ahh . . .

(*The monster is gone.*)

With the passing of the Boyg, the room begins to break up. Armchairs vanish, tables wink out, the sofa fades away.

His mother vanishes.

Only the mirror remains.

And the stairs.

His foot on the first riser.

The guardian dogs, eyes as big as windmills, their name-tags identical: *Hephaestus*—permit Carl to pass by them unharmed.

Mounting. Seven steps. A landing and a turn.

A sealed door.

Knocking.

On the other side, a woman's surly voice. "You can't come in, brat."

"I'll smash it down."

"I don't believe you."

Hurling himself at the door. Hurting himself.

Her again: "Tell me the password."

"Shibboleth." Spoken sarcastically.

A click. Trying the knob. Unlocked.

A slim woman blocking the doorway.

Recognizing her. "Let me through."

"Only if you do what I tell you."

Shaking his head. "Never again!"

"Then I won't let you inside."

"You're not going to stop me."

A wicked smile. "Prove it."

The knife in both hands.

Laughing. "I dare you."

Violating her lips.

Caesarean slice.

*

Stepping over her body. Into the tunnel.

Secure at last: hurdles cleared, barriers down, digressions spurned, dangers braved, phantoms laid to rest.

Confident he'll save Angelica.

The tunnel suddenly collapsing:—*ive, four, three, tw*—

Skittering down the slick conduit, losing footing, slipping, sliding, scraping, tumbling headfirst into Malebolge.

His cries drowned out by the iron bells tolling the Dies Irae, summoning the witches to their bacchanal.

Ronde du Sabbat

The curtain rises on the evil ditches.

The center of the rosette is ringed by critics and celebrant witches, bankers, journalists, magicians and seducers, druglords and flatterers, fortune tellers, racists, evangelists, chauvinists, strikebreakers, goats, oxen, wolves, grizzlies, vixen, dung-beetles, publicists, pigs, hyenas, entrepreneurs, slumlords, jackals, lice, the shaman gurus and their hypocritical priests, tenured pedagogues and harpies, the casting agents, pedophiles, dramaturges and love-dowsers, the plutocrats and cynics: a corporate trust of shawled and sallow butchers of innocence.

Passing across a system of earthen parapet bridges that span the eight concentric troughs, Carl approaches the inner ditch and sees, set up in its center, a low dining board with two masked men occupying couches along either side. At the head of the table, reclining on another sofa, is George O'Brien, a gold vizard pushed back on his forehead. All three of the men are wearing black skullcaps and robes.

"We've been holding a spot open for you, pal," George says amiably, waving his hand towards an empty leather davenport situated opposite him at the foot of the table. " 'Welcome back, my friend, to the show that never ends!' Can't start the meal without you."

Sitting in the indicated chair, Carl asks, " 'What ceremony else,' Horatio?"

"You'll pick up on it, I promise. Would you like me to loan you a mask?"

"Not this time."

"That's your privilege, pal," he says, lowering the gold face over his own, "but I'm afraid you're going to have to wear a *yomil-kha* . . ."

He signals a pair of witches standing nearby. They seize Carl and bind him to his chair, pinioning his limbs with coarse straps. One of them jams a laureate wreath of thorns upon his temples.

"Damn you," he roars, "let me go!"

The Gilded Man gestures again. One of the women grinds Carl's face against her crotch, cutting off his protests and his breath.

The mocking bleat of goats, the chittering of household worms.

The Gilded Man snaps his fingers. The witch releases her prey.

"Anything else you're dying to say, pal?"

Carl, gasping for air, shakes his head.

"Then let's get going. All of us are starving." With a nod of his golden head, the witches begin to chant.

The celebrant takes a knife, turns to the unprotesting gentleman on his left and, grasping him by the wrist, slices open one of his veins. He directs the scarlet stream into a succession of four glowing-hot metal cups.

The bleeder removes his mask. Carl observes an incompatibility of features: beneath a broad, handsome forehead and patrician nose, the weak jawline and pale blue eyes of a dreamer.

The chanting witches distribute the libations. The one who suffocated Carl holds the steaming brew beneath his nose. Its odor is both rancid and oddly sweet.

The wounded man raises his glass. "To the lady I loved." He swallows his own blood. The two men wearing masks say, "Hear, hear!" and imitate his action.

Carl gags as the harridan pours the scalding potion down his throat.

A witch brings the cups to the Gilded Man. He removes his mask, prods a thumb in his own eye and contributes a teardrop to each drink. When the receptacles have been returned to the other three, he makes his toast.

"To the woman who used me."

They drink again, Carl unwillingly.

George turns to his right and addresses the man seated there. "Your turn, Harlan."

The last member of the company removes his mask. Carl peers into a pair of heavy-lidded feral eyes sullen with suspicion and resentment. Harlan's lips twist spitefully as he circles the table and spits into each of the four chalices.

"To the girl I used to fuck."

The crone forces a third nauseous drink on Carl.

Another one of the witches sets a large covered plate upon the table in front of George, who, readjusting his mask, rises and holds his hands above the tray in an attitude of benediction. The hag removes the decorative cloth that shrouds the serving dish.

On the uncovered platter, Carl notes a symmetrical arrangement of five covered dinner plates and, beside them, a separate heap of three small grey-white fingerbones, one of which the Gilded Man picks up and splits in half with a brittle snap.

The cracking signals the witches to end their plainsong. Now the

Gilded Man lifts four lids and sets them aside. One of the plates beneath contains bitter herbs; the second, a sprig of hemlock; the third is piled with chopped apples and almond seeds soaked in cinnamon and piss. The fourth dish bears a female foetus.

Raising the latter plate above his head, the Gilded Man intones, "Behold the child."

"The child is dead!" the chorused witches cry out. "All hail!"

One of the women carries the foetus to the languorous bleeder. Wearily, he signs a cruciform blessing in the air above it and proclaims, "Behold the daughter of the mother who killed her child."

"The child is dead!" shout the witches. "All hail the murthering mother!"

The foetus is passed to the sullen man. He stabs his forefinger into its stillborn vagina and grunts, "The only thing you bitches are good for."

The witches do not echo his sentiment.

The dish is returned to the tray in front of the Gilded Man. He sets his mask aside and looks expectantly across the table at Carl. "Well? Never knew you to miss a cue."

"I thought this was your script, Georgine."

"Come on, Cary, you know better. You're last at table. The next line's yours."

"I didn't audition for it." Carl, struggling in his bonds, glances at the witch standing at his elbow. "I don't care what you do, that's a game I don't play."

George shrugs it off. "The issue isn't critical. All right, so we're dropping the catechism sequence and cutting right to the final reel. Cover your faces, gentlemen, it's show time." The three of them put their masks back on. "Okay, now here's the casting. I'll do the wiseass. Harlan, you're the—"

A surly interruption. "You'd better not tell me I have to play the bastard again."

"The wicked one, anyway."

"You think self-sufficient is wicked?"

"Whatever. Look, Cary here is going to be playing the one who keeps his mouth shut, so don't go accusing me of type-casting."

"Then I'm supposed to play the foolish son?" the dreamer asks drowsily.

"You've got it." George holds his open palms above the fifth dish, the one that is still covered, and speaks through his slitted golden mouth.

"Begin the ritual."
Harsh bells strike.

WITCHES (*In unison*)
Welcome, my lords. Although the cheer be poor,
'Twill fill your stomachs. Please you eat of it.

WISE SON
How come this is all there is?

WITCHES
There's nothing left.

WISE SON
I'm not in the mood for leftovers.

WITCHES
'Twill fill your stomachs. Please you eat of it.

HARLAN (*Glaring at them*)
Why should I?

ELDEST WITCH
We weren't talking to you, goof. What makes you think you were
even invited? (*Ignoring his vulgar gesture and turning to the Foolish
Son . . .*)

FOOLISH SON (*Examining dish*)
But what's inside?

WITCHES
'Twill fill your stomachs. Please you eat of it.

FOOLISH SON
Actually, I'm really not very hungry . . .

"Nice going, it's all yours," says the Gilded Man, sliding the covered
dish across the table so it stops in front of Carl.

WITCHES (*Singing*)
Snow that's white and blood that's red,
   Maidens dying, angels dea—

The carol cuts off. The bells abruptly stop.

Like bubbles of earth, the women disappear, and with them, the sullen man and the dreamer, the bitter herbs, the hemlock, the fouled apples, the foetus. The ditches and the insubstantial pageant fade away.

The Gilded Man endures one scant second longer, just enough time to rip off his mask and smile ironically at his old friend Carl. Then the skin of his frame begins to prune up and draw in on itself like a rind of sun-withered fruit. George O'Brien slowly, silently crumbles into dust.

The binding thongs around Carl's wrists and ankles vanish. As he rises, the sofa he sat on is also gone. All that remains is the table and, on it, the last covered dish . . .

Carl removes its lid and stares at the thing he sees upon the plate.

Angelica's severed head.

Horror becomes sorrow. Tears for waxen skin no longer warm to the stroke of his hand. Tears for blind eyes that once held challenge and desire. Tears for lips and teeth whose fierce kiss reminded him of strawberries and blood. All corrupted now into a rictus of pain.

Sorrow becomes guilt. Contrition for the act of love that turned to secrecy. Perverting the news that should be shouted into whispering lewdness. *Playing "House" with her, using her body like a toilet.*

Guilt becomes denial. *Angelica the manipulator . . . using me for*
pulse . . ."

Carl has heard that after death, fingernails and hair continue to grow. Now, from the roots of her chopped spine and throat, the rest of Angelica's body begins to form, filling in downward from her shoulders to her slippered feet until her entire corpse is sprawled across the table. Her blood-spattered costume looks familiar . . .

". . . still a
nd suddenly
Clutching Angelica to his chest,
shedding the last layer of
onionskin identity,
scrying further
downward
to the
final
pit
a
n
d   *trudging*

over an endless frozen field where, beneath his feet, the remnants of shattered trust are trapped for good.

In the distance, he sees the Devil's gigantic trunk locked waist-deep in the ice.

Carl permits himself a wintry smile. For once, he feels secure in the knowledge of the coming ordeal: *the Thing in the Cellar, the skulls in the mirror, the trinity of teeth torturing Angelica* . . .

"What's your answer, Cary?"

Hell first, then Heaven.

There are three rivers running through the underworld, the Skeamu, the Coulpah and the surging Prytai. In the plain where their muddy waters meet and freeze, Carl comes upon the Lord of Hell from behind. The ripples of the demon's mighty spine are hatched with tiny scars.

Never turning round to look at him, the adversary's angry thoughts fly at Carl like poisoned darts.

> Of all men else I have avoided thee.
> But get thee back, nor

dare to save *my* life?"

Sudden confusion. Reality slipping away.

Who are *you?*

Running to face his enemy.

"Who *are* you?"

her

no longer hidden in secret corridors

Sinners captured in the bitter trinity of HER mouths, impaled on the sharp points of HER incisors . . .

Gored by the teeth of the midmost head: a company of small men, Carl recognizing amongst them the sullen Harlan and the pale weak eyes of the anonymous dreamer.

Charity mixed with selfishness. *Sister George, at least, isn't one of them.*

Clamped in the demonic jaws of the left head: a balding older man, totally unfamiliar to Carl, stoically enduring his fate.

Dangling from Angelica's third mouth, legs kicking backward, the whole skin of his back shredded to pieces, is the sinner who seems to be suffering the most—

who?

—and in the sudden altered light of doubled focus, Carl discovers the final sinner's identity—

Low angle, looking up at her, separate and distinct;
Extreme closeup, trapped in the teeth of her fury.

Daring to fuck me when I said yes.
Daring to try to understand me.
Daring to fail to see why.
Daring to pass judgment.
Daring to forgive.
Daring to care.
Daring love.
Daring!
s
sss
sssss
SSSSSSS
SSSSSSSS
yes
Yes
Yes!
YES!
daring
wanting
needing
(selfishly)
Yes!
trying
wanting
needing
(selflessly)

NO! Ripping him from her mouth, Lilith batters him on the frozen floor of Hell.

Raising his head, he chokes out the word.
"Yes."
NO! With long fingernails, Beatrice slashes him neck to groin.
Swimming in agony and his own blood, still stammers out his answer.
"Ye-es."
NO! Angelica gouging out his eyes and genitals and lungs and heart.
Still, the little heap of ashes and bones—
". . . scars . . . the rapes . . . revenge . . ."
Shoveling shoveling him into
—yes—
wonder and despair, *why*
"Because we're linked."

Animando un poco

"C'est toi?"
"C'est moi."
"I've been looking for you."
"Tell me something I don't know."
"Come back with me, Angelica."

"Come back with me."
"I'm tired of it, Carl."
"So am I. So what?"
"Tired of hurting."
"Tell me something I don't know."

"Angelica?"
"We'd never work."
"You don't know that for sure."
"Gut instinct."
"Come back with me, anyway."

"Come back.
Too late. I'm dying.
No.
Why do you care?
I wish I knew."

You feel the same as I do.
I never said I love you.
You never had to.
I never will.
I know. Come back with me.

"Come back."
"How many times are you going to ask me that?"
"Until you come."
There's only one way I will.
"Name it."

You go first.
"And you'll follow me?"
On one condition.
"What?"
You never look back.

"Agreed."
Then turn around and go.
"Are you behind me, Angelica?
Angelica, are you there?
Are you following me?"
In the Skeamu's dark tides,
Braving Prytai's treacherous flow,
Battling Coulpah and the evil ditches,
Past the thorns, the tombs, the battleground,
The theatre, the plaza, the chamber of the whirlwind,
Seeking Gramma Hannah in the vestibule, not finding her—
"Angelica, are you there?"
No answer.
Not part of the deal.
So:
Traveling northward.
PRO-*ject!*

Gravity compressing into quadrants
Smothering and the spinning
Bars and shafts
honeycomb
cobwebs
down
all
*
up
sensing
not seeing
All Carl *mouth*
The Burning Petals
Must
|

|

urian's Sp
|

ards?''

Noise.
Coldness. Harsh light.
''—chards, can . . .?''
Groaning. The voice too loud.
''—ister Richards, can you open your eyes, pleas—''

....

LÉLIO

or

The Return to Life

'But why abandon myself to these dangerous illusions? O Muse, mistress pure and true: your friend, your lover asks your aid. An end to morbid thought! I shall create . . . if only for myself . . .'

OSTINATO PERPETUUM

"Sie sprach zu ihm, sie sang zu ihm,
Da war's um ihn gescheh'n,
Halb zog sie ihn, halb sank er hin
Und ward nicht mehr geseh'n."

Pat Clayborne stepped out of the elevator first and hurried down the corridor. Trailing behind her, Jan Napier smoothed her skirt and snatched a quick dissatisfied glimpse at herself in the mirror of her compact.

Dummy! Gynger *told* you to borrow some lip gloss . . .

"I hear somebody singing in German," the plump blonde said, her ear pressed up against the door. "Guess he's still alive."

"Not for long." Jan gave the doorbell three short, vicious jabs. "Come on, Carl! Open UP!"

"Hush! The neighbors . . ."

"I don't give a polyester shit about the neighbors!" She pushed the bell for nearly twenty seconds. *"Carl!"*

"He won't answer. Not the door, not the phone. I know, I've been try—" She broke off, eyes widening. "What are you *doing?!*"

"What's it look like? Unlocking the door."

"Where'd you get that key?"

"From Carl. Managing his old pad between sublets," Jan said drily, "is another one of my little job perks."

"We can't just barge in on him! He mightn't even be dressed."

"Talk about your perks. Look, Pat, if you're so darned afraid he'll bite your head off, move aside and I'll head the parade." She brushed past her into the alcove. Striding to the archway of a large, square, book-lined parlor where the music was coming from, Jan looked inside, paused, then turned back to her companion.

"Maybe you'd better not come in, after all. Carl's in no condition for a powwow."

The publicist nodded, obviously relieved. "I'll wait for you downstairs in the coffee shop."

"Okay, but this could take a while," Jan warned, glancing at her employer. He was slumped in a recliner chair staring into space as if he couldn't *remember yesterday or sunset or the last five minutes*.

Carl had on a rumpled grey bathrobe and an old pair of thongs tugged over black gold-toe socks. His hair was more tousled than ever and his whiskers hadn't been touched by a razor for weeks.

Jan switched off the music. He neither protested nor budged. He gave no indication that he even knew she was there. For one panicky second, she was afraid he'd slipped back into coma, but then she caught him watching her as she leaned over to pull up a hassock. She sat down next to him and was surprised to find he didn't smell nearly as bad as he looked.

The depths of despair, yet he splashes on cologne . . . ?

"Earth to Mr. Richards. Are you in there?"

"Jan." His voice was husky with disuse. "Please go away."

"No, sir, that's not what you pay me for."

"Okay, then, you're fired. Now leave me alone."

"I love you, too, chief." The way he winced made her feel perfectly dreadful. "Look, Carl, it's not my idea of a picnic to come over here and upset you, but you've been this way for weeks."

"My choice."

"All I'm asking is ten minutes of your time."

No response.

"Five minutes? I promised Harry Kent I'd call him today."

"Wha-at?"

"Powder Rocks wants you to pick some possible dates. What do I tell Harry?"

Carl pressed his temples, perplexed. "Dates? I don't . . . what are you talking about?"

She hesitated. "You don't want to hear this."

"Not if it's what I think."

"It's what you think."

"Tell those ghoulish bastards—" He stopped himself. "Never mind."

"Don't get so steamed. Harry knew you wouldn't want to go near *Woyzeck* again, but he had to ask. After all, the theatre lost a lot of money—"

"We all lost things," he murmured.

"Yes, well, thanks to Harry, you haven't lost Powder Rocks, not yet. He's been telling the board after all that publicity, the next show you bring in, whatever it is, will rack up healthy box office. But it's got to be soon." The last remark was her own bit of editorializing.

"I can't think about it now."

Jan stifled her impulse to argue. "Will you at least give me a clue what I can tell Pat?"

"I don't care. I'm not talking to anyone."

"For God's sake, Carl, let her release *something!*"

"What? 'I killed Angelica Winters'?"

"You don't actually believe that!"

He shrugged wearily. "I wish I knew what I believed."

"Well, not that!" She moved to put a comforting hand on his arm, but Carl flinched. She drew back, hurt. "You have *got* to stop blaming yourself. The police are satisfied it was suicide."

"I'm not. I was right there, Jan, and I'm still not sure."

"Because you're a goddamn masochist!" She bit her lip. "Oh, Christ, I'm sorry. I came over to help, not to be a smartass."

"You want to help? Close the door on your way out."

"Yes. Okay. Time to move on." Jan stood up. "I'll be at the office, if you need me."

No response.

She started to leave.

"Jan?"

She paused at the archway. "What?"

"Where did they bury her?"

She stiffened. "Why would *I* know that?"

"Because you always know everything."

"Lauderdale," she snapped. "They shipped her body home to her mother." Jan rummaged in her purse, found a newspaper clipping and dropped it on the floor. "That's her death notice. If you want to read it, get your ass out of that chair and pick it up."

"Jan—"

"Like I said, Carl . . . time to move on." Feeding her anger to keep the tears from coming, she allowed herself the luxury of slamming the door on her way out.

> *"Froid de la mort, nuite de la tombe,*
> *Bruit éternel des pas du temps,*
> *Noir chaos où l'espoire succombe,*
> *Quand donc finirez-vous?"*

A *cycle of pain*ful thoughts spooled through Carl's mind.

Angelica, where are you?

You promised you'd follow.

I feel you close by . . .

Where are you, Angelica?

The moon came out from behind a cloud. Pale light trickled through the Asian roll-screen that covered the parlor windows. Carl closed his eyes and regulated his breathing, two three four hold hold, but there was an iron barrier in his mind and the amber glow was gone. Scraps of memory and emotion blocked his concentration, nudging him toward the interchangeable option: Art or Death?

Art: fragments of language pushing at him

(Dark Angel, reborn each night in misery,

You proved to me there is a Hell . . .

You died and left me there.)

pushing at him to scribble them down on paper and shape them into—what? Free verse? Let all the ugliness loose?

No.

A sonnet? Hack away at the pain until it fits the glass slipper?

No.

A play? Dress up the ghosts in other people's bodies?

Maybe.

Only . . .

Only what?

Oscar Wilde: "Art is the consolation prize for the life you crave but cannot achieve."

But you had the life you wanted, Cary.

You got tired of it, remember?

So . . .

Art or Death?

The pale moon spilled through the translucent roll-screen. The *repeated loop* of thoughts spooled endlessly.

> Where are you, Angelica?
> I feel you close by . . .
> Angelica, where are you?

> *"Allons, ces belles éplorées*
> *Demandent des consolateurs,*
> *En pleurs d'amour changeons ces pleurs,*
> *Formons de joyeux hyménées.*
> *À la montagne au vieux couvent*
> *Chacun doit aller à confesse*
> *Avant de boire à sa maîtresse*
> *Dans le crâne de son amant."*

Stuart Pierce stepped out of the elevator first and offered his arm to Diana Lee Taylor, but she motioned him to walk on ahead. Trailing unsteadily behind him, she guided herself by running her hand along one wall of the corridor. She paused to snatch a last anxious glance in the mirror of her compact.

'Minimal facial damage'? Maybe for that miserable quack's grandmother . . .

Pierce pressed the bell and backed away nervously from the door. He made a last feeble attempt to convince Diana to let him stay for the meeting, but once again she shook her head.

He nodded, secretly relieved. "I'll wait for you downstairs in the coffee shop."

Carl opened the door. Diana followed him to the parlor, grimly observing that the *agony called love* hadn't left any tangible marks on him, at least. If anything, he looked better than ever in a crisp mocha shirt, a studded black leather belt looped through designer blue jeans and smart black shoes he'd bought on High Street in Edinburgh. He was clean-shaven and had even made an effort to brush down his hair . . . wait! a touch of grey? Hallelujah!

"Would you like a cup of coffee, Di?"

"I wouldn't mind some tea." In the morning, she actually preferred coffee, but she'd had bitter first-hand experience (literally) of Carl's.

The respite of the tea ceremony was brief. They sat across the room from one another sipping their beverages and doing their best to avoid eye contact. Diana had asked for this meeting, so she knew she ought to speak first, but the words wouldn't come.

Carl finally broke the silence. "So what's the agenda? I assume you want to talk divorce?"

She shook her head. "Uh-uh. I wouldn't've sent Stu downstairs."

"What, then?"

"Don't rush me."

He raised a placating palm. "Take all the time you need, I'm not going anywhere."

"I heard. You haven't budged in quite some time."

"So?"

Diana resisted the temptation to say, "So budge, damn it!" She pointed out, instead, that the board at Powder Rocks was becoming impatient. "After everything that happened, don't you think you at least owe them the courtesy of an answer?"

"I'm not ready to think about a new project."

"You think I am? *Look at me!*"

Carl opened his mouth to say something, thought better of it. A strained pause. He addressed his coffee cup. "You look better than you think you do, Diana."

"Well, that is truly comforting!" She pulled the Veronica Lake curve of hair away from the side of her face. "Take a closer look, Carl. Would you cast *this* as Juliet?"

"No, but I wouldn't have before. Kate or Beatrice, absolutely. Maybe even the Scottish Queen . . ."

Really?

She rearranged the strand and lowered her clenched fingers. "This is a digression. Sorry."

"Digression from what?"

"From my agenda, as you call it."

"Which is?"

"Getting you back on track, mister."

"I'm surprised you even care."

Diana set down her teacup. She felt like throwing it at him. "I can't turn off my feelings as easily as you think, Carl."

As easily as *you* can, Carl.

"I didn't mean that. I meant—" He stopped. "I don't know what I mean. I just don't want to hurt you anymore."

"You can buy stock *that* won't happen again."

He rubbed his temples wearily. "Let's not fight, please. I don't feel well."

Her voice noticeably softened. "You're never going to feel better holed up like this, all by yourself."

"Di, I know that. Intellectually I know that. I just can't get it together."

"You . . . you loved her that much?" Asking it was like swallowing glass splinters.

No response. He stared into space.

"Damn you, answer me!"

"I don't know what to say. The eskimo language has umpteen words to describe snow. We've only got one for the most complicated emotion of all." He gestured helplessly. "What do *you* mean by 'love'?"

"The way you feel . . . felt about An— No, never mind, I don't need to hear that. The way she made you feel."

He fidgeted. "Not all that good."

"That hardly comes as a surprise. Considering."

"What do you mean?"

"Considering the things her ex-husband did to her."

Carl became very still. "What things?"

"She never told you?"

No response.

"Don't look so upset. We shared a dressing-room, remember?"

Not to mention you, you little shit.

"There are some things, Carl, that women don't tell their lovers." They don't like to talk about men like her husband. Or her father. Horrible. All *in the name of love*. No surprise she *no longer trusted tenderness* . . .

She rummaged in her purse and took out a small green hardcover book with a paper marker in it. "Jan missed this one when she packed up your things."

"Thanks."

Diana set the book on the sidetable next to her cup. "I've got to go. Stu's waiting for me."

"Yes, I know." Carl's tone implied more.

Believe what you like, pal.

She started out, but paused at the archway to the foyer. "Carl?"

"What?"

She hated herself for having to ask. "Did you mean what you said before? About me playing Lady Ma—"

"Shhh! Don't say it. Haven't we had enough bad luck already?" A wan smile. "Yes, I did mean it. I can definitely picture you playing the Scottish Queen."

"I hear the word 'but' about to happen."

"You won't get mad?"

"Just spit it out, Carl."

"But only with a lot of coaching . . ."

"La porte de l'enfer, repoussée par une maine chérie, se referme; je respire plus librement. Une brise harmonieuse m'apporte de lointains accords."

He shut off the lights and slumped into his recliner chair. Tonight, for some reason, he felt a bit less depressed. Fractionally.

Some of it, at least, he told himself, *was nothing but illusion.* The serpent and the *brutal nightmare* vistas, for instance: they *were not real.*

Then what is?

Carl's eyes drooped and closed. Now for the first time since he'd emerged from coma and without any conscious effort on his part, the barrier in his mind lifted; he saw the amber glow and descended into the vortex.

Here was the rocky vestibule, but it was empty.

He passed through Limbo and found nothing.

The chamber of the whirlwind was boarded up.

The plaza was closed for repairs.

The theatre was dark.

Down the chute, the bloody plain was gone, the tombstones were toppled, the thorny wood was being chopped down, the evil ditches had been turned into a toxic waste dump. All in all, an improvement—

But where are you, Angelica?

Right where I've always been.

Scrying across the rift: the mountains eroded, the flocks of geese gone south, blue paint flaking off the sun-bleached ox carts, the fields gone to seed.

The crystal cottage's roof was caved in, the walls were tarnished, the jewel-fruit rotted away.

Where are you?

Where I belong.

Where's that?

The *one reality*

       |

       |

       |

   d |
    r|

       y flutter of sound. Carl's eyes opened. He switched on the lights. Across the room, near where Diana had been sitting, he noticed something on the floor. He went over to see what it was.

It was the place marker from the book she'd brought back. The volume itself lay open on the sidetable where she'd put it.

Odd. The windows are shut.

He inspected the edition. It was the second part of Walter Kaufmann's superb translation of the Austrian historian-critic D. L. Oubralz's massive study, *Antiheroes and Their Opposites*. Carl glanced at the open page. One paragraph was lightly pencil-bracketed.

Carl never wrote in his books.

He read the marked passage. "The artist possesses intense awareness of ecstasies he can never aspire to. What denies them? Certainly not corrupt society, but the creator's own relentless hyperideation, without which he cannot hope to scale Olympus. Thus, ironically, God our Father must be supremely impotent!"

Yes, but no. But if it helps you deal with it, Di, think what you like . . .

> "Oh, que ne puis-je la trouver, cette Juliette, cette Ophélie, que mon coeur appelle! Que ne puis-je m'enivrer de cette joie mêlée de tristesse que donne le véritable amour; et un soir d'automne, m'endormir enfin dans ses bras d'un mélancolique et dernier sommeil!"

Gynger Morrison stepped out of the elevator, walked down the corridor and rang the bell to Carl's apartment. He led her into the parlor, where he'd already set out a table of fresh juice, coffee, tea, and an assortment of sliced muffins and jam.

"You know I'm not a morning person," he said, "but I wasn't sure about you, so I laid in a little breakfast. Please, serve yourself." Like a waiter, he stood behind her chair and helped her adjust it as she sat.

"La, sir, you do make a damsel feel welcome," she said in the flirtatious manner of a Fielding courtesan. Gynger helped herself to pineapple juice, coffee and chunks of banana walnut, apple-cinnamon and sweet potato muffins, in an attempt to block off with carbohydrates the tingling chill she felt at the nape of her neck.

Carl wore a pale blue long-sleeved shirt, a pair of black slacks and a maroon jacket, but as usual, no tie. He sat across the table from the actress and medicated himself with his first cup of coffee before beginning the meeting.

"Well, Gynger, you're probably wondering why I called you here this morning."

"I have a fairly good notion. Jan said something about your taking the Scottish play to the Fringe Festival?"

"That's right. We try it out first at Powder Rocks, then Edinburgh, and if we get good enough press, we go off-Broadway."

Trouping an American production of *Macbeth* to Scotland? Tienes cojones . . .

"Are you going to play the lead?" Gynger asked.

"No way. Joe Ferrer could've directed himself in a part that big, but not me."

Gynger patted her lips with a napkin. "So let me guess. You want me to play one of the witches?"

Carl shook his head. "I feel a little awkward. Didn't Jan fill you in on her big decision?"

"You mean, her accepting Val Snyder's offer to work in Seattle?"

"She did tell you, then." .

"I didn't think it was my place to bring it up."

"Did she also say that she recommended you as her replacement?"

Gynger's cup, almost to her lips, stopped in midair. She set it down. "Stage manager?"

"A.D., if we can stand each other close range."

"Jan didn't mention a word about this. I just thought—I hoped— that you wanted me in the cast."

"That wouldn't have necessitated a special meeting." Carl turned up his palms quizzically. "So? Are you interested?"

Gynger rubbed her chin, flattered but puzzled. "Any job offer in the theatre is always thrice blessèd, of course—but stage managing? I don't know, Carl. I mean, my thing has always been acting."

"It's too complicated a show, I couldn't spare you for the witches. Besides, I'm seriously considering using men in those roles. There's Lady Macduff, but I'm picturing someone a lot younger. Then there's Hecate—"

"Whom you're cutting, of course. Everybody does."

"No, actually, I'm adopting the Michael Godwin solution to the Third Murderer question, and that validates the Hecate scenes. Why, would you like to do her?"

Hecate would be a blast!

Gynger hesitated. "I thought Equity doesn't allow stage managers to act."

"Union rules don't apply at the Fringe Festival. We'd have to do some fancy footwork at Powder Rocks, of course."

"Hmm." She *gazed at him* appraisingly. "So what are we talking here in terms of money?"

"That depends . . ."

"On what?"

"On how much Jan told you to accept."

"You'd pay *that* much?" Carl's jaw dropped before he realized she was counter-twitting him. Gynger snickered. "Jan and I never discussed money. I have no idea how much you gave her."

"Honesty *and* a sense of humor? We just might be compatible."

"Thank you, kind sir. If I wasn't sitting down, I'd curtsey." She finished her coffee. "So, not to be crass, but what *are* we talking about in terms of filthy lucre?"

"If you can do Jan's job half as well as she did, I'll match her salary, dollar for dollar."

"I'll tell her that, she'll be pleased."

"Will she? The last time I spoke to her, she seemed anything but." Carl's brow knitted. "Look, Gynger, I know you and Jan are close . . ."

Oh, dear, I was dreading this.

"Can you tell me why she's really leaving?"

"Is this question a litmus test?"

"No. You have every right not to answer."

"I appreciate that. However, I see you're hurting."

"Well, it feels like just one more rejection."

"Oh, it is. Absolutely."

"Why?"

"Carl, I think you're *distressingly aware* of her reason."

He rose and began to pace. "It occurred to me. I tried to write it off as male ego looking for a Band-Aid."

"Well, now that you know, does it make a difference?"

"Not really."

"I didn't think it would."

Carl paused at the window. "A lifetime ago, it might have. Not now. I'm flattered, but the inconvenience outweighs the compliment."

"I won't tell Jan you called her an inconvenience."

"You know I didn't mean it that way." He returned to the breakfast table. "You just reminded me of another worm can, though. Confidentiality."

"Ahh," the actress intoned, "Dame Rumour rears her ugly punim?"

"Well, Jan did mention that you're dating Perry Cooke."

"How lovely to hear someone still use that term. Yes, I'm 'dating' Perry, but we've got an agreement. He doesn't read me his Sunday columns and I don't recite *Hamlet*."

"Okay. I'm satisfied." Carl seemed a little sheepish. "Look, I hope you're not offended, Gynger. You do understand I had to bring this up?"

"No offense taken. This is about Diana, right?"

He started to reply, then censored himself.

"Come on now, Mr. Richards," she said, patting his arm and pretending not to notice him flinch, "if I'm going to become a Jan Napier clone, I have to stand two inches closer to you than your own shadow. Cards on the table. *Do* you trust me?"

A lengthy pause. "Yes."

"So what are we really into here? How much selective blindness am I going to have to cultivate?"

"First off," Carl said sorrowfully, "there's Di's appearance. She dyed her hair copper to 'look more Scottish' and she's brushing it along the side of her face to make Lady M. 'more wild and sultry.' That's the official version."

"Unofficially?"

He rested his forehead on one hand. "There's residual facial paralysis. Very slight, but not to Di. The downsweep's enough to hide it, but she was still self-conscious about it, so, by way of misdirection, I recommended that she change the color, too."

Gynger nodded. Privately, she wondered which of them had decided on red. "Tell me this, Carl—are you and Diana planning to get together again?"

His lips twitched sardonically. "Officially, Gynger, we've never been apart."

"And unofficially?"

"The *truth?* We stay together till the show opens, then we file for a no-fault." He sucked in air. "This is hard for me to talk about."

She felt another urge to pat his hand, but knew she'd better not.

(Yes, I see you. *Whispering.*)

Gynger hefted the coffee pot. "There's enough for one more cup."

"You go ahead."

"I think you need it more than me." She poured the rest of it out for him. "Carl, you *do* know that none of this will ever leave this room? Not even as far as Jan."

"I trust you."

"Thank you." She frowned. "I want to say something, but I'm afraid of overstepping."

He sipped coffee. "Artful hubris is one of the major secrets of becoming a good A.D."

She smiled. "Mr. Richards, I love your vocabulary. Okay, here it is, Carl. You never struck me as being one of those let-it-all-hang-out types—"

"That I'm not."

"But every once in a while, we all need an extra pair of ears, don't we? Maybe with a shoulder thrown in?"

"That's true."

"I've got all three." She waited, but he still couldn't let it out. "How about if I ask a question I already know the answer to? If I'm wrong, I quit. If I'm right, it's up to you."

"Okay."

"Apropos of your working with Diana again . . . are you hoping it'll bring the two of you back together?"

He shrugged. "Hope is a foreign concept."

"You know that's not what I'm asking."

Outside on Amsterdam Avenue, an ambulance suddenly shrieked. Carl waited for the banshee wail to die away before replying. "You're asking me my feeling toward Di?"

"Yes."

"I don't have any. None that are relevant."

"Because you're still in mourning."

His chin trembled slightly. "You *do* understand."

"Better than you think."

"Sometimes—"

"Yes? Sometimes what?"

He tried to wave it away. "It'll sound too crazy."

"Let me guess. Sometimes you feel as if she *never really died at all?*"

He regarded her curiously. "How do you know that?"

"Because she's here."

A long, long, long silence.

Gynger chuckled ruefully. "Now who sounds crazy?" She stood up. "Well, this is usually the time I'm asked to leave."

"You're going to drop a bombshell like that and walk out?"

"I'm saving you the trouble of firing me."

"Why would I want to fire you?"

"Dismal past experience."

"Because you're psychic?"

"No. Because I open my big yap about it."

"For God's sake, sit down and don't be so paranoid."

"Gladly." She reclaimed her seat and waited while Carl, eyes half shut, wrestled with it. She could sense the concepts and columns in his mind jostling into binary order.

He turned to face her. "All right, Gynger, tell me exactly what you mean. Do you have some vague sort of mental impression, or do you actually think you see her?"

"Very shadowy." Like she always was. "But she's there."

"Where?"

"Behind you. Always behind you."

His tremulous smile turned to tears.

> *"O Miranda, no ti vedrem, ormai!*
> *Delle piaggie dell' aura nostra sede*
> *Noi cerceram in vano*
> *Lo splendente e dolce fiore*
> *Che sulla terra miravan.*
> *Miranda, addio, Miranda!"*

Noise of the crowd. Shouting. Applause.

The curtain rose, fell, went up again. Cries of "Bravo!"

Carl, feeling *gloriously, vibrantly alive,* hurried up the aisle with an arrangement of several dozen roses for Diana. She extended her hand across the footlights and *he tenderly kissed her fingertips.*

"Get up here!" she stage-whispered.

"Uh-uh. Maybe in Edinburgh. Tonight's yours." He tried to get away, but his wife, laughing, held on with both hands. Gynger came over to help, but Diana shook her head and *wholly and independently* forced Carl to come onstage and take a bow with his cast.

Noise of the crowd. Shouting. Applaus

erward, lingering backstage while the crew strikes and crates the set, out of the corner of his eye, Carl notices a small object that *shimmered*.

He bends down to pick it up.

The *sudden agony of* recognition.

A golden earring in the shape of a maple leaf.

C'est toi?

C'est moi.

You're still with me?

As long as you never look back.

The stage lights dim. The restless crew departs.

Carl Angelica alone in hazy wilderness.

The naked union of *harmony and flame*

s amis,
je suis souffrant; laissez-moi seul!

[**Dolce assai ed appassionato**]

[Dolce assai ed appassionato]
    "Encore . . . Encore, et pour toujours!"

"This is WNCN and that was *Lélio* by Hector Berlioz. This obscure sequel to the composer's celebrated *Symphonie Fantastique* was ironically named for a comic character in a play that Harriet Smithson, the composer's *'belle dame sans merci'* starred in—"
chk

7:01 A.M.
Marie shut off the clock–radio. She was glad it woke her when it did. Blessed daylight always banished him.
Him?
The man who compelled her to submit to the most degrading acts. The man who abandoned her to pain and anger and self-loathing.
Carl.
Blessed daylight always banished him.
The only thing that remained in her memory to torment her was her mother's old sadistic pun, *Après le mort, on y triste*. That . . . and a thought wholly and independently her own.
Tenderness is the worst rape of all.

Da capo al fine

ENGLISH TRANSLATIONS

Key foreign language passages not in common usage are explained in the text, although considerations of structure, viewpoint and pacing sometimes dictated that the initial appearance be far removed from its eventual translation, as in the case of Gramma Hannah's "Nur die Alten und die Bösen können schlafen nicht." (Only the old and the wicked cannot sleep.)

In the penultimate section (page 229), Carl remembers Osmin's threatening lyric from the libretto to Mozart's *Abduction from the Seraglio*, which, freely rendered, warns that

> We'll behead you, then we'll hang you,
> Thrust you through with spikes of fire,
> Then we'll tie you, burn and drown you,
> Flay your skin with red-hot wire!

Since the final section is patterned after *Lélio*, the intermediary foreign passages derive from that curious artistic hybrid. Here they are, freely rendered, in consecutive order:

Page 245: The mermaid spoke and sang to him,
               "Why do you lure our folk away
               With human art from waters dim
               Into the deadly light of day?"

Page 248: Coldness of death, night of the tomb,
               The eternal noise of marching time,
               Despair that reigns when hope is numb,
                  When will you ever come to an end?

Page 249:   Come on! these woeful beauties crave consolation!
We'll change their drops of sorrow to loving tears.
First, let's go to the mountain and the old convent,
Where each of us must confess
Before drinking a toast to his mistress
Out of her late lover's skull.

Page 252:   Hell's gate, forced back by a loving hand, is closed.
I breathe freely again. A harmonious breeze wafts me
far away . . .

Page 253:   Oh, if I could only find that Juliet, that Ophelia to whom my
heart calls. If I could only find that joy mixed with sorrow
that true love has to offer, then one autumnal evening, I
could lie down in her arms in a melancholy and final slumber!

Page 258:   O Miranda, we shall see you no more!
On the wind-swept shore
We will search for you in vain,
Our most splendid, sweetest flower.
Miranda, farewell, Miranda!

Page 259:   [Interrupted in the text] My friends, I suffer . . .
Please leave me alone.
[The idée fixe recurs]
Again . . . again . . . and forever!